THE FIGHT AGAINST THE SHADOW REAPERS

By
JOSEPH ALAN WORKINGER

Published by True Beginnings Publishing
Copyright 2014 by Joseph Alan Workinger

This Novel is a work of Fiction

ISBN-13: 978-0692273173
ISBN-10: 0692273174

Ordering Information: To order additional copies of this book, please
visit Amazon or CreateSpace, at: ttps://www.createspace.com/4945694

The Fight Against the Shadow Reapers
© Joseph Alan Workinger
Printed in the United States of America

Table of Contents

PART 1
THE BEGINNING

PART 2
THE SECRET

PART 3
THE END

To my grandmother, Dianna,
for always believing in me and supporting me.

Prologue

"Do you love me?" asked Elizabeth Williams as she touched his hand in a seductively way. She was lying down on the ground next to her boyfriend of three months, Eric James.

"Of course I do, sweetheart." Eric replied. He intertwined his fingers with her fingers and kissed her softly on her small, upturned nose. In Eric's mind, today was a perfect day for their date; the bright, warm sun was high in the sky, and the air gave them a cool breeze on the hot summer day.

Abruptly, Elizabeth let go of Eric's hand and stood up.

"If you love me, Eric James, then you would save me from this place. Save me, before I die."

Before Eric could say anything, her auburn hair caught fire. Eyes that had once been sweet and grey turned pitch black, and her sun-bronzed skin turned ghostly pale.

Eric jumped up from the ground in surprise.

"What do you mean? What's going on?"

Unexpectedly, the ground around them gave out, the breeze stopped, and the air turned stale. Then, the temperature dropped, and a lightning bolt struck a tree in the park, quickly igniting a fire that spread with a passion.

Elizabeth's face showed no emotion. She was as still as a rock until the ground under her gave way. Eric jumped down to the ground and grabbed her hand. He was just about to pull her up when she slipped from his hands and fell into the darkness.

PART 1
THE BEGINNING

Chapter 1

Eric James woke up to the sound of glass breaking, wood splintering, and people screaming. Annoyed, he looked at the clock on his nightstand. 12:00.

"What the hell is going on, outside? It is midnight, for crying out loud."

He turned his light on and got out of his bed. As he headed for the window on the adjacent side of the room, he heard an explosion come from outside.

Eric raced to his door and into the hall. Before he reached the stairs at the end of the hall, he heard the front door give way. His mother screamed but then was silenced by a flash of bright light. Eric slowly descended the stairs, and when he reached the bottom, he stopped in his tracks as he saw two people dressed entirely in black run across the floor; black smoke was now coming from his left. Looking down, he saw a small body on the ground.

"Mom?" Eric whispered.

More commotion drew his gaze to his right where two people in black were now fighting his dad. He didn't understand how, but his father and the two people were fighting with fire that was coming from their hands.

Eric's father looked at him and bellowed, on the verge of actually screaming, "Eric, get out of here!"

One of the men turned around and started running toward Eric, while the other one shot several balls of fire at his father. His father crumpled to the ground under the onslaught. At that moment, Eric turned around and ran back up the stairs and into his room, quickly shutting and locking his door

He went to his window, opened it, and was ready to escape just as he saw several dozen men, just like the ones in his house, walking toward him on the lawn, outside. He shut the window and ran to the door, hoping he still had time, but before he could get there, his door was covered in flames. Fear of his own end

1

quickly settled in his heart as tremors began wracking his body. He quickly ran and hid under his bed. He swore his heart was going to jump out of his chest as both sweat and tears began to form a puddle on the wood floor. The door gave way, and one of the men slowly walked into Eric's room.

The man took out a stick from his sleeve and flicked it, consuming Eric in a bright white light and effectively paralyzing him on the spot. As the man slowly walked over to Eric, he put the stick back into his sleeve, picked him up, and walked out of the room. He met up with his partner, downstairs, and left the house by going out the back door.

Once outside, they headed toward the woods surrounding Eric's neighborhood. As soon as they passed by a few trees, the house blew up. Tears were falling from Eric's eyes, even though he was still motionless. Pain and fear wracked him over the loss of his parents, the loss of the home he grew up in, and not knowing what was going on. He saw several large pieces of flaming debris falling like meteors from the sky, landing around them like bombs.

The men that had Eric were now running through the thicker part of the woods. The farther they got in the woods, the more branches they hit, cutting Eric's face in several places. Even though he could no longer see the house, he couldn't stop looking at where it had been.

Soon, more of the moonlight shown through to the ground as the trees thinned. There was a loud crack and a flash of blue light, followed by another explosion that threw everyone to the ground. Groups of people in white robes jumped out of bushes and from around trees. As soon as the men that took Eric realized what was happening, they were up on their feet. In between dodging shots, one of Eric's kidnappers shot a ball of fire in the sky with his hand.

By the time the fireball disappeared, twenty more men and women that were dressed entirely in black arrived and started fighting. The white robed figures were fighting in seemingly impossible ways, moving at dizzying speeds, and freezing groups of black clothed psychos. The chaos was terrifying to watch, and Eric couldn't help but stare with wide eyes at the carnage.

Soon, a tall person in a white robe killed the man that

2

paralyzed Eric by splashing a liquid on him. Eric soon regained movement in his bruised body and slowly crawled to a tree to hide behind it. He tucked his knees close to his chest and closed his eyes, wishing and hoping all of this was a bad dream.

After a few minutes of listening to people zap each other to bits, Eric decided that he needed to get away. He didn't know where he would go, but anywhere had to be better than there. Before he could take one step, though, someone grabbed his elbow. With his free hand, Eric tried to punch the person, but they stopped his hand with theirs and pulled him to the ground. Looking at them, Eric realized that this person had a white robe, but the hood was up, so he could not see the person's face.

"Do not fear me, Eric James. I am here to help you," said a woman with a sweet, calm voice.

She let go of him and pulled down her hood. Through the flashing lights, Eric noticed the wrinkled kindness in her face. Blue eyes were full of fear, and her grey hair was falling out of its bun and into her face. "My name is Sloan Marlin. Please, come with me. You are in great danger, here." Her soft voice urgently implored him to listen.

Eric nodded his head, got up, and followed Sloan into the thicker parts of the woods. She whispered something into a cell phone, and soon, more people in white robes showed up and surrounded them, effectively boxing them in.

Eric looked at his watch to see what time it was. 3:07. It had been about three hours since his parents' death. As he began thinking about this, more tears started falling from his eyes and stinging when they hit the open cuts that mercilessly crisscrossed his face.

Eric's watch said 3:42 by the time they stopped walking. In front of the group was a big, round oak tree.

Sloan turned around and said to the group, "Keep watch and make sure no one followed us."

Sloan walked up to the tree, pulled out a golden stick from her robe, said something under her breath, and flicked the stick. Eric couldn't believe his eyes as the front of the tree opened up like a door.

"Hurry up, before anyone sees us." Sloan commanded, and everyone stepped into the tree.

The inside of the tree was larger than it appeared, and

everything was covered in grey marble. Six fireplaces lighted the large room, sporting large, white flames that floated miraculously inside of the hearths. Eric couldn't believe what he was seeing, because people were walking into the fireplaces. As soon as they stepped in, the white flames swirled around them, and they disappeared.

"What are they doing? They're going to die!" Eric yelled to Sloan. Instead of answering him, she pushed Eric toward the fireplace that was in front of him.

"Trust me, Eric, you will be okay." Sloan said as she walked into a fireplace, herself.

Chapter 2

Eric watched as the group of people in the white robes went into the fireplaces; soon, he was the only one in the room. Doubt clouded his vision as he considered whether or not to follow the group.

"Should I trust this person named Sloan? What if they are trying to kill me, like the other people?"

Eric decided to take a chance and took a step closer to the fireplace. He noticed something off about the white flames, because they looked as if it were almost translucent.

Eric took a deep breath and stepped into the flame. As it caressed him, he noticed that instead of feeling hot, the flame made him feel cold. With another step, he started to see a faint image of Sloan standing there, waiting for him in a large room full of tables and chairs. Within another moment, Eric took another step and was out of the flames and into that room.

While looking around, he noticed that this room was larger than the previous. The walls were made of a white brick that had several large tapestries and paintings hanging on them. Large, white balls of light that floated close to the ceiling lit the large room, and there were large archways to the right and left that led to different rooms.

Four long, glass tables were lined side by side with hundreds of grey chairs. A longer glass table was perpendicular to the rest and was on the opposite side of the room from Eric. It was on a risen wooden platform overlooking the rest of the tables. The middle of this table had a large chair that was embroidered with a large, golden "S" on it. On the wall behind this table, in a large stain glass window, were the words "Aviance School of Wizardry."

On the ground were large, grey-colored rugs under each of the tables. Eric turned around and saw the six fireplaces with the same white flames as in the room that was in the tree. In the middle of the fireplaces, two stone statues guarded a huge, oak

5

door.

"Welcome to Aviance! School of Wizardry," greeted Sloan. "This is the main hall where we all eat and give daily announcements. Now, if you would just follow me to my office."

Sloan started heading toward the right archway. Eric was right behind her, afraid of getting lost in this large place. The room they entered next had no lights on, but Eric could tell that there were several chairs surrounding a television. The cold wood floor turned into a soft, cream-colored carpet.

"This is one of the common rooms in this school." Sloan said as she opened a door. This new room was full of tall windows. Eric couldn't see where they ended. Bright, bronze floor lamps lit up the room. Beside the lamps, the only objects in the room were stairs that were floating. Sloan started up the steps with Eric right behind her.

Sloan explained as they passed the second floor that the second and third floors were used for housing students. They continued going up the stairs until they got to a point where the steps disappeared.

"This is the sixth floor," Sloan explained. "This next floor is my office. Only the teachers and I know the password to get the stair to appear. I hide the stairs to prevent students coming up when I am busy. But when I am not busy, they are available to students."

She pulled out the stick from her pocket, said something under her breath, and flicked the stick. One by one, the stairs appeared, and Sloan started to climb them, and Eric followed her to the next floor. She unlocked the door and went into the room, saying, "Make yourself at home."

Eric walked into the large commodious room. Five windows flanked each side, surrounded by gold painted walls. Grey, plush carpet was spread throughout the room, and a large, wooden desk dominated the middle. A high-backed chair completed the floor décor.

Behind the desk were two spiral staircases that lead to a balcony. Eric's curiosity peaked when he noticed a small, arched metal doorway leading into another room. Underneath the balcony, there was an extremely impressive array of bookshelves and cabinets. More shelves and display cases lined the walls, containing different brooms, knick-knacks, and other kinds of objects.

Sloan guided Eric to the desk and beckoned, "Please, take a seat." Before Eric could say that there wasn't a chair to sit in, a small, red-colored wooden chair appeared out of nowhere.

"Do you want anything, Eric? A drink? Some food?" Sloan asked as she sat in the chair behind the desk.

Eric shook his head and stared down at his feet. His bare feet were covered in mud, grass, and twigs. His pajama shorts were singed from a fireball that must have grazed him in the woods. Eric started to reflect on all of the events that had led up to this point. He just really wanted to be home with his parents. He looked down at his watch. 4:17.

"Excuse me, miss, but can I please just get some rest? I've been through a lot in these few hours." Eric asked as a tear fell from his eyes to his feet.

"Sure. I will guide you to your living quarters. Since school does not start for a few more weeks, you can take some time and grieve. Remember, I am always here for you, Eric. As are the students, here at Aviance."

"This is a school?" Eric asked confused.

"Yes, but for the students who have non-magical friends, it is a summer camp."

"Why?"

"To protect ourselves. The students here, right now, are getting things ready and situated for when school starts."

Eric's head was spinning with information. None of this was making sense, but for some reason, he trusted Sloan. That didn't stop him from being scared, though. He didn't really know if he was safe, here.

As they reached the second floor, Eric asked one more question. "Where exactly are we?"

"We are in a valley deep in the Appalachian Mountains in West Virginia. Hidden from the world, but unfortunately, not from the people who murdered your family."

At the mention of his family, Eric's eyes once again filled with tears.

Sloan walked him down the moonlit hall towards the Freshman bedroom. She opened the door to the living quarters, and then, guided him into the boys' bedroom and said, "Please, try to get some rest, Eric. Everything will be okay, I promise."

Eric walked into the room, and Sloan closed the door behind her as she left.

The bedroom was lit by a soft glow at the top of the ceiling. Rows of bunk beds were on either side of the room, and several windows were on the opposite sides of the room. Dressers were in between the beds, and grey rugs covered the light brown, wooden floor.

Eric found a bed that had nobody in it and lay down. He didn't realize how tired he was until his head hit the soft pillow.

Snow was falling lightly on Eric and Elizabeth's heads while they sat on a park bench. They were drinking hot chocolate out of the pink, plaid thermoses that Elizabeth brought. She had her hair pulled back into a tight ponytail, and a light blue scarf was wrapped around her neck. A white jacket, a dark brown, pleated skirt, and light brown boots completed her look.

Eric's long, curly, light brown hair was wet from all of the snow and looked as if he never combed it. The grey scarf he had around his neck was tucked into his black Guess jacket; the bottom of his jeans were soaked from the snow, as were his black Converse shoes.

"You ready to ice skate?" Eric asked Elizabeth.

"You bet I am, mister!" She replied.

Together, they pulled out their ice skates from the bag and put them on. They held hands as they walked clumsily towards the ice rink.

Skating started slowly at the beginning, but after a while, they picked up the pace. Soon, they were racing, and Eric was in the lead. They continued for a few more laps, then ended the race and started skating more slowly. The streetlights were coming on, and most of the other skaters had left, so they knew it had to be getting late. Elizabeth was getting dizzy from skating in circles, and when she fell, Eric got on his knees to help her back up.

After grabbing Elizabeth's hands and pulling her up with him, Eric saw that she was crying. Softly, he kissed her lips to cheer her up, but when their lips touched, Elizabeth caught on fire. Eric freaked out, jumped back from her, and fell on the ice. She was now moving her hands up and down her arms as if she was cold. There was no screaming as the fire raged on her. In fact, her face was still.

"Eric, please save me. I want to leave this place," she implored without moving her mouth. Then, she turned into ashes and blew away in the cold wind.

Chapter 3

The door squeaked as one of the students walked into the bedroom. Eric had just woken up and was now sitting on his bed with his head in his hands.

"You okay?" asked the kid.

Eric turned around and looked at the skinny boy, whose physique reminded him so much of himself. He had a good three inches on him, though, with short, blond hair that was gelled up. Freckles covered the top of his cheeks, nose, and continued around his dark brown eyes.

"Yeah, I'm fine," said Eric, looking down at his feet.

"Are you sure? It looks like you've been crying."

"I'll be fine as soon as I get something to eat and a change of clothes."

"Don't you have your own clothes?"

"No, I don't have anything left, besides these clothes."

The kid looked like a light went off in his head, pointed at Eric, and blurted, "Oh, you're the kid that arrived in the middle of the night. Everyone has been talking about you. If you don't mind me asking, what happened, last night? I'm Nick Walters, by the way." Nick walked over, shook Eric's hand, and sat on the bed across from him.

Eric took a deep breath, wiped his eyes dry, and began talking about last night. He told Nick about everything from waking up at midnight to walking into the room, last night. When Eric was done talking, Nick got off the bed, went down the aisle, and turned after a few beds. He opened up a dresser and came back with clothes in his hands.

"You look about my size. The jeans might be a little long, but you can roll them up." Nick said with a smile and handed the clothes over to Eric.

"Is there somewhere I can change?" Eric mumbled with embarrassment.

"The boys' bathroom is down the hall and to your left."

Eric got off the bed and left the bedroom. The living room had about eight people in it, watching TV, who didn't even notice he was there. He hurried over to the door leading to the hall, and once in the hall, he walked to the bathroom.

Now that it was daylight, Eric saw that the hall had another door on the side opposite of the floor-to-ceiling windows. Oil paintings were hung on the wall, ranging from colorful abstract work to immense landscapes that were so detailed, they demanded closer inspection.

The bathrooms were beside the stairs that lead downstairs. The girls' was the right door, and the boy's was the left door, indicated with clear, printed lettering. As he walked in, he noticed that it was about the size of his old school's locker room. A large, crystal chandelier was hanging in the middle, lighting up the whole room. Toilet stalls lined the right side, while showers lined the left. Sinks were on the wall with the door.

On the wall across from him, windows and dressers contained soap, shampoo, towels, and wash cloths. Relief consumed him as he took a shower, even though the soap burned the open cuts that littered his face. He then used a toilet stall and got dressed in the grey t-shirt, dark jeans, brown leather belt, and white socks that Nick had graciously given him.

Before he left, he paused in front of one of the mirrors. He looked at the raw cuts on his face. His deep green eyes were red and puffy from crying and looked slightly bruised. He almost didn't recognize himself.

While leaving the bathroom to walk back to the Freshman living room, Eric couldn't help but wonder if he could trust Nick. Sure, he had been kind enough to listen and had been a huge help with clothes, but with what he had just been through, Eric was finding it hard to develop any kind of trust.

When he walked into the living room, he saw Nick and a girl with black hair, highlighted with blue, playing chess under a window. As she looked up, her hazel eyes flashed with curiosity, and Eric almost blushed with embarrassment. The soft green décor of the living room did nothing to soothe his discomfort.

Eric went up to Nick and the girl and inquired about shoes.

"Your feet look too small for my shoes, but I know someone who might have your size," Nick said as he got up and then

11

added to the girl, "Don't cheat," and then, walked into the boys' bedroom.

The girl giggled at the comment, stood up, and held her hand out. She was wearing a black mini-skirt and a loose, white t-shirt that had a flower print. And when she stood up straight, she was about three inches taller than Eric. Eric shook her hand and the girl said, "Hi, I'm Marina Martin. I'm Nick's girlfriend."

"Hi," Eric shyly mumbled to her.

Marina noticed the unsure look on Eric's face. "You can trust us. We are trying to help you, because we know you've been through a lot and figured you needed a friend."

"Thank you, and I do appreciate it. I'm just really confused by all this." Eric said to her with his eyes downcast.

"We can help you."

Nick came back a few minutes later with a pair of white Nike tennis shoes. When Nick handed them to Eric, he sat down and tried them on.

"Do they fit?" Nick asked Eric while he was still playing chess with Marina.

"A little tight but they will do."

"Checkmate! Are you guys ready for breakfast?" said Marina, triumphantly.

"Sure," the boys chorused.

Nick, Marina, and Eric headed downstairs to the main hall. They walked through the common room and into the main hall where all the loud talking was coming from. Students filled the tables and were so animated with their conversations that Eric felt almost claustrophobic. Nick started walking towards the table on the other side, and Eric couldn't believe all of these people were here, already.

The group of three sat down at the far table, which was close to the front of the room and on the side facing a wall. Nick started to talk to someone across the table, and Marina talked to a person on her right.

When Marina was done talking to her friend, Eric asked, "Why did we sit at this table? There were plenty of free seats at the other tables."

"Each table is for each grade. This one is for the Freshmen. The one behind you is for the Sophomores, then the Juniors, and then the Senior table."

12

"When are we going to eat?" Eric asked as his stomach rumbled in distress.

"Headmistress has to make a few announcements, first, and then we get served."

Soon, Sloan walked out of the common room and into the main hall. She had her grey hair pulled back into a French bun and was wearing a light turquoise gown with silver beads. She walked up to the platform and sat in the middle chair.

"Who are the people at that table?" Eric asked Nick.

"Those are our teachers." he replied.

Sloan talked to the teachers next to her, and then stood up. "Five... Four... Three... Two... One... Thank you for getting quiet." Her air of command caused everyone in the room to stop talking, and all attention went to her.

"Good morning, students. Before we start eating, I have a couple of friendly reminders. The first one is that no one is allowed to leave the school without a permission slip from a teacher, parent, or me.

"Next reminder is that all lights have to be out by eleven o'clock. No one is allowed out of his or her bedrooms after that time, unless it is an emergency.

"The final reminder is that cell phones are not to be used in class, and neither is Skype. You can only use these before and after your classes. And then, laptops can only be used if teachers allow you to.

"Now, let us eat and be merry!"

When Sloan sat back down in her seat, more than two-dozen ghosts with silver serving trays came out of the walls surrounding the main hall. The ghosts looked like they were out of the sixteenth century. Some of them were women wearing eloquent, full, red velvet dresses and white bonnets. The men wore grey, military jackets and dark blue pantaloons. You could clearly see the shape and figure of the ghost, but they were translucent. They separated into five groups, went to each table, and set the trays down in the middle of the table.

The trays were filled with dishes of various breakfast foods like Belgian Waffles, pancakes, omelets, cereals, and so one. Eric reached across the table and grabbed a plate of biscuits and gravy. Nick grabbed some French toast, and Marina grabbed a Denver Omelet.

After all the trays were delivered to the tables, the ghosts flew back into the walls and appeared seconds later, but this time, their trays were gold and had golden goblets on them. Once again, the ghosts split up and delivered the trays to the tables.

Eric looked into the goblets and discovered that some of the goblets were full of milk; others were full of orange juice or apple juice. When everyone was done, the ghosts picked up the trays and left the main hall. After the trio was done eating, Nick asked Eric what he wanted to do, today.

"I was actually thinking of going to Sloan's office and talking to her about a few things." said Eric.

"Okay. Well, do you want Marina and I to go with you? It wouldn't be a bother to us. Our first class of the day is the floor below her office," said Nick.

"Class has started?"

"No, school starts June fifth and ends August fifteenth. Freshmen can come in early and take some starter classes, which is what we are doing. We are allowed to sign up for the starter classes before we arrive, but any student can come a few days early to get situated and get things organized," Marina informed him.

"So, if you do want to find out what the classes are like, you are free to join us," Nick said to Eric.

"Sure, why not."

Half an hour later, clocks in the school rang out and announced a warning that classes would be beginning, shortly.

"Shit," Nick hissed, looking pissed at something.

"What's wrong, sweetie?" asked Marina, interlocking her hands with his and hugging his arm.

"I left my backpack in the living room."

As the group was walking back upstairs to get Nick's backpack, a girl walked up to them and started talking to Marina. She was about a head shorter than Marina and had short, blond, curly hair that was being held back by a yellow headband. She also had on a light blue tank top and a pair of grey shorts. She was skinny as a twig, just like Marina.

"That's Marina's BFF, Catlin Chamberlin. They always hang out," Nick said to Eric as they reached the living room.

As Nick went in and grabbed his backpack, Marina

introduced Eric to Catlin. "Hi, it's nice to meet you, Eric."

"Nice to meet you, too." Eric attempted a smile.

"Eric just got here, last night," said Marina.

"Is that so?" Catlin asked.

"Yep."

"How do you like it here, so far?"

"It's fine. I feel like I need a map, sometimes. All of this is just going to take a while to get used to. I thought all magic was made up in fantasy books. I never thought that this could ever exist in the real world." Eric said trying to smile, again.

Nick came out of the living room with his backpack on and started down the hall. By the time he was halfway down the hall, Nick noticed no one was following him. "Well, come on, before we are tardy," Nick joked with a large, goofy grin on his face.

Chapter 4

The group of four walked up the stairs to the sixth floor. When they got to the top, the girls continued to walk to the end of the hall, where everyone else was headed. Nick stopped with Eric and told him he would go get the Charms teacher to help him get to the Headmistress' office.

It was a few minutes till a tall, chubby man walked out of the door at the end of the hall. The man was shaggy-looking, like he hadn't taken a shower in days. His brown suit was wrinkled and had stains all over it.

"How may I help you?" His voice cracked as he spoke.

"I'm new and just got here, last night. Sloan said if I needed to talk to her, I could do so at any time. So, I was wondering if I could go see her, now." Eric explained to the strange-looking teacher.

The teacher looked into space for a few seconds, then snapped his fingers, pointed at Eric, and croaked, "You must be Eric James. Aw yes, I've heard your story from other teachers. I'm sorry for your loss, and I welcome you, here. I am the Charms teacher for this school. My name is Mr. Chine."

Eric bowed his head and said, "Nice to meet you."

"Now, let's see if I remember the password... Oh, yes."

Mr. Chine took a dull red stick out of an inside pocket in his suit jacket, cleared his throat, and said, "Ravioli," and flicked his stick at the missing stairs. Nothing happened.

"Well, I guess that wasn't it. Let me try, again," he said.

Once again, he cleared his throat, and said, "Cream Puffs," flicked the stick, and once again, nothing happened.

"Well, I give up." The teacher's ruffled appearance took on an even more droopy air. But then, he straightened up as if he'd had a revelation.

Mr. Chine held out his hand and said, "Broom." Within seconds, a broom came flying down the hall and landed next to him. He picked it up off the ground and placed the broom in between his legs. He pushed off the ground with his feet and started floating on the broom up to the next floor.

From down below, Eric heard Mr. Chine knock on Sloan's door. It was a few minutes later when Mr. Chine floated back down on his broomstick. When he hit the floor, he got off the broom, looked at it, and said, "That will be all; you can go back, now," and the broom flew back into the Charms room.

"The Headmistress has informed me that the password is indeed not a food, but a number."

Once again, Mr. Chine took out his stick and cleared his throat. Instead of yelling the number, he whispered it and flicked his stick. Finally, the stairs appeared.

"Thank you, Mr. Chine," Eric said to him as he started walking up the stairs.

"You are very welcome, Eric," Mr. Chine said while walking down the hall toward his classroom.

When Eric reached the next floor, the door was open, and he could see Sloan sitting at her desk. By the time he reached the doorway, Sloan raised her head up and said, "Come on in and take a seat at my desk, Eric."

Eric walked into Sloan's office and went up to her desk. Like before, the same chair appeared as Eric was going to sit down. Sloan put some papers away in her desk, looked Eric in the eyes, and asked, "What can I do for you today, Eric?"

"What exactly happened, last night? And I don't have magical powers, so why am I here?" He clasped and unclasped his hands in confusion as he spoke.

"What happened, last night, should have never happened. Those people who attacked you were called the Shadow Reapers. You never should have gotten your powers."

"I don't have any power!" Eric exclaimed loudly, his frustration showing as he almost leapt out of his seat at Sloan.

"You must have powers," Sloan stated, soothingly. "Otherwise, none of this would have happened. The Shadow Reapers would have left you and your family alone."

Eric sat there with his hand on his head, looking down at his feet. His head was hurting because of all the emotions he was feeling. He still had no clue what happened to him, and the more he thought of it, the more confused and powerless he felt.

"Is there anything else I can help you with?" Sloan asked

while she was writing on a paper.

"I was wondering where I could get clothes for school. The clothes I have on, right now, are borrowed from someone. And since this is a school, what will I need? And what classes am I taking?" he asked her.

"In a couple of weeks, you and the rest of the Freshmen will take the SATs. After you take the test, you will get the schedule for this year. As for the clothes and supplies," Sloan said as she pulled out a pen and paper from a drawer and started writing, "...you will have to go down to the village that is just beyond the school grounds. There, you will find the stores I have written down for you on the back of your pass."

"How much does all of this cost? I don't have any money on me. There is a couple hundred in my bank account back at home, but everything else is gone. "

"You do have money, here. All of your money is in your mom's old bank account. Your mother's family was very wealthy, and her family was one of the richest families in the magic community. Now, all of that money is yours."

"My mother went here? What about my father, did he go here, also? How come they never told me about all of this?"

"Yes indeed, your mother went here. She and I were the best of friends. I was at their wedding, and when you were born, she named me your godmother. So, from now on, you will be living with me. We will discuss that at a later time, though.

"You father did not go to this school. He was on a different side when he was young, but that is a story for another time, too. Everything will be explained when the time comes," Sloan said with a kind smile on her face.

"One more question, if you don't mind?"

"I do not mind a bit. Ask away."

"I'm only 14, so why do I have to take the SATs? SATs are for Juniors and Seniors. I'm just getting into Freshman year, this school year."

"Those SATs and our SATs are different. Our SATs stand for Special Ability Test instead of Scholastic Assessment Test. If these tests say that you have a special ability, then you get put in the SA classes."

"Oh, okay. I think that is all the questions I had, right now. Thanks for your help, Sloan," Eric said to her. His lips were smiling, but his face looked sad. In reality, he didn't feel like smiling, at all, but he attempted it with an effort.

"You are welcome, Eric. And remember that I will always be here for you."

Tears were now falling from Eric's face. It finally hit him that his parents were gone... that he would never see them, again.

"Do not cry, Eric. I know things are hard, right now, but things will change for the better. Trust me, Eric. I understand you miss your parents."

Sloan got up from her desk, walked over to Eric, and put one hand on his shoulder and the other one under his chin. She moved his head so she knew he was looking at her, and gave him a small, caring smile.

"I just can't believe they're really gone. Everything is happening so fast," he croaked with emotion, tears still streaming down his cheeks.

Sloan went to a table on the right side of the room and grabbed a box of tissues. She handed them to Eric; he blew his nose, and wiped his cheeks.

"Thanks. Can some people go with me down to the village?"

"Sure. Give me their names, so I can tell their teachers they will be gone for the rest of the school day."

"Nick Walters, Marina Martin, and Catlin Chamberlin," Eric said as Sloan wrote down their names.

Sloan and Eric exchanged their goodbyes, and Eric left her office in search of his friends.

Chapter 5

By 10:30, Eric, Nick, Marina, and Catlin headed downstairs to the main hall to leave the school. Two large, grey stone statues guarded the large oak doors that headed outside. One was a sculpture of a thin, young-looking lady in a toga. The other was of a man on a horse.

"Halt. Who goes there?" said the sculpture of the man on the horse.

Eric was shocked to see a stone figure was actually talking and looking at them.

"Students of Aviance." Nick said back.

"State your reason for leaving."

"We are going down to the village of Hillthrope."

"Show me ye pass."

After the pass was flashed at him, the man bowed his head and went back to being a statue. The woman got off her platform, opened the large door, and whispered, attractively, "Have a nice trip to the village, young ones!" A gush of warm air hit them as they stepped through the door.

Just beyond the school's boundaries was a thick forest. The grass, outside, was a deep green color and smelled like it had been freshly mowed. Flowers of different colors and variety lined the walls of the school and the path to the village.

"So, how far is the village?" Eric asked while looking doubtfully at the mountains in the distance.

"The village is in the same valley, but it's half a mile away. There are several magical communities and towns, here, in this part of the valley."

The further down the pathway they walked, the clearer tops of houses and chimneys appeared ahead of them. The thick trees of the forest thinned and gave way to reveal a clear way into the colorful buildings, ahead.

Halfway to the village, Nick decided to ask, "So, where do you have to go?"

Eric pulled out the sheet of paper from his pocket and read the list. "Hillthrope Bank. Joey's Bookstore. Glock's Cauldrons, Pens, and more. And Phoenix Clothing Store."

"Okay. That will be easy to do. We'll go to the bank, first, 'cause that's the first building we come across." said Nick.

"Be careful of how you talk to the workers, Eric. They can be very hot-headed. I had a cousin who smart-mouthed, and they took all his money," said Catlin.

"That's terrible! How can they do that?" asked Eric.

"I don't know, but they do that all the time."

"That's just sick."

Finally, they got to the village of Hillthrope. The bank was a large, purple, stone-covered building at the end of a row of wooden taverns. Metal bars covered the dark windows. A dull grey, metal door had the words *Hillthrope Bank* written in golden capital letters.

Inside of the building was just as bright as it was outside. Several huge chandeliers hung from the elevated ceiling, and a huge, silver bank safe was on the far wall. The marble floors and stonewalls were all turquoise. Purple-painted wood counters were lined from wall to wall about ten feet in front of the safe. Several tall, skinny people were standing behind the counters, counting money. When Eric was close to one of the open registers, one of the workers looked up.

"Name," he said in a harsh tone.

"Eric James."

"There is no account registered to that name," said the bank teller after typing on a keyboard.

"It would probably be under my mother's name," Eric pointed out to the man wearing a grey suit with a white tie.

"You cannot access someone else's account without their permission."

"But she's dead. Listen, Sloan said I could access the account, since I'm part of her family."

"Is that so?"

"Yes, it is," Eric said raising his voice, a little.

Marina tapped his shoulder and whispered in his ear, "Keep calm. They won't give you anything if you make them mad."

Eric took a deep breath and asked, "Is there any way I can get the money from my mom's account?"

21

"What is her full maiden name?"

"Amelia Christine May."

The worker tapped his long pointy fingers on the keyboard a few times and then inquired, "Do you wish to remove all of the money from this account and make your own?"

"Yes, that would be fine," Eric said to the bank teller.

"Full name, please."

"Eric Arthur James."

He tapped a few more times on the counter and then handed Eric a silver card, the size of a debit card. "This is your bank card. Do not lose it, because you will not get another one. Good day."

The silver card had a black magnetic strip on the back. Eric's name was on the front, and the letters H and B were in gold on the top of it. As soon as they were out of the bank, Eric put the card in his front pocket for safekeeping.

Nick said, "I hate them. Most of them are rude and creepy."

"I've heard rumors that some of them never sleep," said Catlin.

"That's just weird," Eric said.

The buildings on either side of the street were mostly two-story buildings. They had a Victorian style to them, and the bricks they were made of were all different colors for different buildings. One was red, one was blue, one was grey, and one was brown, and so on. Each of the storefronts had two, large display windows with different items in them, and the stores' names were on the windows and on the doors.

"Where next, Eric?" asked Nick, looking into one of the store's window.

"A place called Glock's Cauldrons, Pens, and More," Eric said, looking at the piece of paper.

"OOOOHHHHH!! That is right next to Britt's Diner!! I love that place! They have amazing milkshakes," Marina exclaimed as she and Catlin rubbed their stomachs.

"We need to eat lunch, there, after this store," Catlin hissed with enthusiasm.

"Agreed," Nick said as he ran his hand through his hair.

"Well, I guess we're eating at Britt's Diner," Eric said.

It took a few minutes for them to get to Glock's. The display windows were full of notebooks and small, round pots full of pens.

They opened a door, and a small bell chimed throughout the store. An old, dwarfish woman with a grey-haired bun situated on top of her head came from around the register to ogle the young assortment of customers. Eric looked around at the various items that covered the walls. Large pots were on the table, in the middle. A register, where the woman came from, was in front of the window.

"What can I help you with, dearie?"

"I'm just starting out, here, so I don't really know what I need," Eric told the woman.

"Well, I can get'cha some of the essentials. You'll need to come back after you take your SATs, dearie," she said to Eric, as she walked to the table with pots. Once there, she said, "First off, you will need a number two cauldron," and grabbed a bronze pot. She continued puttered around the room, collecting random pens and notebooks to put inside the cauldron.

Once she was done, she went back to the register and punched some things into it. "Your total is one hundred and thirty-dollars and fifty-five cents."

Eric handed the old woman his card, and she swiped it across the top of the register. She handed the card back and gave Eric his items.

"Thank you, dear. Have a nice day," she said, handing him his sack full of items.

"You, too," Eric replied as he opened the door, causing the bell to ring, again. Once out in the streets, the group turned right and headed to Britt's Diner for lunch.

The diner was reminiscent of the fifties. Red and white leather bar stools were under the white marble bar. The same red leather was on all of the chair seats and booth seats. The booths lined the front wall and the side walls. Regular, round white tables were in the middle of the room. The bar was on the far side of the room with the kitchen behind it.

Neon lights were everywhere around the room. A neon sign that had the name of the diner was hanging in the windows. Black and white tiles covered the floor. Large black and white photos were hung on all of the walls, along with some old records. A small jukebox on the bar was playing some old rock 'n' roll. Several people, who were already seated, were looking strangely at Eric as they walked in.

"Take a seat anywhere, huns; I'll get to you, real soon," said a young redheaded woman in a poodle skirt that was serving an older couple at one of the tables.

Eric, Nick, Marina, and Catlin sat in one of the booths under the window. Once they were all seated, they picked up the menu and looked through it.

"What's good, here?" asked Eric.

"Their double ranch bacon burger is real tasty," said Catlin.

"I say their Wisconsin cheese quarter pounder is delicious," said Nick, licking his lips.

"Well, I think that their baby back ribs are to die for. If you like ribs, you should get them," Marina said, drooling a little.

The redheaded girl came over to their table and asked what they wanted to drink and if they wanted any appetizers.

"We'll take your supreme cheesy fries, and I'll have a medium lemon milkshake," said Marina.

"For you, sir?" said the waitress, looking at Nick.

"A large, orange milkshake."

"A medium cookies and cream milkshake," said Catlin.

"I'll take a large vanilla shake, please," Eric said to the waitress.

"I'll get those to you as soon as I can," the waitress acknowledged with a brilliant smile.

When she walked away, Eric asked, "So these SATs... are they hard?"

"No, they are extremely easy, especially if you have a known special power, like Nick," said Marina, nudging Nick with her elbow.

"What power do you have, Nick?" Eric asked.

"Astral Projection, which means I can have my physical body in one spot but another copy of myself in another. I can also do Molecular Immobilization, meaning that I can freeze things."

"Wow, that's really cool!" said Eric, not really believing it.

"I'd show you, but we are only supposed to use our powers in school." Nick said, looking disappointed.

"I don't think I have powers, because neither of my parents did, and I know I can't do any of the things you can," Eric said, hanging his head, a little.

"That's probably because you never really tried to harness your powers, yet," said Catlin, cheerfully.

"And one, your mother was a powerful witch, here. And two, if the Shadow Reapers were after you, then you have power, kid." said Marina.

"My mother? What? If my mom was powerful, then how come she never used her powers?"

"She couldn't. Not after what she did," Nick said.

"What did she do that was that bad?"

"That is a story for another time. So are the Shadow Reapers. You don't really talk about them and what your parents did in public," Catlin said.

"You promise to tell me, later though, right?"

"Yes, we promise," said Nick, "This is something you need to know."

"One more thing. What is up with the sticks?"

"What sticks?" asked Marina.

"The sticks everyone keeps flicking around."

"Oh, you mean wands! Wands help you with spells and potions. Freshmen get theirs in the first week of school in Potions class."

Soon, the waitress came back with their drinks, and they ordered their food.

Chapter 6

After eating their food, they meandered down to the next shop, called *Joey's Bookstore*. Eric was still confused about the magic stuff, and he honestly thought that everybody was crazy. No one was making real sense.

As they tried to cross the street to get to the store, a yellow taxicab cut them off. Nick got mad at this and waved his hands in the direction of the cab. Instantly, the cab stopped moving. To Eric, it seemed that no one else around seemed to notice that it wasn't moving. In fact, nobody but the group was moving, either. Eric couldn't believe his eyes.

"Nick, you have to learn to control your powers. Now, unfreeze the cab before you get in trouble," hissed Marina.

Nick waved his hands, again, and everything around them unfroze.

"There... happy?" he asked, still a little perturbed at the situation.

"Very," Marina said and kissed him on the lips.

"It wouldn't have happened if he didn't cut us off," Nick said, taking a few breaths, trying to calm down.

"You know, if anybody knew we did that, we would be in severe trouble." Catlin said to Nick.

As the group walked, they passed a music store that was playing some pop music.

"I love this song!" Marina and Catlin chorused, slowing down to listen.

"I hate this song. This artist is more annoying than Justin Bieber and Rebecca Black, combined," Eric groaned while dramatically rolling his eyes at Nick.

Catlin and Marina stopped in their tracks, turned around, and almost shrieked, "Do not diss our Bieber!"

"Sorry, it won't happen, again." Eric mumbled, noticeably blushing from the verbal attack.

"And besides, how can you hate Katy Perry?" asked Nick

before singing the chorus of the song.

Eric rolled his eyes, and Marina giggled. "Don't make me transform you into a frog."

"Can you even do that?"

"Yes, I have the power of Metamorphosis."

"And I have the power of Divination- the power to see the future. I have premonitions, but they are never anything big. I mainly just see what I did on a test. Stuff like that," Catlin said, dismissing her own powers with a toss of her head.

Eric's eyes widened. "Wow, but I thought you didn't have a special power, Marina," he said, surprise coloring his voice.

"Okay, so I don't know if I can turn you into frog, or not, but I sure can try."

Soon, the four of them reached the storefront, and Nick stopped in front of Eric, crouched down a little, and waggled his hands. "Prepare to be amazed," he said, drawing out the words in a mysteriously ominous voice.

The front of the store had no windows. It was a solid, yellow brick, except for a wide, darkly wooded door. On it was *Joey's Bookstore* in silver lettering. Marina opened the door for everyone, and as Eric stepped inside, he was surprised by how bright it was. It took a few moments for his eyes to adjust to the light, but when they did, he gasped with amazement. Floor to ceiling golden bookshelves were full of different-sized books covering the walls. The floor was made up of solid, polished, golden bricks.

Eric couldn't see the ceiling of the store, though. It looked like there wasn't a ceiling. Instead, the bookshelves seemed to tower off into infinity. On the far side of the store, a spiral staircase went from the bottom to the third floor, and in the middle of the room was a small area for the cashier's counter.

Before he knew it, Nick and Marina were at a bookshelf that said *New Arrivals*, and Catlin was near the mystery section. Eric was unsure what to do, so he walked to the cashier's counter to ask for help.

"How may I help you, young man?" said a husky-looking old man that was wearing a white shirt and jeans.

"I just need the essentials for school," Eric told the man.

"What grade are you currently in?" asked the man.

"I'm a Freshman."

"Well, since you haven't taken the SATs, I'll give you the books that every Freshman needs. Then, when you get the results from your SATs, you can come back and get those books."

When the old man was done talking, Eric followed him as he started walking toward a bookshelf. Stopping here and there at random bookshelves, he proceeded to hand Eric an assortment of titles. *Charms: First Year. DASR: Beginners. Potions with Limits. How to Fly.* And *History of Magic and Its World.*

Once he had all of his books, Eric followed the older gentleman back to the register counter. His friends were waiting on him with books in their hands. After being rung up and paying, Eric and his friends left the breathtaking building.

As they were going to the last store, *Phoenix Clothing Store,* Eric asked, "Can I ask you guys a question?"

"Sure. Ask away," said Nick.

"Who are the Shadow Reapers?"

Nick cast a worried glance at Catlin and Marina, with a look that seemed to say, 'Should we tell him?' After a moment's laden pause, he acquiesced, "We'll tell you when we get back to school."

Eric accepted this, noticing the reluctance in Nick's voice and the sudden uncomfortable atmosphere that settled upon the group. They shopped in relative silence, but Eric's friends helped him choose his outfits for school. He also ended up buying some things for bed, some nicer things for parties, a couple pairs of shoes, and a few accessories. When they were finished, they started to head back to school.

Chapter 7

At 4:07, they arrived at the school. A tall, white-marbled stone knight was guarding the outside of the school gates, providing an intimidating display.

"Stand ho! Who goes there?" asked the knight.

"Friends of the grounds." said Marina.

"State yer names."

They all stated their names, but when Eric said his name, the Knight said, "Unidentified name," and then, disappeared.

"What happens, now?" asked Eric.

"It goes and contacts the Headmistress," said Catlin.

The knight reappeared and said, "You have been identified, Eric James. Welcome to Aviance." The door opened, and they walked in.

Once they were all inside, they trekked up to the Freshman living room. There were a few students watching TV, while some were lying on the floor, reading books and studying. Eric went to the boys' bedroom to put away his new clothes and supplies, while his friends sat down on a couch near a window. When he returned to the living room, a few students walked out of the room with books in their arms.

"How long do classes last for? My last school started at 8:00 and ended at 3:05. It's almost 4:30, and people are still going to class." Eric said as he walked over to them, trailing glances at the students who were leaving.

"They're probably going to the library to study, but they could have scheduled classes this late. The latest class ends at 8:00," said Catlin.

When they were the only ones in the room, Eric asked, "When can we talk about the things I asked about, earlier?"

"We can talk about it, now, if you want," Nick said as he stretched his arms up and behind his head.

Eric nodded his head. "Yes, please."

"What do you want to talk about, first?" Nick asked, as he

got even more comfortable on the couch.

"Tell me about my mother and father."

Nick took a deep breath and began. "Your mother made history here in the magic community. When she took her SATs, she was put into all of the SA classes, but that's not how she made history. She made history by falling in love with your father. During her years here, she found love, but her love was forbidden. She was a White Knight, as are we, but the one she fell in love with was a Shadow Reaper."

"What's the difference between the two?" Eric asked, getting confused.

"You'll learn more about this in history class, but basically, after the witch hunts in 1692, the Shadow Reaper felt threatened by the world and decided to take over. The White Knights formed to stop them, and ever since then, we have tried to stop them.

"Your parents tried to keep their romance a secret, but they got careless and were found out. After that, she was forbidden to see him, ever again.

"After she graduated from Aviance, your father proposed to her. People from both sides tried to stop the marriage, saying that the only way they could go through with it was if they gave up their magic. This didn't stop your parents, though; they gladly gave up their powers if it meant they could be with each other.

"Soon after the marriage, they had you. It was rumored that you were to have powers from both sides. Meaning, you not only can do the things we do, but you also have the power of fire, as well. And with those powers, you could end the fight between the two sides. With this information, people from both sides wanted to get their hands on you and use you for their side, but they could never find you."

"Why couldn't they find me?"

"No one knows," Catlin said in the brief silence that followed the question. "The people who killed your parents, the Shadow Reapers, formed soon after Aviance did, in 1699. Aviance had a teacher for the power of fire, named Vesta De'Lore. An unknown person promised Vesta a great deal of power and control if he came with him. Vesta soon broke away from Aviance and formed his own magical community. Over the years, he has formed an army to take us down, so he can take over the world. Along the way, he has formed a few tricks we haven't figured out, just yet, like how they travel. We know they use the shadows to move, but it involves some sort of portal."

"How is he this old and still living?" Eric asked, confusion marring his features.

"An extended life was part of the gift he was promised," said Marina as she stared out of the window.

"Where is his community? Why can't you guys just go there and attack them?" asked Eric.

"No one knows where they are. Only the Shadow Reapers know," said Nick.

"And every moment he isn't stopped, more and more innocent Numes, normal non-magical people, and White Knights are killed," said Catlin.

"Why hasn't Vesta been stopped?" asked Eric, his eyebrows drawing together in anger and pain as he remembered how his parents had fallen by this organization's hand.

"You think we would be able to, wouldn't you? But we can't. We have been fighting for so long that our powers have grown weak. What we need to end this is someone with a lot of power," said Marina.

"Was my mom powerful?" asked Eric, looking down at his feet, thinking of the last time he saw her.

"I've heard she was more powerful than any other witch or wizard, alive," said Nick.

"Yeah, my mom said that she had the power to stop the whole world with the twist of her nose," said Catlin.

This news made Eric smile, sadly. Tears prickled at his eyes, and his nose started to tingle, causing them to begin spilling down his downcast face.

"Why are you crying, Eric? You just found out that your mom was super powerful. Be happy," Marina said.

"I am happy to hear that... it's just that it makes me sad that I never knew the magical part of her life. I have another question for you guys, if you don't mind."

"Sure, go ahead," Nick said.

"Why is school in the summer?"

"Because we still have to go to regular school. Right now,

our Norm friends think we are at summer camp," Catlin said as she turned on the TV.

"Why can't we tell them we are here?" Eric asked them.

"That would mean telling them we are magical, and we don't want to start another witch hunt. We don't tell them for our own protection. If it got out that there really is a thing called magic, people would want to take advantage of us and our powers," said Marina.

"Then, how did you find out you were all magical?" Eric asked them.

"We trusted each other enough. We knew that having special powers wouldn't come between us," said Catlin, hugging Marina.

To Eric, this just all sounded nuts. There was no way he could have trusted someone that much. All he'd ever dealt with were people who seemed incapable of trust.

As the five o'clock evening news came on the television, the group of friends decided to head down to the main hall for dinner. By the time they got to the hall, the teachers were already at their table, and most of the students were seated. As the trickling of students into the hall slowed to a stop, Sloan stood up. It was hard to tell, but to Eric, it looked as if Sloan was crying.

"Attention students," she said, letting students quiet down before she started talking, again. "Tonight is another sad night for us as a community. Two Numes and five White Knights have been killed. There was an attack on the wizard town in Ohio, called Chesterville."

A few people at different tables let out a small scream, and several people started to cry. All of the students pulled out their cell phones and started to type text messages to whomever they knew in that area.

After a while, Sloan said, "Let us, please, stop and think of those who have been lost."

People bowed their heads and prayed for the families who had lost loved ones.

"Let us eat and be happy for our freedom, but be sure to keep those who have lost their freedom in your prayers," Sloan said before she sat down, signaling the ghosts to come out, like they did at breakfast.

"What does Sloan mean when she says that the dead lost their freedom?" Eric asked the group as he grabbed a plate of meatloaf and mashed potatoes.

"The Shadow Reapers kill people's bodies, but they keep the souls as slaves for their community," said Catlin.

"That's just wrong! Nobody should be a slave in the afterlife!" Eric sneered, outraged.

"I know it is. My mother is one of those slaves," said Catlin as she bowed her head.

"I'm so sorry. I can't even imagine how that feels, knowing that they are still out there," Eric said to Catlin, patting her shoulder, awkwardly.

"Eric, I don't mean to be rude, but your parents are slaves, now too," she murmured back.

Eric's face went white and emotionless

"Dude, you okay? We just thought you would have figured it out when we told you about it," Nick said, leaning a bit closer as he studied Eric's reaction.

"I'm fine, I think. I just wish there was something we could do to set them free."

Even though it was sad, everyone knew that there was nothing that could be done for the lost ones.

"Wait, what's the difference from the Spirit Slaves and the ghosts, here?" Eric asked.

"The ghosts, here, are volunteers. They are some of the first students that came to Aviance." Catlin explained.

After they finished their dinner, the group of friends headed upstairs to the living room. They sat on the couch that was in front of the TV and watch it until 11:00, when they went to bed.

The sun was setting as Eric and Elizabeth walked along the beach, hand in hand. The ocean's waves rolled onto their naked feet in tender caresses, and the cool breeze made the hot night feel just right for them as they continued down the beach.

"I've enjoyed this, Eric. I'm glad you and your family invited me down to Florida for vacation," Elizabeth said as she adjusted her neon yellow swim wrap.

"I'm glad you came. It just wouldn't be the same without you. Want to go on one last swim for the day?"

"Sure!" Elizabeth said as she removed her wrap to reveal a royal blue bikini.

Eric quickly removed his light green t-shirt that matched his green and white plaid shorts and raced Elizabeth to the ocean.

A little while later, the soft pattering of rain drove them from the water, and when the couple reached the sandy beach, the sky lit up with lightning, quickly followed with the roar of thunder in the background.

They quickly ran up the beach to the hotel, but halfway up the stony path, the air changed from hot to freezing cold. An electric charge made the hair on the naps of their necks raise in alarm, and the air stilled, like death, while lightning came crashing down on Elizabeth.

Covered in blue fire, Elizabeth fell to the ground, convulsing violently.

"Elizabeth!" Eric fell to his knees in shock of what just happened.

"If you love me, Eric James, why haven't you saved me?" Elizabeth said to Eric, her voice accusing and whispering in despair.

"What do you mean, Elizabeth? I don't know how to save you!"

Elizabeth stopped moving, all together, with her eyes wide open, staring into the sky. Her voice moaned, "If you don't save me, soon, I'll die."

Thunder exploded, and lightning struck Elizabeth in the chest, making her body explode into ashes.

Chapter 8

The next morning, Nick woke Eric up a little before 8:30. The memories of his dream flooded his head, making him sweat. After taking a few minutes to get his mind focused on the day, he got up off his bed and went to his dresser. In his agitation to get his clothes out, he knocked his cauldron off the top, spilling all of the pens and notebooks. Several people who had been sleeping jerked up in surprise.

"Sorry," Eric mumbled to the kids, gathering up the spilled items and stuffing them in his backpack.

When he was ready, he walked into the living room and noticed Marina sitting on the couch watching *The Today Show* on the television with Catlin. Both of them were already dressed and ready to go.

Several other kids were sitting around the room doing various other activities, like playing on phones, computers, reading, or watching another television show. Eric slipped out into the hall and to the bathroom, barely registering a couple of boys that were chatting in front of him as he walked.

In the bathroom, he noticed with relief that the shower soap didn't hurt his cuts as badly as it did, yesterday. When he got dressed, he sighed with relief. Being in his own clothes took a huge weight off his chest; not that he didn't appreciate the help that had been offered to him, but he'd started feeling like a charity case.

Back in the living room, Nick was sitting beside Marina, and Catlin had left the room. Other than that, the room was empty.

"Good morning, Eric," Marina said to him with a smile as he sat down by Nick.

"Morning. Where did Catlin go?"

"She got a call from her dad."

"Oh. So, what are you guys doing, today?"

"We were going down to breakfast as soon as Catlin gets

done. Then, we have a few more classes. You can join us if you want."

"Yeah, I'm sure the teachers won't mind. After all, it is only the second day of the starter classes," Nick said.

"Okay, that sounds fun."

The person on the TV was now talking about how the gas prices were getting so high. Soon, a commercial for laundry detergent came on, and Catlin walked out of the girls' bedroom.

"My dad called to inform me that he is going to France for the summer because of work."

"Well, that's cool. Where does he work?" Eric asked.

"He's part of the FBI."

"That's awesome!" Eric said.

"Yeah, except that I don't see him all that much. I spend more time with the maid than I do him. But anyways, let's go down and eat breakfast."

As the group walked to the main hall, Eric told them about his dream.

"What do you think it means?" he asked the group.

"I don't know. Maybe, we could ask the Divination teacher. I bet you she will know." Marina told Eric.

At about 9:30, Sloan came into the main hall in a full-length, golden ball gown. Silver beads glittered on the top, and her gray hair was down and pulled back with a silver headband. She stood behind the table and gave the daily announcements.

"Five... Four... Three... Two... One... Thanks for getting quiet.

"Freshmen, do not forget that your SATs are in a week. My stairs will be unlocked, so students can come up and put their names on the sign-up sheet. That is all of the announcements for right now. Let us eat and be merry."

Once again, the ghosts came out of the walls and delivered breakfast to the students and teachers.

When they were done with their breakfast, the foursome chatted about the trip into town that they'd taken, yesterday. Catlin and Marina were talking about some of the books they'd seen in the bookstore when Nick asked about Eric's hometown.

"Deer Knoll? It's a small town. You can stand at one side and clearly see your friend standing on the other side of town. What about your hometown?"

"It's a town called Riverview, in Virginia, which is a weird name for it since there is no river near it. Marina and Catlin live in Riverview also, but they go to a different school than I do."

"Sounds like a big town."

"It's larger than the surrounding towns."

When Nick and Eric stopped talking, Sloan tapped on Eric's shoulder.

"Eric, I need to see you after breakfast in my office. You did not do anything wrong. I just need to talk to you about some things." Sloan didn't wait for a response; as soon as she was done speaking, she walked out of the main hall.

"What was that about?" asked Marina, her eyes a little wider than normal.

"She wants to talk to me about something."

"What did you do?" whispered Nick.

"I don't know. I couldn't have done anything wrong. After all, I was with you guys all day."

"We know you did nothing wrong; we were just teasing you." Catlin said, placing her hand on his and giggling softly.

As soon as their hands touched, images flooded his mind.

"What's wrong? Did I shock you, or something?" she asked him.

"No. It's just…"

"What is it, Eric? You can tell us? We're your friends." Nick told him.

Eric smiled at them and said, "I know you are, and I'm grateful to have you guys. It's just the way Catlin touched me. It reminded me of my old girlfriend. And when you touched me," he said, looking at Catlin, "strange images flooded my head."

"Okay, you have to tell us about this girl," said Marina.

"Her name was Elizabeth Williams. We'd been dating for a few months, but it felt like forever, in a good way. We were in love. I actually thought we were going to get married after high school. But, last year, she was kidnapped. It happened in the middle of the night, during a thunderstorm. The kidnapper never gave her parents a ransom note, or anything. After about three months, the police told her parents and me that the kidnapper probably killed her," Eric told them.

"I'm so sorry, Eric. I didn't know," Catlin said to him

"How could you, we only met yesterday? I usually don't talk

about it, but I like you guys. You've been very friendly."

"I know how it feels to lose someone that was that close to you, like that," said Marina with her head bent down.

Nick put a hand on her shoulder to comfort her. "You don't have to talk about it, Marina."

"But talking about her keeps her memory alive. I lost my sister, Eric. It was about 9 years ago, but it feels like yesterday.

"Her name was Summer, and she was seventeen. I was five. She was really tall, skinny as a stick, and very athletic. It was her Senior year in high school, and she was driving over to her boyfriend's house to tell him that she got a soccer scholarship to Grace College.

"When she was almost to his house, some Shadow Reapers attacked her car. Everyone thinks that Summer swerved to avoid hitting a dog, and what caused the explosion was how the car hit the tree. I was so torn apart when the police told my family."

The group was silent until Eric asked, "So, is Summer one of those Spirit Slaves now?"

"No. She wasn't directly killed from their magic. You see, she wasn't wearing her seatbelt, so she flew out of the car when it hit the tree, and that's what caused her death. If she had been wearing her seatbelt, she would be a slave, right now."

"Ever since she was kidnapped, I keep imagining I see her everywhere," said Eric.

"So did I, until it finally hit me that she was gone."

At five till 10:00, everybody got up from the tables and started to go to classes. Eric walked his friends up to the sixth floor, where they said their goodbyes. As Nick, Marina, and Catlin went to their class, Eric climbed the stairs to Sloan's office.

As Eric neared the door, he could hear two muffled voices. When he offered a tentative knock, he heard Sloan say something, and a loud bang echoed from behind the door. Soon, the door flew open, and an almost morbidly obese man in a black suit stormed out of the office. He ran his large, puffy hands over his greasy comb-over, gave Eric a disgusted look, and marched down the stairs.

"Who was that?" Eric asked Sloan as he walked into the office, casting uneasy glances at the stairs.

"That man is your Metamorphosis teacher." Sloan said,

walking over to her desk to sit down. "He is extremely upset that you are here."

"Why?" Eric asked with surprise as he sat down in front of her desk.

"Because he thinks that you should not have powers, because your parents gave up theirs when they married."

"When they were killed, I did see something strange, now that I think about it. When my father was being attacked, he did something with his hands. I don't know. It hurts too much to think about it."

"That's fine, Eric. But from what you just told me, it sounds like your father was using magic, so, they must have had powers. But the question is, did they regain their powers before you were born? Otherwise, you wouldn't have powers. You must have them, though, because the scroll gave us your name."

"What?"

"There is an old scroll hidden in the school, and only I know of its location. Once a year, it gives me the names of children who are the age of fourteen. Their addresses will appear on the list, and I invite them to our school, because these children possess magic."

"Two days ago, your name was written on that list. Right away, I knew who you were, and so did the Shadow Reapers."

"So, because they were after me, what does that mean, exactly?"

"It means that you could have the power of fire. This means that you can conjure up fire whenever you want, and you have the ability to control it. I will have to make sure that you get tested for that power. Speaking of that, would you like to sign up for that, now?"

"Sure," Eric said as he grabbed a pen from his backpack and signed up for the 1:30 spot on Monday.

"Is that all you wanted?"

"No."

Sloan rose from her desk and walked up the stairs to her balcony. She grabbed a few packages from a table and walked back down.

"The reason I asked you to come up here is to give you these," Sloan said as she handed Eric the packages.

Both packages were wrapped neatly in brown paper. The

top package was small and rectangular, while the second was about the size of a briefcase.

Eric laid the packages in his lap and stared at them until Sloan said, "Well, open them!" as she sat in her chair.

Eric picked up the small package, first, and started to tear of the brown paper. It was one of the brand new iPhones. Eric sat the phone carefully on Sloan's desk, so it didn't break.

After he tore off all the paper on the second gift, he discovered that it was a MacBook Pro. Speechless, Eric just stared at Sloan.

"You're welcome," she said with a brilliant smile.

"This is way too much, Sloan. I can't accept this."

"You will need the laptop for school, and I figured that you had a phone, before, so I decided to give you a new one. Think of it as a welcome gift."

"You give all of your students gifts like this?"

"Well no, but you're my godson. I figured it would make living with me a little bit easier."

Eric smiled, put his new laptop on the desk, and walked over to Sloan to give her a hug.

"Thank you for taking me in."

"I promised your mom and dad I would if anything bad happened to them. And besides, I am getting lonely in my big house."

"Don't you have a husband?"

"No."

"I'm sorry. So where do you… or uh, we live?"

"We live in a town near Washington D.C. called Twins Brook. I teach at the school during the regular school year. The people in the town are very friendly, so I doubt that you will have a hard time finding friends."

"Okay. Sounds like my old town."

"Just a little bigger, though," she said with a smile. "Now, if you do not mind, I have some paperwork to do."

Eric picked up his presents, thanked her again, and headed towards the Freshman living room. On his way, he started to program his phone with some of the contacts he knew by heart.

Chapter 9

Eric was sitting in the living room and playing on his new laptop when his friends came in after their morning classes.

"Wow. Where did you get those?" asked Marina.

"Sloan gave them to me," Eric told them.

"Well, that's awesome! You guys about ready for lunch?" asked Catlin.

"Of course, just let me shut down my laptop and put it away."

As soon as Eric came back, the group traveled down to the main hall for lunch. On the way down, Eric told him about his new phone and gave them all his number.

When they got to the main hall, Eric realized that Sloan and the teachers weren't at their table, like they usually were, and he didn't understand why.

"The teachers are preparing for their next class," Catlin explained.

And at 12:30 sharp, the ghosts came out and delivered the students' food.

"What classes do you guys have, next?" Eric asked as piles of sandwiches, fries, chicken nuggets, macaroni and cheese, and pizza were laid down on the table.

As Nick grabbed a slice of supreme pizza, he said, "It's a beginner class to Flying."

"Do all of you have the same classes?"

"Yep."

"How?"

"Well, we do right now, 'cause we got to sign up for these classes before we came, but we might not when school actually starts." said Marina.

"Oh, that makes sense. So, can I come with you to that class?"

"Sure. We get to ride, today!" said Marina.

"Oh." Eric's demeanor completely changed, turning from excited to morose in a matter of seconds.

"What?" Catlin said, giving him a funny look.

"I'm afraid of heights, and I'm extremely clumsy." He looked away from her, turning slightly red at the admission.

"You'll be fine. I know this sounds weird, but a broom is very easy to control, once you get used to it. And you don't have to fly real high."

"Okay, so, where is this class?" Eric asked.

"It's outside," Nick said to Eric.

"Okay, do I need to bring anything?"

"Nope, just your body!" Catlin giggled.

After lunch was over at 1:00, the foursome walked through the archway that was near their table and into another room. Then, they passed through a small, metal door that led to a large, metal room that had a few small windows on the left side.

"What is this room used for?" Eric asked as a few more people walked in behind them.

"It used to be where they taught the Fire Manipulation class, before Vesta went evil, but now, it's used to teach students how to fight against the Shadow Reapers," said Marina.

"How do you know all of this?" Eric asked.

"There are books in the library that talk about the history."

They walked to another metal door that was on the right side of the room. From there, they entered a small garden. It was full of different-colored plants that were almost trying to reach out of the confinement of their beds, effectively covering the edges of the stone path.

"This is the Potions' garden. We grow things in here that we need for the class. And the door on the opposite side, you see it? That leads to the Potions class. We pass the regular door to it every day when we come down to eat. It's in the common room, by the stairs," explained Catlin.

Eric just nodded his head and continued walking. They walked through a gate that lead out of the garden and continued down to another fenced-in area.

"Hurry up, students. Class is about to begin!" Sloan yelled to kids just coming into the garden.

"Sloan teaches this class, too?" asked Eric.

"Yep," said Nick in a high voice.

"What wrong with him?" Eric asked Marina.

"Oh, he's just scared. When we practiced at home, he fell off his broom," she answered him.

"How far off the ground was he?"

"A foot." giggled Catlin.

Nick turned his head and gave Catlin a dirty look.

"That's not high. That's not even scary to me," whispered Eric into Catlin's ear.

When they reached the fenced-in area, Eric saw several other kids around his age that were standing beside brooms. Marina and Nick stood on one side and Eric stood on the other side, next to Catlin.

"Now students, remember what we keep talking about. You have to believe you can fly before you try to take off. Otherwise, you will fail and fall. Try to clear your mind and picture the broom flying off the ground. Once you have enough courage in your flying ability, you can skip this step and just get on the broom and fly."

Eric closed his eyes and tried to picture the broom flying off the ground. After a few seconds, he peeked and saw his broom still lying on the ground.

This is so stupid. You can't fly, he thought to himself.

He closed his eyes, again, and inhaled as he thought, *Fly*. And he kept repeating that word in his mind until Marina cried out, "You did it, Eric!"

Eric opened his eyes and saw it still lying on the ground, but everyone else's was flying with them on it.

"What are you guys talking about? It hasn't even moved."

"But it was flying, Eric. When you opened your eyes, your connection was lost. Soon, with practice, you will learn how to just say or think *broom* for it to fly for you," Sloan said to Eric, patting his shoulder.

She turned her attention to the rest of the students, raising her voice, so that everyone could hear her. "For those who have a strong connection and think they want to fly, go right ahead. Remember, all you have to do to take off is to kick off with your feet. Once you are in the air, I want you to do ten laps around the school."

All of the students, besides Eric, kicked off the ground and flew away, and for the rest of the class, Sloan made them do obstacle courses while she helped Eric make the connection stronger.

After class, Marina and Catlin decided to go to the fifth floor library to study and read. Eric and Nick trekked to their living room, where Nick played a video game on the TV. Eric sat down with his laptop and started to play with it, getting more and more concerned as the minutes dragged on.

After a while, Eric said, "They think I'm dead."

"Who?" asked Nick.

"Everybody from Deer Knoll. They keep posting on my wall on Facebook saying *RIP* and *You will be missed.*"

"Why would they think that?"

"They must have thought I died in the explosion."

"What are you going to do?"

"I don't know. What do you think I should do?"

"Tell them what happened, but just leave all the magic details out," suggested Nick.

"Okay."

Eric typed for a few and then said, "Tell me if this sounds okay. *I am not dead. I escaped from those people before my house exploded. I kept running through the woods till I got to the interstate. Once there, I hitchhiked to my godmother's summer camp where I am, now.* Sound okay?"

"Yeah, but if you don't mind me asking, how come you are the only one that they are talking about on there? From what you told me, the Shadow Reapers burned your whole community."

Eric looked up Deer Knoll's newspaper and found an article on that night.

"Apparently, people's houses did catch fire, but right after the explosion, fire trucks arrived. The Shadow Reapers ended up disappearing before the cops got there."

"But was anyone else killed that night?"

"No," Eric said as he shut his computer and bowed his head.

"Well, what do you say we text Marina and tell her and Catlin to meet us on the fourth floor so we can go to the Divination teacher?"

"Sure."

44

Chapter 10

At a quarter to three, the four friends walked into the Divination room. The windows were covered with dark curtains, and the darkness that encompassed them gave an impression of twilight, barely allowing them to see the desks split up into three rows of ten. Crystal balls sat on each desk, and candlesticks were around the room, giving just enough light to see.

"What can I do for you four?" said a woman that was sitting at the teacher's desk.

She looked like an old-fashioned gypsy, complete with big, golden hoop earrings and multi-colored bangles on her arm. She had a brown, leather vest over her loose, white blouse, and a green and gold skirt fell down to her brown, leather boots.

Foreboding nipped at Eric as he stepped closer to her and said, "Last night, I had this awful dream. My old girlfriend and I were walking along this beach. Out of nowhere, she gets struck by lightning and then, dies. Before she dies, she asks me if I love her. I tell her I do, and then, she yells that if I did, why haven't I saved her."

"Pull up a chair, my young one," she murmured, softly.

Eric took a chair from a desk and sat across from the teacher.

"First off, my name is Mrs. Grey. I know that you are Eric James. Now tell me, what is this girl's name?" Her voice was soothing, like honey, and Eric felt himself relax.

"Elizabeth Williams."

Mrs. Grey waved her hands around the ball and mumbled, "Ostendite mihi puellam petit. Does she have red hair and grey eyes?"

"Yes. Do you see her?"

"Yes." Mrs. Grey frowned, sadly.

"Is she alive?"

"The person you once knew as Elizabeth Williams is not

45

alive. You do not want to know what is left of her. I'm sorry, Eric." Mrs. Grey got up and went to one of the bookshelves and pulled out a book. "I'm going to give you this book. It can tell you how to decipher a dream. It sounds like she is trying to tell you something, but I can't figure it out by just what you told me. Do you remember any other dream?"

"Not that I can recall," Eric said with downcast eyes.

"Hopefully, you will have a few more so you can use this book. Good luck, Eric James, and I'm sorry for your loss. Come back anytime you need to talk about this kind of stuff."

Eric said, "Thank you for your help," took the book, and left with his friends. When they were out of the room, Eric asked, "How can she be alive but dead at the same time?"

"Coma?" Nick suggested with a frown.

"Well, whatever it is, we are sorry. We will help you try to find her if you need our help," Catlin said to Eric, patting his shoulder softly.

"Thanks guys. I just wish I could figure out if I had dreams like that, before last night."

"You could probably figure out what she is trying to tell you if you remembered," said Marina.

"Yeah. Well, I don't really feel like going to classes with you guys for the rest of the day. I'll just go to the living room and read this book."

"We understand. We will see you later, Eric," Nick said as he walked down the stairs.

Eric went downstairs to the second floor Freshman dormitory. Instead of staying in the living room, he went to the bedroom to lie on his bed.

"Eric! Wake up! Eric!" Elizabeth screamed, jolting him up in surprise.

Was he awake, or was he still sleeping? Looking around, he saw the boy's dormitory, but Elizabeth was here too, standing at the foot of his bed.

"Listen, Eric," she implored him. "This is a dream, honey. I'm sorry to disappoint you, but it's the only way I can talk to you."

"But..."

"No, don't talk. Listen. That woman you talked to, earlier,

is right. I am dead but not really dead. I don't really understand it, either. Before I leave, again, I need to tell you a few details before you wake up.

"The night I was kidnapped, I was taken by the Shadow Reapers. Vesta is keeping my body for something."

Elizabeth started with surprise, looking around in fear.

"I'm about to leave, now. My spirit is getting weaker. I love you, Eric James. I always have and always will."

The door slammed open, drawing their attention, and a ghostly, pale man walked through, wearing an all-black tux.

"Your soul will burn in hell for this, daughter!" The man raged at Elizabeth, almost frothing at the mouth. Then, he calmed as he turned his black, empty eyes on Eric. "And for you," he breathed, still seething with barely-controlled rage, "You will be mine, and you will die, along with your parents... along with the rest of this school."

He waved his hand, and Eric's bed caught fire.

Eric woke up sweating. The room smelled like burning wood, now, reminding him of the terrible dream that he'd just had. Looking around, Eric realized that it was night, and everyone was deep asleep.

Chapter 11

When the weekend came a few days later, Eric decided to go talk to Sloan. The stairs to her office were conveniently down, so he went straight up, knocking on her door.

"Eric, what a nice surprise. Can I help you with something?" She smiled and asked when she opened the door and let him in.

Eric was pale and drawn, with messy hair that he obviously hadn't combed for days. His eyes were red, and the bags under them spoke of little sleep. Slowly, he walked over to Sloan's desk.

"I was wondering if I could go home," he murmured, looking at the raindrops that were hitting the windowpane.

"Eric, you would be in a lot of danger if you even stepped foot in your old town."

"I want to go home. I want to visit my parents' grave, and I want to see what's left of the house," he said, now looking at her.

"I am sure that you have seen the photos."

"I want to see it in person."

Sloan took a measured look at Eric, weighing the request and getting a worried look on her face. "If it means that much to you, I will figure something out."

"Thank you, Sloan." Eric sighed with relief.

Sloan picked her desk phone up and started to talk to one of the teachers.

Eric sat there, looking outside while the rain started hitting the window at a harder pace, fast and furious. The wind was picking up, and thunder roared in the distance as he toned the conversation out.

All he seemed to be able to think about was the loss of his childhood home... that recent dream... the loss of his parents... and the fact that those he loved were now the slaves of the twisted freak that had visited in his dreams. The words he'd spoken hung heavy in his heart, and Eric felt so alone and helpless.

Tears started to form in the corner of his eyes as he dwelled upon the thoughts that swam through his head. Eric furiously scrubbed at his eyes with the back of his hands, attempting to push away the emotions and remain strong for the coming visit.

By noon, Sloan had gathered a few teachers that Eric didn't know yet, and everyone stood together in the main hall. The storm had passed, and the sun was shining, again. Sloan had changed from a bright yellow gown to a thin, light blue t-shirt and tan dress pants.

The six of them were standing in front of the fireplaces that had brought Eric here, and one by one, the four teachers stepped in and disappeared, followed by Eric and Sloan.

The fire cleared to reveal the tree, again, and Sloan took on her air of command, telling two of the teachers to go ahead of them and two to follow behind. As Sloan opened the tree, sunlight spread into the room, lighting up the atmosphere in a cheery light that didn't touch Eric's saddened heart.

Stepping out of the tree was quick as the four teachers took their positions to cover Sloan and Eric. They hurried through the woods, and although their pace was swift, Eric noticed that some of the woods looked burnt.

They took a path leading to his neighborhood, and by 12:34, they reached his house. Burnt wood was everywhere, and nothing was still standing. Yellow caution tape lined the perimeter of the property, and as Eric surveyed the destruction, tears fell from his face. He was soon overpowered enough to fall to his knees.

Quietly, Sloan walked over to him, sat beside him, and comforted her godchild. She waited a few minutes before she reminded him that they couldn't stay here for long. When she helped Eric back up, they headed toward the local cemetery.

The cemetery was only a few blocks from Eric's house, but to make things quicker and less conspicuous, the group cut through the bushes. It was 12:57 when they walked into the back entrance to the cemetery.

His parents had a simple, white marble tombstone with gold leafed lettering. Their names, pictures, birthdays, and death date were on it, bringing home the fact that they were no longer in the land of the living. It made Eric feel better, though, when he saw all of the flowers that were placed on their graves.

He sat on the warm ground as his eyes filled with tears... tears of longing for his parents... tears of fear... tears of sorrow... they all came to him, leaving him feel raw, as if someone had rubbed him down with sandpaper.

"Why didn't you tell me about any of this?" He asked the graves. "They expect so much out of me, and I don't want to do this. I'm scared."

He heard nothing in response, though. As if they truly were dead, nothing but the breeze answered his sobbing form.

He sat beside his parents' grave for a while, but all too soon, Sloan walked over to him and told him that it was time to return to the school.

Chapter 12

A week later, all of the Freshmen had arrived and were gathered in the main hall before breakfast on a Monday morning. They all sat at their assigned table, getting to know one another and waiting for Sloan to come down and give directions. The roar of the crowd was considerable.

At about 7:00, Sloan came into the main hall and walked up on the platform. In her authoritative voice, she said, "Five... Four... Three... Two... One... Thanks for getting quiet." Her eyes scanned across the new members of the school, all of them captivated by her. "Good morning, Freshmen. For the SATs, today, I will be splitting you into five groups, based on the times you have selected.

"If you chose the time spot of 8:00 to 10:00, you'll need to go to the fourth floor. The Divination room will be your testing area, this morning. 10:00 to 12:00 spots need to go to the Metamorphosis room. This is on the fourth floor, as well. 12:00 to 2:00 spots need to go to the Molecular Immobilization room, on the fifth floor. 2:00 to 4:00 spots need to go to the Astral Projection room on the fifth floor, as well. The last group, 4:00 to 6:00, needs to go to the Telepathy room. You'll be able to find this on the fourth floor.

"Once you are in your assigned rooms, the teacher will take you, one by one, and give you the test. You need to stay in the room until everybody in your group is done. Once everyone is done, then you can go back to the living room to further get to know one another.

"Those groups that are scheduled at a later time are free to do whatever they wish till their group needs to start. And remember, if you don't have any special powers, don't get discouraged — you do still have magical powers, or you would not be here. After everyone is done, I will give you a letter telling you your results and what you need for those classes. Then tomorrow, I am giving you a free day to travel down to

Hillthrope to get those supplies. After that, you can start scheduling classes. Just come see me before the week is out. That is all you need to know for today. Good luck!"

Sloan walked out of the main hall, and the first group of students started to head to the Divination room.

"I'm in the third group. What group are you guys in?" Eric asked, hoping that at least one of them would be in the same time-slot.

"Second," said Marina.

"Fourth," said Nick.

"First. So I got to go. I'll see you guys, later," said Catlin.

"Bye, Catlin. Good luck!" Nick said as she walked out of the main hall to the fourth floor.

Eric and Marina wished her the same as she walked out.

Eric, Marina, and Nick stayed down in the main hall for breakfast. After that was done, the group walked up to their living room to wait out their time slots. Nick started telling Eric how to harness his powers.

"For Astral Projection, I picture two things. I picture where I am now, and then, I picture where I want to be. Confusing, I know.

"With Molecular Immobilization, I just wave my hands in front of an object and think *freeze*. I'm not sure about the other powers, but I'm sure they are the same. If you want it to happen, just picture it in your head and make it happen."

"Thanks for your help, Nick, but I'm sure it's useless. I don't even know about half the powers they're talking about." Eric rolled his eyes, a little, not even willing to believe that he could have anything at all special about him.

"You'll be fine. I've heard that they are explaining it to the groups. I'm going to run; I'll see you guys, later," said Marina.

"Thanks for your help. Have fun."

After Marina left, Eric asked, "Does she always do that?"

"She runs when she gets stressed out about something, whereas, I play video games."

"That's how she stays so skinny, even though she eats a lot," Eric said, laughing.

Nick played a video game, and Eric was reading a mystery book as they waited. As 10:00 came, Catlin came back screaming with joy.

"Guess what, guys!!!" Catlin screamed as she entered the living room.

"What?" Eric and Nick asked.

"I can Astral Project myself, and I'm Telepathic, along with being able to tell the future!!"

"I don't know what that means, but good job!" Eric said.

"It means that I can read minds, and I have this power that allows me to be two places at once!" Catlin explained.

"Oh cool! How did you read the other person's mind?" Eric asked her.

"You know what, I don't even know. Mrs. Grey thought of a sentence in her head and told me to tell her the sentence. I closed my eyes and opened my mind, and it felt like I could go into everybody's mind that was there. After a little searching, I found her voice, and I heard what she was thinking. Sounds stupid when I say it, but it makes sense to me."

"That is really cool, Catlin. My mom is Telepathic, and she enjoys finding out what people think about her in her book club. And also, doesn't hurt to have it when you're a parent," Nick told Catlin.

Catlin and Nick laughed at his joke, while Eric just stood there with a depressed look on his face.

"What's wrong?" Catlin asked.

"Nothing. I'm just not over my parents' death, quite yet. If you don't mind, I'm going to go explore the school a little more."

"Okay. You can talk to us, you know that, right?" Nick said to Eric.

"I know. I just feel like taking a walk and sorting out these feelings."

"Text us if you need us." Nick said as Eric left the room.

As he walked out of the room, Eric felt a few tears escape his eyes. Brushing them off his face, he couldn't help but sniffle, a little. Today was just too overwhelming for him. He had no clue what he was supposed to do for the tests.

After mindlessly wandering for a few minutes, he made his way up to the fifth floor and went into the library. As he walked through, he couldn't help but be reminded of a smaller version of *Joey's Bookstore*. There were large, alder wood bookshelves all around the room, and the librarian's desk was near the front of the room, with public computers behind it. In the center of the room was a wooden, spiral staircase, leading up to higher levels. Surrounding the staircase were desks for students to sit at.

Browsing the library seemed like a productive thing to do while waiting for noon to come. While browsing the second floor of the library, he came upon Aviance's old yearbooks. Looking at the years, he grabbed one that would have had his mom in it and took it downstairs to a desk.

Eric flipped through the yearbook, looking for his mom, and found her in the Sophomore section. She looked so young in this picture, and Eric hardly recognized her.

"I miss you so much, mom. Why couldn't you tell me all of this, sooner? I feel out of place, here. I don't know anything they are talking about, and I just really wish you were here," Eric whispered to himself.

"Eric?"

Eric looked behind him to see Catlin standing there, looking concerned.

"What are you doing, here?"

"I want to know what's wrong."

"I just want to be left alone," he said, turning away from her and flipping through the yearbook.

"Why? Why can't you just talk to us?"

"I was going through my Twitter, and I was remembering some things about my old school. Never trust the people who befriend you the quickest," Eric murmured, just loud enough for Catlin to hear.

"What is that supposed to mean?"

"When I entered middle school, I tried to make new friends. The ones who befriended me the quickest ended up stabbing me in the back."

"So you don't trust us."

"I just don't know you."

"In time, you will, Eric. Trust me, I can see the future, but for now, you need someone to talk to. You are going through a really difficult time, but trust me when I say that Nick, Marina, and I won't backstab you. We, ourselves, have been backstabbed by people that we trusted, and would never do that to someone.

I'm sorry if you don't trust us, yet, but just know we are here for you."

"Okay."

"I will see you, later, in the living room. Text me if you need me."

Catlin left the library after their talk to leave Eric alone. She hoped that her words would comfort him, but right now, all Eric wanted was to be able to talk to his parents. He knew that he couldn't, and that was the problem.

Soon, noon came, and he left the library, heading to the Molecular Immobilization room for his SATs. Four windows were on every wall, except for the one with the door. White, lacy curtains covered all of the windows, and the walls were the color of light mustard. Several white cabinets were fixed on the walls, and long, light-colored benches were moved back to the wall.

Four other kids were in the room with Eric, watching the young woman before them. The teacher looked as if she was in her early twenties, with curly, red hair that was wild and long. Her hourglass figure was shown off by her tight, green cocktail dress, and her height was elongated by the three inches that came from her dark blue pumps.

"Hello, students. My name is Miss Carton. I am the school's Molecular Immobilization teacher," she told them and then, whispered in a conspiratory voice, "That's fancy talk for *freezing power*." Smiling, her voice returned to normal. "Now, this is how it's going to go. I'll call you guys up based on the time you signed up. I will tell you about every SA power and how to use it in detail, and when I'm done, I will tell you that you can try to use that power.

"First person up is," Miss Carton looked at her clipboard and continued talking, "Britney Delaine."

A plump, dark skinned girl wearing tight, dark skinny jeans and a purple t-shirt walked up to the teacher.

"Okay, Britney. The first power will be Molecular Immobilization," Miss Carton said as she walked to one of the cabinets and grabbed a small, green glass ball. "When I count to three, I will drop this ball and you have to stop it.

"Now, to stop it, there are many ways to do it, magically. First off, you have to believe you can stop it. When I drop it, I want you to keep repeating *freeze* and throw your hands out to it."

Britney nodded her head and said, "I'm ready."

Miss Carton raised the glass ball above her head and said, "Three... Two... One..."

As soon as Miss Carton dropped the glass ball, Britney's hands went out to freeze the falling glass ball. The ball slowed down when Britney threw her hands out, but fell to the white, shiny wood floor and broke to pieces.

"Good try, Britney." Miss Carton said as she pulled out her wand and waved it over the broken glass.

The pieces of broken glass came back together and flew into the air, landing in her hands, again, complete and reformed. She put the ball back into the cabinet and grabbed a larger glass ball. Unlike the other one, this one was crystal clear.

"The next power is Divination, which is the power to tell the future. Now, this one is a little harder to test, but yet, simple all at the same time. Take the crystal ball between your hands and look deep into it. If you see something playing out before you, then you have the power of Divination."

Britney took the crystal ball in her hands and stared into it for a few minutes, until finally, she shook her head and said, "I don't see anything."

"That's perfectly fine. Let's just move on to the next power, which is Telepathy. This is the power of reading someone's mind," Miss Carton said as she put the crystal glass back into the cabinet. "For this, you will have to open your mind. I will think of a sentence. You will have to tell me what sentence that is by searching for my voice in your head.

"When you open your mind, it opens pathways to different places. Right now, you will hear everyone's voices if you have the power. I want you to search through the voices for mine. Okay?"

"Okay."

It was a few minutes till Britney said, "A journey of a thousand miles begins with a step?"

"Very good, Britney! Now, let's try Astral Projection. This is the power that comes in handy in battles. Or tricks! Astral Projecting is when your body is in one place, but you produce another copy of yourself, called an apparition, in another spot.

At first, you will appear as a ghost, but after some training, you will have a solid figure. You ready to give it a try? It's just like the other powers. Think, imagine, and do."

"Sure."

After a few minutes, Britney collapsed on the floor. Everyone screamed. Miss Carton pointed to a faint outline across the room.

"Now, picture yourself back in your body," Miss Carton said to Britney.

Britney soon found her body and stood up.

"Last, but not least, is the Metamorphosis power, which is simply changing one thing into another. Go ahead and give it a shot. Try to transform one of the benches into a dog."

Britney focused hard on the bench for a few minutes, but nothing happened.

"Well, that was it. You are done, Britney."

Eric waited till 1:30 for his turn at the test.

Miss Carton walked over to the cabinet to get the glass ball as she told Eric what to do.

"This is the Molecular Immobilization test. I will hold this glass ball and count down. When it drops, I want you to freeze it."

She counted down, and Eric didn't think this was going to work, but the glass ball instantly froze when he tried. After that, he believed that he could do the rest of the tests.

When it came to the Metamorphosis test, he tried hard and ended up transforming one of the benches into a bench that walked around the room.

"What were you aiming for?" Miss Carton asked as she returned the bench to normal.

"A dog," Eric said, shyly, and kids around him laughed.

Even though that made his confidence go down, he projected himself clear out in the hall when he did the Astral Projection test.

When she introduced the Telepathy test, Eric felt confident but also scared because he wasn't real sure on how to use the power. He took a deep breath in, closed his eyes, relaxed his body, and opened up his mind. In his mind, he could see the shapes of the people that were in the room. He searched out Miss Carton's body, and he could hear what she was saying. He opened his eyes and repeated Miss Carton's sentence, "Life isn't about finding yourself. It's about creating yourself."

She wrote some things down on a clipboard and walked over to the cabinet, grabbing the crystal ball. When Miss Carton handed Eric the crystal ball, she explained what to do. Eric grasped it tightly in his hands, cleared his mind, and looked straight into the ball. He tried for several minutes to see something, but he couldn't.

But then came the Fire Manipulation test.

"Now Eric, I'm not sure how to work this power. Just don't catch anything on fire, please," Miss Carton said to Eric as she grabbed a fire extinguisher from another cabinet.

"I highly doubt you have this power, but then again, it was being said that you shouldn't have any powers, at all. You've proved that wrong, so far," she said, walking back to Eric and readying herself.

He didn't really know how to work it, either, but he figured that it worked like the rest of them. Eric imagined fire coming out of his right hand, wanting to believe he had this power, but at the same time, he knew what would come of it if he did. Imagining the worst, he thrust his hands forward and to everyone's amazement, fire was coming out of his hands for a good two feet.

Before anything got damaged, Eric stopped the fire. When he looked around the room, he saw that everybody backed up as close to the wall as they could, even Miss Carton. Some of them looked as if they were afraid he was going to harm them. Others looked as if they wanted to harm him, instead.

Eric understood why, though. He had the power that had killed thousands of people's family and friends.

Eric dropped his head, hunched his shoulders, and sat down on a bench far away from everyone. He could still the whispers, though.

"Oh my god, he's a freak…"

"He shouldn't be here…"

"He doesn't belong…"

"Stay away from him, or you'll get hurt…"

When Eric's group was done testing, he went back to the living room. Right away, he spotted Marina and Catlin looking at him. He stopped in his tracks as they approached him.

"How did it go?" asked Marina.

"You shouldn't be seen talking to me."

"Why?" asked Catlin.

"Because I'm a freak, and it would hurt your image. After that test, people are looking at me like I have a third eye, or something. I... I'm just going to bed." Eric said as he walked away with his head down.

The next day, Eric spotted Nick, Marina, and Catlin sitting in the living room, watching a soccer game on the television.

"Hey, can we talk?" Eric asked as he sat down in a chair next to them.

"Sure. What's up?" Nick asked.

Marina muted the TV, and Eric began to speak.

"Like I explained to Catlin, I'm not used to this friend thing. I haven't had many friends, before, and when you guys just instantly started to be nice to me, I sort of felt like I was your charity case."

"Not at all, Eric. You were sad and alone. The least we could have done was be nice to you," Catlin said.

"Yeah, we don't see you as a charity case. We just wanted to be friends with you; we thought that that's what you needed, as well. Someone you could go to while you were hurting," Marina told him.

"We would never do anything to harm you, Eric. You can trust us," Nick added.

Eric felt happier knowing that he had friends who trusted and cared for him. He got up, hugging and thanking them for being his friends.

When they got their SAT results back after breakfast, the four of them, along with all the other Freshmen, went down to Hillthrope to get their books and supplies that they still needed for school.

Chapter 13

A couple of days after the SATs, more and more people started to show up at the school. The starter classes ended, and students were ready for school to start.

It was Monday, June fifth, and everyone got up at 7:00 to get dressed and ready for breakfast. It was like a regular first day of school, with people in the halls catching up on their lives. Everyone was dressing nicer than they would be the rest of the school year, and students were panicking, because they didn't have enough pens.

At 7:45, Eric dressed in grey plaid shorts and a light yellow shirt and made his way down to the main hall to eat with his friends. The hall was even louder than usual with all of the new arrivals, and most of the seats were full, already. Eric was relieved to see that his friends had saved him a seat. They'd chosen to sit up toward the teachers' table, on the side closer to the Sophomore table. Like normal, they all sat together; Catlin sat next to Marina, and Eric sat by Nick.

Marina's curled hair was down, but a lock from each side was tied in the back with a dark blue ribbon that matched her t-shirt. She was also wearing a black pencil skirt and dark blue Converse shoes. Catlin had her blond hair flipped over her left shoulder, exposing the back of her neon pink wrap dress. Eric could also see that she was wearing bright orange high heels.

Much like Eric, Nick was dressed in navy shorts, plain grey Nike tennis shoes, and a white t-shirt that had some kind of video game logo on it. Also, like normal, Nick's short hair was spiked on top.

"Thanks for saving me a seat," Eric said to the group.

"No problem," Catlin told him with a smile.

"Does anyone know when we get our schedules?" asked Eric.

"I don't know," Nick said

"I think we get them after breakfast," Marina told the group.

"I actually asked a Sophomore, and they said that the ghosts deliver them to you after you eat," Catlin said.

"I wonder if we have any classes together?" asked Eric.

"I figure we got to have a few classes together. If not any regular classes, then we surely will have some SA classes together," said Nick.

At 8:05, Sloan entered the main hall, walked up to the teachers' table, and gave the daily announcements to the gathered students.

"Five... Four... Three... Two... One... Thanks for getting quiet." Sloan said as a hush enveloped the room.

"Good morning, students, and welcome to Aviance. Today is the first day of school, so make it count. Please, don't be late to your classes on the first day. Remember that you only get ten minutes between classes, so use them wisely. After everyone is served, the ghosts will come back out and give you your schedules.

"If you have any questions, concerns, or changes that need to be made to your schedule, my stairs will be unlocked for this week, allowing access for you to come up and schedule a time to meet about it.

"I have a few daily reminders before we eat. One, no one is allowed to leave the school without a permission slip from a teacher, parent, or me.

"Two, all lights have to be out by eleven o'clock. No one is allowed out of his or her bedrooms after that time, unless it is an emergency.

"The final reminder is that cell phones are not to be used in class and neither is Skype. You can only use these before and after your classes. And laptops can only be used if teachers allow you to do so.

"Now, let us eat and be merry!"

The ghosts came out of the walls dressed in festive wear and delivered the food. After the food and the drinks were delivered, the ghosts came back out with stacks of paper.

"How do they know who is who?" Nick asked.

"Yeah, how do they know? I mean, there are about two thousand kids, here," said Marina.

"Well, however they do it, it's amazing. I know I would never be able to do it. It's a miracle that I remember your names," Catlin joked with a giggle.

"I read in the library the other day that the ghosts actually have to remember each face and name, because they are our security system," Eric informed them.

"What book did you find that in?" asked Catlin, quizzically.

"A book called *101 Facts about Aviance*. It was very interesting. I also learned that the stairs disappear if we are attacked," Eric told them.

"Wow. That's really interesting. I might have to check that out," Catlin said to him.

Finally, one of the ghosts floated up to the four of them and handed their schedules over. Nick and Marina compared theirs, as Eric and Catlin went over theirs, together.

"We have Astral Projection, Telepathy, Potions, and History together!" Catlin exclaimed to Eric, smiling over at him excitedly. "But when are you supposed to have your Fire Manipulation class?"

"Cool! Sloan told me that she would help me with that after school on the weekends."

At 9:00, a small bell went off, and everyone left the main hall, walking toward their first periods. This meant that Eric, Catlin, and Marina headed toward the Potions class, while Nick went to the sixth floor to Charms.

Chapter 14

At 9:10, the bell rang, again. The teacher hadn't yet arrived, so the students sat wherever they wanted, clumping together into groups that they were familiar with. The desks were a dark red-colored wood, with a dark red chair attached by a metal bar. The three friends, Eric, Catlin, and Marina, sat in the middle of the second row.

Eric looked around the room, noticing about ten cabinets placed in between windows. The lights on the ceiling made the wooden desks look really old, as if they were stained by long-dried blood.

Eric was getting slightly annoyed by the people who were tapping their feet loudly on the wooden floor, but five minutes after the bell rang, a tall, skinny man in a blue suit and black Converse shoes walked into the room. Eric sighed with relief as he examined the man. His short, brown hair was gelled in a messy style, and rectangular tortoise shell glasses sat on his long, pointy nose.

"Good morning class, my name is Mr. Smith. John Smith, to be exact. Now, it looks as if you are all here, so let's get to it, shall we? Students, if you would just pull out your cauldrons, we will get to work."

Everyone in the room grabbed their cauldrons out of their bags and put them on the desk.

"Good, now what I want you to do is search the room for different items you like, including objects, colors, herbs, flowers, or anything else you can fit in the cauldron, after everyone is done with that, I will tell you what to do, next."

Everyone sat at his or her desk confused as to what Mr. Smith wanted. Finally, a blond-headed girl sitting in front of Eric raised her hand.

"Yes, Evergreen," he said after looking at the roster, "What is it?"

"Well sir, what exactly are we looking for? How many

63

things do we need?"

"You need at least four objects. Tell me, Miss Evergreen, what is your favorite color?"

"Plum."

Mr. Smith swiftly turned around and rushed toward one of the cupboards and rummaged through it till he found a large dark purple bottle.

"Pour a few drops into your cauldron."

Amber took the bottle, unscrewed the cap, and poured a few drops into her cauldron before handing it back to Mr. Smith.

"Now, what is your favorite flower and herb?"

"That would have to be foxglove. And my favorite herb is mint."

Once again, Mr. Smith ran to a cupboard that was behind the students and pulled out two small cloudy colored containers.

"Put in a pinch of each."

Amber took the containers, put the pinch of each in her cauldron, and gave the containers back to Mr. Smith.

"Now, what is your favorite object?"

"Pearls."

"I want you to put three pearls in your cauldron." Mr. Smith told Amber after he took out a small wooden box out of a cupboard to the students' left and handed it to Amber.

"Okay, now students, after seeing Amber pick her favorites, you should be able to, now. So go at it!"

Everybody got up from their desk and went in search for their favorite things. Mr. Smith played *My Favorite Things* from *The Sound of Music* while everyone searched.

Eric grabbed his cauldron and went in search for his favorite things. He found a metal container full of broken crystal and put a few shards in. He found some lavender flowers and some sage and put them in, also. All he had left was some forest green dye, which he found in a cupboard near the main door that held all different kinds of dye.

Once Eric found everything, he sat back down at his desk and waited for everyone else. Once Catlin and Marina sat back down, Eric asked what they put in.

"I put in some dark pink dye, a few onyx gems, a spoonful of stevia, and some lilies." Catlin said.

"What about you, Marina?"

"Well, of course, I put in the dark blue dye. I also put in a small pure silver bar. I also found a piece of fleece! I love fleece."

"Apparently." said Eric.

"Oh, shut up. I also put in two heads of white roses, along with a tablespoon of cayenne. But does anyone know why we have to put herbs in?"

"Stupid question, Miss Martin, but I'll still answer it." Mr. Smith said to Marina and then smiled at her.

"I didn't see you there, I'm sorry."

"Don't be, nothing to be sorry about. Now, the reason you put herbs in is because it represents something about you. You will find that out, later in your years of life," Mr. Smith told Marina, and then, walked away.

Once everyone was seated, Mr. Smith stopped the music and stood up.

"In the cupboard on the wall to your left there are enough Bunsen burners for everyone. Please, go get one, and we will begin cooking some magic."

Once everybody got one and went back to their seats, Mr. Smith said, "Now, there is a knob on the Bunsen burner. I want you to turn it a little to the left, until you hear a hiss come out, while I pass out the matches."

Eric turned the knob till he heard the hiss. Instead of waiting to get a match, he decided to use his firepower, instead. He pictured a small flame in his mind, and then, he snapped his fingers. He opened his eyes and saw his index finger had become a small torch. He lowered his finger down to the burner and lit the gas.

"How did you do that?" Catlin whispered to him.

"Magic," he replied.

"Impressive," Marina said.

"Very impressive, Eric James, but until you get more control over that power, I don't want you to use it in my class, is that understood? Now put it out," Mr. Smith said as he handed Catlin a lit match.

"Um, sir, I don't know how to."

Mr. Smith took out his brown, wooden wand and waved it over Eric's hand. Small drops of water landed on Eric's hand and extinguished the flame.

"Like I said. Get it under control, Mr. James."

After handing out the matches to everyone and putting out a desk that someone caught on fire, Mr. Smith returned to the front of the room.

"Now, put your cauldron on top of the Bunsen burner and turn your gas up until the flame covers bottom of your cauldron. Once everything has melted in your cauldron and it starts to boil, I want you to whisper these words, 'These are my favorite things', and blow into the cauldron. I'll let what happens next be a surprise."

They put their cauldrons on the Bunsen burner and waited while all of their ingredients melted. It was about five minutes after everything melted that the mixture started to boil. When Eric's mixture started to boil, he bent over the mixture and whispered, "These are my favorite things," and blew into his cauldron.

The mixture started to increase volume till it hit the top edge of the cauldron. Once at the top it started to decrease, leaving a small green colored crystal stick about nine inches long.

"Once it looks cool enough to touch, you can take it out. Students, this is your wand. Your wand is not indestructible, but it takes a lot to break it. This does not mean you can neglect it. Be careful with it," Mr. Smith stressed to his students.

Eric blew on his wand a little bit to let it cool down and picked it up. It felt weird in his hand, almost like there was a bond between it and him. Eric carefully spun the wand in his hands to examine it. Inside of the wand were little specks of the lavender flower and the sage leaves.

"Before the bell rings, please make sure you wash out your cauldron and put back the Bunsen burners. And read chapter one in your book, by Wednesday, when we will have a quiz over it."

"I'll take your Bunsen burner for you, Catlin," Eric said.

"Thank you, Eric; do you want me to wash your cauldron for you?"

"No, I got it, but thank you."

Eric took the Bunsen burners and walked with Marina to the cupboard to put them away. On the way to wash their cauldrons, Marina asked, "Do you like Catlin?"

Eric smiled at Marina and continued to wash his cauldron.

"I'll take that as a yes."

"Please, don't tell her." Eric said, looking at her with wide eyes.

"I won't, but I think she already knows," Marina whispered, smiling at him.

"Has she said anything?" Eric said, spilling the water in his cauldron on the counter.

"Not much. I have to go to class, now." Marina said as she stuffed her cauldron in her bag and ran out of the class.

Chapter 15

Eric sat in the main hall, reading the book that Mrs. Grey let him borrow- *Decoding a Dream*, when his phone alarm went off, letting him know that it was time for his next class. He closed the book, turned the alarm off, and gathered his books, being careful to look at his schedule to make sure he was going to the right class.

Putting on his book bag, he walked to the commons room that led to the Defense Against the Shadow Reapers classroom. His new shoes squeaked as the carpet in the commons room turned to wood, and his eyes adjusted to the dimly lit room. The room had changed since the last time he had been here. Tall, robot-like creatures lined the right side of the room against black walls. The room was divided into two parts, with the front half of the classroom being empty, except for the robots. There was tape on the floor, making it look like a basketball court.

Eric walked toward the back of the room where the desks were lined up, facing the robots. Most of the seats were already taken, and since none of his friends were in the class with him, he was worried that he would have no one to talk to. He sat down at one of the empty seats near the front of the room and went through his book back, taking out the textbook for the class. A notepad, pen, and a yellow highlighter were also removed, and as he sat reading the syllabus for the class, he couldn't help but hear the people behind him, talking.

"He doesn't belong here. He is endangering us all," said someone with a very high and squeaky voice.

"I heard that he is a spy for the Shadow Reapers. I tried to tell Sloan this, but she refused to hear me out. This school is going down the dumps," said another person who sounded like he was from New York.

As this went on, Eric tried to ignore them. They were getting inside his head, though, igniting his already frail emotions. He closed his eyes just as tears were forming, deciding to get up and leave the classroom. A tapping on his shoulder stopped him, and Eric turned to see a familiar-looking girl.

"They're only talking trash about you because they fear you. I've seen you around, here, and I know you're not a danger to this school." She cocked her head to the side, looking at him with a smile. "You're just like most of us. You didn't know you had powers until you got here, and you don't know how to use them, I understand."

"You're Amber Evergreen, right? You were in my last class." Eric wiped his eyes on his shoulder and looked back at her.

"Yeah, and I saw you light the Bunsen burner with your powers. I thought it was actually cool."

"Thanks. I seriously didn't even think anything would happen if I snapped my fingers like that." Eric offered a tentative smile.

"See, you're not any more dangerous than anyone else around here. So, don't listen to them. At least you didn't catch a table on fire with a match," Amber murmured with a giggle as she went back to her seat.

A few minutes later, the teacher came in and shut the metal doors, which made the room a little bit darker. Eric stared out the small windows on his left to the raindrops that were hitting them, thinking about the conversation that had just happened.

When the teacher got to the front of the classroom, she shuffled at some papers on her stainless steel desk, chose some, and then said with a soft, quiet voice, "Sorry, I'm late. My name is Mrs. Brown."

Her white high heels clacked on the floor as she walked to the front of the desk, and when she sat down, she pushed her grey hair out of her face with her wrinkly hand and started to talk about the class.

When she was finished, she stood up and straightened her blue blouse. "Today, we are going to begin with the Shadow Reaper dummies. We won't be practicing with them, today, but I want you to get familiarized with them. They are extremely dangerous, and I want you to get a few lessons of Charms and Potions underneath of your belt, before we practice with them."

She walked to the back of the room, grabbed one of the

practice dummies, and rolled it to the front of the room.

They looked like a metal person, and Eric was freaked out about just how realistic it was. The creature was being held up by more metal that was wrapped around the whole body.

"These are called Shadow Reaper Bots, SRBs for short," Mrs. Brown said as she picked her yellow wand up, waved it over the SRB, and exclaimed, "Animari!"

A red dot appeared in the right corner of its chest, and with every second, it was growing and looked as if it was pumping like a heart. When it stopped growing, red lines started to come out of the dot and covered every part of the SRB. When the red lines reached the head, the eyes opened to reveal two black holes. The mouth opened, and it sounded like it took a breath.

All of the students jumped in their seats and screamed in fear. Mrs. Brown had a smile on her face and chuckled as she said, "I love the Freshman reaction to that!"

"What is that thing?!" someone yelled.

"This is a robot that acts like a human Shadow Reaper. We can't practice with something that won't act like a Shadow Reaper, so the need arose to invent this thing. If we practice against something that acts just as they act, we will know how to defend ourselves." Mrs. Brown stated, matter-of-factly. Then, she added, "It is made entirely out of steel, except for the heart. The heart is the heart of a Shadow Reaper."

At this point, several people screamed, again.

"How can you do that? How can you take several hearts, like that?" asked one of the students that was sitting by Eric.

"Those hearts were retrieved from the bodies of Shadow Reapers that were attacking us. They were near death, anyway, so we decided to take those hearts and use them in the SRBs." Mrs. Brown informed the class.

"Now, the spell I used isn't the only thing you can use to awaken it. Not only is it dangerous because it is alive and has a mind of its own, but it awakens when you startle it. That means, if you hit them, bump into them, or do anything to them, you have a chance of awakening them. So, be careful.

"But let's talk about how they fight. Once awoken, they will fight the metal that is wrapped around them. And if you don't get them out, they will force their way out."

"They fight with fire, like the real Shadow Reapers, but this fire won't burn your flesh. It will burn clothes and spread like normal fire, but it will feel cold when it comes in contact with the skin. So, you are in no immediate danger.

"But the real threat is in this. The SBRs are as mean as the Shadow Reapers. They will do anything for a kill, but as long as you pay attention in class, you will be fine." The teacher stated as she paced before the class, her heels clacking authoratively. "Now, before this one tries to get out, I will put it back to its hibernating state."

Mrs. Brown took her wand, waved it over the SRB, said, "Somnus," and the red lines started to disappear, as well as the red dot on the chest. Its eyes closed, and it stopped trying to escape.

It was nearly time to go when Mrs. Brown gave out the homework.

"I want you to read chapter one, which is background information on the Shadow Reapers. I want you to also complete a study guide on it by tomorrow," she said as she passed out the study guide.

Chapter 16

As soon as the bell rang, Eric got out of his seat, left the Defense Against the Shadow Reapers class, and headed upstairs to the second floor to get his books for the next class. As he entered Freshman living room, Eric briefly spotted Catlin, Marina, and Nick all playing a video game. He was going to go over and say hi, but he looked at his watch and figured he was going to be late for his next class.

He quickly stuffed his books into his book bag and ran out to the hall and up the stair to the sixth floor. Several other kids were running towards the same room he was going to. The classroom was large, but it had so much stuff in it that it made it look cramped and minuscule, compared to the other classrooms. The small, wooden desks were arranged in a circle around the teacher's desk, and the teacher was sitting at his desk, fiddling with a pile of papers that had just fallen over.

Raindrops were pounding the windows that were covering three of the walls, and the room smelled like old books and fresh coffee. Eric made his way to an empty seat that was near a window in the back. He sat down and pulled out a book that he had been reading and continued from the spot he left off.

He was almost finished with the book when the teacher stood up and said, "Oh my, it's time to start class." Eric put away his book and pulled out his textbooks, while looking at his watch. Class was supposed to start twenty minutes ago, which meant they had half an hour left. Eric looked at the teacher and realized that he recognized him. It was the teacher who helped him out the first day.

"My name is Mr. Chine. I am your Charms teacher. This is where you will learn not only how to fight with your words, but also learn how to do some pretty cool things, like this!" he said as he pulled out his brown, wooden wand and said, "Mundabit."

Loose papers from all over the room started to move towards the center of the room to where Mr. Chime was standing. Dust and books flew upwards to the ceiling. Eric was freaking out, because it looked like a tornado in the room.

The tornado of papers, dust, and books soon stopped and all landed in neat piles on his desk. Even his wrinkled suit now looked like it was recently ironed, and his usually messy hair now looked combed and neatly parted. The cream-colored, wooden floor was shiny, and the windows were spotless. The room was no longer cluttered with junk, but was spotlessly clean.

"As you can see, magic can help you with even the simplest tasks, like cleaning a room, and to learn how to do these, you first need to learn Latin. The more advanced you are in Latin, the more charms you can cast. So, with that in mind, please pull out your textbook and turn to page 17, so that we can begin."

Mr. Chine waited for everyone to take out their textbooks and turn to the right page. Once everyone had their book open, Mr. Chine began his lesson.

"Now, the first thing you need to learn is that a charm is cast by using one or two words. For example, the charm I used to clean this room, and me, was just one word. Clean. So basically, this year, you will learn some basic Latin."

Mr. Chine spent the rest of the time teaching the students some simple verbs and objects. At the end of the class, he stood at the door, handed out a packet, and said, "This packet is a list of words. I want you to translate all of these and start practicing these charms. By the end of the year, I will test you on these."

Eric took the packet from him, put it in his book bag, and then, headed toward the main hall for lunch.

Chapter 17

ric's Flying class was canceled due to the rain and the storm that was coming in, so he spent the next hour in the library with Catlin. They sat down at one of the study tables and started to do some of their Charms homework.

When it was reaching 2:00, they decided to put their books away and head to their next class. When they reached the entrance, they spotted Marina and Nick walking down the hall.

"Hey guys, wait up!" Eric yelled to them.

When Eric and Catlin caught up, Nick asked, "So, how's your day going, so far?"

"Not bad. Defense class was really cool. The SRBs are *so* scary!" Eric said to him.

"I know, right! They creep me out." Marina said to them with a grimace as she was texting.

"I have a feeling that this class is going to be a bore." Nick groaned as they entered the classroom.

"Why, I don't know anything about this kind of history." Eric said as he sat down in a seat next to his friends.

"Yeah, but it's a History class, and history is boring," he said as he pulled out his books.

The teacher introduced himself as Mr. Abbot. He was a short, plump old man with thick glasses. He was wearing a grey-stripped button-up shirt and navy blue dress pants.

As Mr. Abbot droned on about what was going to be happening in the class, this year, Eric's gaze wondered around the room, taking in the map-covered walls. The room was large enough to fit about thirty students in, and the maps were varied, some being of the United States, some of just the East coast, and others being maps of the world.

Mr. Abbot had turned around to write something in the whiteboard when Catlin quickly placed a note card in front of Eric.

Can you please be my tutor? It was written in pink pen.

Why? Eric quickly wrote back, underneath, and quickly placed it back on her side of the desk.

Before Catlin had time to write anymore, Mr. Abbot turned around and started giving his lecture. Eric opened his notebook and started taking notes.

"1692 was the height of the Salem Witch Trials. People feared our powers, much as they do, now. What they refer to us bewitching them was really us trying to help them. In 1688, a fellow witch, Goody Glover, was having an argument with Martha Goodwin. Goodwin was accusing Glover's daughter of stealing linen while she was washing them. When people talk about the dispute between Glover and Martha Goodwin, they assume it was over missing linen, but actually it was over power.

"You see, Martha Goodwin was sick; real sick. The doctor had told her she only had a few days left. She went to Glover to ask if she could have her powers, so she could stay alive. When Glover tried to explain to her that having powers didn't help you stay alive, Martha turned on her. She poisoned herself and her siblings to make them seem like Goodwin bewitched them."

Mr. Abbot turned to the whiteboard and started to talk about the timeline he had drawn that went from the year 1688 to 1692. He talked about all of the famous people, like Roger Toothaker and Bridget Bishop, and how modern history had their stories wrong.

"At the end of 1692, when the Salem Witch Trials were calming down, the remaining witches in jail decided to make schools dedicated to teaching young witches and wizards to use their magic and how to hide it from the outside world.

"In 1693, when the governor pardoned those still in jail, they started building the school. Of course, back then, they couldn't say it was a summer school, so when construction was finished in 1798, they said it was a factory for kids to work at. Of course, they only 'hired' those who had magic."

Mr. Abbot was asked how that changed when they created child labor laws, but he said he would get to that in a later class. Then before class ended, he told everyone to read the first chapter in their textbook.

"Told you that class was boring," Nick said as he put his books into his bag.

"Nah, it was interesting. I didn't really get all of it, but yeah." Catlin got her phone out and checked it.

"Yeah, interesting. That's why I have drool ALL over my empty notebook," Nick complained.

"That's because it's factual. It's not a video game about zombies," Marina said as they walked out of the room into the hallway.

"Hey, why do you need me to tutor you?" Eric asked Catlin.

"I just don't do well in classes. I learn more from a hands-on approach, and it seems like most of these classes are textbook-based," she told him before she darted away with Nick towards the library for the Study Hall class.

As Eric and Marina walked to the Freshman living room to get their books for their next class, Marina asked, "Are you going to help her?"

"I don't know. I'm probably not the best person to ask to be a tutor. I don't make that good of grades, and besides, I'm not even sure I'll have time to."

"I'm sure you'll be fine. You seem smart enough."

"Thank you?" he said, giving her a puzzled look.

Eric exchanged his current load for the next class' books, met up with Marina, again, and headed for the Metamorphosis classroom on the fourth floor.

Chapter 18

At 8:30, the four friends were in the living room, going through their day with each other as they studied for tomorrow's classes. Eric was in a downcast mood, due to the events of the day.

"Mr. Goodman, the Metamorphosis teacher, really doesn't like me. Every time he looked at me, he gave me this weird look." Eric said, propping his feet up on his backpack and glaring at the pen in his hand.

"Maybe, you had something in your teeth." Nick teased.

"He's done this, before, though. A couple weeks ago, when Sloan gave me my phone and laptop, he said I shouldn't be here."

"You can't prove that, Eric," Marina said to him as she gave him a stern look.

"But that's what Sloan told me. I heard them fighting about it, because I was right outside her door."

"Is it because of your dad?" Catlin asked while she was filling in an answer to her homework.

Eric nodded his head, solemnly. "He fears that I am endangering the school by being here. Let's just change the subject, please."

"Someone already got hurt in our DASR class," Nick said while he was playing a video game.

"Yeah, who was he? I didn't recognize him, at all." Catlin said.

"His name is Keith East. He isn't smart, at all. Apparently, he took one too many footballs to the head," Nick said.

"He may be dumb, but boy is he nice to look at," Marina said, gazing off into space.

"Excuse me?" Nick said to her.

"I'm sorry, Nicky, I love you. You know that; it's just that he is SO hot."

"And I'm not?"

"In your own geeky, nerdy way, yes you are hot."

"And on that note, I leave." Catlin said.

"Me, too." Eric agreed.

"Do you want to go to the library and study?" she asked him.

"Sure."

Catlin and Eric grabbed their books and walked out of the living room, heading to the fourth floor. They weren't the only ones going to the library to study. It seems that every other student was, also. As they got closer to the library, though, it became apparent that the students were going to the game section of the library.

"We better go upstairs. I can tell it's going to get loud down here," Catlin said, giving one of the kids with sagging pants and a baggy shirt a dirty look.

"Yous gots a problem with me?" baggy-pants snapped at her.

"Not that you can do anything to me if I did," she said, continuing to walk to the stairs.

Catlin guided Eric to a corner that had a row of tables and chairs, where they decided to sit across from one another. Eric was reading the first chapter of *Potions with Limits* while Catlin was doing the section guide for the Defense Against the Shadow Reapers class.

It was about 10:00 when Eric and Catlin got done with everything they needed to do. Eric asked, "So, what did this Keith East guy do to get hurt?"

"The period hadn't even started, yet. He was lucky the teacher was in the classroom when it happened. You know the practice bots that we are going to use later in the year that Mrs. Brown talked about?"

"Sure."

"Well, Keith was walking, and he tripped and fell onto one of them. That woke up the bot, and it started to attack him. The poor boy caught his pants on fire."

Eric burst out laughing, grabbing his side. "Wow," he chuckled, after getting a hold of himself. "I'm really glad that wasn't me. I would be so embarrassed."

"Oh, he was. After Mrs. Brown saved him from the fire, he asked to be excused, and we never saw him after that. Oh hey, I almost forgot, Mrs. Grey asked about you, today."

"Really? What did she want?"

"She asked if you had any more dreams since she last saw you. I told her I didn't know, because you hadn't said anything about them."

"I haven't, lately. The last one I had was the night I first saw Mrs. Grey."

"What happened in it?"

"I don't remember much. Elizabeth said something about the night she was kidnapped, and then, a man came into the dream."

"What man?"

"He was really pale and tall. I'm pretty sure he was wearing a black tux."

"That sounds like Vesta."

"I don't really remember. He could have looked differently."

Eric finished all his homework and was reading more of *Decoding a Dream,* while Catlin was finishing her homework.

"Are you done, already?" Catlin asked as she erased something off her papers.

"Yeah, I was going to study some more before bed, but all of my study guides are done. Why, you need help?" He asked as he turned the page.

"Yeah, I'm stuck on number thirteen for our Defense class homework. It's asking *what's the best way to treat a burn from a Shadow Reaper?*"

"Oh yeah, I remember that one. What do you think the answer is?"

"Well I think it's the answer is C- Apply a healing potion to the area and use a cooling charm to get rid of the sting," she said, rubbing her head, looking confused.

Eric took out his paper from the book and looked at what he had as an answer. "Yes, that's right. Good job!"

Eric shoved his paper back into the book as Catlin thanked him for his help. She continued to finish her homework as Eric went back to reading.

"It's about eleven, children. The library will be closed, soon," said one of the librarians.

"You ready?"

"Yep," Eric said, gathering all his books and papers.

When they had all of their things cleaned up, they walked

out of the library and headed toward their living room. On their way down the hall, Catlin told Eric how nervous she was about her up-coming quizzes.

"I've never been good at school. I know you haven't known me for long, but I tend to have a lot of blond moments," Catlin told Eric.

"I'm sure you will do fine."

When they hit the fourth floor, Catlin spent a little time looking at Eric from the corner of her eye. Finally, she asked, "Do you like me?"

Eric stopped in his tracks and dropped the books that were in his hands. "What? I. What?" He stammered, not knowing what to say.

Catlin smiled at him. "You heard me. Do you like me? And I don't mean as a friend, either."

Eric could feel the blood rush to his cheeks as he bent down to pick up his books. "Who told you?"

"No one. But that answers my question."

"Listen, Catlin, I do like you more than a friend, but I don't think I'm ready to date, just yet."

"I understand."

The two walked to the Freshman living room as quickly as they could to avoid awkwardness. When they finally reached the room, they said their goodbyes and headed to their bedrooms.

Chapter 19

A few days later, it was the weekend. It had been the only weekend that the four of them had free, since they all had tests coming up. It seemed like the last one for a while, so they decided to spend it, together.

"I think, since it's a nice day, we should go out and play some soccer," Marina suggested.

"Sure, but I'm not that good at it," Eric said, putting down a book.

"I just painted my nails," Catlin said, looking at them and wiggling her bright pink fingernails.

"I'm fine with playing, as long as I play with a controller," Nick said, not taking his eyes away from his computer.

"How do you get anything done?" Eric asked with his eyebrows raised.

"Multitasking."

"You need to go outside and get some fresh air," Marina said to him.

"But the graphics suck," he countered back.

Marina rolled her eyes and shut his laptop off. Catlin quickly changed into an old, bright orange t-shirt, some old khaki shorts, and white Puma shoes.

At 10:30, they walked downstairs to the main hall, laughing and pushing at each other, playfully. Marina was bouncing her soccer ball off her head when they reached the man on the horse, who greeted them.

"Halt, who goes there?"

"Students of Aviance," Marina said, still bouncing the ball.

"What is your reason for leaving?"

"We're going to play soccer."

"All right. Have fun, and be careful."

The statue opened the door, and they left the school, breathing in the fresh air and admiring the view. They walked around, attempting to find a suitably flat area to play on.

"So, how long are we going to play? I have to get back to my simulated family before they die," Nick said as he jokingly punched Marina.

"As long as it takes to beat you and Eric's butts."

"Well, that's not going to take long," Eric said as he tightened his shoes.

"Dude, you have to be less harsh on yourself. It's not good on your confidence," Catlin said as Marina kicked the ball to her.

"I know that, but I suck at everything I do."

"I'm sure there's several things your good at," Nick said as he stole the ball from Catlin.

"I'm good at sports," Marina said, chasing Nick.

"I'm good at getting a bargains when I shop. These shoes? Half off, online," Catlin said as she guarded their goal.

"I'm extremely good at video games," Nick said as he shot the ball past Catlin and into the goal, "And apparently, at soccer."

"There's nothing that I'm really good at. I get good grades, but I'm not that smart," Eric said, getting winded from all of the running he was doing.

"Square root of 690," Catlin said as she tried to kick the ball toward Marina.

"26.267. Why?" he asked as he rested for a while.

"Dude, you're smart," Marina said as she sat on the ball.

"Super smart. Like, you need to be my freaking tutor, smart," Catlin said as she went to lie down on the grass.

Eric lay down on the grass with the rest of them, smiled, and said, "I love you guys."

"Before we get all gushy here, who's up for a *Twilight Zone* marathon, tonight?" Nick asked.

They all agreed to meet up for the marathon, and then, went back to the game. Marina had the ball and was doing a trick where she caught the ball between her calf and her butt and then kicked it with her other foot so that it flew over her head.

"That's cool! Can I try?" Eric asked walking over to her.

"Sure, but I just mastered this trick, like, last year," she handed the ball over to Eric and then told him how to do it.

"Okay, what you want to do is place the ball so that it is balancing on your ankle. Then you want to lift it so you can move your leg to catch it between your calf and butt. Once it's there, you have to lift your leg up and let go so you can kick the ball with your other leg," Marina said as she watched Eric.

Eric had balanced the ball and was trying to lift the ball so that he could catch it with his calf, but as he tried to lift it, he fell on his butt, and the ball hit him in the face.

"Are you okay, dude?" Marina asked as she rushed over and helped him up.

"Yeah, I'm fine. Told you guys I'm a klutz," he said with a smile as he wiped the dirt off his pants.

Catlin kicked the ball out of Eric's hands and then said, "Are we playing this game, or not?"

Eric smiled at her and raced her for the ball, while the others took off after them. Eric was about to kick the winning goal, when Marina intercepted the ball and kicked it all the way to the other side, where Catlin was waiting.

Chapter 20

It was the week of midterms, which meant that June was ending. Eric and his friends were stressing out because of all the homework that was pilling up, the projects, and the large tests. It was two days into the week, and they still had five tests to get through. There were two classes a day that lasted two hours each.

It was 8:00 in the morning, and Marina was walking around the living room balancing her soccer ball on her head while she was studying for her Metamorphosis midterm with Eric. Nick and Catlin were going through Eric's flashcards he made for the History midterm.

As the time for the first class was arriving, Eric, Marina, Catlin, and Nick were getting stressed. They packed their notes into their book bags and headed for the History classroom. They sat down in their regular seats, and Marina started to fidget with her pencil as Mr. Abbot handed out the test.

"Would you stop?" Eric asked her.

"I am nervous. Right now, all I really want to do is run, but I can't, so deal with it," she said with an angry glare.

"Whatever," he said under his breath.

As Eric was taking his test, he couldn't shake off the feeling that his friends were angry with him. All week, he'd had this feeling. They were more distant, only talking to him if they had a question about the study material. He tried to talk to them about it, but they completely ignored him.

As he kept thinking about it, he was being filled with anger. He couldn't stop it. He was trying to cool down, but it wasn't working. He made his hands into fists and put them under his desk, closing his eyes and taking a deep breath. Eric heard someone gasp, and he opened his eyes.

He didn't know how it happened, but his hands were on fire. He wasn't trying to do it. Eric was afraid that he might hurt someone, so before he had a chance to, he ran out of the room.

He ran down the hall to the bathrooms, and by the time Eric was in the bathroom, the flames had spread up his arms. The anger inside of Eric was building up, and for the first time in a while, he felt something other than doubt and sadness.

He was angry at so many things. He was angry that his parents had lied to him. He was angry that his parents were gone. Angry because, once again, he had chosen the wrong friends. Angry because he had just walked out from a test. The flames were still spreading and were now covering his upper chest and his head.

Eric knew how to put out the flames, but for some reason, it felt good to be angry. Soon, the flames covered his whole body, the heat of the flames made him black out and fall.

Eric was still on the bathroom floor. The flames were gone, though, and the bathroom was freezing. He didn't know if it was his eyes, or if there really was fog in the bathroom. He stood up and walked to one of the sinks, turned it on, and washed his face. With some paper towel, he wiped his face, and then, looked into the mirror.

Instead of seeing his face, it was a face he'd seen, before. A long, skinny, hollow, and pale face stared back at him, with eyes as black as coal. The hair was black, as well, and was combed over to one side.

"That's it, Eric. Fuel the anger. Give in to the anger," the man whispered to him without moving his lips.

"Who are you?" Eric asked.

"You will find out in a few weeks. Until then, you have a choice to make. Join me, or stay with the enemy."

"Eric, are you okay?" Nick asked Eric as he helped Eric up off the bathroom floor.

"Get away from me," Eric growled as he pushed Nick away.

"Dude, I'm just trying to help you."

"I don't need your help. Just leave me alone."

"Fine. Whatever," Nick snapped back as he left the bathroom.

Eric waited a while, since his head was a little fuzzy, and left the bathroom when he was feeling a little surer on his feet. He decided not to go back to his History class, but instead, went to the living room. As he walked, he texted Sloan and informed her of what happened.

I will talk to Mr. Abbot, later, and ask him if you can retake the test. Sloan replied.

Okay. Thank you.

I do think we need to talk in person about what actually happened, today. Meet me in my office, after dinner.

Eric reached the living room and headed straight for his bed. His next test was in an hour so he decided to study for it. The Metamorphosis test was going to be easy. They had to transform a rubber ball into whatever the teacher said.

Anything, right now, was better than thinking about what had happened, so Eric lay on his bed and held the rubber ball in his hands, closed his eyes, and pictured in his mind a large metal shield and sword. When he opened his eyes, the small rubber ball had transformed into a large, shiny metal shield and a long, heavy sward.

He closed his eyes, again, and imagined the rubber ball as it had been. The weight of the sword and shield lifted, and he felt the rubber ball return to normal in his hands. After working on a couple more transformations, his eyes felt heavy, and he started to doze off.

Chapter 21

Eric woke up to a strong gust of wind blowing on his face and the sound of traffic. The night sky twinkled with stars that seemed to reach down to him and whisper for him to awaken. He was shocked to see that he was no longer in Aviance or Hillthrope. Instead, he was in an old convertible. His head felt like a sledge hammer was pounding it, and he couldn't see straight.

He didn't believe his eyes when he looked at who was driving the car. Elizabeth Williams had a dark, olive-colored scarf over her auburn hair and a black dress on. She glanced over at Eric, an unreadable expression on her face. "Finally, you're awake. I was beginning to think that sleeping potion killed you."

Eric tried to respond, but nothing came out of his mouth when he opened it. He also tried to move his hands but realized his hands and feet were tied together.

"Don't try to talk. It will be useless. I put a charm on you. Now, listen to me. You HAVE to listen to me. In a few miles, I am going to pull over, so we can talk more about the subject. I want you to know that you are in danger, and I am trying to save you before you die." Her expression had turned from unreadable to insistent. There was almost a hint of mania to it.

Eric looked at the clock on the dash and saw it was 3:30. It wasn't until 4:43 that Eric's vision finally stopped swimming, and Elizabeth pulled over to an old, abandoned farmhouse.

Elizabeth got out of the car and opened Eric's door, untying him.

"I'm only untying you because I trust that you won't try to leave," she said, looking around, nervously.

Eric just sat in the car looking at Elizabeth with a confused expression on his face.

"We can't talk long. I don't know how safe this place is, and I don't know when my father will catch on that I'm gone."

Elizabeth's attention focused solely on Eric as she pleaded for him to listen to her. "Something big is happening, Eric. Something that you have to stop, before it gets out of control. Before I tell you what happens, though, I have to tell you that I'm sorry. I am so sorry for what is going to happen. I don't think you will ever forgive me for it, and I don't blame you.

"What I'm about to tell you, I'm telling you to save your life. Vesta is planning to attack. He knows it's his time to die, so he plans on taking as many of the White Knights as he can with him. As long as you're prepared, that won't happen.

"Vesta is saying he will come in the middle of the night when the moon is dark and shadows are alive. With him, he is bringing an army of four hundred. He says four because four means death."

Elizabeth checked her watch. "The sun will be rising, soon, which means I will be leaving, again. This is the last time we will meet this way."

Elizabeth got back into the driver's seat and started the car as Eric closed his door. She started driving back the way they had come from.

They could see the sun start to rise in the mirrors when Elizabeth said, "One last warning. The one you like is in deep danger. Something bad is going to happen to her; something you will never forgive yourself for."

Chapter 22

loan stood before her students, gathering herself before speaking. "Five... Four... Three... Two... One... Thanks for getting quiet. Now students, I know you are probably wondering why I canceled your tests for the rest of the afternoon and called you here."

"In just a few hours, the sun will be going down, and the new moon will be going up. A reliable source has informed me that the Shadow Reapers will be attacking us. So, in the remaining hours that we have, I need you to focus and keep calm while we get ready for battle.

"In your bedrooms, there is a closet. This closet is full of white robes similar to the one I am wearing, now. Put on the one that has your name on it, and then, come back down. For those of you who do not know, these robes are your armor. It will protect you against their fire powers. You are dismissed."

The older students got up quickly and rushed toward the stairs. The Freshmen had worried looks on their faces and hurried to their bedrooms to get their robes.

Once everyone was dressed and was back down in the main hall, Sloan gave out further instructions.

"I am assigning each grade with a teacher. Freshmen, you are with Mrs. Brown. Sophomores, you are with Mr. Day. Juniors, you are with Miss Carton. And Seniors, you guys are with Mr. Goodman. The rest of the teachers have been instructed to go down to the village and get some more help if we need it. Now, please go to your classrooms for practice."

Everyone got up as quickly as possible and ran to the classrooms they were assigned to. Each classroom was emptied and had about ten of the practice bots in them. For the remaining five hours, they practiced their DASR skills. At 9:00, the sun started to go down, and the students sat in the main hall, waiting for the Shadow Reapers to arrive.

A few ghosts came around the room and offered

refreshments while they waited. No one took them, because most of the students were sick to their stomachs with fear. Half an hour later, a ghost came flying through the main hall and went straight up to Sloan.

"Students. The time has arrived. The statues have spotted movement in the forest. I have some advice for you. Don't go into the shadows. They are unsafe. Please, get ready for the first attack. Good luck. And Eric James, please come with me."

Eric gave Sloan a confused look, and Sloan returned with a kind smile.

Eric got up from the table and rushed to Sloan

"What do you want me for?" Eric asked Sloan.

"Walk and talk at the same time, please," she said as she walked toward the Potions classroom. Once inside, they went out the door that led to the garden, and then, quickly toward the forest.

"I have to keep you safe. If you die, then there will be no hope we will ever beat Vesta and his Shadow Reapers."

"But I can't just watch while my friends are slain."

"You will not be watching - you will be helping me kill Vesta. And by killing Vesta, you will be helping your friends. Besides, Freshmen are not allowed to fight."

"I'm not strong enough to fight him."

"I know that, but he does not, and he does not know that you also have Fire power. Now, please follow me into the forest."

Eric stopped in his tracks "The forest? You just got done telling us to stay out of it."

"Yes, I know that. I promise you that you will be fine," Sloan said, covering her mouth so she wouldn't choke on the smoke that had started billowing out of the forest. The Shadow Reapers had started to burn trees.

"I don't want to do this. I never wanted *any* of this to happen," Eric exclaimed, getting mad.

"You have to," was all that Sloan said.

Sloan walked into the forest as Eric heard a thundering explosion that hurt his ears, followed by screaming from inside the school. He looked back over his shoulder and saw plumes of smoke over the top of the school, and a tear started to form in his eye. Eric wiped the tear off his cheek and walked toward the forest to help Sloan.

"Sloan, where are we going?"

"Shh. Duck down and watch where you step."

They went deeper into the forest and circled to the front of the school. Fire was everywhere. Some of the students were trying to put out the side of the school that caught fire. The smell of burnt flesh was getting to Eric and bringing back memories of his parents' death. Eric's ears were hurting because of all of the explosions and the screams from innocent people.

"Are you here to kill me?" said a cold and empty voice.

Suddenly, everything got quiet. It was like time, everywhere, simply froze. There wasn't even a small breeze in the air. Eric looked toward the school, and no one was moving. The apparent freeze didn't affect him and Sloan, though.

"I know you are here to kill me, Sloan, but what I don't know is why you brought a useless boy with you," said the voice, again. It seemed to come from everywhere and nowhere, at the same time.

"Sloan, who is that?" Eric asked.

"My name, *stupid boy,* is Vesta De'Lore. Now, *fear me!*"

Eric fell to the ground, shaking and crying out in pain.

"Let him go, Vesta." Sloan said.

A pale, tall man dressed in a black tux walked out of a shadow and chuckled sinisterly, "Why should I do that?"

"Because, I said so," Sloan murmured in a voice that carried authority. She pulled out her wand and flicked it at Vesta, creating a strong gust of wind that came out of the tip of the wand and knocked Vesta off his feet.

As soon as Vesta hit the ground, he made a small grunting noise, and Eric stopped shaking. Eric stood up and ran to Sloan.

"Is he… is he dead?" he asked her, clutching at her robes.

"Use your power and give us a little light. Then, we will find out." she responded.

Eric shook his left hand, and then, a small fireball was floating in his hand. He extended his hand toward Vesta. A branch that was stuck in the ground was sticking out of Vesta's chest. Bright, shining blood was covering his chest. Vesta moved his head to look at Eric and smiled at him with blood running down his chin.

"You must be the son of Rory James and Amelia May, Eric James. You do not yet realize your importance. You have only begun to discover your powers. Join the Shadow Reapers, and we will complete your training. With our combined strength, we can end this battle and bring order to the magic community."

"You killed my parents!" Eric screamed at him as he pulled back the hand holding the fireball, ready to throw it.

"Do it, boy. Kill me, and give into the anger," Vesta said, showing off a cold smile that chilled Eric to the bone.

Sloan stepped toward Eric and whispered, "You do not have to kill him. I have seen how this plays out, and you do not have to do this."

"Stupid, *weak* little boy," Vesta snapped at him. "You will never amount to anything. You and your friends will die at the hands of Shadow Reapers."

"Shut up!" Eric screamed at him.

Sloan stepped in front of Eric and raised her wand above her head. "Ardeat Apud Inferni!"

Vesta's body burst into black flames. When nothing but bones remained, they crumbled into dust. Time unfroze, and the wind blew away the dust of his bones. Eric looked toward the school and saw that the rest of the Shadow Reapers had disappeared at the same time Vesta did.

Chapter 23

A few days after the fight, the damages were tallied up. Sloan had gathered everyone in the main hall, and Eric was sitting alone at the end of the table. It was the first time, since the fight, that Eric had actually taken in the damage.

The front of the school had taken the most damage and was almost gone. The main hall smelled like charcoal, due to the floor being singed. Many seats were empty, due to the deaths that occurred. During the fight, a Shadow Reaper had found his way into the school, ferreted his way to the Freshman, and had killed a handful before he was taken down.

"Three... Two... One... Thank you for getting quiet. Even though we have won the battle, we must still mourn our losses. It is a bittersweet time, but we must go on. The first thing we have to do is repair the school, so we can get back to our lessons.

"Tools and building materials are being sent to us from Hillthrope and will be here, shortly. Once they arrive, I will separate you into groups and assign you to a construction worker. Those of you who are advanced enough to use Charms to help you build may do so. Those who are not, there will be tools for you to use."

When Sloan was finished, she walked away toward the stairs, and everybody got up. Eric sat there and pulled out a book from his book bag and began reading. As he was reading, he noticed a couple of people sitting across the room staring at him. He glanced to see who they were, and the only faces he recognized were Marina, Catlin, and Nick's.

This was the fifth time, this week, he has noticed them staring at him. Ever since the fight, people were looking at him differently, and Eric knew why. They all thought he was the one who killed Vesta, but his friends should have known the truth. Eric was annoyed that ever since the fight, they had been looking at him differently. It was like they weren't even his friends, anymore.

Yesterday, Eric tried to use his telepathic power to try to understand why, but the only thing he got out of them was the word *two-faced* which made Eric really angry. He had no clue why they were calling him that, and it hurt tremendously.

Eric was contemplating on whether or not to send them a text to chew them out. He imagined what he would say, and even typed it out a couple of times but never had the courage to press send. Even though their shunning hurt, he couldn't shake the feeling of loneliness without their friendship.

Eric slammed his books shut, shoved it into his book bag, and then stormed out of the hall. He had no clue where he was going to go, since the library was closed and the living room was considered 'unsafe'. Eric just needed to go somewhere other than where they were.

He ended up finding a spot in the Potions garden, where no students were milling about. It was half destroyed by fire, and half of it looked as if it had been trampled. No one was here, though, which suited Eric just fine.

He sat down against a wall that looked stable and waited for the construction people to get here. While he waited, he thought about why they considered him two-faced.

"I am who I am. I'm shy and socially awkward. I don't make friends easily, because I don't trust people. They are the ones that are two-faced. They say they are my friends and that they will always love me, no matter what, and then, they pull this off! I should have never trusted them. Books were fine enough all these years, and they are fine, now. Who needs friends?" Eric said talking to himself.

He sat, finished *Decoding a Dream,* and was planning to give it back to Mrs. Grey when he got the text message saying that the construction workers had arrived. Eric walked back into the school and into the main hall. Most of the students and teachers were in the hall when he arrived.

Sloan walked into the main hall with Mr. Smith, carrying a large chalkboard between them. They hefted its awkward size in-between tables and deposited it beside the main door that was half destroyed. She reached into her pockets and pulled out some papers, unfolding them, and pinning them on the board.

She waited a while for everyone to arrive. Once the majority of the students were seated, Sloan began to talk.

"Three... Two... One...Thank you for getting quiet. There are two lists on here. One is the list of groups you will be working in."

Sloan closed her eyes, took a breath, and continued by saying, "The other list is the list of those who did not survive the fight." She then left to talk with one of the construction workers.

Eric got up, along with everyone else, and went to see what group he was put in. Several people, including Nick, Catlin, and Marina, were looking at the list of the deceased. Eric glanced at it, and the only name he recognized was Amber Evergreen.

Eric was surprised that she'd died, because she had been the top of his class and had been doing exceptional in the Defense Against the Shadow Reapers class. A feeling of remorse crept into Eric, but he shoved it down and searched for his name on the group list. When he found his name, he was furious. Eric marched over to where Sloan was and started to yell at her.

"You put me in *their* group?"

"I understand that you are in a fight with them, but they are your friends, and you need friends, Eric," she said, trying to ignore him.

"No, I don't. Are you going to do nothing about this?" he said, getting annoyed.

"I have more important issues than your friend drama, Eric, and as your godmother, I am telling you to make up with them. As your Headmistress, I am telling you to stay with the group I assigned you to."

Eric stormed off and walked over to where Nick, Catlin, and Marina were standing, listening to a construction worker. When Eric was with them, the construction worker identified himself as Pat. He told them that, today, they were going to be working on the first floor walls.

Over the next couple of days, Eric worked silently with them. He didn't talk to them, and they didn't talk to him. They would exchange a few angry glances, but that was about it. Eric was glad he was working with a hammer half the time, because it was taking away his anger.

Chapter 24

By July the fourth, the students of Aviance, along with the community of Hillthrope, helped rebuild the front of the school. Within that time, the students that were harmed in the fight were healed and were back in school.

As the evening approached, the students were helping plan the annual dance, and this year, they were celebrating the death of the Shadow Reapers, as well as remembering those who were lost in the fight.

"Are you going to the dance, tonight?" Marina asked Eric.

"Oh, you're talking to me, now?" Eric countered back, bitterly

"We had a fight. I'm sorry."

"Had a fight? We are still in it. Now, get away from me before I light you on fire," Eric said, bumping her shoulder on the way to his Telepathy class.

"We are not done talking."

"Oh, we are so done talking! You screwed me over!" Eric yelled, visibly seething.

Eric arrived at the class right before the bell rang, and the only seat left was next to Catlin.

"I'm only sitting here 'cause it's the only seat left. Do not think I'm not mad at you, anymore," he whispered as he sat down.

"But Eric, I'm sorry."

"No, you're not."

"I am."

"No, you're not! You lied to me! You guys said you were my friends, and then, you, Marina, and Nick started ignoring me for some strange reason!" Eric's outburst was drawing the attention of the class, and the teacher cleared her throat. Eric looked up at her. "Miss Tyler, I need to talk to Sloan," he said, feeling heat starting to build up in his body.

"I'll tell her you're on your way," Miss Tyler said, picking up the phone on her desk.

Eric walked out of the room and down the hall to the stairs, waiting for the stairs to appear. It was a few minutes until Eric heard Sloan walk out of her office, and then, Eric saw the stairs appear. He rushed up them to Sloan's office and went to Sloan, hugging her, fiercely.

"I can't do this, anymore," he said, almost sobbing with the rush of emotion that was overtaking him.

"Do what?"

"Be here with them. It brings me so much pain. They were the only friends I had, and I don't make friends easily, you know."

"Let us sit down and talk about what happened," Sloan told him softly and walked over to a grey couch that Eric had never noticed, before.

"It started a few weeks ago, around the start of midterms. They stopped talking to me and started leaving me out of their plans. The only time they talked to me was when they needed help understanding a subject. They stopped treating me as a friend and more like I was an object they could use to study. And then, after the Shadow Reapers came, they stopped talking to me, all together, and started calling me *two-faced* in their heads. I try to put distance between myself and them, but they keep showing up to yell at me."

"It sounds like you are over-reacting, a little. They are your friends, Eric. Everyone has been through a lot. Maybe, they are the ones that need some space to deal with the deaths of their classmates. Are they trying to talk to you, now?"

Eric thought about what Sloan had just said to him, and responded, "Yes, they are trying to apologize, but if they needed space, why didn't they just tell me? I would have understood. Instead, they just cut me out. And what happens if I forgive them, and they do the same thing, again? I couldn't handle that, especially if Catlin cuts me out, again." Eric lowered his head and shook it, slowly.

"Why do you say that?"

"Because I like her, and she says she likes me."

"If you like her, then accept their apology. At least, find out why they did it all."

"Okay."

"Are you just saying that, or are you actually going to do it?" Sloan asked, putting her hand on his arm in concern.

"I'll do it," Eric said as he hung his head down, again.

"Good boy. I'll tell Miss Tyler that you won't be returning, today."

"Thank you."

Eric hugged Sloan once again and left her office, heading toward the library. Once there, he turned on his phone. There were thirty-two messages, with most being from his friends back in Wisconsin. Ten of them, though, were from Nick, Marina, and Catlin.

He deleted all of the messages without even reading them. Then, he texted his supposed friends, saying that they needed to meet before the Fourth of July dance, tonight.

Ten minutes after eight, Nick, Marina, and Catlin walked into the library and headed toward the table where Eric was sitting. Agitation had gotten the better of him, and he snapped.

"Do not talk. I've heard enough of your voices for a lifetime, now, and it's my time to talk.

"I don't know what I did to deserve what you are doing to me. I never did anything to you. I helped you guys when you needed it. I thought I was your friend, and you decided to cut me out of your lives. Why? I have no god damn clue. I thought I was ready to forgive you and move on, but the pain you have caused me is just too much to endure. And every time I see your faces, it causes me even more pain.

"Well, thanks for nothing, and I hope all of you go to hell," Eric slammed his fist on the table, grabbed is books, and got up and left the library.

Eric walked to the second floor and lay down on his bed. He plugged his headphones into his phone and turned up the volume to drown out the world.

Eric fell asleep until Nick walked in and took Eric's headphone out of his ears.

"What are you doing?" Eric asked him.

"You weren't answering your phone."

"Yeah, 'cause I'm pissed at you. So, take a hint and get out of here."

"I can't do that till you accept our apology."

"That will never happen. There was no reason why you

started ignoring me. Now, leave me alone and go to the dance with your little sweetheart."

Eric put his headphones back into his ears and closed his eyes.

At 9:53, Eric got out of bed and changed into his pajamas and was reading a book.

"Eric, can we talk?" Catlin said as she walked into the room. She was dressed in a tight, light yellow strapless dress that fell to her knees. She had on dark blue flats and a dark blue headband pulling back her hair from her face.

"No."

"Well then, at least listen to me."

When Eric didn't say or do anything, Catlin started to talk.

"I do like you, but it's not what you think. We weren't ignoring you."

"Oh, please just shut up. Yes, you were -- I'm telepathic, remember? I know you were all ignoring me, because you were saying it in your head. You even called me two-faced."

"I'm sorry, Eric, I really am."

"What you are is a bitch. Now, get out of my sight," Eric turned his attention back to his book and ignored Catlin.

Chapter 25

Eric continued to ignore Nick, Marina, and Catlin's apologies, but ignoring them was starting to get at him. Whenever he was in the library studying for the final exams, he found himself going back to times when they were friends and thinking about going and accepting their apologies. But then, he would see the three of them together, laughing, and he continued hating them.

It was the eve of the last day of school. Everyone in school was doing their last minute studying before the eleven o'clock curfew. Eric was up in Sloan's office, practicing for the Fire Manipulation final with her that would take place, tomorrow.

They were practicing fireball throwing when a ghost came floating through the wall with a panicked look on her face.

"Miss Marlin?"

"Yes, Vicky?"

"A storm approaches. A strong storm. A different storm. A black storm," said Vicky. She looked scared and very lost.

"Are you sure? This cannot be."

"I am sure, Miss Marlin."

"But we defeated them." Sloan said with a concerned look.

"But they are coming."

"How fast will they be here?" Sloan said, looking scared.

"Soon. They move swiftly."

"But it is not even dark, outside. It's only just dusk."

"I know. It is strange."

"Warn the rest of the ghosts and the statues. I will tell the students."

Before Sloan got to her phone to make the announcement, the whole school shook. Power went out, things fell off walls and cabinets, and kids screamed. Sloan ran out of the room in her full-length, dark purple dress, revealed the steps and ran down them.

"Eric, they are approaching the school. Help me alert the

students."

Eric ran down the stairs behind her. He looked out the window and could see the black masses walk toward the school.

Eric quickly opened doors and yelled, "Shadow Reapers are attacking."

When he got to the Freshman door, he saw Nick, Marina, and Catlin all huddled together underneath a window. He told everyone what was happening and then rushed over to his friends.

"Listen, I honestly can't stand you guys, and I can't forgive you for what you have done, but if we make it through this, I'm sure we can figure something out," he said before preparing for the battle.

"Thank you, Eric." Catlin said with a half caring and half scared look.

Eric ran into the boys' bedroom and got his white robe, along with the others, and then ran down to the main hall, where Sloan was pacing the floor.

The school was still being hit by fireballs and lightning as Sloan talked.

"Students of Aviance, your time is here. Please, be safe and be smart. Use your powers wisely and fight in groups. Never get separated."

As Sloan finished, part of the front wall crumpled. People screamed and yelled, while others jumped to their feet and used their powers. Eric, Nick, Marina, and Catlin were some of the few that jumped up to their feet.

The four of them followed a few others, outside, to help the others that came from the community to fight.

"They seem stronger, this time!" Nick yelled over the sound of young children in the village, screaming.

"There are more of them!" Catlin yelled as a fireball hit the ground, near them.

Eric felt his phone vibrate multiple times in his pocket but ignored it.

A large wall of fire lighted the area around the school, and the air was thick with smoke and ash.

As a group of Shadow Reapers approached the group of friends, Nick froze them, and then Eric caught them on fire with a fireball, while Marina and Catlin put stun charms on a few of them that were trying to attack from behind them.

The group escaped the fight for a few moments behind a wall of the first floor of the school that still stood. Eric pulled out his phone from his pocket and looked at the text message. His phone said it was an unknown number, but Eric knew that that number belonged to Elizabeth. It seemed like the whole world paused. Eric wasn't scared, anymore, because he knew that Elizabeth was okay.

"Guys, Elizabeth contacted me."

"What did she say?"

"She has important information for us. Information that can help us win this fight. She wants to meet me on a hill that is just beyond the school."

"Does she mean the hill that's behind the Potions classroom?" Nick asked.

"That's the only one that is near the school."

"You can't go, Eric." Marina said

"Why not? I trust her."

"I've seen this situation in a premonition before. It's not her. It may look like her, but it's not. Trust me, Eric," Catlin said as ashes started to fall on them.

"I just know it's her. If you guys really are my friends, then trust me when I say that this *is* her. I have to save her," Eric said as more of the school collapsed beside them.

"Let us at least help you get there."

"Okay."

They moved toward the back of the school. As soon as they turned around the corner, several Shadow Reapers were waiting for them.

Two of the Shadow Reapers caught Nick and Marina on their sides and brought them to their knees as they screamed in agony. Catlin pulled out her wand to do a charm, but a Shadow Reaper knocked it out of her hand with a fireball. She got down on her knees to find it while Eric shot a fireball and killed them.

"Did you find your wand?"

"Yeah."

"Are they okay?"

"I don't know," Eric said, trying to look at them through the thick smoke that separated them.

"You stay here. I'll be okay."

"Are you sure?" Catlin said as the second floor fell to the ground.

"Yes. Just get them to safety," Eric said in between two coughing fits.

"Where? Everything is under attack."

"Get them inside."

"Are you nuts? The school is crumpling."

"Don't you know a charm that will make the walls stronger?"

"Kind of, but it won't last for long."

"I'll be back as soon as I can. I'll help you, then."

"Be safe."

"I will. I love you."

"I love you too, Eric James."

Eric grabbed Catlin, pulled her close to him, and kissed her on the lips. A lightning bolt cracked, and part of the third and fourth floor fell to the ground. Eric pulled apart from Catlin and ran to the hill where Elizabeth was waiting for him.

He ran as fast as he could to the hill, and every once in a while, Eric would see a Shadow Reaper and would throw a fireball at them, knocking them out of his way. He worried about his friends when he felt the ground shake and heard the sound of brick crumpling, but he pressed on, knowing that at the end of his fight, Elizabeth would help him.

A single figure was standing at the top of the hill. She was in a black, full-length halter cocktail dress, with a long, black cape. Her auburn hair was longer than it had been in his dream, and it was flowing in the wind. She stood watching the fight, and no emotion was on her face. When Eric saw the figure, he ran faster, adrenaline rushing through him.

"Elizabeth!" he shouted. He was so happy. He knew that his girlfriend was safe, and they could be together, again.

Her head snapped to him, but there was still no emotion on her face.

"Elizabeth." Eric gasped, his body starting to feel fatigued from his efforts to reach her.

She was closer, now, and Eric could see that she looked tired. Her eyes were black, and her tanned skin had gone pale.

"Elizabeth, are you okay?"

Eric was opening his arms to her, and when they were close

enough, he wrapped his arms around her. "I love..."

Eric took a sharp breath in. Pain blossomed, and he felt like he couldn't breathe.

"Elizabeth," Eric gasped out. "How could you have done this? I love you," he said in a raspy voice, before he went unconscious.

Elizabeth kicked Eric, so that he was on his stomach. She reached down and pulled the knife out, walking away in silence. As soon as she was out of sight, several Shadow Reapers came out of the nearby woods, picked Eric up, and dragged him into the darkness of the trees.

PART 2
THE SECRET

Chapter 1

"Eric, hurry up. I want to leave in five minutes," Sloan yelled down the hall to Eric's bedroom.

"I'm working on it, Sloan," Eric barked back as he picked up his wand from his nightstand.

He pulled his suitcase onto his bed with his free hand, and as he pointed his wand at the empty suitcase, he said, "Dilata profundum."

The inside of the suitcase grew three times as deep as it was, without the outside being affected. Eric put his wand back down and started packing the folded clothes that were scattered on his bed.

It was May twenty-ninth, Eric just got out of school two days ago, and they were heading off to Aviance. Sloan wanted to get there early to check out the new construction after the school had been destroyed during the fight, last year.

Half an hour later, Eric was done packing everything and carried his suitcase and his book bag downstairs to the living room. Sloan was sitting on the couch with her suitcase and purse, waiting for Eric while she checked her email on her phone.

"We are going to be late. It is bad for the Headmistress to be late, Eric," Sloan said to Eric as she got up and picked up her suitcase.

"Just put the suitcases in the trunk of the car, and we will be on our way," Sloan said as she walked out of the front door.

"How are we getting there, exactly?" Eric asked her while he followed her retreating form.

"If you recall, last year, you arrived at the school through a tree. Well, there are trees all over the country, one for each state. Ours is in Rock Creek Park, and the trip will take about forty minutes. After I park the car, I'll be putting a charm on it, so that it goes disregarded. After that, we'll go to the tree, enter it, and arrive at Aviance," Sloan explained to Eric as she put her suitcase in her brand new, grey Jeep Grand Cherokee.

No one talked as they drove to the park, and when they got there, Eric helped unload the suitcases. He couldn't help but be thankful as he carried his load into the woods and encountered little to obstruct their journey. He continued to follow Sloan for about twenty minutes, until she stopped walking in front of a tall and very wide dogwood tree. The massive tree had to be over a hundred years old.

Sloan took out her wand from her purse and said, "Aperire ostium."

Like he had seen multiple times before, the front of the tree split open like two doors. Sloan picked up her bags and stepped into the tree. Eric grabbed his bag and suitcase and followed her, his shoes squeaking on the gray marble that covered the floor and walls. As he had expected, the inside was larger than it looked, outside, and six fireplaces were fixed around the room, lit by the familiar white flames.

Before Sloan walked into the hearth, she looked at Eric and said, "Do not screw this up. You screw up, here, you *will* have to take the punishment I give you. This is not high school, Eric. Here, you are expected to be mature, so act like it."

Eric watched as she turned and walked into the fire. The white flame engulfed Sloan, and when the flame went down, he pushed the heavy luggage through and waited for a moment before stepping through, himself. The cold, white flame became translucent, and he could see that people were walking around the new main hall.

Eric came out of a fireplace that was to the left of the main door. As he looked around, he could see the newly painted, beige walls of the main hall. The floor was covered in a dark brown carpet that cushioned everyone's footfalls, so that the only echoes were of voices. New marble statues were standing by the large, French glass door, and he noticed that the closest one was a mermaid that was brushing her hair with a coral comb. On the other side of the doorway was a marble statue of a pirate with a sword in one hand and a telescope in the other.

Two, white wood double doors had been built on the left and right walls, and two, glass spiral staircases stood on the far wall on the ends of the golden table that belonged to the teachers. The chair in the middle was large-backed and had an

'S' carved into the back. The wall behind the teachers' table was all stained-glass and had 'Aviance School of Wizardry' written in it. Through the wall of glass, you could see plants that Eric assumed were from the Potions garden.

The four tables for the students were all made out of silver, as were the chairs.

"Impressive. And I see that they saved my chair," Sloan observed as she headed towards the stairs on the right side of the room.

Eric followed her up the stairs and to the second floor, toting his luggage behind him.

"I want you to get your items sorted out, and then, I expect you to be down in the main hall in an hour for dinner." Sloan commanded to Eric as he walked into the commons room of the second floor.

Instead of acknowledging her, he smirked behind her back and looked around at the new construction. Floor to ceiling windows lined the wall between the stairs, giving a view to the woods that still bore burnt-out marks from the battle, last year. Across from the windows were the floor bathrooms. The warm, red wood of the hallway cast warm reflections on the light brown floor, giving an energized atmosphere for the students.

Eric cast a glance at the Freshman room on the right side of the stairs and smirked, again, heading over to the Sophomore living room, to the left. As he walked to the white door, he noticed several other students that were walking that direction, as well, with some of them carrying larger amounts of luggage than him.

Eric opened the door and walked into the Sophomore living room. The grey-blue walls and thick, white carpet went well together, and the brightly-painted modern art that was hanging on the wall gave the room a modern flair. A forty-nine inch, flat-screen TV was mounted on the wall opposite the main door, and there were already students lounging in the two, navy blue couches in front of it. The dark brown end table was piled with belongings, and students were going through the birch wood bookshelves and horsing around in chairs and couches around the room.

"Hi Eric! We thought you were dead! You never answered our texts over the break!" exclaimed Marina Martin.

Marina, Nick Walters, and Catlin Chamberlin were sitting at one of the tables in the room, playing cards. They hadn't changed, at all, since last year, which made Eric laugh.

Catlin was still that insecure, little girl in pink. Eric could tell by the way she held herself and the way she fidgeted with her cards. Nick was still the lazy gamer with the high metabolism, although this year, he looked as if he hadn't had a haircut in months. His short, blond hair from last year was now covering his eyes. Marina was still the high-energy jock. She had a few cuts and bruises on her arms, undoubtedly from a soccer game.

Ignoring them, Eric continued to walk to the adjacent wall where a door that had *Boys' Bedroom* was standing wide open. He entered it, but before he closed the door, he heard Catlin mumble, sadly, "Your vision was right, Marina. I thought he was our friend. I guess my vision was wrong."

This made Eric grin in delight as he went to go choose a bunk bed.

The walls of the bedroom were painted navy blue, and the floor was covered with the same white carpet as the living room. The bunk beds were made of birch wood, and the sheets were royal blue. Eric walked to a bed at the end of the room, claimed the bottom bunk by writing his name on the board on the footboard, and unpacked all of his items.

After he put the last of his clothes in his dresser, Eric decided to lay on his bed to text some of his friends from his high school. At six, he got up and walked down to the main hall. To Eric's right, as he walked down, he could see that all the teachers were sitting at their table, and Sloan was standing up, ready to speak.

All the students were already at their assigned tables, and Sloan glared at Eric as he walked down the last few steps. Eric took his time getting to the Sophomore table, relishing in the disruption he was causing. As he came upon the table, he noticed that only two seats were left; one by Catlin, and the other by a group of people that Eric hadn't met, yet. Eric sat at the far end of the table, next to the people he didn't know.

"Sup," said one of the guys, his Bob Marley t-shirt proclaiming *Herb Heals* in bright, green lettering.

"Sup?" Eric said back to him.

"My name is Zack Roberts, and you're that Eric James kid, right? The one with the fire power?" Zack had green, bloodshot eyes. His face was covered in acne, and his hair looked like it hadn't been washed in a few days, if not longer.

"Yeah, that's me. Why?"

"Dude, you're like, famous."

Eric was a little confused. Only last year, they'd all hated him for having fire manipulation power, but now, he was famous? A smile spread across his face as he thought about it, so he didn't question it further. He liked the title of being famous. To him, it meant power, and he couldn't get enough.

"Five... Four... Three... Two... One... Thanks for getting quiet." Sloan said as the hush spread across the room.

"I would like to welcome you to the new and improved Aviance. As all of you know or should know, Aviance was destroyed in battle, last year, and the kind people of Hillthrope have donated resources and material to build this new school. It's so wonderful to see the magical community come together, like this." Sloan gestured around herself to the new hall with a large smile, and the students and teachers erupted into applause and cheering.

Finally, Sloan raised her hands for silence, and the whole room became still. Then, she continued, "The stairs to my office will now be there, permanently, and there's now a waiting room. Just sign up for a spot, and I will be with you as soon as I can.

"The first announcement before we eat is this: due to the recent circumstances, security has been advanced. There are several ghosts that are roaming the woods, on the lookout for Shadow Reapers. There are also a few statues that have joined the patrols. The main door will be locked at five o'clock in the evening, except on the weekends. At that point, they will be locked at eight o'clock. After the first day of school, the fireplaces behind you will be put out, as well.

"Secondly, you are forbidden to go into the woods. The woods are filled with shadows, and that is how the Shadow Reapers get around. You do not need to worry, though. The school has been protected, so the Shadow Reapers cannot get into the school by shadows.

"Thirdly, if you need to go to Hillthrope, you will need a teacher's note or a note from me. You will tell the main entrance statues what places you need to go to, and two ghosts will guide you down to the village.

"The last announcement is that, this year, we are announcing Aviance's first soccer team. Each grade will be able to sign up for either a boys' or girls' team, and will compete against the other grades. There will also be a Band, Choir, and other assortment of activities we will offer, this year. All of the sign-up sheets are in the waiting room on the wall.

"Now, let us eat and be merry!" she exclaimed, warmly and with a kind smile on her face.

Like last year, when Sloan sat down, about two dozen ghosts came out from the walls in the main hall with glass trays in their hands. They went to each table and delivered the food to the students, and then, disappeared back into the walls. They came back out, again, with the glass trays full of crystal cups with drinks in them.

Chapter 2

After dinner, Eric walked back up to the living room and plopped down on the couch to watch some TV while he texted some friends. It was a little after 10:00 when Eric decided to go to bed and shut off the TV. All the boys were peacefully sleeping in their beds, and Eric was the last one up on the floor.

As Eric walked down the middle of the aisle, he stopped dead in his tracks at Nick's bed. A disturbing smile crept onto his face as he pulled his green crystal wand from his back pocket. It was chipped a little from abuse, but it worked just fine.

Eric turned to Nick's bed and whispered, "Astringimus pressis funes," and flicked his wand at Nick. Ropes came flying out of the tip of his want and wrapped itself around Nick.

Grinning to himself, Eric stuffed the wand back into his back pocket, went to his dresser, put his pajamas on, and got into bed.

Eric woke up in a dark room with water dripping on his head. Two, floating fireballs were in the hall outside of the room, and as Eric's eyes adjusted to the poor lighting, he realized that he was in a cell. Iron bars made up two of the walls, while the other two were made of a cold, almost slimy rock. Even the floor was cold, hard, and damp. Water was dripping from a crack in the ceiling. Eric almost gagged at the smell of mildew, and the small, dirty plate sitting by the door didn't help, since it held a mold-covered piece of bread.

Harsh footsteps came down the hall and spiked an overwhelming panic in Eric. He crawled to the far side of the cell and got as close as he could to the wall without hurting the ankle that was chained to the floor.

A tall woman with long, curly auburn hair walked down the hall. A black headband held some of her hair back, and an ankle length, black lace ball gown covered her body. Her black stiletto boots were the source of the loud clicking.

This girl had no emotion on her very pale face, and her eyes were pitch black, reminding Eric of twin abysses glaring back at him.

"Are you going to do what you are asked, today?" asked the woman in a harsh but sweet tone.

Eric looked up at her, and then, he looked back down at the floor.

"Have it your way, then," she said as she began to unlock the cell door.

The woman walked into the cell and towards Eric, relishing in the fear she was causing. As she came closer and closer, he started to tremble more violently. The girl stopped a few inches from him and spat at him, rolling his petrified body over with her foot and stomping viciously on his stomach.

Eric let out a loud and muffled scream as her stiletto heel stabbed him. He felt a warm fluid cover his stomach, and even though he couldn't see very well in the darkness, he could tell that his torn, dirty shirt was now soaked in fresh blood.

"Someone sew him back up," the woman barked the order when she stepped out of the room and looked at him, again.

Eric woke up the next day by the sound of someone screaming. He shot up in surprise, but when he saw that it was just Nick, he grabbed some clothes for the day and walked out of the bedroom with a devilish smile on his face.

He checked is iPhone as he walked into the living room, noticing that five texts were waiting on his reply. Two were from old friends, and three were from unknown numbers. Eric answered them as he walked down the hall to the boy's bathroom.

The walls and floor were made out of a light brown wood, giving the bathroom a manly feel. Seven sinks lined the wall to the right, and four windows with dressers underneath them were on the far wall. In between the dressers were laundry hampers, and seven toilet stalls lined the wall to the left. Seven showers were on the wall that held the door to the hallway, giving a little bit of privacy as you walked through the hooded doorway and into the bathroom.

"Did you see what happened to Nick in the middle of the night?" said one of the boys that were standing at a sink, shaving.

"Did you like my artwork?" Eric said as he walked to the dresser to get a towel and some soap and shampoo.

"That was you?" said another boy who snapped his head around to look at him, puzzlingly.

Eric nodded his head triumphantly.

"I thought you guys were friends."

"Nope," Eric said as he stepped into a shower.

Eric got dressed in a baggy, old brown t-shirt, torn black shorts, and some black skater shoes. When he was done, he left the bathroom and headed back to the living room.

"Thanks for tying me to my bed, Eric." Nick said to Eric as he walked down the hall toward the bathroom.

"No problem." Eric said as he pushed Nick's clothes out of his hands.

"Oops, let me give you a hand with that." Eric reached his hand out to the pile of clothes and threw a fireball on top of it.

Nick quickly stomped on his clothes to extinguish the flames and cursed at Eric as he walked away.

Chapter 3

At 8:30, everybody was already downstairs in the main hall as Eric walked down the staircase.

"And that was the last of the announcements. Let us eat and be merry!" Sloan exclaimed her normal finish to her speech as Eric entered the main hall. She was about to sit when she noticed him.

"Nice of you to join us, Mr. James." Sloan said as she gave him a look that said he was in trouble.

He looked over his shoulder at her, rolled his eyes, and walked away. Eric sat across from Zack, again, to wait for the ghosts to drop off his breakfast as he and Zack talked.

"My buddy brought some Kansas grass from his hometown," Zack whispered conspiringly. "You want to meet us in the second floor bathroom and have a fire safety meeting?"

"Sure. Sounds like a plan, dude." Eric said to him as a ghost sat a plate of scrambled eggs and toast in front of Eric.

At 9:00, breakfast was over, and people started to leave the main hall. As Eric started up the steps, someone tapped his shoulder. He turned to see a short and thin girl in short shorts and a purple lace-backed t-shirt. Her brown, curly hair was loose around her shoulders.

"What do you want?" Eric said with disgust as he looked at her.

"My name is Jamie Chamberlin. I'm Catlin's little sister, and you're Eric James, right?"

"Once again, what do you want?" he asked, losing patience.

"I want to know *why* you broke my sister's heart and *why* you are treating her and her friends like crap."

"Well, that's just none of *your* fucking business, is it, kid? Now, go away before I turn you into a pile of ash." Eric said as he began to cover his hands in red-hot flames.

Jamie let a little squeal out and ran up the stairs as quickly as she could to avoid being burnt to a crisp. When Eric got to the second floor, he headed towards the boys' bathroom. There were three boys in there standing by the open windows. One was Zack, who was wearing a baggy red and blue shirt and black skinny jeans.

"This is John Anderson," Zack said, pointing to a kid on his left.

John had short, straight strawberry blond hair that was so messy, it went in every direction possible. He was wearing a white Lincoln Park t-shirt with a black, long-sleeved shirt underneath it. He had khaki shorts on and dirty white converse shoes.

"And this is Damon Cowell," Zack said, pointing to a guy on his right.

Damon had short, dirty blond hair and grey eyes. He was wearing a worn-out, grey shirt, jeans with holes in the knees, and green skater shoes.

"Make sure you lock the door." Zack said to Eric.

Eric locked the door behind him and walked to the windows.

When Eric got closer to the boys, John pulled a baggie out of his pocket.

"This is the finest grass in this part of the country," Damon said with an eager glint in his eye.

John pulled out paper from his bag and started to roll up joints. When they each had a joint, John handed the baggie back to Damon, and he put the marijuana back into his pocket and pulled out a lighter from his other pocket.

He tried to light his, but when his lighter didn't work, John asked, "Hey Eric, can you give us a light?"

"Sure." Eric held up his finger to the end of the joint and snapped his fingers. As he did, a small flame covered the tip of his index finger, which he used to light the joint. After he was done with the others, he proceeded to light his own.

Five minutes later saw to it that the joints were gone. The boys were lying on the floor, giggling and laughing like little school children. Eric felt lightheaded and had a paranoid feeling of being watched. He turned around, quickly, and thought he saw his twin across the room, staring at him. He blinked, and his twin was gone.

"Hey, who's in there? Let me in," said a loud and stern voice outside the bathroom.

"Shit. Shit. *Shit,*" Zack whispered vehemently as he stumbled to his feet.

They tried to get to their feet, but they kept falling to the ground.

"What are we going to do?" Eric whispered.

"I can hear you talking in there!" said the guy outside the door.

The guys tried to run to the windows, but then, heard the voice say, "Recludam hoc ostium," and the door flew open, banging against the shower stall.

"Gotcha. You boys are coming with me," said Mr. Goodman, the Metamorphosis teacher.

He flicked his wand at the boys, and chains flew from the wand, wrapping around each of them. Mr. Goodman grabbed a hold of Eric's arm and pulled him out of the room, with the chains pulling the rest of the others with them, like a chain-gang. The irate teacher walked the boys up the staircase to the seventh floor, and the whole time, all four boys were laughing uncontrollably.

Mr. Goodman sat the kids down in the waiting room chairs against the wall, and left through the doors into Sloan's office. From where Eric was sitting, windows lined all the walls, except the wall to his right. That wall had a single door in it that read *Headmistress Sloan's Office* on it. A few posters about discipline were neatly arranged around the door, along with a corkboard with sign-up sheets on them.

The walls, floor, and furnishings were all white, and the furniture was all made of metal.

"My ass hurts," Zack giggled from his chair.

The other boys burst out laughing, again. As they calmed down, Eric looked out of the window, behind him, and noticed the new greenhouse that the school had built. A large, glass chandelier hung in the center of the ceiling, lighting the whole room. One of the other boys noticed him looking out the window and giggled.

"What?" Eric said, grinning in his drug-induced stupor.

"I wanna hock a loogie on that glass down there," he said in between fits of giggles.

The boys erupted into a fit of laughter as Mr. Goodman

walked out of Sloan's office. The teacher sternly snorted and flicked his wand at them, releasing the chains. With a disgusted backwards glance, he walked down the staircase.

"Mr. Jones, please come with me," Sloan said when she came out of her office.

John got out of the chair and tried to walk straight into the office but ran into the doorframe. No one laughed, since the mirth had seemed to drain out of them at the view of Sloan's passive face. One by one, the boys where called into the office. They would stay for a few minutes, and then, come out and immediately go to the stairs. The last one to go in was Eric.

"Mr. James, please come into my office."

Eric got up from his chair and clumsily walked into Sloan's office.

The office had changed, since the last time Eric stood here. The right and left walls had five windows set into them. The golden yellow walls were accented with sage green curtains that draped over the windows. Sloan's golden desk and high back chair was now positioned underneath the balcony that led to her private room.

On the far balcony wall was a French door with white curtains. Neatly positioned around the room were oil paintings of oceans and mountains, and bookcases and cupboards lined the walls and held an assortment of magical items and books. Several gold floor lights with a sage green shade on them sat around the room.

Sloan was dressed in tan dress pants that fell just below her ankle. Her brown, high-heeled boots made no sound on the thick carpet, though Eric wasn't sure if he'd have noticed it they had, or not. She wore a pink sweater with a light blue dress shirt under it, and her silver hair was pulled back into a ponytail.

She guided Eric to the golden desk in the back of the room and sat in her chair, motioning for Eric to sit down. Like last year, as Eric went to sit down, a chair appeared out of the blue. This one, though, was golden with a plump, green cushion on the top.

"As your godmother, I say this. *How the hell could you do this? This could ruin your whole damn future!*" Sloan roared forcefully at him. She took a deep breath to calm down, and continued, "And as your Headmistress I say this. I am very disappointed in you, Eric James, and I have no other choice but to punish you for your actions. You, and the rest of your new friends, will be assigned to a different teacher. That teacher is allowed to use you in any way he or she wants to.

"This punishment starts, right now. And *your* teacher is Mr. Goodman."

Eric groaned and rolled his eyes.

"I wouldn't be late with the teacher who *hates* you." she said.

Eric got up, walked out of Sloan's office, and headed down one level to the Metamorphosis classroom, hatefully grumbling the whole way.

Chapter 4

Eric slowly walked down the last few steps to the sixth floor. The new sixth floor had two glass staircases, like all of the new floors, except the top one. As he came to the hallway, he glanced across the hall to the new Telepathy classroom and behind him to the bathrooms. A little further down, the Metamorphosis classroom door yawned its mouth, like a lazy beast that was only waiting for him to step through to his demise. Eric sighed and slowly walked that way, glancing at a doorway that led to the second story of the library.

Between the two staircases was the same floor to ceiling windows that were on most of the floors, giving a view of the dark woods. Eric grinned as he glanced around at the crimson red walls and dark brown, wooden floor. The combination fit his mood. Some students were studying on some dark brown leather couches that lined the hall, and several, dark wood lights were attached to the walls, lighting the hall.

Eric's slow pace eventually brought him to the Metamorphosis classroom, and he belligerently knocked on the door. He heard several loud footsteps come towards the door, and Mr. Goodman opened it with a whoosh of air. Now that the stupor had started to wear off, Eric noticed the teacher's light brown Argyle polo shirt and dark brown dress pants. His dark, cold green eyes were fixed on Eric's head. Mr. Goodman slid his hand over his graying comb-over in agitation as he walked away from the door.

"You follow me when I walk, boy," he barked at Eric.

Eric followed behind him as he walked down a row of desks towards a bookshelf full of old, dusty books.

The Metamorphosis classroom was large in space, but was cluttered with miscellaneous objects that were scattered haphazardly in odd places around the room. Grey and white-checkered marble covered the floor, making it look like a chess table. The walls were painted a creamy white, and a large

120

wooden desk sat at the front of the room, next to the door. A wall-to-wall chalkboard was behind the desk. The opposite wall had four windows on it. A dozen, glass ceiling lights lit the room. On all the walls were shelves covered in nothing but books and/or miscellaneous items. Eric couldn't get over the clutter.

There were three rows of seven desks for students that were facing Mr. Goodman's desk, and behind the student's desks was an area designated for practice.

"I want you to organize *all* of my books, alphabetically," Mr. Goodman said, and then, walked towards his desk.

Eric looked at all the books around the room and softly said, "Fucking mother of hell."

"What was that, Mr. James?"

"Nothing, sir, just admiring your extravagant collection."

Mr. Goodman rolled his eyes, grunted, and started to go through some papers that were in a messy pile on his desk.

Eric started by taking everything off of all the shelves in the room. He put the miscellaneous objects, like a small, silver cannon ball and a golden elephant figuring, on the desks in the center of the room. All of the books were then spread out all around the room in piles, according to title. He put the A's by Mr. Goodman's desk and went clockwise around the room.

Once all the books were sorted, he sat down by the A's and sorted them, alphabetically, putting them on the shelves. By the time Eric was finished with the F's, dinner had passed, and the sun was gone, replaced by a full moon. His stomach growled from hunger as he placed the rest of the books back on shelves, awaiting more organization.

"See you tomorrow at four in the morning, Mr. James." Mr. Goodman yelled at Eric as he walked out.

Eric rolled his eyes and mumbled some curse words under his breath. He couldn't believe that they were making him get up *so* early. He couldn't even remember the last time he had to get up at four in the morning.

"Eric James, right?" said a voice from behind Eric as he approached the stairs.

"Yes, who are you?" he asked as he turned around.

"Damon Campbell. We met in the bathroom, earlier." Damon said as he was walking out of the Telepathy room.

"Oh yes, I remember. You were the one with the weed, right."

"Yep."

"You have some lipstick on your neck, by the way."

Damon wiped the lipstick off his neck and said, "Who knew a punishment could be so fun."

"Nice, and if rumors are true, how many does that make it, right now?"

"Eight."

"Impressive."

"Stick with me, and maybe, you can get as high as me." Damon said as he nudged him in the side with his elbow.

"More than one way, I'm sure. Hey, how do they not know you're dating them at the same time?"

"Now, that's a secret I'm not willing to share. Besides, if a teacher ever realized what I've been doing, I'd be toast, for sure. Like banned from the school, toast."

"Why do you say that? It can't be that bad," said Eric in a softer voice as a kid walked past them.

"Well, for one, I'm screwing one of the teachers. That's enough to get kicked out and my powers taken away. But some of the charms and potions I use, they aren't taught, here. My older brother taught them to me years after he graduated. And they aren't taught, here, for a reason." Damon said with a devilish smile on his face.

"Dude, you *have* to show me some of them!"

"Only if you don't tell where you got them from."

They agreed, shook hands, and walked together down the stairs to the second floor, Eric's stomach growling all the way. On their way, they exchanged phone numbers and talked about the kinds of girls Eric was into.

Before they entered the living room, Damon asked, "Library, two o'clock?"

Eric nodded, and they casually entered the living room. The only people in the room were Nick, Catlin, Marina and someone else that Eric couldn't see. The four were huddled close together around one of the tables. Eric looked at them and when Nick, Catlin, and Marina looked at Eric, the fourth person disappeared.

He didn't really think much of it, just thought they were

messing with him. He went in the boys' bedroom and walked to his bunk. He opened up the bottom drawer on his dresser and pulled out a bag of potato chips and lay on his bed. As he ate his potato chips, he stared up at the posters of the Black Veil Brides band and some other bands that were on the bottom of the bunk above him.

Eric quickly changed into his pajamas, and then went to bed. Before he dozed off into sleep, he saw something that caught his eye. He could have sworn that he saw a black figure at the foot of his bed, looking at him. But then, Eric blinked and the figure was gone. He looked around the room to see if anyone else was up, but everyone was asleep.

Chapter 5

A long, leather whip hit Eric against his thigh, creating a long, deep cut. Blood was flowing down his thigh as the tall, pale redhead yelled, "Are you ready to give in, yet?"

The woman was wearing a long-sleeved, knee-length, black lace dress with a black leather gathered skirt. Black high-heeled boots snapped cruelly on the floor. Her long, fiery red hair was curled and covered by an elegant lace veil.

Eric was tied to a cold, wooden table in the middle of a white tile room, and seven pale people dressed in all-black tuxes were taking notes on a clipboard. Two Spirit Slaves stood forlornly apart from the others, tied together by metal chains. To Eric's surprise, the Spirit Slaves seemed to be more solid than the ghosts he'd seen.

The woman raised the whip, again, and hit Eric across the chest. A small rip opened up in his shirt and fresh blood started flowing, further staining his filthy clothes. Eric was in agony, and tears washed down his dirt-covered face. A small amount of blood came out of the corner of his mouth, leaving a metallic taste in his mouth.

"Who are you?" Eric weakly screamed at her.

"Don't you know who I am? I'm offended. After all, you were my first and only love." She reached up and took off her veil, throwing it on the floor.

Eric slightly gasped, making his chest hurt. He coughed loudly, and then said, "Elizabeth, is that you? W-w-w-why would you do this?"

"Because I want your powers."

"How do you know about that?"

"Because I too have powers. I have SO much power, Eric. Much more power than you. Well that is, after you tell me how I can get your powers. And you'll do that for me, won't you?" she asked as she gently caressed his face with the back of her *hand.*

When he said and did nothing, she removed her hand and slapped his face where a large cut was. Eric screamed in pain, only seeing white. His face went pale, and then, he went limp. The flow of blood from the cut had thickened and was dripping down his cheek.

"He's no use to me like this. Take him back to his cell," Elizabeth commanded as she walked out of the room. When she stepped out of the door, two of the guards that where in the room followed her.

The Spirit Slaves, a woman and a man dressed in worn-out black pants and shirts, untied Eric from the table. The woman had dirty blond hair that was stained with blood and mud, which looked like it had been recently cut with dull scissors. Her eyes were solid white, and her kind face was covered in Eric's blood.

The man had long, shaggy salt and peppered hair that hung past his shoulders. His face bore stress lines, and a long, salt and pepper beard hung from his chin. His eyes were black, but not as black as a Shadow Reaper. There was almost a hint of grey in them.

The woman helped Eric off of the table and supported his left side, while the man supported his right. They left the white room and entered a long hallway, where black metal torches with white flames lit the narrow space. The walls of the hall were made out of black bricks, and the floor was covered with black marble.

They continued their halting journey down the hall, until it came to a T. The Spirit Slaves led Eric down the left hall, which was as barren of any sort of paintings or decorative nature as the last. The torches were fewer, as well, which added to the despair Eric was feeling. He knew this hall well, not just because of the people screaming in agony, but because of the puddles under his feet.

This was near the cell where Eric was being held to suffer, and the farther they walked, the stronger the smell of urine, body odor, fecal matter, and blood grew. The Spirit Slaves placed Eric in his cell at the end of the hall, and as they set him down, he opened his eyes.

"Mom? Dad?" he said weakly before coughing up a large

amount of blood.

The two Spirit Slaves gasped, their faces brightened a little, and then, the woman said, "Yes hunny, it's us!"

"Listen, we can't talk much longer without getting in trouble, but I want to tell you that you need to be strong. Be strong for us, Eric. We know things are bad, and I'm sorry to say that it will only get worse before it gets better," his dad said to Eric.

"I may be dead, but I still have a little bit of my powers. I keep it hidden. But Eric, sweetie, I want you know that there will be more losses in the future if you are not strong. We will help in whatever way we can," his mom said. She bent down and placed her translucent hand on his cheek as he passed out from the pain.

Chapter 6

A few days later, Eric and his new friends were still serving their punishments. Getting up at four in the morning was wearing Eric thin, and it showed in his red, baggy eyes and pale skin. No amount of energy drinks could help the sleep loss he was suffering from.

It was the Saturday before school started, and all of the Freshmen had arrived and were taking their SATs, today. Most of the other students had arrived and settled in, and because of the SATs, the older students were given a free pass from Sloan to go down to the village. Eric, Damon, Zack, and John had decided to skip their punishments and go down to visit a local bar. Before they left, they gathered around Eric's bed and planned how they were going to get away with skipping detention.

"As you guys know, I have the power of Astral Projection. All you guys have to do is use the charm that Mr. Chine taught us, last year, to make a clone of yourselves. Once we are done, we can send the copies to go to our punishments." Eric told them.

Damon, Zack, and John all looked at each other, and then, stared at Eric with dumbfounded expressions on their faces.

"Do you not remember the charm? You guys are going to get killed. The charm is for those who don't have the power of Astral Projection."

They continued to look at him like they were lost. Eric gave up on trying to teach them and just did it for them. He pulled his green crystal wand out of his pocket, aimed it at them, and then said, "Perfectum exemplar te."

A single clone formed in front of them. Eric gave them their commands and sent them on their ways. Damon, Zack and John left the bedroom, and before Eric left the room, he did the same for himself.

Before they left the living room, Eric put his laptop in his book bag. As he looked around the room to make sure no one noticed them, he saw a phone with a bright pink case. He walked over and quickly put it in the pocket of his dark blue hoodie. He picked up his book bag, again, and headed out. As Eric shut the door, he could hear Catlin ask, "Where did my cell phone go?" which made Eric smile a sly smile.

They walked down the stairs to the main hall and to the glass door that led outside. The mermaid was combing her hair, as usual, and the pirate was looking through his telescope.

"Who are you, and where are you going?" asked the mermaid as she looked into her mirror.

"I'm John Anderson."

"Zack Roberts."

"Damon Cowell

"Eric James, and we're going down to the village."

Without double-checking the list of students permitted to leave, the pirate took his sword and waved it in front of the door. The door made a loud clicking sound, and then opened, and the four friends walked through. The warm, humid air, which smelled like freshly mowed grass, hit them as they walked out.

A group of students were walking a little ways in front of the boys, and when the school doors shut with a thunk, behind them, a small, skinny girl turned to look. She yelled an excited, "See ya, later!" to the group she was with and ran to John.

She was really short, and her bleach-blond hair was straight, with crimson red bangs that seemed to hover just above her eyelashes. Her tight, red and black plaid tank top was cut just a few inches above her stomach, which screamed for attention. Her black, skinny jeans had several holes in them, some at the top, near the pockets, and holes over her knees. Some old-looking black flip-flops made slapping sounds as she walked.

She was walking in between Eric and John, sticking her hand in John's back jean pocket and kissing him on the lips. They stayed lip locked the whole way down to the village. When they finally got to the edge of the village of Hillthrope, John and his girlfriend left the group and headed towards a black painted building that happened to be a music store.

"So, who exactly was that?" asked Eric.

"That was John's newest girlfriend, Erica Fisher." Damon

said.

"What happened to the other one?" asked Zack.

"John gave her an STD, but don't start telling people that, though, because it would ruin his credibility with the ladies." Damon said, sarcastically.

"What if we weren't the ones that spread it? What if someone found out about it and told everyone else?" Eric suggested.

"Who? John knows everyone that goes here."

"Someone who knows everyone's secrets. Someone with a secret identity." Eric said in a devilishly way.

"What do you have planned?" asked Damon, curiously.

"Get me to a bar, and I'll tell you my plan."

The group of three continued to walk down the main road of Hillthrope. They passed *Joey's Bookstore*, *Britt's Diner*, a couple music stores, and a shoe store. Only a few buildings were left on the road when they stopped, and Zack led them down an alleyway, between two buildings on the right. The smell of week-old garbage wafted around them in the damp and dirty darkness, and when they came to a door on the side of the building to the left, Zack knocked.

A young guy with black hair and a black beard opened the door. His white t-shirt stood out against his black, skinny jeans as he seemed to emerge out of the darkness, beyond. Zack handed him something that Eric didn't quite see, and the guy stood aside to let the group in. Their eyes adjusted as they went in, revealing a small storage room full of all kinds of beer, wine, vodka, and more. The guy led them to a door on the other side that opened up to the main room of the bar.

The lighting was low, and the floor was covered in peanut shells. The smell of body odor and pee assaulted them, but Eric ignored it. An older man dressed in an old, grey t-shirt that was covered by a dirty, white apron, stood behind the bar as he served drinks to a couple of older guys. Zack led them to a table in the corner, far from any of the windows.

Eric pulled his laptop out from his book bag and turned it on, quickly pulling up the school's webpage.

"Okay, so here's my plan. On the student section of our webpage, I'm going to add a gossip page. I'll make it so that it won't be traced back to any of us. Once it's up, I'll hack into

Sloan's account and get everyone's phone numbers and email. That way, whenever there's a new post, it will be automatically sent to them."

"Gossip? Are we in elementary school, again?" John asked, taking a swig of his drink that just arrived.

"This isn't a tabloid gossip or school girl rumor I'm talking about. Trust me; I know ways on how to get stuff out of people. People trust me too much," Eric smirked, rolling his eyes.

"Sweet. But where are we going to get all of the gossip?" asked Damon, ordering a beer from the waiter.

"This school is basically high school. Gossip spreads like an STD, here. That is where I'll get the little stuff like people cheating and sex scandals, but for the most part, I'll be digging up people's secrets they never wanted exposed. I have the first few posts already in mind."

It took Eric a few hours to hack into the school's system, but it wasn't that hard. Once he was in, he transferred all of the cell phone numbers to his computer's contact list. The next thing he had to do was create the site.

The site was called *Gossip Central*. Eric wanted to wait until tonight, at dinner, to post the first tidbit, so he could see everyone's faces went they saw what the gossip was.

The guys finished off their final drinks and headed back out through the storage room. On their way out, they all grabbed as many bottles as they could and put them in their bags.

Before the gang went back to Aviance, they stopped at *Joey's Bookstore* and *Glock's Cauldrons, Pens, and More* to pick up their school supplies for the start of school, next week. By the time they got to the school, it was almost 5:00. The knight statue from last year was still there, guarding the front of the door, and yelled at them for being late for dinner.

"Is that alcohol on your breath?" asked the knight.

"So what." Zack said to him.

"The Headmistress will be informed of this."

"Whatever." Damon responded as he swayed, a little tipsy.

The knight opened the door for the kids, and they stepped into the school. When they walked into the main hall, Sloan stopped talking and everyone turned to look at them. The boys slowly walked over to the Sophomore table and sat down.

"As I was saying, before I was interrupted, Aviance is

adding some non-magic, extracurricular activates, this year. With the rebuilding of Aviance, this last fall, I have decided to add soccer, baseball, and softball fields behind the school. I want it to be known that these fields have an anti-magic field. As soon as you step into them, your magic stops working.

"I have also added a Choir, Band, a Key Club, a Drama Club, and an Art Club. You can sign up for these in my office until the first day of school. On the first day of school, you will get a letter of when and where those clubs will meet.

"That is all of the announcements that I have for tonight. Let us eat and be merry!" Sloan said, sitting as the ghosts came out to serve the food.

"Are you ready?" Zack asked Eric.

"You bet."

Eric took out his iPhone and opened up the web browser, typing away. A few minutes later, he pushed *Publish*. Within a few seconds, every phone in the school started to go off.

Everyone pulled out their phone and looked at their new text message.

Innocent little Catlin Chamberlin and the dumb jock Keith East had a pregnancy scare after only weeks of getting back together, this year. Guess Keith was confused about how to put on a condom. But then again, Catlin has never even seen a condom... or a penis, before that night. *cough* too stupid to function *cough*

-GC

Catlin slammed down her drink, got up from the table, and ran to the stairs, crying. Marina ran after her, while Keith, looking confused, was getting high-fives from all of his friends.

"How did you know that?" asked Damon.

"I found this, today." Eric said, holding Catlin's phone in his hand.

Chapter 7

The next day, the students were determined to find out who *GC* was. Ever since the first text, Eric decided to lay low and stay under everyone's radar to make sure he didn't get caught. He was still attempting to find more secrets, though.

It was just after dinner on Sunday; Eric was still sitting in the main hall and was reading the book *The Art of War*. As he was reading, he was listening to the band that was practicing in the main hall. Some of the players sounded like professional players, while others sounded like dying elephants.

Eric glanced over in their direction to see who all had signed up. Catlin was in the first row, playing the flute, even though Eric couldn't really hear her. There was a nerdy boy from Eric's Metamorphosis class that was playing the French horn. The back row, though, is where the most terrible sound was coming from. Jamie Chamberlin had an old, rustic-looking trumpet in her hands and was blowing way too hard, making it sound flat and like a cat that was slowly and meticulously being run over by a car.

All of the sudden, Eric was disturbed by someone cheering behind him at the Freshman table. It was a group of geeks, including Nick, playing a video game on their computers. Computer games were never something Eric was good at, but at that moment, he missed playing them with his friends like he had, last year. He shook the feeling away and went back to his reading.

After a few more minutes, Eric couldn't stand the noise, anymore, and decided to go outside. He walked to the door and waited on the mermaid to let him out of the school.

"Reason for leaving?" she asked him.

"It's too loud in here, and it's a nice day out."

She accepted this and unlocked the door for him. Eric pushed the door opened and was hit by the hot and thick air. He breathed in the fresh air and went to sit by a tree that was near the school. He opened the book, again, and started to read.

Near Eric, a couple were sitting on a blanket and doing homework, together. A little further away by the path to the village, a new, small man-made lake had been put in a few days ago. It wasn't that big or deep, but there were still a few students swimming in it.

Eric had just started a new chapter of the book when a bunch of Senior guys came running around the corner of the school. He assumed that they were getting ready for soccer tryouts, since they were kicking a ball ahead of them. Some of the younger girls chased after them, trying to get their attention. As they passed Eric, he noticed something odd behind them. A familiar, black shadow was walking toward him. As it got closer, it sent shivers down Eric's spine. He quickly pulled out his phone and took a picture of it.

When the boys' team had left, the shadow disappeared. Eric looked around to see if anyone else had seen the figure, but everyone was acting as if they hadn't seen anything. Eric franticly pulled up the picture on his phone. The feeling of going insane was gnawing at him, but the picture was clear as day. The face was blurry, but there most definitely was a man standing there.

"Who is this man?" Eric mumbled to himself.

A few minutes later, Eric's peace was interrupted by a group of girls going around announcing the soccer tryouts that were happening in half an hour.

"Sophomore and Junior girls' soccer tryouts! Starts at three!" they declared, excitedly.

They continued screaming it a few more times, and then left. Several large groups of girls left the school, headed to the soccer field, including a group of cheerleaders, some of the teammates, and the pep-squad. Eric snorted, deciding to remain where he was.

As it was nearing 4:30, Eric recognized Mrs. Brown, the Defense Against the Shadow Reapers teacher, walking around the school property, giving the thirty-minute warning before the doors were locked. Eric gathered his stuff, walked to the front door as the knight unlocked it, and went inside. The cool air of the school greeted Eric as he stepped in.

As Eric reached the Sophomore living room on the second

floor, he could hear loud music playing. All he wanted, today, was some peace and quiet. He sighed and opened the door, immediately being assaulted by figures dancing to an annoying song by One Direction. As they twirled, Eric saw that it was Nick, Catlin, and Marina.

"What are you guys doing?" Eric asked as he turned down the volume, a little.

"We are celebrating."

Eric was going to ask why, but he could tell by the way that Marina was smiling; she must have gotten a spot on the girls' soccer team.

Rolling his eyes, Eric went into the boy's bedroom, heading to his bed to put his book bag on top of his dresser. He pulled out his computer and plugged it in to charge, opened up the school webpage and navigated to the *Gossip Central* site. He read some of the hate comments he was receiving and created a new post.

Within a few minutes, he hit 'send' and closed the site. He started his Charms homework that was due yesterday. A few seconds later, his phone alerted him of a new text.

Wanted: The identity of this figure. Could it be a student from Aviance or a Shadow Reaper? I just want to keep y'all safe. For now. Jk. I love the gossip that never ends, here! Anyways, this figure has been spotted several times walking around the school and in the shadows of the school. Be careful.

-GC

Chapter 8

The next day was June fifth, the first official day of classes. Eric was walking down the fourth floor to his first class after lunch, Charms. He had his earphones in, listening to music while he was texting. His own little world was rudely interrupted by someone coming up behind him and tapping his shoulder.

Eric removed his earphones and turned around to see Mrs. Grey, the Divination teacher, standing there looking sad in her dark grey sweater and black pants. Eric figured that Sloan had told her to scare him straight by saying *bad things will come if you continue down this path.*

"I haven't seen you since last year. I assume this means that the dreams have gone away?" She asked him in a soft and caring voice that sounded a little bit creepy, as well.

Eric looked at her for a second, confused at what she was talking about, but then, it hit him. She was talking about the nightmares he had about Elizabeth, last year. He told her that the dreams stopped after the last battle last year, and that the book that she loaned him really helped. He wanted to tell her about some of his more recent dreams he had been having, but he was afraid that she was either going to give him another book to read, or that she was going to say he had been smoking too much weed and that was the cause of the dreams.

She was about to leave, but before she did, she added, "Watch your back, Eric James. Bad times are upon us."

Eric had a frightened look on his face as Mrs. Grey walked away, fiddling with her straight, long blond hair that she had in a ponytail. He shook off the feeling and headed to his Charms class, which he was now late for thanks to her. He ran to the classroom and opened the door. A rush of warm, humid air hit him like a blanket as he stepped into the small, cluttered room.

"Why isn't the air on?" Eric said angrily under his breath.

"Well, if you had made it to class on time, you would know

135

that by now. Please, take your seat, Mr. James." Mr. Chine said cheerfully.

Eric hurried to the only seat that was available, which was next to Marina. Marina greeted him with a smile, but Eric ignored her.

"As I was saying, before, wind is a very useful element in combat against the Shadow Reapers. With their main power being fire, you can use wind in two ways. You can use it to put out a fire, or to turn it against your opponent."

Mr. Chine turned around toward the chalkboard and wrote, *Ventus.*

"This, ladies and gentlemen, means wind. This is a charm that you cast upon yourself that will last only for a few minutes, so use it wisely."

Mr. Chine picked up his old, red-colored wand from his desk and continued, "Point your wand at your throat, recite the charm, take a deep breath in, and then, blow out with all your might!"

At that, Eric began to gag at Mr. Chine's cheerfulness. To Eric, Mr. Chine was a good teacher, but the way he taught was overwhelming. He was just too cheerful and peppy for Eric's taste, and the way he dressed and looked spoke for itself. He might as well have lived in a barn. When he was near, you could see dirt under his fingernails, stains on his dress shirt and blazer, and his shoes were scuffed up. Never in Eric's life had he had a teacher that was like this.

"Eric, would you mind playing the role of the Shadow Reaper?" Mr. Chine asked him.

This happened to Eric, constantly. Last year, when he was asked to, he refused, knowing that he could put others in danger. But this year, he was used to it. He stood up and walked to the front of classroom, taking his position next to Mr. Chine. Eric cleared his mind and waited for Mr. Chine's signal.

Mr. Chine raised his wand, once again, to his throat, said, "Ventus," and took a deep breath. When he was ready, he nodded his head, and Eric covered his hands and arms with flames. As he did, a few people still gasped in surprise, but not like they did, last year.

As Mr. Chine exhaled, papers on his desk flew around the room, the flames that covered Eric's arms were extinguished, and Eric was knocked to the ground. Mr. Chine closed his mouth and took a bow. Eric stood up, brushed the dust off his clothes, and took his seat. For the rest of the class period, the room smelled like Mr. Chine's breath... Onions.

When the bell rang, Eric ran out of the room to escape the smell, but as he approached the stairs, he saw a few Seniors and Juniors that seemed to be looking for trouble. Eric tried to ignore them by using the other staircase, but as he walked by them, one of the larger ones grabbed his book bag and pulled him toward them.

"We need to talk, freak," said the one that grabbed him.

The guy was wearing old, ripped up jeans, a shirt that said *YOLO* on it, and a baseball cap, skewed sideways on his head. There were three guys on either side of him, who were dressed like him.

"Who are *you* to call me freak?" Eric replied, a little annoyed.

"My name is Jake DeLinsky," he said in a threatening way.

"Never heard of you. Do you always walk around with people who are pretending to be your friends?" Eric said, looking at his watch.

"Was that supposed to hurt my feelings? Unlike you, I have real friends."

"Highly doubt it, but whatever. What do you possibly want from me?" Eric asked, not really caring about the answer.

"What I want is for you to kill yourself," he said coldly.

This statement shocked Eric. Every muscle in his body froze, and his eyes widened.

"Wh-wh-what did I do to you?" Eric nervously asked.

"You do not deserve to be here. You are a freak and an abomination. *You deserve to die*, not the thousands of us that are fighting against *your* kind. And if you don't kill yourself, then I will make your life here a thousand times worse than it is already. You got that?" Jake hissed at Eric.

"I am not going to kill myself. It's closed-minded people like you that should kill themselves. I am a work of art. I am a new breed of White Knights. I have the power of *both* sides."

As Eric was talking, the anger inside of him was building up, and he was unaware that flames were beginning to spread up his arms.

"You don't hate me. You fear me, and for a person like you, someone who's not afraid of anything, that threatens you. Doesn't it?"

Eric took a step closer to them. By now, sweat was beginning to form on Jake forehead, and a few members of his group had run away. Eric raised his hand up to Jake's head and took a step closer to him.

"Dude, I'm sorry! Don't hurt me!" Jake begged, closing his eyes in fear.

"I didn't hear that first part; what did you say?"

Eric's hand was seconds away from touching Jake's eyes.

"I'm sorry! I didn't mean it!" Jake pleaded.

"That's what I thought. Don't you *ever* mess with me, again, or I just might kill you." Eric said before he walked away.

Chapter 9

It was the end of the first week of school, and the damage was just piling up. Eric was serving double dentition. He was still organizing Mr. Goodman's classroom for smoking pot in the bathroom, and was now cleaning all of the new band instruments under Mrs. Grey's eyes for skipping three of his classes and for threatening Jake.

It was Friday night, and the Seniors were throwing a party to welcome the Freshmen and for celebrating a start to a new school year. Eric was supposed to be working on the pile of homework he had to make up for skipping classes, but he was invited to go to the party with his friends, and Eric could never refuse a chance to go to a party.

At 7:38, Eric was standing with Zack outside the school and by a long table that held the refreshments and snacks. The outdoor statues were dancing, which was a bit comical for the knight. Both Eric and Zack were dressed in black dress shirts and pants, while Eric was wearing a white blazer on over his black shirt. New, white Converse shoes matched the blazer.

Damon was flirting with Miss Tyler across the room, where he was DJing, and a couple were arguing on the dance floor. As Eric watched, his interest was piqued when he notice that the couple was Nick and Marina. As he casually watched the fight, he started to have the feeling of being watched, as well. Looking around the room, he noticed that several students were looking at him, hatefully. Honestly, Eric shouldn't be here. Sloan had told him earlier that day that he was banned from all student activities, due to bad behavior.

"Just shut the hell up! I'm out of here!" Marina said as she picked up her diamond blue, sleeveless ball gown, stepped on Nick's black dress shoes with her silver stiletto heels, and rushed out. Nick, looking shocked and confused, ran after her.

"What are you doing?" Zack asked Eric as he pulled his phone out of his blazer pocket.

"I'm just texting a few *hundred* people." Eric replied with a cruel smile on his lips.

Within minutes, cell phones all over dance floor went off, and everyone stopped to look at them.

It seems that Aviance's favorite couple, Nick and Marina, have called it splits. How long will this last until Nick comes begging for her to take his balls back?

-GC

Eric stepped out onto the dance floor and tapped on Jamie Chamberlin's shoulder, who was standing with a bunch of other girls. Her long, curly brown hair was in a tendril bun, and her light pink, baby-doll dress fell to her knees. Grey wedges were on her feet, and she was cocking one foot on the toe of her shoe.

"May I have this dance?" he asked her as he put his hands on her lower back and pulled her closer toward him.

"If I dance with you, then you have to answer a few questions for me," she said in her annoyingly high voice as she tried to pull away.

"Hit me," Eric said as the DJ started playing *A Moment Like This*.

"Why are you treating my sister and all her friends like shit? They were so nice to you, last year."

"Lose your parents and then talk to me. Watch as they are being taken down and you can't do anything to help them. Talk to me when you have smelled you parents' bodies burning in the fire that has just burned your house that held everything you ever loved. Those things change a person. Your sister and her friends were nice to me, but they took me in when I was weak. I can't trust my judgment, last year. People change, Jamie."

"But how can you trust your judgment when you're always drunk and high all the time, now?"

"Those things keep me alert and awake," Eric said as his eyes drifted over to a shadowy figure by Catlin and Keith.

"Could you at least try to be nice to my sister and her friends?"

"Why would I do that?" Eric said, now looking into Jamie's eyes.

"Well, for one, they still care for you. I don't know why, but they do. And secondly, because I asked you to."

"And why should I listen to you? You're just a tiny little

Freshman."

"Because you like me," she said with a playful smile.

"Prove it."

"Well, we are still dancing, even though the song ended a few minutes ago." Jamie fluttered her eyelashes.

"Oh," Eric said as he leaned in closer to Jamie.

Their lips met in the middle. Eric slid his left hand up her back and placed it on her neck. Jamie resisted at first, but then gave in, kissing him back.

"Hey, I have an idea, follow me." Eric said with a devilish smile as he headed back into the school.

Jamie slowly followed him back into the school. Eric headed right towards the Potions room. Once they were both in the room, Eric opened the door to the new greenhouse and motioned with his hand for Jamie to go through.

The humid air hit them as they stepped in. Eric stepped in after her, grabbed her hand, and opened the door that led to the practice field in the back.

"Where are you taking me?" Jamie asked him as they passed the soccer, flying, and baseball fields.

"To a small meadow in the woods."

"We're not allowed in the woods. There could be Shadow Reapers in there."

"I'll protect you," he whispered to her, tightening his grip on her hand.

When they stepped into the woods, it was pitch dark, so Eric raised his right hand up and snapped his fingers, covering his hand in flames. Jamie let out a little squeal, and Eric pulled her closer to him. He let go of her hand and wrapped his arm around her waist. Jamie was now holding tightly onto his blazer, afraid to let go.

"I'm scared, Eric, I keep hearing things behind us," she said softly, so soft Eric almost didn't hear it.

"Don't worry, it's just the animals," he said as he, himself, saw something move in the corner of his left eye.

They followed a small, narrow pathway that was almost being taken over by surrounding bushes for about ten minutes, and then, they came upon a small meadow with tall grass that flowed in the warm light of the night sky.

Eric stepped into the meadow and pulled out his wand from

his jacket pocket, said, "Natantis luminaria," and waved his wand around the meadow. Tiny little lights filled the woods surrounding the meadow.

"That's beautiful. Where did you learn that? Catlin hasn't taught me that, yet."

"I studied a lot over the winter. Now, come on and sit down with me," Eric said as he took of his blazer and laid it on the ground for them to sit on.

Jamie walked into the meadow, sat down by Eric, and looked up and gazed at the stars in the sky.

Eric laid back and watched the stars with Jamie. Soon, Jamie lay back, too, and Eric supported her head with his arm and puller her close. The sound of the party diminished, and the smell of a warm summer night surround them with the sounds of nightlife. They could hear the sound of rushing water and frogs croaking from a river, nearby. The lights in the woods slowly went out as Eric started kissing Jamie.

"I don't feel comfortable doing this. We should get back to the school, before they know we are missing."

"Are you always a goody-goody?" Eric asked her.

"No."

"Then, prove it." Eric said as he pulled out a small silver flask from his pocket, took a swig of it, and then handed it to Jamie.

Jamie took a few swigs of the alcohol and handed it back to Eric. When it was empty, Eric pulled his wand out and waved it over the flask, filling it back up. They started drinking, and soon, everything was blurry. It wasn't long before the alcohol and warmth of the night made them both fall asleep.

"Stop!" Eric yelled at Elizabeth as she flicked her long, red wand at him. Bolts of electricity flew from the tip of the wand and headed toward Eric. He screamed and seized in pain as Elizabeth shot him, repeatedly.

Elizabeth had Eric in the white tile room, again. She was dressed in another black dress. This dress was tight on her chest but had a flowing skirt that fell a little above the knees. Her feet were covered in dark red, leather boots. Her red hair was straightened and held back with a black lace bow.

"Tell me what I need to know. All of this will stop, and we

can be together, again."

"I don't understand what you want!" he yelled at her.

"Your powers!" she yelled back.

"W-w-why?" Eric asked, weakly stumbling on his words.

"Because, if we get your powers, then we can defeat you and your stupid White Knights and get this stupid war over with, like my father wanted."

"Your father? Your father was a Nume. He worked as our math teacher. Don't you remember?"

"He's not my real father. Vesta De'Lore is my biological father. He and my mother had a short-lived love affair. In that short time, she became pregnant with me. Two years ago, Vesta took me from my normal life, awoke my powers, and told me that one day, all of this would be mine. He also said that I would be the key to get you to surrender your powers to us."

"Even if I knew how to, I never would tell you."

"Then, you will be killed."

"You can't kill me. You love me. Nothing could ever change that. Not even the hate in your heart."

"You are wrong. I will kill you, Eric James, if I need to." Elizabeth said as she leaned in to kiss him on the lips.

Eric's eyes rolled back into his head, and his back arched in some sort of seizure. Foam started coming out of his mouth.

"Somebody keep him alive for more testing!" Elizabeth screamed before she walked out of the room, again.

Chapter 10

Eric woke up with a killer headache and looked around. Realization dawned on him as he remembered what had happened, last night. Grabbing his phone, he texted Zack.

Did you get the pic, last night?

Yes, here it is.

Zack then sent a picture of him and Jamie, last night, with Eric in his boxers and Jamie in Eric's shirt. He saved the picture on his phone and created a message from *GC* for everyone. Eric lay back down and pushed *send*, hiding his desire to wickedly grin about it. Within seconds, Jamie and Eric's phones went off, waking up Jamie.

She angrily grunted as she took in her surroundings and looked at her phone. An ear-splitting scream broke the clearing's tranquility. Eric moaned and got up, acting like he'd just been woken.

"Why on Earth are you yelling?" Eric irritably asked.

"Tell me this isn't true? And who could have taken this photo? We were alone, last night," she asked frantically, getting her stuff together.

Eric took her phone and read the message.

Looks like goody-goody Jamie Chamberlin gambled with party boy and lost her V card. Way to go, but what is big sis going to say about this?

-GC

"I don't remember anything from last night, but the picture looks real," Eric told her.

"What was in that flask?" she quickly asked.

"I don't know. I stole it from Mr. Goodman's room."

"This was a really big mistake. How could I have been so stupid?"

"You're related to Catlin, whose highest grade is a D-. It's in your genes to be stupid."

Jamie picked up the flask from the ground and threw it at

144

Eric's head, took of Eric's shirt that she was wearing, and got back into her dress from last night. Her sobs could be heard as she ran away.

"Don't get lost," Eric sarcastically yelled at her as she disappeared into the woods.

Eric heard something from his left and jumped to his feet.

"Who's there?" Eric said as fireballs started to form in his hands.

A small, dark mass moved in the shadows of the woods.

"What are you?" Eric yelled at it with a little bit of fear in his voice.

It moved closer to Eric but disappeared when it hit the sun.

Eric gathered his clothes up from the ground and started to dress as he walked through the woods. Zack was waiting for Eric at the greenhouse door when Eric walked through the last lines of trees.

"Thanks, man," Eric greeted him as he walked inside.

"Never ask me to do that, again. You guys were totally wasted." Zack said as they walked back into the school.

"I don't even remember anything from last night, man."

"Hey, don't you have a make-up class with Sloan, today?"

Eric looked at his watch and saw that it was 2:46.

"Shit."

Eric had fourteen minutes till his class.

"I'm never going to make it. Can you tell Sloan that I'm not feeling well and can't do anything, today?"

"I don't think she'll buy it, but I can try."

"Thanks."

Eric and Zack walked up the stairs to the second floor, where Eric left off toward his bedroom and Zack headed to Sloan's office. As he walked into the living room, he saw Catlin and Marina sitting on the couch, near the TV.

Catlin was wearing tight yellow, knee-length shorts with a white t-shirt and yellow Converses on. Her eyes were puffy and red, with messy hair falling into them as she sobbed. Marina was wearing a blue lace, sleeveless shirt with a white tank underneath it. She also had white short shorts on and black flip-flops. Marina had her arm around Catlin's shoulders, hugging her close to try to comfort her.

As soon as Catlin saw Eric, she jumped off the couch and

ran to Eric.

"How the hell could you do that to my sister?" she yelled at Eric as she slapped him with the back of her hand.

Eric smiled and put his hand on her shoulder and said, "She was too easy."

Before Catlin could slap him, again, Eric caught her wrist and burned it with fire.

She screamed in pain as Eric let go and walked into the boys' bedroom. He grabbed a white t-shirt and tan shorts and headed towards the bathroom, not even bothering to check on Catlin. After taking a shower and changing, he tried to get the smell of alcohol off of his breath by brushing his teeth five times. It wouldn't go away, though.

When he was finished, he went to the sixth floor library to do some homework for Monday. He walked into the study room and noticed that a few other people were already in the room. Most of them looked at him with disgust and anger on their faces, but Eric just gave them a sarcastic smile and sat at an empty table to work on his History homework.

Halfway through the reading assignment for his Charms class, a skinny girl walked into the room. She was wearing a red t-shirt and jeans, with shoulder-length, wavy dark brown hair pushed back behind her small ears.

She looked at Eric, and he shot her a smile. She smiled back and walked towards him.

"Is this seat taken?" She asked, shyly.

"No, it is not." Eric said to her as she sat down across from Eric.

"My name is Blair DeLinsky. And you're Eric James, right?"

"Yeah, how do you know me?"

"Well, after the text from GC this morning, I think I know you well, but, you are also in my Potions class."

"Oh, okay. Yeah, I think I have seen you a couple of times in that class."

"You mean the couple of times you've actually been in the class?"

"Potions aren't my thing."

"And apparently, sleeping with random girls in the woods is?"

"GC, whoever the hell it is, got that all wrong. That girl took advantage of me. She gave me this flask and said it was only water, but I think she added something to it. I only remember certain things from last night."

"She seems awful." Blair said in a flirty tone.

"She is. Were you at the dance, last night?"

"No, I was studying."

"You study a lot, I take it?"

"Not really. That party just seemed lame," she said, tossing a bit of her hair out of her face.

"From what I remember, it was."

Blair laughed, her voice almost like tinkling silver.

Eric leaned closer, grinned at her, and asked, "Would you like to go out sometime?"

"That would be nice. Here's my number." She said as she wrote her number on a page in Eric's notebook.

At 4:50, they collected their books and headed to the living room. On their way, they talked about how Blair was on the soccer team and had gotten the position of team captain. She told Eric that in her hometown, she was the JV captain.

Once they dropped off their things, they started to walk down to the main hall for dinner. Together, they walked to the Sophomore table and sat next to each other.

Eric looked over at the Freshman table and saw that Jamie's eyes were puffy and red. He then looked over at Blair and smiled. They talked about how much they hated Potions, this year, waiting on Sloan to come down the stairs.

"He's not even letting us do any of the cool potions, like he did last year." Blair said to him.

"I know. It's like they don't even care that we could be attacked at any moment. How is a potion that heals us effectively help us in a fight? I mean, it's not going to help us get rid of them." Eric said back.

Blair laughed, lightly laying a hand on Eric's shoulder. He smiled at her as she murmured into his ear, "I don't know why I was so afraid of you, last year. You're actually really nice."

"You were afraid of me because I have the same power that the enemy has. And because of that, I could be a spy. That's why everyone is afraid of me."

"I'm not. At least, not anymore," she said, looking into his eyes.

"Is that so?" He asked while he moved his hand closer to hers.

Before anything else could happen between them, Sloan walked down the stairs into the main hall.

Tonight, Sloan had a light blue-grey, full-length dress with a square neckline and short sleeves. Her silver grey hair was recently cut just below her shoulder and was tied back with a grey diamond hair clip.

"Five... Four... Three... Two... One.... Thank you for getting quiet. I hope everyone who went had a great time at the party, last night.

"Announcements begin with a reminder to all students. The woods are off limits to *everyone*. Not just for selected people," she said, looking directly at Eric. "The woods are a treacherous place. It is unguarded. If you go in there, you are at risk of a Shadow Reaper killing you. They move in the shadows of the woods, and they move sharper then a mighty fox, always ready for a fight.

"Lastly, due to the enormous amounts of drinking and drug use this year, every day, the teachers will go through each grades' living and bedrooms in hunt of any illegal substances. If we do find any, your punishment will be strict," she concluded her announcement and sat down.

While they were eating dinner, Eric's phone went off. It was a message from Damon, who was sitting on the opposite side of the table.

wot iz w d chick?

The chick has a name, and it's Blair. Eric texted back.

I knO hu it iz. dud hr bro iz da 1 tht threat u.

Maybe this is my way to get him back.

Ur sik

Eric ended the conversation, there, and turned his phone off.

When Blair and Eric were finished with their meals, they decided to go back up to the living room. They walked in silence up the flight of stairs, and when they reached the living room, they said their goodbyes, and Blair left to go to the girls' bedroom.

Eric plopped down on one of the couches near the corner of the room and pulled out his computer. He had an essay for his

DASR class and was in the middle of writing a sentence when he noticed someone walking toward him. Catlin had changed into an old, grey shirt that said *Grey Wood High School* and a pair of sweatpants. Eric tried to ignore her, but she sat down right next to him and began to talk.

"I love you. Or at least, I *loved* you. Except for the times when we were under attack, last year was the best time in my life. You were one of my best friends. You actually helped me understand that if I just try hard enough, then I could do *anything*. And toward the end of the year, I had this thought that, maybe, there was something between us. That maybe you were getting better, and maybe we could be together. I know mistakes were made. I am sorry for the mistakes I have made that made our friendship diminish.

"I know you're busy, so I'll leave you with this. Everything that I had thought last year has changed," Catlin said in a hushed but stern voice, "You mean nothing to me, and you will continue to unless you get help. What you're doing is sick. You're life sucks, and we get it. *Get over it.* There are people out there whose lives suck more than yours. Stop with the *pity me* act and get your act together."

Eric shut his laptop, looked her in the eyes, and said, "Why do you even care?"

"I've asked myself that question since the day I met you," Catlin said before she got up and left.

Chapter 11

ric was lying on the cold, hard ground in pain. Warm, fresh blood was dripping down his face. He had no clue if it was day are night, and he couldn't even remember the last time he actually slept because he was tired, instead of passing out from all of the pain.

The sound of chains being dragged on the ground and the sound of screams were deafening. A few days ago, Eric was caught trying to talk to the person that was in the cell next to him. He had been tortured for hours, after that, and the person he was talking to had his tongue ripped out and his fingers crushed.

Eric no longer talked or struggled when they came to get him. He let them do what they wanted, and he got to live. But he was beginning to wish that they would just kill him, already. At first when he was put into this cell, he had high hopes of being rescued. But after what he can figure as ten months of this torture, his hopes had diminished. He had come up with the conclusion that his friends and family were not coming for him.

He was beginning to think of his friends and family and the short time that he was with them, when he heard the horribly familiar sound of heels coming down the hall.

"Good morning, Eric," said Elizabeth's eerie, warm voice.

Eric turned his head away from her.

"I know that you have questions, and since you are going to be here a while, I might as well answer a few of them."

Eric looked at her in confusion and asked in a weak voice, "Why now?"

"Think of it as a random act of kindness."

Eric had a coughing fit and asked, "Why do the Shadow Reapers still exist? Vesta De' Lore is dead."

"He is not dead. He is alive in me. He is the reason why I am here. He gives me extraordinary powers."

"What the hell is that supposed to mean?"

"Vesta isn't dead. Last year, you only killed his body. You did not kill his spirit."

"I-I-I don't understand," Eric said, coughing up even more blood on the ground.

"Your stupidity used to be cute. Now, it's just annoying."

"I am not stupid," he said, out of breath.

"But you are. You always have been, and you always will be. You are stupid enough to think that your so-called 'friends' are trying to rescue you, and you're stupid enough to think that you ever meant anything to me." Elizabeth leaned against the cell door, getting a little more comfortable, and then, continued, "You see, I felt sorry for you. You were lonely and depressed at school. And if I'm being completely honest here, which I am, someone dared me to ask you out. I knew that you would say yes. After all, I was popular. Head cheerleader. And now, look at me. QUEEN OF THE SHADOW REAPERS. And you, my slave. You mean nothing to me, Eric. You never have."

While she was talking, Eric gathered his strength and stood up. He grabbed her long, red hair and pulled on it, while he stabbed her at the base of her head with the broken spoon he stole from his last meal.

Elizabeth let out an evil laugh, pulled out the spoon, and then, turned around and looked at Eric.

"Do you seriously think you can kill me? And with a plastic spoon? Like I said, you're very stupid."

Elizabeth walked away with blood dripping down her neck. As she came upon the guard, she said, "He gets no food till I say so."

They nodded, and she headed back upstairs.

Chapter 12

A few days later, Eric was sitting in the living room watching a rerun of *Family Guy*. Mr. Smith was going through everyone's stuff. Luckily, Eric had hidden his stash of alcohol underneath a floorboard under his bed. It was almost 8:30 when Eric received a text from Blair.

I'm going to be a little late for our date. You can go ahead and go to the library. I'll meet you there <3

I have a better plan. Just meet me in the main hall when you're done. He replied to her.

He got off the couch and started to walk out of the living room. On his way, he spotted Catlin, Keith, Nick and Marina. They were sitting at a table in the common room that was on the second floor. Nick and Keith were sitting on one side with their backs against Eric, while Marina and Catlin sat across from them.

Eric quickly ducked behind a large, leather chair that sat facing the stairs. He pulled out his phone and quickly took a picture of the four of them. As fast as he could, he got up and darted toward the closest staircase. Once he was in the clear, he pulled out his phone and looked at the picture. He devilishly smiled at it and attached the picture to a group message.

AWW. It's a double date. But do Catlin and Marina know that underneath the table Nick and Keith are holding hands? I think it's about time these two came out of the closet. Oops, I guess I just told everyone. Sorry guys.

-GC

After Eric hit send, he got up and quickly went down the stairs. He was headed to a table to sit and wait for Blair when he felt someone tap on his shoulder. He turned around and saw Blair. She was wearing a light purple maxi dress, and her dark brown hair was curled and was held back by a light grey silk scarf.

"You look nice." Eric said, fumbling to put his phone back

into his pocket.

"Thanks. I didn't know where we were going, so I wore this old thing." She said, giving him a shy, yet flirtatious smile.

"Speaking of that," Eric said, looking around the room to make sure no one was watching.

When he was sure no one was in the room or coming down the stairs, he grabbed her hand and walked her towards one of the marble statues that was between the last two fireplaces. The statue was of a small child who sat on a large toadstool, reading a book. Eric pulled out his wand from his back pocket, pointed it at the girl, and said, "Mihi revela absconditis tuis," swirling his wand around the little girl's head.

The little girl closed the book, stood up, and walked away from the toadstool. As she did, the toadstool started to grow, revealing a wooden door in its stem.

"Wow," was all that Blair got out.

Eric grabbed her hand one more time, opened the door, and walked inside. Right as Eric stepped inside, there were stairs that led down to the only light source available. As they descended down the stairs, the cool air got a little colder, and Eric could see goose bumps start to form on Blair's bare shoulders and arms.

Halfway down, Blair worriedly asked, "How are we gonna get out of here?"

"Don't worry. All you have to do is just open the door, again, and everything will be fine," Eric said, trying to calm her down.

As they were reaching the bottom of the stairs, Eric put his hands on Blair's eyes and whispered, "No peeking."

He slowly guided her down the last few steps, and when she was off the stairs, he asked, "Are you ready?"

"Yes," she replied shyly and nervously.

Eric removed his hands from Blair's face to revel a large room that was filled with large piles of objects that were covered with white sheets. The room was lit with several small lights that hung on the white walls. Blair walked around the large, cold room for a moment and then murmured, afraid to disturb the tranquility, "What *is* this room?"

"It's the basement. It's where they put all of the extra stuff, like desks and books." Eric said as he pulled a white sheet off one of the smaller piles to reveal an old, wooden table and chairs and a small wicker basket.

"How did you find out about this?" Blair asked as she sat down in the seat that Eric pulled out for her.

"I know everything about this place. After all, I do live with Sloan," he said, sitting down across from her.

Eric opened up the small wicker basket and pulled out two shot glasses, a flask, and two plates with sandwiches on them. He handed a plate and a shot glass to Blair, and then, put the basket on the floor next to him.

"What's in the flask? Water?" Blair asked, giving Eric a mischievous look.

"It's not like we're going to get caught. There's only enough in here for a couple of drinks," he said, pouring a brown liquid into the glasses.

"You just might turn me into a real rebel after all, Eric," she said, giving him a slight devilish smile.

"From what I've heard, you're worse than a rebel."

"Maybe, that's why I like you. Because you're not so innocent, either."

They sat, talked, drank, and ate for what felt like hours. When Eric looked at his watch, he realized it was nearing 11:00.

"It's getting late." Eric said, informing Blair of the time.

"I-I-I don't think I c-c-can make it to my room like this," Blair said between hiccups.

"We could crash here for the night. There are a few beds near the back of the room."

"You don't think they would mind?" Blair said, still hiccupping.

"I'm sure it'll be fine, as long as we put everything back."

Eric stumbled out of his chair and walked over to Blair to help her out of her chair.

As they walked to the back of the room, the air got colder and moister. The whole back wall was lined with unused, single beds. Eric removed the white sheet that was covering the nearest bed and climbed into it. Blair was swaying back and forth, unable to keep her balance. She was about to fall backwards when Eric reached for her hand and pulled her toward him.

She fell right on top of him, making the plastic covered mattress make a loud crinkling noise. Her glazed-over eyes met with his. They both started to breathe a little heavier. Eric looked back and forth from her eyes to her soft pink lips. Blair leaned in a little bit towards Eric, and he did the same. Their lips met in the middle.

"Eric, I don't know about this," Blair said as she pushed him away.

"It's fine. You can trust me. Everything will be fine."

"Can I?" she said as Eric undid the zipper of her dress.

"Yes," he said as he took off his own shirt.

They both lay on the bed for a few moments, just examining each other's bodies. Eric slowly moved his thumb over the cuts that were on Blair's thighs and stomach. Blair shivered as he did this. Blair felt strangely comfortable with him, and he felt the same about her.

Chapter 13

ric woke up with a major headache. While sitting up in bed, he tried to recall what all had happened, last night. When he looked at his watch and saw that it was almost noon, a strangled gasp released itself from his gut.

"Shit," Eric said, jumping out of the bed and putting his clothes back on.

He quickly ran across the room, bumping into some of the furniture, and up the dark stairs. On his way up, he stumbled a few times, falling on his knees. When he finally reached the top of the stairs, he opened the door and walked out as secretly as he could, so people wouldn't notice him appearing out of nowhere.

Eric thought he was in the clear until he saw Marina come down the stairs. Marina was in her soccer uniform and was bouncing the ball on her head as she headed toward Eric.

"Walk and talk," she said as she grabbed Eric by his arm and walked to the main door.

The statue that usually guarded the door was gone, so Marina and Eric just walked out of the school. Marina bounced the ball off her head, and it landed in front of her.

"I don't know why you are acting like this, but you need to knock it off. You don't need to prove anything, here, so stop acting like a player and start acting like the Eric I knew, last year," she said, kicking the ball toward the soccer field.

"Bitch, don't even tell me what to do. You don't get to judge how I choose to fix what you broke, last year." Eric said as he fought Marina's grip.

"We didn't *break* anything, last year."

"Yeah, so you just stopped talking to me for what reason, again?"

"Because we knew you were going to change, this year, but we didn't know it was going to be *this* bad."

"So you're telling me that you had a vision that I did something bad to you guys in the future, but instead of telling me about it and trying to stop it, you stopped talking to me, and you made the situation worse? Yeah, I trust you to be the *future* of the White Knight army."

Marina just looked at him with a dumbfounded expression on her face. She was just about to talk, again, when Eric said, "And to be completely honest, this is who I am. Last year, I was damaged because everything in my life had changed. I look back to that time, and I don't even know who that person was. This is who I am. And since you don't like it, kindly fuck off."

Eric took his free hand and wrapped his fingers around her wrist. He then let go of all the anger that was building up in him, releasing it out through his hand. The moment he did, Marina let out a deafening scream. Several of the students that were nearby stopped what they were doing and rushed over to help. Eric's hand was still covered in fire when he let go. He shook his hand to extinguish the flame and walked away, not even bothering to look back.

His phone vibrated in his pocket, he pulled it out to read the new text message that was from Blair.

Hey! Last night was amazing! Whenever you get a chance we need to meet up to talk!

Eric still had not recollection of what happened, last night, and was hoping to get some more out of Blair when they met up. He told her that he had a meeting with Sloan in a few, but after that, he was free.

Hope that doesn't mean you got in trouble, again. I'll see you in the library?

Sure, he responded and put his phone away.

Eric walked back into the school and walked to the stairs. He was near the fifth floor when Sloan was coming down.

"Eric, I was just on my way to find you. I just heard from another teacher of your little accident. At least, I *hope* it was an accident," Sloan said with a disappointed look on her face.

"I wish I could say it was, but it wasn't."

Sloan didn't say anything else until they reached her office. And even then, they still didn't say much. Eric sat down in front of her.

Sloan sat down and pulled out a pad of pink paper and wrote some things down before saying, "I am done with being lenient with your punishments. You cannot go around this school thinking that you can do whatever you want and not get in trouble for it.

"You have gotten away with too much, already this year. Do not think I do not know. I know about how you hacked the schools records and how you are pulling pranks on other students. And starting now, you are going to stop all of this. Otherwise, I will have to take extreme measures.

"Starting today, you will pay for all of the damage you have caused, so far. You will hand over your phone and computer. You will start going to all of your classes, and you will finish this school year with all B's or higher. Do I make myself clear?"

"Yes ma'am," he said as Sloan handed him a slip of pink paper.

"That is the total damage that you have caused, this year. As you will see, it is extensive."

"How am I going to pay for this? It's over a thousand dollars!"

"Should have thought of that, before. Now, please hand over your phone."

Eric reached in his pocket, pulled out his phone, and handed it to Sloan.

"I will give you fifteen minutes for you to go and get your laptop. If you fail to bring it to me, I will find it myself."

Chapter 14

"I knew you were going to get in trouble at some point," Nick said as Eric walked out of Sloan's office.

"Don't you have a date with Keith to go to?" Eric responded, still walking away.

Nick started to walk with him, and as they went down the stairs, he said, "You know that rumor isn't true. I love Marina with all of my life."

"Then, why did you guys break up?"

"Believe it or not, we were fighting over you."

"I'm flattered, but I'm not gay, and Marina isn't my type."

"Ignoring that comment. She believes that this is the real you, and that you were playing us, last year. I think you're just depressed, and that this is your way of dealing with it."

Eric stopped in his tracks, looked at Nick, and growled, "What if it's neither, and there's nothing you can do about it?"

"But we can try," Nick said with a wolfish grin.

Eric ignored him and continued on to the second floor. The halls were mainly empty, except for a few students walking and reading. The cold air of the air conditioner hit Eric as he walked into the Sophomore living room.

The room was completely empty when he entered. He walked into the boys' bedroom and quickly grabbed his laptop from the top of his dresser and left. On his way out, he saw Blair sitting down on a couch by the window with her laptop.

Eric told her he had to do something, but he would be right back.

"I thought we were going to meet up in the library?" she said, looking confused.

"But it's such a lovely day, today. I thought we could take a walk outside, if that's okay with you!"

"Sounds wonderful!"

"I'll be right back!"

"Hurry up!" she yelled to him as Eric ran out the door.

Eric quickly ran back upstairs to Sloan's office. His quick pace had eaten up the fifteen minute window by the time he reached the office door. He knocked but didn't wait for Sloan to respond as he went right in. He was shocked to see that Catlin and Marina were talking to Sloan.

Sloan cleared her throat, and the girls turned to look at him. Eric couldn't help but notice the new, white bandage on Marina's arm, and he tried to hide the smirk on his face as he walked up to Sloan's desk.

"Thank you for that information, girls. I will look into the option of getting a track field."

Catlin and Marina got up and headed towards the door. When they met Eric, they bumped into him, almost knocking him down. Eric regained his balance and continued walking to Sloan's desk. He put his laptop on Sloan's desk and started to head back toward the door.

He was about to turn the doorknob and leave when Sloan said, "Don't leave just quite yet. Mrs. Spelling, from our library, is on her way here to talk to you. It seems that your bank account has been emptied, so you're going to have to find a job to pay off what you owe the school. Fortunately, the library has an open position."

Eric rolled his eyes and walked back to Sloan's desk.

"What will I be doing?" Eric asked as he sat down.

"You will be putting books back on the shelves."

Eric sat down and looked out the windows that were to his left. He was waiting for Mrs. Spelling to come when he looked at his watch. It was almost five o'clock. He knew Blair was going to be mad at him.

Half an hour later, there was a knock at the door, and in walked a short, skinny woman who looked to be in her early fifties. When she reached the desk, she greeted Sloan. They offered their hands like old friends, both standing. After a parting smile to the woman, Sloan offered her seat to Mrs. Spelling and left the room.

"Sloan has told me all about you. If it were up to me, I wouldn't hire you, but she has ensured me that you will behave. But if you do not behave well, I will report you to Sloan. Since tomorrow is Monday, you will start work at six in the morning and finish at eight for breakfast. Then, you will come back at nine that night and work till close. This will be your schedule for the weekdays. During the weekend, you will be working from noon to close."

Eric thought that the hours were unfair but decided not to argue. Mrs. Spelling continued to tell him more of the rules of his job. It wasn't till around seven that Mrs. Spelling dismissed him and let him go. As soon as he left Sloan's office, he ran down the stairs to the Sophomore living room.

He reached the second floor in record time and made his way to the door, stopping to prepare himself for what Blair might do to him for skipping out on their date. He slowly opened the door and stepped inside. The room seemed empty, but Eric could hear the sound of someone breathing hard.

Eric pulled out Marina's iPhone that he'd swiped from her pocket when she bumped into him, earlier. He quickly unlocked it and opened up the camera as he slowly got down on his knees and crawled over to the couch that the sound seemed to be coming from. He slyly raised the phone over the back of the couch and quickly took a picture of whatever was happening on the other side of the couch.

Once he took the picture, he quietly crawled to the boys' bedroom door. He opened the door and continued to crawl into the bedroom, quietly shutting the door behind him. Several others were in the bedroom as well, and when they saw Eric on his hands and knees, they gave him a weird look. He shot them an indifferent shrug and stood up, walking over to his bed. He quickly unlocked the phone and opened up the photo that he'd taken. Red hot rage filled his blood when he realized what he was looking at.

With speed and an aggression that consumed him, he closed out of the photos and opened up the Internet. *Gossip Central* was only a few clicks away, and it took him only a few minutes to create a new post. He savagely hit the post button. It took a couple of minutes until Marina's phone vibrated, and Eric opened the message to read it.

Cheater, cheater, pumpkin eater. Seems like goody two shoes Blair DeLinsky isn't so good, after all. You should know by now that secrets don't stay secrets for long around here. Nick isn't the only one who's in the closet.

-GC

Along with that message was a picture of Blair making out with a girl that Eric didn't recognize. He was hurt, but it felt amazing to get revenge. After locking the phone and laying on his nightstand, it vibrated a few times as he got ready to go to bed. The messages were from Marina's friends, asking if it was true that Nick was gay. Eric figured he had done enough damage for the day, so he left it alone. He grinned evilly as he set his alarm for five in the morning and went to bed.

Chapter 15

The alarm went off as scheduled, and Eric slowly got out of bed, wiping at his eyes and trying to wake up. As his gaze shifted over to his alarm clock that he'd shut off, an idea came to him. He stifled his giggles as he set another alarm to go off in twenty minutes, set the volume on high, changed the tone to a high-pitched squeal, and hid the clock in the room.

He left the Sophomore living room and headed toward the bathrooms with a sneer on his face. Getting a glare from the freshly rising sun, Eric looked out the window on his right to see it starting to shine through the woods. The sky was clear and boasted that almost mesmerizing blue that only dawn could offer. As he was looking out, Eric thought he saw something move at the corner of his eye.

Eric dropped his clothes on the floor and ran to the window. He frantically looked all around the yard, but it was still too dark to see much. There was a creepy crawly feeling at the nap of his neck that he couldn't shake, and the feeling of being watched from the corner of his eye made him turn cold and hot, cold and hot.

He looked around the yard a couple more times and decided that he was just being paranoid. Turning away, he picked up his clothes and continued to the bathroom. The lights were off when Eric opened the door, and everything was deathly quiet as he quickly took a shower and got dressed. As he headed toward the fifth floor, he had just over fifteen minutes to be there on time.

It was a silent walk for Eric. No one would be up for another hour, and Eric reached the oaken library doors with five minutes to spare. He turned the brass doorknob to get in, but it wouldn't open. He huffed in irritation and knocked on the door, waiting for someone to let him in. It was only a minute before Mrs. Spelling unlocked the door.

"I told you there was a dress code," Mrs. Spelling said as she walked him to the back room.

"Sorry, laundry day. What is wrong with what I'm wearing?"

They walked behind the checkout counter and into a room that was full of shelves overflowing with books.

"For one, I told you no shorts and no shirts with writing on them, especially ones with cuss words on them."

Eric glanced down at his black and red t-shirt that said *Fuck it all.*

"For today, just wear it inside out. Now, down to business. This room holds all of the books that have been returned or have been found out of place. It is your job to put them back on the shelves out there."

Mrs. Spelling walked out of the room and left Eric to do his work. With a huff, he complied with the finicky librarian and turned his t-shirt inside out. He then grabbed a small, metal cart and pushed it to a shelf marked *Fiction* and started putting them on the cart.

The cart squealed as Eric pushed it over to a chair, sat down, and began putting them in order. It took him a few minutes to finish, and he grunted as he started to push the cart out into the library. When he reached the Fiction section on the second floor, he slowly shelved the books, getting the hang of what to do. At that point, he smirked, thinking that the job would be extremely easy.

Around ten minutes later, he was done with the cart and headed back to the back room, with the cart squealing even louder than it had, before. When he reached the back room, he stood dumbstruck as he gazed upon the pile of books that had appeared on the shelves for sorting. It had to have grown three times, since he had left.

"What the hell?" Eric slammed his fists on the cart.

"People returned some books," Mrs. Spelling said as she poured herself a cup of coffee.

"What? Did the entire school return *all* of their books?"

Mrs. Spelling rolled her eyes, finished filling her cup of coffee, and left the room. Eric shot her retreating form a glare and walked over to the shelves full of books, starting to put more on the cart. Because he was so far behind, he decided to use both shelves on his cart and his Astral Projection power.

Both Eric and his Astral Projection form continued to work

164

this way until Eric's shift was over at 8:00. He dismissed his Astral Projection and headed down to breakfast. The closer he got to the hall, the more his stomach rumbled. He knew his timing would be late, so he would most likely get the food that nobody wanted. He cringed at the thought of oatmeal. When he reached the main hall, he was ten minutes late. Sloan was already seated, and the ghosts were gone. The students were all talking and eating, and as Eric walked to the Sophomore table, he noticed something odd in the corner of his eye. It was a dark, translucent figure that looked to be standing right behind Sloan, but as soon as Eric turned to look at it, the figure disappeared.

Eric shook his head, thinking that it was probably all the weed he'd been smoking that was going to his head. He sat down next to a couple of classmates he didn't know and grabbed a plate of scrambled eggs and a glass of milk. He ate and eavesdropped on the conversations going on around him, realizing that the dance to celebrate the year being halfway done was coming up. This also meant that midterms were coming, and Eric was not prepared for that.

As 9:00 was approaching, Eric left the main hall to get his supplies for his first class of the day. While he was walking, Zack and Damon caught up with him, and they talked while they walked.

"Sorry about Blair, but I tried to warn you," Damon said as he checked out a Freshman that walked by.

"But hey, the past is in the past. Are you planning on going to the dance, this weekend?" Zack asked as he handed Eric a metal flask.

"I figured I would go for a few hours. See how much trouble I can stir up," Eric said before he took a drink from the flask.

The whiskey burned as it when down Eric's throat, making him feel warm all over.

"We could help you with that. I can call a guy and get something to spike the punch." Zack told the group as Eric handed the flask back to him.

As they reached the second floor, Eric gave them Marina's phone number and told them he would text them later to make plans. Eric then quickly ran down the hall to get his books for his first class.

Chapter 16

The bell had just rung when Eric stepped inside the Astral Projection room, and because he was late, the only available seat was in the front, next to Catlin and Nick. When Eric realized this, he rolled his eyes and walked toward the seat.

Mr. Day wasn't in the room, yet, so people were still talking. Eric put his head down on the desk and was about to close his eyes when Nick started talking to him.

"So, Sloan talked to us about how you are wanting to turn your attitude around."

"God, your voice is so annoying in the morning," said Eric as he laid his head back down on the desk.

"Is that alcohol I smell on your breath?" Catlin asked as she began to pull out her phone.

"What do you want me to do?" Eric asked, not wanting to get in trouble, again.

Catlin put away her phone and said, "Well, we talked to Sloan, and she thinks it would be good for you to be a part of the decoration committee."

"Well, isn't that just right up your guys' alley? The one who is in love with pink, but doesn't even know how to spell it, and the aspiring gay decorator. It's no wonder you are losers, but if it gets me on Sloan's good side, then whatever." Eric said and then laid his head back on his desk.

Mr. Day walked in the room a few minutes later and sat at his desk. He apologized for being late and got things ready for the lesson, shuffling around papers and reading his lecture notes.

Eric raised his head to look alive. He wasn't shocked at what he saw. Mr. Day's curly brown hair was still in an Afro. It seemed he only had five outfits, and today, he was wearing a brown shirt underneath a blue, button-up shirt and blue jeans. Some of the students thought he was the greatest and the coolest teacher ever, but to Eric, he was just another person that dressed like a nerd from the 80s.

Mr. Day walked to the whiteboard that was behind his desk and erased the **RYAN BELL RULZ** that was written on it. Turning around, he took off his thick-framed glasses and cleared his throat.

"Today, we will not be practicing anything. Instead, I have been told to tell you about something that I usually don't tell my students until their Senior year."

"But if it was important, why were we not taught this, last year?" asked Catlin, a confused expression on her face.

"Even though I do feel like it should be one of the items that should be discussed in the first year, I also feel like I shouldn't be scaring my students, so that they don't use their powers."

Mr. Day waited for any more questions, and when no one raised their hands, he walked back to the whiteboard. He picked up a marker and started to draw a large stick figure.

"This is you," he said as he pointed at the stick figure.

"Every time you use your Astral Projection power, you create another copy of yourself that is linked with your brain," he said, drawing tinier stick figures with lines that attached them to the original stick figure.

"Now, since every one of your Astral Projections are linked up to your brain, you have total control over every one, which is very helpful in battle. But it is also your weak spot.

"I've told you, before, that if you die in battle, your Astral Projections also die," said Mr. Day as demonstrated this on the whiteboard by erasing the original stickman.

"But what I haven't told you is what happens to *you* if the Astral Projection is killed."

The room was silent as Mr. Day redrew the stick figures. Usually, the classroom was full of people talking and practicing trying to get more than one Astral Projection. But right now, it seemed like no one was even breathing. The silence was almost deafening.

"Before I tell you what happens, let me see if any of you know."

Mr. Day sat on the front of his desk with his arms crossed. He looked around the room at his students.

"No one? I'm sure some of you know, but you just don't want to say it. It's scary to think about, let alone have it happen to you.

"Do you guys remember, last year, when I demonstrated that you and your Astral Projections both feel the same? It doesn't matter who it happens to, you both feel it?"

Eric nodded his head along with everyone else, and before Mr. Day even began talking again, several people gasped.

"I'm sure that by some of your reactions, you have figured out what I'm about to say. And let me tell you, what you can imagine in your head is much more painful in person.

"When an enemy attacks your Astral Projection and ends up killing it, there's no difference in how many you have. You all feel it, and it feels like you are dying. That's because a part of you dies, along with it."

Mr. Day took the eraser and erased one of the smaller stick men. He then started to erase the line that connected the small stick man to the larger one.

"And the part of you that dies is the part that controls your Astral Projection powers."

As Mr. Day erased the other small stick men, Eric asked, "So, what you're saying is that we lose that power?"

"Yes, that is correct, which is why this class is very important. And is why you shouldn't skip this class, Eric James."

People around Eric laughed, causing him to feel embarrassed, and he slumped down in his seat. Mr. Day asked if there were any more questions, but before anyone had the chance to ask one, the bell rang. Eric quickly collected his stuff and headed to his next class.

Chapter 17

Eric was sitting in the small Telepathy class that was on the sixth floor. The smell of barbecue potato chips seemed to seep into his pores, and he cringed at the thought. Catlin was sitting next to him, like always. Usually, it was Zack who sat next to him, which would stop Catlin from trying to talk to him. Zack got to class too late to grab the seat, today, so Eric expected an ear-full from Catlin. When it came, he was far from surprised.

"I knew that Blair was trouble. I knew she wouldn't be good for you!" she said in a cold *told-you-so* way.

"Oh, would you just shut up, already." Eric said under his breath.

"Last year, she almost failed all of her classes. I heard her brother gave her the answers to the finals, so that she could pass," Catlin said, shuffling papers as she got ready for the class to start.

"Yeah, is that so? Well, I heard that you are a bitch. I also heard that you get special treatment from the teachers, because you are dumb. You throw up everything you eat, and I know that you have a thick scull, since you think that we are still friends."

"I'm just going to ignore that and rise above it."

"You go right ahead, sweetheart."

Miss Tyler walked into the classroom a few minutes late, as usual. She sat down at her desk and waited while everyone's noise quieted down into silence. After that, she stood up and turned to the whiteboard behind her, picked up a marker, and wrote **Charms Through Telepathy**.

As in every class, Miss Tyler never spoke a single word to her class. Instead, she used Telepathy to teach. Everybody in class closed their eyes and opened their minds to connect with hers. When Miss Tyler felt everyone listening, she began.

When you are in a battle, saying a charm out loud can hurt

169

us. If they know what spell we are using, they could quickly counteract it, which is why the Telepaths are so important. We can get into their minds and do the damage from there.

Once inside their head, not only can we read their mind to see what their plan is, but we can also cast charms on them from inside. It's a little tricky to do, but let's give it a go. What we will be trying, today, is casting a simple spell that freezes your opponent. Cerebrum frigore.

Now, to do this successfully, you need to aim your wand at them. And to do this, you need to have your eyes open, which is something we've been practicing. Don't worry if you can't quite do it with your eyes open, today, since you will be across from your partner.

Remember that if you chose to do it with your eyes open, you still have to keep the connection to their mind open, as well as your connection to what is going on around you! Good luck! And if you need help, don't be afraid to ask!

Eric opened his eyes and adjusted to the sudden brightness of the room. By the time he had stood up to go partner up with Zack, Catlin had already grabbed his arm and claimed him as her partner.

Zack shrugged his shoulders and mouthed, "Don't kill her."

Eric rolled his eyes and prepared himself for the torture that was going to happen in the next half hour. She pulled her desk closer to his and cheerily asked, "Do you want to go first, or should I?"

"I don't care."

"Okay, I'll go first! And then, you can do me!"

"I will never *do* you."

At that comment, Catlin shot Eric the rudest look she could manage on her pretty face and kicked him under his desk. Then, she smoothed out her expression and began the exercise by closing her eyes and trying to connect with Eric's mind. It didn't take her long, and when she did, she slapped him for what he was thinking.

It took a few minutes for her to get the charm to affect Eric, but when it finally took hold, Eric couldn't control anything, anymore. He couldn't see, couldn't move, and couldn't feel. The only things he could do were breathe, hear, and think. Essentially, his brain was cut off from the rest of his body.

"Miss Tyler, how do I undo the charm?" Eric heard Catlin ask.

Immediately after hearing that, Eric started to freak out.

"You know how, Miss Chamberlin. Now, unfreeze Mr. James before he has a heart attack."

Eric felt Catlin enter his mind, and as soon as she did, he almost spat venom at her, *I hate you, bitch. Just wait till I get my hands on you!*

You can't afford to get into anymore trouble, and you know that if you do anything to me, I will tell Sloan. I talked to her before this class, and she told me that you are on your last strike.

I'm not going to do anything that would get me in trouble. I'm trying to clean up, remember?

Eric entered Catlin's mind through the connection that Catlin had made. He envisioned himself standing in front Catlin, pointing his wand at her. He flicked it in her direction and then said, *Cerebrum frigore.*

Eric opened his eyes and touched Catlin's sun-kissed skin, which was cold to the touch. He smiled at his work, but just when he was about to unfreeze her, the bell rang. He began to pack up to leave when he heard Catlin yell inside his head, *You better unfreeze me, Eric!*

Eric, once again, imagined standing in front of her and flicking his wand. He said, *Regelo,* and opened his eyes. Catlin immediately hurried to gather her stuff and get out of the classroom for lunch. Eric did the same and followed her.

"So, how's Keith doing? Are you two still working things out?" Eric asked her.

"He's good. I'm sure you've heard that he's the captain of the boys' soccer team, this year! And we are doing fine; there was never anything to work out."

"So, you're fine with dating a guy who is more interested in guys?"

"My god, Eric, he's not gay! And since you keep asking, I can only assume that you are the one that's gay," Catlin said, getting upset with him.

"You should know me well enough to know that I'm not gay."

"You've changed a lot this past year, Eric. I honestly can't say that I do."

Catlin saw Marina and Keith down the hall and ran towards them, leaving Eric alone. He was walking to the stairs heading to the main hall when he heard someone call his name.

"Eric James? I know you hear me. Please talk to me." Blair said as she placed her hand on Eric's shoulder.

"Can you not. The only thing I want to do is punch your face in with a fireball," Eric said as he shook off Blair's hand and started down the stairs.

"Can I please explain?" Blair frantically said, chasing after him

"You cheated. End of story," Eric said in a harsh voice.

"But I can explain. She meant nothing to me..."

"Like that makes it any better!" Eric growled, interrupting her.

"She came on to me, and we weren't doing that well."

Eric stopped in his tracks, turned to her, and said, "So, because *you* felt that the relationship was falling apart, you decided to make out with a random girl. How does this make any sense to you?"

"I made a mistake, and I am very sorry that I hurt you."

Blair shyly stepped closer to Eric, but when he realized what she was doing, he stepped away and said, "You made your decision. I don't give second chances. Now, fuck off."

Chapter 18

Blair finally left him alone, and Eric made his way down to the main hall for lunch. Sitting near the front, he took of his book bag and hung it on the back of the chair, still seething about Blair and her inadequate apology. While looking around, he saw that the ghosts hadn't started bringing out food, so he decided to study for the quiz that was coming up for History.

As hard as he was trying to study, he kept getting distracted by all of the loud talking that was going on. Most of the other students were talking about the first boys' soccer game of the year. It would be Senior boys versus Freshmen boys, which was scheduled to be at 7:30. According to some of the girls that were sitting close by, "Everyone is going to be there." Eric was going to have to miss it, since he had his last class during that time.

Eric checked his watch and saw that lunch should have started five minutes ago. Sloan wasn't even present to do announcements, which was strange. At that thought, the ghosts started to come out and deliver food and drinks, and Jake DeLinsky and another kid were walking down the staircase. Eric recognized the other kid as a Freshman that was commonly known as *Speedy.*

When they made it down to the main hall, they stood by the teachers' table. Jake took a whistle out of his pocket and blew hard on it, making a deafening noise that bounced off of the beige walls.

"Listen up! We've talked to Sloan, and we have an announcement to make!" Jake yelled over the clatter of dishes. The students, however, had effectively been silenced.

"As you all should know, the first soccer game of the year is tonight! I speak for both teams when I say this; it would mean a lot to us if you all showed up to support your fellow classmates."

"There's more good news, as well! Just before we came

down here, we got something approved. After lunch, we would like to invite you down to the soccer field for the pep-rally!" Speedy told everyone.

"And don't worry about your classes, Sloan said that she would give us all a pass for the day. With that being said, we need those of you in Band to come and help boost class spirit!"

Jake and Speedy bowed, patted each other on the backs, and went to sit at their tables. The hall filled with cheers and excitement. Eric put his books away and decided to skip lunch. Grabbing his book bag, he headed to the Sophomore living room.

The room was empty and cool; not anything like it normally was, and Eric sighed with contentment. He sat in his favorite spot in the room, which was the sofa on the far wall that sat near the windows. Stretching out, he opened the window that was beside him to let the warm, summer air inside and pulled out a book that he'd checked out from the library to read.

About thirty minutes later, Eric's classmates started to come into the room, disturbing the sweet silence. Getting mad at all of the noise they were causing, he pulled out his headphones and his phone from his book bag and started listening to his music.

"Are you going to stay up here, all day?" Catlin asked Eric.

"What's it to you?" Eric answered, giving her the cold shoulder.

"I just think that you spend too much time alone. Come with us. Please? It could be fun!"

"Don't you have to be with the Band?" Eric asked as he put his headphones away.

"Yeah, but you could sit with Marina and Nick."

Eric thought about it for a few minutes. "Maybe next time, but thanks. Thanks for asking."

Catlin smiled, and Eric smiled back. He gathered his stuff and left the living room and headed to the library. On his way up the stairs, he ran into Jake DeLinsky.

"Where are you going, freak?" he asked him with a sneer, taking hold of Eric's book bag and attempting to pull it away.

"What did I tell you about calling me names?" Eric asked as ripped his book bag out of Jake's hand.

A bit of fear popped up in Jake's eyes as he took a step away from Eric.

"That's more like it. And for your information, I'm headed to the library. I have no intention of watching small-minded people chase after a ball. I can do that on a farm," Eric said as he started up the steps, again.

On his way up the stairs, he could hear Jake make a snide comment under his breath, which made Eric angry. He was reaching the sixth floor in his huff when he encountered Sloan, who looked like her professional self in white khakis and a light blue blouse. There were some papers in one hand, and her cell phone was in the other.

"Hey, Sloan, can I ask you something?"

"Make it quick, Mr. James. I do not have much time."

"I was actually wondering if we could move my Fire Manipulation class up to now."

"Not possible. I have to go to the pep-rally. Why?" She asked, concerned.

"If I do it, now, I'll have more time to study for some of my tests that are coming up."

Sloan sighed and let Eric hold the papers that were in her hand while she started typing away on her phone. As an afterthought, she added, "I will send you an email over the things we were going to learn, today, and I will send you the file for the readings. You will take a test, tomorrow, over what you have learned from it all. You can use the Defense Against the Shadow Reapers classroom."

Eric thanked her, gave her back the papers, and walked with her to the first floor. When they made it, Sloan turned to him and said, "I am giving you a chance, here. Do not blow it."

Sloan left the building, and Eric headed toward the Defense Against the Shadow Reaper classroom. As Eric opened the heavy metal door, cold air hit him. The room was dark, except for the glowing red hearts of the Shadow Reaper bots. Eric ran his hand along the wall to find a light switch.

When his hand finally hit something that felt like a light switch, he flipped it, groaning at the brightness of the light. His eyes burned as they adjusted. He made his way over to a desk and pulled out his laptop, opening it up to his school email account.

This was the first time that he had actually used his school email, this year. He had over a hundred unread messages. The most recent was from Sloan.

Subject: Fire Manipulation Class

Eric opened up the file that was attached and waited for it to download. The wait was considerable, and he couldn't help but think of Jake and the hate and pain he'd caused to build inside of Eric. Finally, Eric couldn't stand it, anymore. As much as he tried to brush off the anger, it kept building, but he knew what he could do to fix it. It wouldn't be hard.

Eric opened up the school's main page and headed to the Gossip Central page. He logged in and started to create a new post.

Jake, Jake, he's our star! But he's not a very good one. I've done some digging, and it seems that Jake DeLinsky and 'Speedy' have been using some 'sport enhancing' drugs. I guess now 'Speedy' is going to have to change his name to 'Druggy.' Don't worry, guys, I've already gotten rid of the drugs and placed them in Sloan's office.

-GC

Eric hit send and waited for the damage to begin. Of course, he didn't have proof that they were using steroids, nor did he drop any off in Sloan's office. But that what made it a good plan. Once Sloan saw the post and realizes that the drugs weren't in her office, she'd assume that Jake and Speedy stole them back. Or, at least, that was the plan.

The file that Eric was downloading had finished, so he opened it and began reading the three pages that Sloan had sent him. Eric was excited about what he was learning, today: fire whips. After he quickly read about the skill, he began to practice. Usually, Sloan and Eric practiced with the SRBs, but Eric didn't feel safe using them by himself.

Instead of using the robots, he decided to just practice getting the hang of the exercise. Eric moved the desks out of his way and stood in the middle of the room, raising his arms out and closing his eyes. There in his mind, he stood alone in a dark, cold room as he focused on his powers.

Eric envisioned bright orange flames forming around his shoulders. He made the flames spread out down his arms and to his hands. From there, Eric envisioned the flames growing and forming a long whip in his hand. After the whips had grown to his liking, Eric opened his eyes.

Even though his arms and hands were covered in flames, he didn't feel anything. In fact, it just felt like he had long sleeves on. He looked at his hands, and in each of them was a three-foot long whip made of flames. Eric read that in order to do this right, he had to imagine that the flames were solid.

He moved his hands, and with them, the whips followed. They felt solid and heavy, and as Eric moved them across the marble floor, they left little trails of flames. The next thing that Eric had to test was seeing if they moved as fluidly as a whip did. He quickly raised his right hand over his head, with the whip sliding across the floor, near his feet. As quick as he could, he slammed his hand down diagonally toward his left foot. Within a blink of an eye, the whip flew over Eric's head and hit the floor with a loud bang, sending sparks flying.

Eric extinguished the flames, rested for a few minutes, and started again. Until the hour was over, Eric worked on getting the flames and whips to appear more quickly.

After working on the exercise for a while, Eric glanced at his watch and noticed that it was five minutes after the bell should have rang. Sloan must have had them shut down for the day, since classes weren't meeting. He extinguished his flames and shook his arms out, glad of the absence of the extra weight. He was about to close his laptop up and leave when he noticed an icon blinking, telling him he had new mail. It was from Sloan.

Subject: Next Class Period

Since your next class is cancelled, I have informed Mrs. Spelling that you will be picking up an extra hour of work, today.

"Shit," Eric spat as he quickly gathered his belongings and ran.

Chapter 19

A few days had passed, and Eric was in his Metamorphosis class, watching Mr. Goodman turn a wand into a sword. It was three days until the party and two days until midterms. Mr. Goodman had finished demonstrating and had told the class to pair up into groups to practice the technique. Eric was walking over to one of the girls that had been eyeing him when Marina stepped right between them.

"Cock-block much?" Eric asked her as she grabbed his hand and dragged him towards a corner, near a window.

"If anyone needed to have their dick cut off, it would be you," Marina said with a dark expression on her face.

"I no longer want to practice with you, anymore," Eric said as he put his hands over his crotch.

"We need to talk about Saturday, and since you don't have a cell phone, and you have no more free time, this is the only time we can talk."

Eric pulled out his wand from his cargo pocket in his shorts and held it in both hands. As quickly as he could, he pictured it becoming a large, foam sword. Before he could get his wand to transform, though, Marina had tapped him with her foam sword.

They tried again, and as Eric closed his eyes, Marina said, "So, we were thinking about an eighties theme for the party."

"If we want no one to show up, that's a great theme. We need a theme that is popular," Eric said as he swung his foam sword at Marina.

Eric transformed the sword back into his wand as Marina said, "Well, Nick talked about a sci-fi theme. That could be cool."

"Cool, if you are a nerd, but not everyone, here, is a sci-fi fan. It's not like you're even trying."

"Fine, what do you suggest, then?" Marina asked as she swung her sword at Eric.

"What about something patriotic, since the party is near the

178

fourth?"

Marina gasped and jumped up and down. "We could do a 'Surfing in the USA' theme! And it could be beach-themed, as well!"

Eric just looked at her with a blank face, and then, hit her with the sword so hard, it almost knocked her over.

"Just for that, you are doing the flyers and the decorations for the party."

"I hate you so much. You know, I don't have to time to do that kind of stuff."

"Do you not get breaks at work?" Marina asked, sarcastically.

Eric ignored her and focused on beating Marina with the sword. When the class was over, he quickly left the classroom and headed towards the Potions classroom. Eric was just glad that they weren't doing anything in that class, today.

All of the herbs had been destroyed a couple days ago, and it was some Freshman rumor that pinpointed Jamie Chamberlin as the culprit. She'd mixed the wrong ingredients, which had effectively wiped out all the classroom plant life that had been above the soil. While they were waiting for new ones to grow, Mr. Smith had them working on a paper about the uses of lavender and chives.

Eric reached the Potions classroom a few minutes before the bell rang, at 6:10. He sat down at one of the empty lab tables and waited for Mr. Smith to come in and take them to the computer lab in the library. While he waited, he took out a piece of paper and started to sketch the poster.

Mr. Smith walked into the classroom at 6:10, pulling his glasses out of his blue suit jacket pocked and placing them on his long and pointed nose. He went to his desk, sat down, and started taking attendance.

When he got to Eric's name, he called it out, and Eric answered with, "Here."

"Three days in a row, Mr. James. That's a record, this year." Mr. Smith replied in a monotone voice before moving on to the next name. There were some snickers from the other students.

A few minutes later, he was finished with the list. Mr. Smith got up, gathered his things, and told the class to start heading toward the library. Eric still had his notebook out, sketching the poster, and by the time he had gathered his stuff and left the classroom, he was the last one to leave.

As he reached the sixth floor, he was the last one still in the hallway. Eric ambled along, taking his time, but as he walked by the girls' bathroom, he heard two people arguing. He wouldn't have thought anything of it, but a male voice caught his attention.

Eric put his books back in his book bag and slowly sneaked into the bathroom. As soon as he was in, he closed the door and put his full weight on it, taking out his wand, quickly waving it around his head, and said, "Invisibilis," a spell he learned from Damon.

Slowly, his body started to turn transparent. When his full body was gone, he started to walk toward the yelling. He only had minutes before the charm wore off, so he quickly snuck around the corner to see what was going on.

Damon Cowell and Brittney Walker, a Senior, were standing in the middle of the bathroom, yelling at one another.

"You cannot go around the whole school saying we had sex, last night!" yelled Damon as his face became red with anger.

"You can drop the whole *I'm a virgin* act. The whole school knows you're a man whore," Brittney said as she shifted her weight to her left leg.

Brittney walked over to the mirrors, where Eric was standing, pulled out some lipstick from her tiny purse and fixed her makeup. As she bent over to lean into the mirror, her short mini skirt revealed her thong.

"I'm not saying that I'm a virgin. I'm saying you're lying. You kissed me, I pulled away, and then you left. That's all that happened, and you know it." Damon growled as he walked towards her.

"I would have thought you wouldn't have minded me spreading that rumor around, unless you don't want someone to know?" she said in a mysterious way, shooting a wink at him.

Damon knew what she meant by that, and Eric could tell by the way Damon looked at her. And it took him a while to figure it out, but Eric understood, as well.

"What do you mean?" Damon asked her. His voice cracked at the end.

"You should be more careful of your timing when you make

out with a teacher. When you came into Miss Tyler's room the other day, I was in there too. I'm her student aid, that period. Dumbass."

Damon looked at her like he had just been caught burying a dead body. His pupils were dilated, and he had sweat dripping down his forehead.

"I-I don't- I don't know what you mean," Damon stuttered, barely getting any sound out.

At that time, the main door opened up and in marched Miss Tyler.

"What is going on in here?" she asked, stepping in between them.

"Nothing, I was just leaving," Brittney said as started heading towards the door.

As she passed the teacher, Miss Tyler grabbed her arm and whispered, "If you say anything to anybody, I will-"

"You'll do what. Harm me? Either way, you're going to jail. Sicko." Brittney yanked her arm free and walked out of the bathroom.

When they heard the door slam, Miss Tyler said, "She's right. We need to be more careful."

As she wrapped her arms around Damon's thin waist, he asked, "Can we do anything about her?"

"I guess I could wipe her memory, so that she doesn't remember the last couple of days."

Damon placed his hand around her waist and drew her in. As they went in for a kiss, Eric pulled out Marina's phone and took a picture. He could feel the charm wearing off, so he silently left the bathroom. As he closed the door, he removed the charm and headed to the library.

"Where have you been?" Mr. Smith asked as Eric walked into the computer lab.

"Nature called," Eric said sarcastically.

"Well, next time nature calls, put it on hold," Mr. Smith responded.

Eric sad down at an empty computer and logged in. He opened up his email and saw that he had a new email from Marina with *Party Changes* as the subject.

Since my phone is still MISSING. *cough * *cough * This is the only way I can talk to you when we're not

together. I talked to Catlin and Nick, and we like the 80s theme better. So, we are going with and 80s theme.

Eric rolled his eyes and deleted the message. He opened up a new document on his computer and started on the posters for the party, but the whole time he was working, he was also thinking of when to give the news about Miss Tyler and Damon to everyone.

Chapter 20

It was the day of midterms, and Eric was given the day off of work, so he could do some last minute studying. Everywhere he went to study, though, people were talking about the party. It was sickening. Every class he was in, he sat behind couples that were talking about what they were going to wear, where they were going to eat, how the girl was going to do her hair, and so on. By the time first period started, Eric already wanted to throw up. He couldn't wait for the next two days to be over with.

Eric was sitting in the Astral Projection classroom, waiting for the class to start. He was one of the first to arrive, because he'd tried to get there early enough to avoid sitting next to Catlin and Marina. The moment he sat down, though, they walked in. Nick sat on his left, and Catlin took the seat on his right.

Eric rolled his eyes as Nick said, "Hey, buddy, ready for this test?"

"Don't talk to me," Eric hissed through his teeth.

"Someone's in a bad mood," Catlin said, reaching across Eric's desk to hand Nick a pen.

"Do you mind getting out of my personal space?" Eric growled, pushing her hand out of his face.

"You know what? I think I know what is wrong with Eric." Nick said across the space to her.

"What would that be, besides the large stick up his ass?" Catlin responded.

"I think he's upset, because he doesn't have a date for the party."

"Wouldn't be surprised if he didn't. He's friendless. No one likes him. Not even the people he gets high with."

"You know what would be a great idea? Since you and Keith are no longer together, you two should go together!"

"I would rather die," Eric said to them.

"I think that is a perfect idea, Nick! We would look SO

cute!"

"I'm going to puke," Eric said as he pretended to gag.

"We'll talk more about it later, okay?" Catlin asked Eric.

"Whatever," Eric said before he stopped paying attention to them.

Nick and Catlin continued to talk about the party even after Mr. Day walked in. It was a few minutes later when Mr. Day began speaking about their test.

"As I have said before, your test for today requires you to have at least two Astral Projections," he told the class.

When he was done taking attendance, everyone got up and headed towards the practice area near the back of the room. Eric slowly walked back with them as he read some last minute tips from his notebook. Everybody took their positions and waited for Mr. Day's command.

Eric stood near the back corner of the room, behind Marina and Catlin. He put his notebook down on the ground and looked outside the windows to the dreary, rainy morning. Eric watched the trees from the woods sway in the heavy wind.

Mr. Day walked to the back of the room with his clipboard and gave some advice. "Time is of the essence. The quicker you get your Astral Projections out, the quicker you can attack. Remember that one Astral Projection is easy, and the more you have, the trickier it gets. Just remember some of the tricks we've been working on, so far."

Eric knew the tricks. With one Projection, you just imagine yourself somewhere else within the area. With more than that, you have to see the bigger picture. Picture the room or place with the different copies of yourself around that room or place.

Eric did what he could in the shortest time possible. He opened his eyes and the room was full of people. Some people had four or five, but most had two or three. Eric was glad there weren't any twins in his class, and he was sure Mr. Day was glad, too.

Mr. Day walked around the room grading on how many Astral Projections everyone had and how strong they were. When he got to Eric, he sighed.

"Two and a half? I had higher hopes for you, Eric, after what you did, last year. But since you've missed most of the classes, I guess this is all you can do. You better hope you do better in this class, or you'll be taking it over, again."

When Mr. Day walked away, Eric rolled his eyes and shot him a dirty look as he got rid of his Astral Projections by imagining the room to be empty. He left the practice area and sat down at his desk with the others that had already been graded. When Mr. Day was finished with his grading, he dismissed the class.

Eric rushed out of the classroom as quickly as he could, but he still couldn't escape Nick and Catlin. They ran up to him and wrapped themselves around his arms.

"Are you not aware that I have a class to get to?" He asked them while trying to escape their grips.

"Come on, your next class is literally right there," Nick said, pointing to the Charms classroom that was between the staircases.

"And since it's right here, you have a few minutes to chat," Catlin said, guiding him down the stairs.

"Sure, let's chat. Let's chat about how you and Keith are no longer together, Catlin. Or let's talk about how you and Marina are no longer together, Nick. What happened, there? You guys were the perfect couples," Eric said, sarcastically.

"Actually, Marina and I are actually dating, again," Nick said, happily.

"I'm so happy for you." Eric rolled his eyes.

"And as for Keith and I, it turns out that he loved me more than I loved him," Catlin said, sounding distant.

"How sad," Eric said with as little emotion as he could.

Eric looked at his watch and grunted.

"Listen, if this is about the party, we can talk at lunch. I really need to get to my class, and I really don't want to escape by MY means." Eric said as he clenched his hands into fists. Nick and Catlin gasped and let go.

"This isn't about the party. This is ab-" Catlin was saying before she was interrupted.

"Then it can wait," Eric shot back before walking away.

As Eric walked away, he could hear Marina's nervous sounding voice greet them. Eric rolled his eyes at the thought of being in the same classroom as her. He remembered the last time they took a test in the class. The whole time they were taking the test, she was shaking her legs. How freaking annoying.

Eric walked through the door into the brightly lit room and sat down at a desk that was near the back, next to the window. He sat his book bag down next to him and pulled out his flashcards, studying the notes that he'd written on them. The rain had stopped, and the hot air had cooled down, so Mr. Chine walked around the room and opened the windows.

When class began at 10:10, Mr. Chine explained that today, they would take the written portion of the test. The practical and oral test would be given, next Monday. He then explained that the written test would be two parts. The first part was going to be matching, and the second would be figuring out what charm to use in different situations.

Some people had last minute questions about some of the vocab words. Instead of just telling his students the straight answers, he helped them figure it out, which is why Eric liked him so much. Mr. Chine was more focused on the learning part, rather than the memorization part of teaching.

Mr. Chine passed out the test and sat down at his desk, pulling out a book. Eric skipped to the end of the test to see how many questions there were. There were fifteen matching questions and twenty theoretical questions. Feeling confident in his studying, Eric picked up his pen and started on the second part of the test, first.

When he was done with the theoretical part, Eric looked at his watch to see how much time he had left. It was 10:45; he had 15 minutes to finish the test. The matching part of the test was easy, but as he got closer to finishing, he got stuck on a few of the last words. He started looking around the room while he thought about the answers.

A shadowy form caught his eye, and he noticed it standing near Marina. She was working on her test with her head bent down over her paper, but next to her right side, there was something Eric couldn't really see. He knew something was there, but it was shapeless and translucent. Marina flinched and in a blink, whatever Eric saw was gone.

"Eric, eyes on your own paper," Mr. Chine said to him.

People laughed as Eric went back to his test. When he finished, he turned his paper upside down and laid his head down on his desk. The bell rang a few minutes later, and Eric got up, grabbed his book bag, and turned in his test. He left the room looking for Marina, and when he saw her, he ran up to her and pulled her aside.

"What the hell was that?" Eric said, pushing her against the wall.

"Let go of me before I start screaming," Marina said with a serious look in her eyes.

Eric let go but still insisted to be answered. "What the hell was that thing next to you in class?"

"I have no clue what you are talking about. There was nothing next to me. I think you are imagining things, Eric, so maybe you need your head checked. You might need to go to the nurse."

"You answered that a little too quickly. I don't believe you."

"Believe me or don't believe me, but there is no way *you* can prove otherwise," Marina said as she pushed him out of her way.

Eric bit his lip and angrily sighed as he watched her stomp away. When she was out of sight, he headed to his next class, Telepathy. Since the classroom was two floors up, he had time to think about what exactly he'd seen. He began to form a theory of what was going on, and if he was right, he was going to have to stop what was going on, before things got bad.

To stop it, though, there were things he had to do and some people he had to take care of, before anything else happened. As he walked into the staircase, he pulled out Marina's phone, opened up the web browser, and started his work.

Chapter 21

"I have some good news to tell you, Eric." Elizabeth said, walking into the white tiled room. She was wearing a small, black-jeweled tiara on top of her curly, red hair. She lifted up her skirt of her black V-neck gown and revealed her black, knee-high heeled boots.

The sound of her steps echoed loudly in the cold room. Eric was strapped on a metal table in the middle of the room, and his mouth was covered with a patch of duct tape. Sweat was dripping down his brow as he nervously looked at Elizabeth, fearing what she was going to do to him next.

Elizabeth walked over to a counter, opened a drawer, and pulled out a scalpel. Eric's eyes widened as they focused on the scalpel. Elizabeth even went as far as to sashay her hips as she walked closer to him.

"We have done some testing, and it turns out that the key to your powers is your blood. So, I intend to take your blood." She said as several more people dressed in black uniforms walked in.

She placed the blade of the scalpel just below his right wrist. Someone stepped next to Elizabeth with a suction tube to collect as much of the blood as possible.

"Is everyone ready?" Elizabeth asked.

Everyone nodded their heads, and with an evil grin, Elizabeth pushed down the scalpel and began to cut from wrist to his elbow. At first, Eric tried to scream, but the pain overcame him. His eyes rolled back into his head, and he passed out. When they collected as much of the blood as they could without killing him, Elizabeth handed the scalpel over to the person on her left. Before she left the room, she said, "Make sure he stays alive. We need him for more blood."

Eric woke up screaming in pain. His right arm felt like it was going to fall off, with pain so intense that he felt like he could hack his arm off and not even care. When the pain faded, he looked down at his watch and saw that it was 7:48. He had less than fifteen minutes to get ready for the party. Casting a glance out the window that was near the couch, he saw that it was storming, outside. Eric glanced at his phone that he'd gotten back from Sloan, yesterday, and saw several missed calls from Catlin and Marina.

"Shit!" He hissed the word as he frantically called them back.

"Where have you been? You were supposed to be in charge of decorations!" Catlin yelled angrily as she barged into the living room.

Eric hung up his phone and put it away. He couldn't take her serious in her large, pink tutu and the oversized, neon yellow sweater. When he looked at her newly bleached and teased hair, he lost it and started cackling.

"I feel asleep. Sorry," he wheezed, trying to catch his breath from laughing.

"Get dressed, Eric. We're supposed to be down there by the time the party starts." Catlin huffed as she turned around and left the room.

Eric was still giggling as he walked into the boy's bedroom and to his dresser to grab his clothes. It was nearing 8:00 when he left the bathroom dressed in acid washed jeans, a graphic button-up dress shirt, and a mullet wig he had picked up at a wig shop in Hillthrope.

"We decided to move it into the main hall, rather than to delay the party," Marina said to Eric as he reached the main hall.

Most of the tables had been removed, except for three. The teachers' table was still were it was, there was one in front of the DASR doorway that had the food on it, and there was one in front of the Potions doorway that had drinks on it. There were about twenty chairs on the far wall on either side of the main door.

The whole room was covered in bright, neon-colored streamers. Some of the lights above the dance floor were replaced with black lights. There were posters from hit 80s movies on the walls, there was a large boom box on the teachers' table that had a stack of CDs near it, and there were pictures of street art and old video games posted on the walls.

The rain sounded like hail when it hit the windows, and thunder and lightning cracked as some of the students came down the stairs. The lights, above, flickered with a power surge as Catlin started to play some dance music.

"Just what we need. A power outage," Marina said as she fixed her bright pink leggings and her bright green shirt.

Eric walked over to the drink stand to help set it up. At 8:00, Sloan walked down the stairs in a neon orange peplum dress. Her grey hair was in a side ponytail. She smoothed out her dress as she walked over to the teachers' table and stood in front of her chair.

Sloan started talking about some of the rules for the night, going on about how there would be no use of drugs or alcohol, no making out, no going beyond the third floor, and that the party would end at 11:00. As she was talking, Eric overheard a couple of the older students, Emily Fouler and Carrie Garber, gossiping about what had happened earlier that day.

"Did you know that Damon Cowell, Zack Roberts, and Miss Tyler were dismissed from the school, around noon?" Emily whispered to Carrie, conspiringly.

"Yeah, do you know why, though?" Carrie cocked an eyebrow at her, showing the other girl that she knew, herself.

"You mean the rumor that they were sneaking around at night, together?" Emily giggled.

"Yeah, I heard Sloan called them *meetings*, although I'm sure we could put other words to it," Carrie tried to stifle a snort.

"Were you at dinner when it was announced?" Emily asked.

"Nah, I was late. I took a nap and slept in. What was said?"

"Sloan said that if anyone else was caught doing anything similar, their punishment would be the same. They'd have their powers swiped away, along with their memories," Emily told her with wide eyes. A little fear had crept into her voice.

Carrie's indrawn breath told Eric that she was scared of those consequences, as well. He lost interest in their personal conversation as their voices lowered, but his mind was still on the swiped powers and memory wipe. Eric really had no clue how they could do that; probably with a potion, but he didn't care that much. Sloan finished her speech, Catlin started playing music, and people started to dance. Eric was in the middle of pouring a drink when Catlin walked over.

"You know that people can pour their own drinks for a while, right? I mean, you are supposed to be my date," she said as she stood next to him and looked up into his face with a fluttering of her eyelashes.

"I'm in charge of the drink station. What if someone tried to mess with the drinks?" Eric hinted, sarcastically.

"You're no fun. Who am I going to dance with?" Catlin said, throwing a little tantrum.

"You could dance with me, baby," said a young, nerdy Freshman that had parachute pants on.

Catlin gave him a kind smile. "Maybe, in a few minutes. I have to go change the CD."

The Freshman smiled back and walked toward a group of other Freshman that were giggling at him.

"But seriously, we need to dance together at least once, tonight. You know that in half an hour, the Band and Choir take over the music. I'm free, then," she said with a smile.

At 8:20, the Band and Choir started walking down the stairs to set up. Ten minutes later, they were ready, and Catlin turned off the boom box. The Band and Choir took over with their version of *Time After Time*. As they started playing, Catlin walked over to Eric, grabbed his hands, and pulled him toward the dance floor.

When they reached the middle of the dance floor, Catlin reached up and placed her hands around the back of Eric's neck. She pulled him toward her, and he wrapped his hands around her waist.

"You know, I'm sorry about what happened between us, last year. We... I should have never abandoned you. Especially since you had gone through so much," she said, looking deeply into his eyes as they started to dance.

"Why did you?"

"Because of something Marina saw in one of her visions. And I knew we shouldn't have listened to her. I even told her that the future could change. People could change."

"But you still listened to her."

"I didn't really want to. Trust me, Eric. I—I—I love you. I tried to make it up to you by trying to call and text you, but you never answered me."

"I honestly didn't know how to respond," Eric told her as

they slowed down their pace.

"I don't blame you. I wouldn't know, either. And so far, this school year has gone really shitty. I miss you. I miss the late night study sessions," Catlin laughed to herself and continued, "I'm not doing that well this year, school wise. Nick and Marina have tried to help me, but it's just not the same."

"What can I say? I'm a good teacher," he said as he wrapped his arms tighter around her waist.

Eric tilted his head and leaned in closer to Catlin's face. His eyes shifted from her eyes to her lips. He could smell the fruit punch that she had, earlier. Catlin tilted her head the other way and leaned in the rest of the way.

"Are you sure you want to do this? After all, I am dark and twisted," Eric said as their lips began to touch.

A few seconds passed before they broke away for some breath.

"I can so handle dark and twisty," Catlin responded with a twinkle in her eye.

When the Band and Choir ended their song, Eric and Catlin stopped dancing and went back to their stations. But once Catlin put in a new CD, she walked over to the drink station to give Eric some help.

"So, what does this mean?" she asked while pouring someone a drink.

"Seriously? You really want to be *that* girl?" Eric asked, giving her a beatific smile.

Chapter 22

It was 9:30, and things were slowing down for Eric, causing a haze of boredom to start choking at him. Grinning to himself, he decided to pull out some of his emergency stash of vodka from his back pocket and pour some into the big, glass punch bowl when no one was looking. He stirred it around and started giving away drinks, again.

Within the next few minutes, everything got really interesting. Suddenly, everyone was thirsty, and once they tasted the new punch, they kept coming back for more. Soon, everyone was tipsy. Eric chuckled as he looked around the room. Mr. Smith was dancing with his necktie around his head. Miss Carton was passed out in a chair. Sloan was stumbling around the room, sloshing punch on the floor, and most of the kids were bumping into each other, trying to dance to the music.

In the corner, by the DASR room, Eric thought he saw something. When he turned his eyes back to investigate, he narrowed them, attempting to peer into the darkness. Thunder roared and shook the walls, and when lightning struck, it burst into the corner, allowing Eric to see a little bit more of what he was looking at. It was still unclear, due to the alcohol.

Although he was foggy-headed from all of the vodka, he left the drink station to see if he could get a better look at the corner. When he was close enough, he saw a pale, dirty figure that looked like a ghost but seemed to flicker in and out. Eric went to step towards him, but as he did, thunder cracked, and all of the lights went out. Fearing that what he saw could cause harm, Eric decided to attack it.

He shot several fireballs into the corner, and as he did, everybody around him screamed and scattered. Eric struggled to walk over to the corner to see if he had hit the shadow figure. Adrenaline was pumping the liquor through his system, making him even foggier. When he got to the corner, the flames were extending to the ceiling and were spreading across the walls. As he tried to focus his vision, Eric realized that there wasn't a body.

Eric turned around and crossed the makeshift dance floor as a loud noise popped, signaling the lights to flicker back on. Eric frantically looked around the room, searching for the ghost figure. There! He spotted Nick, Marina, and Catlin talking to the figure by the teachers' desk. He was just about ready to throw another fireball when Sloan grabbed him by his arm.

"What have you done, Eric James!" she yelled as she pulled him towards the staircase that lead to her office.

As Sloan dragged him toward the staircase, he looked toward Catlin, Marina, and Nick. They were standing there, staring at Eric with fear and confusion coloring their faces. Sloan pulled Eric onto the staircase and quickly walked him up to the seventh floor, silent the whole way.

"Not only are you in trouble for spiking the punch, but you caught the school on fire." she said as they entered Sloan's office.

"You can't prove I did it." Eric slurred his words as he talked.

"Yes, I can. I also know something else about you. Something I have known for quite some time, now," she said with a blank expression.

"Know what?" he growled, getting angry.

"You have not been yourself in a while, Eric," Sloan said very calmly.

"What do you mean?" Eric said, raising his voice.

"Look into the mirror." Sloan said as she got up and walked over to the right wall. On the wall was a ceiling to floor length mirror that was next to a window.

"As soon as I knew your secret, I cast a charm on the doorway into this office," she said, pointing to the office door. "You see, this charm makes it so that I can see someone's true form if they have used a shape shifting charm. But how exactly did you do it? How did you fool everyone for so long? After all, you don't have our powers."

"That was the simple part. I used potions and charms to make it look like I had the same powers as Eric."

"So, Mr. Smith was right. You were the reason why ingredients for potions went missing. Anyways, step in front of the mirror and tell me what you see when you look into the mirror."

He stood in front of a mirror and looked at his reflection. He smiled a devilish smile when he saw it. "I haven't seen *this* face in a long time."

Eric quickly turned around and lunged at Sloan. He pushed her to the ground and pulled out a knife from his front pocket. He placed the knife on Sloan's throat and said, "Any last words?"

Sloan screamed for help, but before she could get much out, Eric kneed her in the stomach. As she screamed in pain, the door busted open with a crack! Nick, Marina, and Catlin ran into the room, trailed by a ghostly figure. Now, though, the ghostly figure was more visible, and Eric could see more details in the face. He recognized that face. It was his own.

Chapter 23

"We know you're not Eric James. So, before we kill you, tell us who you are." Marina said to the pale-skinned person standing next to Sloan's unconscious body. The person was wearing the same clothes Eric was wearing an hour ago at the dance.

"And if I don't?" said the man as he twirled his knife in his hand.

"Then, I'll torture you," Eric said weakly.

"You can't do anything. You're too weak to even wipe your own ass. Besides, I know you're just an Astral Projection… and a poor one, at that."

"We'll then, if you know that, then you understand that I know the location of the Shadow Reaper base."

"No, you don't. And even if you did, it's too late. We have won."

"I overheard some of my guards talking about it. And besides that, I've been talking to my parents."

While Eric was talking to the man, Sloan was crawling away towards a cabinet that was full of potions. Eric kept the man talking until Sloan was able to get the one she wanted.

"I bet you didn't know that my friends, here, can read your mind. And that's how they figured out you weren't actually me. Not to mention that two of them can see the future."

The man now looked at them, realizing all the mistakes he had made in the past few months.

"They also know that right now, you are thinking of several different ways you could take us down and several ways to get out of here, alive. But you've made a mistake. *Now*!"

Sloan threw as many of the bottles at the man as she could. The bottles broke on contact, and the man fell to his knees in pain. He screamed in pain for several minutes. His body went up in flames, and then, exploded into ashes. Thunder and lightning crashed, once again, and the lights flickered for the second time that night.

Eric's ghostly figure had faded away as Marina and Catlin rushed to help Sloan with her injuries. At Sloan's request, Nick rushed to get the nurse, Mr. Smith, Mr. Day, and Mrs. Grey.

"Why did you wait for so long to do something? Eric could have been saved, by now." Catlin asked Sloan as she helped to her chair.

"I first figured that something was wrong, last year after the battle, when you guys came to me when the fighting had ended, telling me he was missing and had gone to meet Elizabeth. When we found Eric in the forest, he said nothing about her and kept acting strangely, as if he didn't know me. I couldn't read his mind right, and at that point, I just thought something had happened to him, that night. Maybe, he had hit his head or had his memory erased." Sloan closed her eyes and shook her head. "I tried a few charms on him, and nothing happened. He didn't get better, only worse. But then, you two showed me evidence that he wasn't the real Eric, and that is when I started to form a plan.

"And as of right now, that plan is closing the school. That is what is best for the students, the school, and for the community." She told them as Mr. Smith, Mrs. Grey, and Mr. Day walked in with Nick.

"You have made the decision, then?" said Mr. Day.

"That I have, Mr. Day," she said sadly.

"You can't close the school!" Nick said.

"I have to. We are all in grave danger, here. The Shadow Reapers have found out how to get our powers. In days, they will have an army of half breeds."

"We can fight them!" Marina said, trying to cheer up the group.

"I don't think that is wise at this moment. We are at a disadvantage now that they have both powers." Mr. Smith said as he sat down at Sloan's desk.

"What exactly are we to do? I've seen the future, and if we do nothing, it will become very dim," said Mrs. Grey.

Sloan sat down at her desk and put her head in her hands.

"I do not know," Sloan said, getting frustrated. She cupped her face in her hands and leaned her elbows on her desk.

"There has to be something we can do," Mr. Day said as he

placed a hand on Sloan's back.

"There is, but it's too risky." Sloan sounded defeated and tired as she raised her head to look at them. "Mr. Day, Mr. Smith, and Mrs. Grey, can you please round up all of the students for me down in the main hall?"

They agreed and left the room. Nick, Marina, and Catlin were all standing by Sloan's desk, waiting for her to say something... anything.

"You know I would let you three stay if there was a way I could keep you safe, but there isn't. I am afraid that in a year's time, we will all be gone. Please, go downstairs while I make arrangements."

The three slowly walked out of the room. Nick held onto Marina as she let out a small tear.

"This is truly the end, then." Catlin said as she held on to her friends.

When they reached the main hall, all of the tables and chairs had been placed back where they belonged, and everybody was there, sitting at their assigned tables. Everyone looked scared. It was well past midnight, the thunderstorm had passed, and the moonlight lit the yard, outside. Everybody was silently talking to one another. Besides Catlin, Nick, and Marina, no one had a clue what was going on.

For the students, it felt like a lifetime before they saw Sloan walking slowly down the stairs. A hush fell over the entire room as everyone stopped whatever they were doing and stayed still and quiet with wide eyes. Sloan walked to the middle of the teachers' table and began to speak.

"Something horrible has happened. One of our students was kidnapped, late last year. You would know him as Eric James. We didn't know it at that time, because a Shadow Reaper took his form and fooled us all. We have, however, been contacted several times by the real Eric, and he has told us about what they were planning. I will admit to you that it's not good." Sloan took a moment to sigh, sadly, and continued. "Since we have found out about this, we have made many plans on how to stop it. My main duty, though, is to protect my students." Sloan took a deep breath and looked at the teachers. They all nodded their heads for her to carry on.

"That is why I have decided to close the school. Students,

you are to go and pack your things as fast as you can. Your parents will be contacted, and once they arrive, we will move on to the second step of the plan." After she finished her speech, she quickly turned around to wipe the tears off her face, and headed toward the stairs with tears still flowing.

As Sloan left, students felt both confused and scared. Students hugged one another as they got up to go pack. Kids of all ages were now crying. Instead of going to pack, Nick, Marina, and Catlin decided to go back to Sloan's office.

When they arrived, Mr. Day, Mr. Smith, and Mrs. Grey were already in the office. Sloan, herself, was at her desk, talking to someone on the phone. The other teachers were walking around the room, talking on their cell phones. From the conversations, they must have been calling parents. When Sloan was finished on her phone, she invited them into her office.

"You should be packing," Sloan said to them. Her face was swollen from crying, and she had bags under her eyes.

"Sloan, we have to get Eric back."

"Do you not think I know this?" she yelled at them as she stormed across the room. She opened the door to her room and slammed it behind her.

The threesome looked back and forth at each other with wide eyes. They'd never seen Sloan make any outburst like that, before.

Mr. Smith hung up his phone and turned to the kids. "I've told her the same thing. We tried to come up with some plans, but none of them would work."

"If something would work, I would have seen it when I looked into the future. But all I see is death," said Mrs. Grey as she dialed another number.

"But what if what she saw was the plan?" asked Marina, looking like she had come up with a plan.

"What do you mean?" Sloan said as she burst out of her bedroom.

"What if that is our plan?" Marina said, getting excited.

"Our plan is to be murdered? How is that going to help?" Mr. Day said.

"Not exactly. What I'm thinking is we let them think that we are dead. Pull a Juliet. Make them think we have all died."

"Juliet? Like from Romeo and Juliet?" asked Nick with a

confused look on his face. He was convinced that Marina had snapped under the pressure.

Marina rolled her eyes and whispered, "So you *did* read it. I'm so proud of you!" to Nick.

"Can we make a potion to do this?" Sloan asked Mr. Smith, clearly skeptical, but still trying to have some hope.

"I think it's possible. It might take me a while to figure out the right combination, but yeah," he answered as he grabbed a paper off of Sloan's desk and started writing.

"But how would we do this?" Sloan asked them.

"Eric could help. Next time he comes, we'll tell him of our plan. He can inform the Shadow Reapers of our fake death. They will surely come to see. Once it's assured that our death is true, we start working on saving Eric."

"It is not really rational or practical, but it seems possible. We will need to gather some outside reinforcements. I will ask any of the remaining Seniors and teachers if they want to volunteer, and see if there is any way that the potion will protect us from fire, just in case they try anything. I also must warn the others. If they're after us, then surely, they are after all of the schools." Sloan said with foreboding.

"Wait—there are *other* schools?" Catlin asked, confused.

Sloan took a deep breath. "Did you honestly think we were the only ones? You *were* supposed to learn this, later in the year, but there are schools in every country. And they are all just like us; hidden from the world. They just are not as involved as we are in this war."

Around four in the morning, the group came down the stairs. Sloan and the teachers took their places at the head table, while the kids walked to their seats, noticing just how scared and worried everyone was. Some of the parents had arrived and were sitting with their kids. Others were huddled in groups. A couple more students came down the stairs and laid their luggage with the others by the fireplaces, preparing for their tree journeys to areas further away. Sloan waited until everyone was accounted for before she began to announce the plan.

After she had outlined the plan, she added, "After we fake the deaths, I will need any Seniors and teachers that are willing to stay and help. Everyone else is free to leave."

As soon as she finished, most of the Seniors raised their

hands to volunteer. This made tears well up in Sloan's eyes. She dismissed the volunteers to bed.

Chapter 24

A few days later, all of the potions were made. Now, they were waiting for Eric to show up. Marina had a vision of him coming, but the only clue she had of the date was a fourteenth. During the wait for Eric, those who were involved in the rescue mission were practicing their DASR skills and trying to improve them as fast as possible.

On the fourteenth of July, a thunderstorm was approaching the school. Catlin and Marina both were sitting in the main hall hoping Eric would arrive, today. If not, volunteers would start to be sent home, tomorrow. It was near 9:00 in the morning, and the wind was picking up. Rain started to hit the windowpanes, and it was getting darker, outside.

Marina was walking around the room, kicking her soccer ball and trying to stay calm as she talked to Catlin, trying to come up with a plan to rescue Eric. From the corner of her eye, she saw something move. She turned to see a vague outline of a body on the floor and pulled Catlin along to it as quickly as they could.

"Eric, I know you don't have much time, so we are going to say this as fast as we can." Marina said to the transparent outline of Eric's body.

"You have to tell the Shadow Reapers that their plan worked; that we are all dead."

His pale face looked confused, and he tried to talk but was too weak. Marina got up and ran to the stairs. Catlin stayed with him and reassured him. "Don't worry, everything will be fine."

His figure was beginning to fade away when Catlin moved her hand to his face to comfort him. Before he faded away, she whispered, "I love you."

By 9:30, Sloan had gathered everyone into the main hall. She was wearing a sage green, full-length dress. The ghosts were standing against the walls with glass cups full of blue liquid on their trays. Sloan explained how the potion would work and how long it would last. She then instructed the ghost to hand them out. After waiting for all of the cups to be passed out, she straightened her back with courage and said, "I guess this will be the last time I say this." She paused while a few tears dropped from her eyes. "Let us eat and be merry."

She raised her glass, and so did the rest of the students. She waited a few minutes, taking in the moment, and then, drank the potion. Before drinking theirs, a few people said, "Bottoms up," to try to lighten the mood.

"Tell Elizabeth I have a message for her." Eric said to the guards outside his cell. When they didn't listen, he got up on his knees and crawled over to the cell door.

"Did you not hear me? I said I have a message for Elizabeth. It's from Sloan Marlin." The guards looked at him. One of them asked, "What is it regarding?"

"Your spy."

At this, the guards took off to get Elizabeth. Within a few minutes, they arrived again with Elizabeth.

"How did you get in contact with them?" Elizabeth asked.

"I have been in contact with them from the beginning. I have the power of Astral Projection and Telepathy, dumbass."

"How? I cast a spell on you to stop that!" she yelled at him, getting frustrated.

"I'm powerful. More powerful than your whole army."

Elizabeth's hands shot through the cell door window and around his neck. Slowly, flames started coming from her hands, licking at Eric's exposed flesh. He started screaming.

"Tell me the message!" she yelled as she let go of his neck.

"I don't know why you're mad! Your plan worked! They are dead, but with your success comes a downfall. Your spy died with them."

"Collateral damage," Elizabeth said with a smile before she walked away. "Go see if what he says is true. And make sure to bring backup, in case it's a trap," she said to one of the guys that came with her.

Within an hour, Eric was taken out of his cell, tied up, and blind folded. He was guided down hallways and up stairs to Elizabeth's cold and dimly lit office. Someone ripped the blindfold off of Eric's face. A small team of bodyguards stood with them in the large office that was in the top of the building. Hanging balls of fire were near the black, marble ceiling. The metal chains they had around Eric's ankles scraped the grey, marble floors as he walked, reminding him of so many horror flicks that he had seen, seemingly years ago. The only things that were in the office were a large desk, a chair, a bookshelf, and a large mirror on the side of the wall.

Elizabeth stood in front of the mirror and waved her hand across it. The glass turned black, and then, Eric saw a group of Shadow Reapers in the mirror. Elizabeth was talking to them in hushed tones, and when she was finished talking, the Shadow Reapers walked away. Elizabeth started to walk into the mirror, and a few minutes later, she came back and sat down at her desk.

"My dearest Eric. Sorry about the mess. I'm having this place renovated since I am the Empress of the world. And since your message turned out to be true, you have the honor of going with me to burn the bodies." Elizabeth said as Eric collapsed from the weight of the chains and hit his head on a cold, wood floor.

He lifted his head and realized that they were now in the main hall at Aviance. Eric looked at where he had come from, and what he saw was a small, dark shadow in the corner. As he stood back up, he saw several people just lying on the ground, and the scent of gasoline hit his nose. They weren't moving, at all. Tears started to stream down Eric's dirt and blood-covered face. Elizabeth came through the hole, next, and her bodyguards followed.

"You can do the honors of burning the first body, Eric." Elizabeth said.

Eric just stood there looking at the bodies.

"Go ahead, now. Burn them!" she cruelly yelled at him.

When he did nothing, she raised her arm and shot a fireball to where Sloan's body was. As soon as her body caught on fire, it spread to the surrounding areas.

"Now that they're finished, for good, let's move on to the other schools."

"There are other schools?" Eric asked.

"You didn't honestly think that you were the only ones, did

you? There are several other schools throughout the world. And soon, they will be mine. After the schools are gone, I'll take down the governments."

"And then, what will you do? The world will be yours. There's nothing more for you to take over."

"You silly boy. I never realized you were so dumb. You honestly think that's what I'm trying to achieve?"

"Then, what is your plan?" Eric asked just before he was pushed back into the hole.

"You'll see if I decide to keep you alive that long," she said with a sly face.

"What does it involve?"

"Destruction."

Elizabeth didn't say anything else to him. All she did was smile at him.

"Before we move on to the next school, I want to be sure that we have the reinforcements that we need. I don't know what awaits us, there."

Chapter 25

Soon after the Shadow Reapers left, the potions wore off, and the fires were extinguished. After they were sure they weren't coming back, Sloan put a plan into action.

"After you leave here, you cannot do magic under *any* circumstances. In a little while, after you pack, we will be using a charm that will change your identities. Once you have your new identities, you need to leave, and leave fast. This spell only changes how you look and sound to Numes and Shadow Reapers. To White Knights, you are the same. For those who choose to stay and fight, we will be using a different charm that I will explain at a later time."

Sloan began to walk down when someone yelled, "What's going to happen to the school?"

Sloan looked back at the crowd and said, "I am afraid that Aviance will be closed, for good." She then walked away before any of the students could see the tears running down her face. Catlin, Marina, and Nick all followed Sloan up to her office.

"What's the plan?" Marina asked when they arrived.

"We attack them, obviously," Nick said, sitting down on a couch.

"But we can't just charge in there. We'll get killed, instantly," Catlin said as she nervously played with her hair.

Sloan sat down at her desk and laid her head in her hands.

"I honestly do not know what we are going to do. I should have known that something was up from the very beginning. Vesta seemed too easy to get rid of, last year. None of this would have happened if I'd realized something bigger was going on under the surface," Sloan said to them.

"You can't blame yourself, Sloan. No one saw it coming. Eric thought that Elizabeth was good. After all, she did warn us about their first attack," Catlin said, trying to comfort her.

"But that fight was not the real one. It was a trick to make us think that they were gone. None of us were expecting another fight from them."

"Do you think what Eric said was true? That Elizabeth is now the ruler of the Shadow Reapers?" Nick asked after a few minutes of silence.

"Anything seems possible, anymore, but they have a monarchy. If she is now the ruler, then she had to be the daughter of Vesta," Sloan informed them.

Sloan raised her head and had a surprised look on her face.

"Of course. It all makes sense, now. Elizabeth must be somehow related to Vesta. When Vesta was killed, he kept saying *Do it. Kill me.* He wanted to be killed, so that Elizabeth could take over."

"But how?" Marina said, confused.

"You guys told me Eric was having dreams last year, right?"

"Yeah."

"Dreams of Elizabeth?" Sloan asked to make sure her facts were right.

"Yes," Marina and Catlin said, together.

"What if Vesta used Elizabeth as bait. She was used to get Eric to trust her. If Eric trusted her, then he would listen to her, which is what happened. He trusted her and told us about the first fight. Maybe, once Vesta knew we were ready for his attack, he knew it was time for him to go.

"Once he was dead, Elizabeth took over. She returned to Eric in his dreams a few more times to reinforce that trust." Sloan paused for a few moments, and then, asked, "What exactly happened, last year, in the final battle?" Sloan asked them.

"Eric got a text from Elizabeth," Catlin told her.

"How do you know?" Sloan asked.

"I was with him. The message said something about her needing his help. I told him not to go, but he did, anyway. He disappeared for a few hours, but then, we found him in the woods, and he was fine."

"But he was not fine. We now know that Eric wasn't him. Elizabeth had gained Eric's trust. If she needed his help, he would have gone to her and helped her. And when he went to her, she captured him. I am sure that is what happened, last year."

"It did seem like right after Eric disappeared, the fight

ended," Nick said.

"That's because they got what they came for," Sloan said, chiming in.

"But how is knowing this going to help us get Eric back?" Catlin asked.

"I do not know, yet, but we figured out just what is going on," Sloan said with a defeated and scared look on her face.

"But we don't know what they are planning to do with him."

"I do. They want his powers. He is the only one with the powers of both sides. His blood is the key to them having our powers, along with theirs. And if they find that out, it is going to make it that much harder to fight them," Sloan said with a haunted look on her face.

"Why couldn't they take anyone else?" Catlin asked.

"If they put our blood in theirs, it would take away their power."

"So we have to figure out a plan before their whole army has our powers," Marina said, looking scared as she held Nick's hand tightly.

"But as Catlin said, we cannot just barge in and take him. That would be a suicide mission," Sloan said as she looked out the window.

Chapter 26

By 4:00, most of the students had gone with the exception of those who still needed a new identity, and those who chose to stay and fight were sitting in the main hall, waiting to hear Sloan's instructions. Even though most of the students left, the room was filled with not only students but with other volunteers from Hillthrope and other communities, and when Sloan came down with Catlin, Marina, and Nick, she began to cry at the sight of the people who were willing to risk their lives to save the magical communities.

Catlin, Marina, and Nick were going to go sit down with the others when Sloan said to them, "You helped me figure this entire plan out, so you can help tell these people what they are about to do."

They were shocked at what Sloan had just told them. They walked with Sloan up to the teachers' table and sat down next to her chair. Sloan continued to stand and told everyone what had happened to Eric. She told them about what the Shadow Reapers planned to do with his blood, and how they had captured him.

When Sloan was done talking, she gestured to Nick, Marina, and Catlin and then said, "These three students helped me figure all of this out, and they helped me form a plan. They are here to explain exactly what we have decided to do."

Sloan sat down, and the three of them stood up.

"Since we know how they tricked us with the fake Eric, we figured we would do the same," Catlin said, stumbling a little on the words.

"What she means is, we transform ourselves to look like Shadow Reapers," Marina said to the crowd.

At that, Nick took over. "Once we do that, we can sneak into their hideout, hopefully without getting noticed. Eric has told us about some of the things we need to know. He is at the bottom floor of the building, but he doesn't know just how many floors there are.

"Sloan, Marina, Catlin, and myself will be the ones who go for Eric. The rest of you guys are lookouts and scouts. We need you to search the building and find out any useful information you can about what they are planning. We also need you to make sure no one catches on to what we are doing. Mr. Smith has come up with a potion that will act like a teleporter. If you get into any problems, throw it on the ground and you will be teleported back here. Are there any questions," Nick said, looking them in the eyes.

"How are we going to transform into them?" Someone asked them.

Sloan got back up and answered the question, "With the same charm they used. It is a charm that we do not teach, but we are very aware of. Mr. Chine and myself will place the charm on you. The charm lasts until someone takes it off of you. The only thing it will not do is give you their clothing. But the owners of Phoenix Clothing Store has provided us clothes that match their uniforms."

Sloan waited for any more questions, and when there were none, she asked one more question. "Is there anyone who would like to take back their offer and leave?"

When no one left, she continued once more by saying, "Then, let us begin."

Right away, Sloan stepped down and joined Mr. Chine. She asked for people to line up in front of Mr. Chine or herself, so that they could put the charm on them.

When the line formed, they went to work. They pulled out their wands and said, "Transformantes in Umbra Messor."

As the three of them waited in line, Nick said, "This is the first time that playing video games has ever come in handy."

"You play *Minecraft*. That's not very much of a strategy game," Catlin said as she rolled her eyes.

"I play a little *Call of Duty*."

Marina made a funny face at them, and Nick asked, "What's wrong?"

"I want to run. I am too stressed to be in one spot," she said as she jogged in place.

As they waited in line, Nick saw something out of the corner of his eye.

"Eric!" Nick said, jumping out of line and running toward

him.

"Nick, I don't have long. I have managed to give you a little help once you're inside. Take this and give it to Sloan," Eric said in a very weak voice as he handed Nick a piece of paper.

Before Nick could ask about the extra help, Eric had faded away. Catlin and Marina were next in line when Nick ran back into the line.

"What did he want?" Sloan asked before casting the spell on Catlin.

"He said that once we are inside, he has provided us with some extra help. He didn't say what kind of help, though, and he also gave me this paper to give to you," he said, handing it over.

Sloan took the paper and looked at it. She looked confused for a while, then said, "That clever boy. He has given us a way to use their shadow portals."

"How could he have done that?" Marina asked as Mr. Chine transformed her.

Sloan looked at her and said, "His father."

Chapter 27

O nce everyone was transformed to look like a Shadow Reaper, the proper clothes were distributed. It was nearing dusk as everyone gathered in the main hall with pale faces and black clothes.

"Now, I know it's getting late, but if we are going to do this, then we need to do it soon. Before I say the spell that will activate the shadow portal, you will have a few minutes to have a bite to eat and drink," Sloan said.

On cue, the ghosts came out of the wall with their silver trays and handed out turkey sandwiches, bags of chips, and some bottles of water.

"I miss him," Catlin said, looking out the window.

"Eric?" Marina asked as she finished off her sandwich.

"Yeah."

"We all do." Nick tried to comfort her.

"I know, but I liked him," Catlin said as she fiddled with her empty chip bag that she held with her extremely pale hands.

"I thought you liked Keith?" Nick asked.

"I did, but not like I do Eric. I knew it, last year, but I never told him. I didn't know when it would be appropriate."

"He liked you back," Marina said, looking at her.

"How do you know?" Catlin asked.

"He told me, last year, but he didn't know if he could let go of Elizabeth."

"I'm pretty sure she's moved on, by now," Nick said, trying to make them laugh. The joke fell flat, though. No one was in the mood.

"Yeah, but I wish I could have done something to let him know. Instead, we just cut him off."

"But we did that because of the vision I had, remember?" Marina asked.

"Yeah, which sort of came true, this year. He *was* caught smoking pot," Nick added.

"But that wasn't him, and we should have known that. After all, we were his friends!" Catlin said as a tear escaped her eye.

"You must really like him," Nick said to her.

"I do," She answered.

"Then, tell him," Marina said as she tried to comfort Catlin.

"I will, if he's still alive by the time we get to him."

"You can't be like that. You have to stay optimistic. He's going to be fine; he's smart and a strong fighter," Nick said to her.

"You guys have seen him, lately. His apparitions are weaker than they've ever been. And from what details we can see, he looks bad."

"That is way we are attacking, now," Sloan said, interrupting their conversation.

"Five... Four... Three... Two... One... Thanks for getting quiet. In just a few seconds, I will be opening the portal. As soon as it's opened, we need to rush in as quickly as we can. I have no idea how long the portal stays open. Once we are in, we need to move swiftly. If we move too fast, however, we might blow our cover. Too slowly, and we might miss our chance of finding out their secret. And don't forget to use the potions if you get into any trouble. I do not want to lose anymore individuals than we already have." Sloan walked across the main hall to the mirror that Marina, Nick, and Catlin recognized from Sloan's office.

When she was directly in front of it, they could see her shiver at her reflection. Pulled out her shiny, golden wand from her inside blazer pocket, she said, "Aperi umbra ostium," as she waved her wand in front of the mirror.

Dark clouds started to form in the corners. They started to spread across the mirror, and as the clouds started to reach the center, they swirled together. Everyone stayed as still as they could as they watched a black vortex form. When the mirror was all black, the vortex calmed down, and the mirror revealed a black-stained wooden wall.

A small sound came from the wall that sounded like people walking. Sloan waited for the sound to pass before she stepped into the mirror. When she was in, she looked to make sure it was clear, and then, she motioned for the others to come along.

Everyone got up and formed a two-person line in front of

the mirror. Catlin, Marina, and Nick where one of the first ones to enter, and when they stepped through the mirror, they realized the portal had opened up into a hallway that seemed to go on for a long ways. The hallway was dimly light by pots of fire hanging from the ceiling and had a long, crimson red rug on the floor.

When everyone was through, Sloan told them to break into their teams and start their jobs. A group of ten people started to walk down the hallway one way, and Sloan guided her group down the hall the other way. Marina was nervously sweating, hoping that nothing would go wrong. Catlin was gripping the escape potion so hard that she thought it might break in her hands. And Nick was making sure they weren't being followed.

It took them a while, but they reached the end of the hall where there were two sets of stairs. A thick, glass door blocked off the stairs that were leading up.

"Those must lead to Elizabeth." Nick quietly said to them.

"How do you figure?" Sloan asked him as they headed down the stairs.

"Something important must be up there if they have it blocked off, like that."

The next floor looked exactly like the last, except for the blocked off staircase. As they walked down the hall, they heard footsteps, and then, they saw a group of kids walking toward them, carrying books.

"You guys are going to be late for class," one of the girls said to them.

As that group walked up the stairs, Sloan, Marina, Catlin, and Nick all breathed a sigh of relief and continued walking down the hallway to the stairs leading downwards. As they passed by the solid, metal doors, they glanced through windows, seeing classrooms that were packed with students.

When they reached the next floor and saw that the classrooms were still packed, they realized how outnumbered they were. It wouldn't matter if they had everyone from the communities and the school; they still would be overwhelmed by greater numbers.

Chills went down their spines as the feeling of being out numbered sank in, but they continued on. As they walked down the stairs, again, the layout of the floor changed. Two rooms that were marked dorms took up most of the floor. Two other smaller rooms were by the stairs that were marked bathrooms. This layout continued for three more floors.

Still, the feeling of being greatly outnumbered haunted them. Catlin was getting shaky and tried to calm herself down but couldn't manage to slow her breathing down. As they were reaching the staircase, someone grabbed her shoulder, making her almost cry out in shock.

"We need someone's help," said Mr. Day.

Fear lit up on their eyes as they turned around.

"It's okay, we're safe. Our team ran into some trouble. We think we are on a lead to something, but we are being questioned."

"I need to keep these three safe. I cannot help, but Catlin can." Sloan said.

She looked at Catlin who was beginning to protest and said, "I've seen your grade in Astral Projection. You are doing very well. I believe that you can help us and them, both."

Chapter 28

Sloan, Nick, Catlin, and Marina had finally reached what they assumed to be the main floor. The room was ten times as big as what Aviance's was. There was a large, glass table between the two stairs with only one chair at it. The rest of the room was full of dark wooded tables and chairs in rows of five. Large torches on the black marble walls lit up the cavernous room.

As they walked through, they noticed there were no more stairs. They knew Eric was on the lowest level, but this was not it. They didn't want to stand still too long; otherwise, they would be sitting ducks.

Just as they were about to go get the others, they heard a weak, quiet voice.

"We are here to help you," said a tall, thin, middle age woman who was translucent.

"Amelia? Amelia May?" Sloan asked the ghost.

She nodded and continued, "Eric told us you were coming. My husband is making sure it is clear, downstairs. Once he knows that it is all clear, he will open the door to the stairs."

Amelia walked over toward a corner of the room that was opposite of the stairs and waited for the others to follow. There was a design in the marble floor where she stood that was different from the rest. A circle with lines drawing near the center decorated it.

They waited for a few moments, watching Amelia's downcast eyes. Finally, she looked up at them. "Everything is clear, down there. Rory is going to open the stairs, but when he does, we will have to move fast. There's no telling how much time we'll have."

As she finished, the circle where Amelia was standing was collapsing to form a staircase to the level, below. As soon as it stopped moving, Sloan stepped forward and started down the stairs. This new area was dark, cold, and damp. The smell that greeted them made them nauseous.

It smelled like urine, fecal matter, and burned hamburger, mixed with a dead animal left on the side of the road. They all tried to hold their breath as the continued down the stairs to the lower level of the basement, but the acrid stench invaded their lungs and seeped through their pores. When the stairs ended, a very tall and skinny man, who was also translucent, greeted them.

"Hello, my name is Rory James, Eric's father. Now come, follow me. And whatever you do, try to ignore the people around you," he said to the group as he guided them down a long corridor.

It was dimly lit by torches and very cold. On the left side, there were cells full of bodies. Some were dead, and some were still alive. Every cell was as full as the last, and from each came cries for help.

This sight brought tears to Catlin's eyes. She wiped her face dry and held on tighter to Marina and Nick.

"What if we're too late? What if the damage is done? What if he dies?" Catlin whispered to them.

"We can't give up hope," Nick quickly said through gasps in his breathing.

They continued down the hall, but something changed on their right side. What used to be just a wall was now a floor to ceiling window that revealed a torture chamber. Marina turned her head to look in, and when she did, she gasped and buried her head into Catlin's shoulder.

What she saw in that room would scar her for life. There was a single metal table in the middle, surrounded by cabinets that had surgical supplies on it. The light above the metal table was still on, focused on the limp body that was covered in blood. A couple of flies flew around the head of the body that had obviously been dead for a while.

They had reached the far corner of the room, but before they got to the far cells, Rory had stopped them.

"You need to prepare yourselves for what you are about to see. He is in an extremely bad state. I know that you have seen him, before, but this does not compare to his apparitions. During the last few days, it's taken a turn for the worse," Rory said in a quick, but calm manner.

Tears started to form in Catlin's eyes, again. When Rory was finished talking, he continued to walk down the hallway. They reached the corner and looked into a cell that looked empty. At closer inspection, they noticed something in the dark corner. The door to the cell had three bulky, metal locks that Sloan said took three different spells to unlock.

Sloan walked to the door, pulled her wand out of her blazer pocket, pointed it at the first look, and whispered, "Reserare hoc pessulus." The lock opened and fell to the floor, making a loud crashing sound.

Everyone looked around to make sure no one had noticed. When the coast was clear, Sloan continued. She lowered her wand to the second lock and said, "Hunc dimittis crinem." Again, the heavy lock fell to the ground.

Sloan quickly continued, in fear that they might be caught, soon. She lowered her wand to the last lock and said, "Aperire hoc capillo atque hanc ex homine." The last lock fell off, and the door opened. But as soon as it did, they heard someone coming down the hall.

Catlin slipped into the dark cell, while the others turned around to cover her. The corner cradled a pale body in ragged and torn clothes. Dirt and dried blood covered most of Eric's body. Dirty bandages were held poorly in place where jagged and seeping wounds were. Catlin placed two fingers on his neck to check for a pulse. When she touched him, Eric's eyes shot open as he flinched and opened his mouth to try to scream. All that came out was a soft, muffled sound.

There was a pulse, but it was very weak. If they wanted to get him out, alive, they were going to have to do it fast. Just as things were going smoothly, the cell door shut behind her.

"Now, you didn't think I would miss the big rescue party, did you? After all, I love a good party," said a cold, dark voice from behind her.

Catlin quickly pulled out a weak healing potion from her pocket and poured it into Eric's mouth. She picked him up and whispered, "Come on, Eric, we need you. Please drink it."

Catlin turned around to face the door. Sloan, Nick, and Marina were standing where they were, before, but they were not moving. Amelia and Rory had vanished. There, before Catlin, stood a girl in a tight black dress with a very pale complexion and fiery red hair that was flowing down over her shoulders.

"I don't think we've had the pleasure of meeting. I'm Elizabeth Williams, Eric's girlfriend. And you are?"

"What did you do to my friends?" Catlin angry screamed at her.

"I froze them with my new Molecular Immobilization power. Isn't it neat? I have all different sorts of powers, thanks to my boyfriend."

Catlin sat Eric back on the floor and fiddled with her wand that was in her hand. Elizabeth noticed it and said, "What are you going to do, put me to sleep? After all, you are no threat to me."

"We'll see about that. There's one thing you don't know; that I'm best friends with Eric, and best friends share everything, even spells that we shouldn't be learning in school. That is why I should be a threat to you."

Catlin raised her wand above her head and swiftly swung it toward Elizabeth while yelling, "Augue."

A large, blue fireball came soaring out of the tip of the wand. It went straight through the bars of the cell door and hit Elizabeth straight in the face. Within seconds, her whole body caught on fire, and when she lost her concentration, Sloan, Nick, and Marina were unfrozen.

Sloan, Nick, and Marina quickly threw the transportation potions on the ground. Catlin got down on her knees and held onto Eric's hand. She pulled out her own potion and was ready to throw it on the ground when she got hit in the chest by a fireball.

"Bitch!" Elizabeth, who had been extinguished by a guard, screamed as she stood there, watching Catlin's body being covered up with flames.

Eric woke up, realizing what had happened, and started to scream. He took a hold of Catlin's hand.

"I love you," He weakly whispered to her.

She nodded and looked at the potion that was in her other hand. Eric grabbed it from her hand, kissed her, and then threw it on the ground. As soon as it hit the wall, it broke, and Eric was transported back to Aviance.

Chapter 29

Sloan and a few other teachers rushed over to Eric as they saw him appear. He was lying on the cold, wooden ground, staring up at the burnt ceiling with tears running down his face. He could see that they were talking, but he couldn't hear what they were saying. All he could hear was Catlin's scream when she first got hit.

Eric blinked and realized he was now in a new room; a room that he didn't recognize, before. It was very bright and very warm, something that he wasn't used to and had wanted for what seemed like an eternity. People wearing green masks over their mouths and green caps on their heads stood over Eric.

They were still trying to talk to him, but this time, he chose not to listen, for he didn't care what they were saying. A person that was to the right of his head placed a plastic mask over his mouth that produced a sweet smelling air. His eyelids got heavy, and as he shut them, a tear fell from his left eye.

When he awoke, his throat hurt, his head felt full, and he was in a new room. It was smaller than the last, and from what he could tell, it seemed to be a patient room in a hospital. He looked down at his arms and saw an IV tube running from one hand. Two, large white bandages on his arms covered the large wounds that had been inflicted. He could hear the beeping of the machines that were behind him, measuring his pulse. The room smelled like rubbing alcohol and the cleaning solution that Eric's mom would use in the kitchen.

Out of the small, narrow window in the door, Eric could see someone pass by. He tried to cry out, but his throat was too sore. His head was a little clearer, now, and he tried to remember what had happened. A sob choked him, because the last thing he remembered was seeing Catlin being burned.

He searched around the room, trying to get any clue of where he was. There was a window on the wall behind him, but it was fogged up due to the humidity, outside. There was a call button that hung at the end of his bed, and Eric tried to grab it, but his IV line wouldn't let him bend that far.

That was when he noticed the hospital wristband around his right wrist. There was something strange about it, though; his name was down as Jonathan Seth O'Conner. He read farther and found out that he was in Boone Hospital Center.

Someone knocked on his door, and before he could do anything, the door opened. Eric was shocked, but happy, to see Sloan walk in. She gave Eric a warm and kind smile as she walked in and sat down in a chair that was near the left side of his bed. She reached across to Eric and grabbed his hand, holding it loosely, so as not to bump his IV needle. The greatest thing about it was that she held it like a mom caring for a sick child. It warmed Eric's heart.

"Hello, Eric. I am glad to see you're awake. You were come and go for a while, there. You had an infection from all of the cuts that were left open. Now, I know you are very confused, right now, but all that's important is that you are okay."

Eric looked at his wristband, and then at Sloan with a puzzled expression. He tried to voice a question, but his vocal cords were so dry that it was futile.

Sloan's eyes crinkled up in a smile as she patted him. "You do realize that I can read your mind, right?"

"We had to lie about your name. For now, that is your new identity. If we used your real name, Elizabeth would have found you, and we cannot lose you, again. I have talked to your doctor, and you will be discharged in a few days if everything continues to go the way it has been, today."

Eric wanted to ask about Catlin, but he was afraid about what he might hear, so he didn't bring it up. Instead, he turned on the TV and started to watch it. The only channel that he could get was a local new channel.

"Welcome to the news at five. My name is Jessica Robbins, and this is day five after the assassination of our president and the destruction of the East coast."

Eric's eyes widened in fear, and his pulse began to race, which showed up on the monitor. He started to breathe heavily as he tried to scream.

"Eric," Sloan said to him, trying to calm him down. "Please, stay still. We are in no danger, here. Like I said, before, things will be explained later when we are in a private place. But yes, this is Elizabeth's doing."

Eric looked back to the TV where there was now footage of a helicopter flying over a blacked and crumbled city that used to be Washington D.C.

PART 3
THE END

Chapter 1

"*Here you are. Chef Salad for the lady. Rib-eye steak, medium with a side of fries, for the gentleman," said the young, vibrant waitress as she set plates of food in front of Elizabeth and Eric.*

It was April twenty-third, Eric's birthday. Elizabeth had taken him out to one of the fancier restaurants in Dear Knoll. **Kellie's Restaurant and Bar.** *It was a cold evening for the end of April, but the restaurant was nice and warm.*

It was small and family owned, but it was nice looking. It had an old, rustic country feel to it. The tables were covered in red and white plaid sheets. Old, rusty farm equipment hung on the white walls. Old, wooden wagon wheels that were hung from the ceiling had lights strung on them. A local country radio station was playing an old song that Eric recognized from his childhood.

"Are you ready for the pre-calculus test, tomorrow?" Eric asked.

"What do you think? I've missed most of the chapter, because I was sick!" she responded after taking a drink of her lemonade.

"Well, after we are done here, you could come back home with me and study," he suggested shyly.

"I have other things planned for us after this," she replied with a devilish smile.

"Don't make it too late; it is a school night!"

"Don't worry. We're just going to go see a movie."

"What movie?" he asked, taking a bite of his steak.

"You'll have to wait and see!" she said, taking one of his fries with a wink.

They sat, finishing their dinner, and when they were done, Elizabeth paid the bill.

"You really don't have to do this," Eric said as they were paying.

"It's your birthday. I will pay. You always pay!" she responded, giving him a quick kiss on the lips.

As they walked out and to Elizabeth's beaten up Chevrolet, she whispered a soft but insistent, "I love you!"

"I love you, too! Don't you ever forget it," he said, pulling her toward him.

They got into the car and started to drive to the movie theater that was in the town over: Greenwood.

"Please don't get us pulled over. Remember that you shouldn't be driving anyone, yet."

"We'll be fine. I'm a good driver," Elizabeth said as she pulled out of the parking lot.

It was reaching eight o'clock when they got to the theaters. It was a huge building attached to an even bigger mall. Elizabeth parked the car, and they started walking to the main door of the building.

"If you love me so much, why don't you save me?"

"What?" Eric asked, confused.

"I didn't say anything, silly!"

"Yeah, you did. You asked me why I'm not saving you."

Eric stopped in his tracks and pulled Elizabeth in his direction.

"We're going to miss the beginning of the movie if we don't hurry up!" she giggled.

"What do you mean? Save you?" Eric asked, getting a little frustrated.

Elizabeth stared deeply into Eric's eyes, looking concerned. She was about to say something, but suddenly her face went from being sun-touched bronze to being snow pale. Her eyes, once grey, turned into black holes.

"You didn't save me in time. The time has come, Eric. You have been told what to do, and you didn't do it. There is only one way to stop this, now."

"Elizabeth, what are you talking about? What on Earth is going on?" Eric asked, very scared and confused.

Suddenly, the air got extremely warm, and the wind picked up. Car alarms started to blare, and the town tornado sirens went off. Over in the distance behind Elizabeth, Eric could see a small twister. It was small, but he could see the damage that was being done by it.

Eric started to panic as the twister headed toward them, wrecking the town as it moved. With cat-like reflexes, he grabbed Elizabeth's wrist and tried to run to the theater for shelter, but when he grabbed her wrist, his hand went right through it.

"I'm sorry, Eric. I really am. Remember that I love you," she said softly, barely heard over the sirens.

Chapter 2

Eric's head hit the car window, waking him up. He was confused of where he was at, but then, the memories of the last few months flooded his head. He was in Sloan's new, red Dodge Avenger, driving up the bumpy stone driveway to their new house, which was also being used to house students and teach them.

After Eric had been discharged from the hospital in August, they moved several times trying to hide from Elizabeth. Sloan, Eric, and the others that had chosen to stay with them to fight, had changed their identities a countless number of times since they left the hospital. The White Knight army split up into ten groups over the United States. Each group had around fifty students and volunteers from the communities.

Currently, Eric was known as Aaron Clay Greene. Sloan was known as Martha Alice Greene. Their home was located a few miles outside of the town of Republic, Missouri. It was a large, two-story house that was on seven acres of farmland. The house was perfect for housing the fifty students and the five teachers that Sloan had chosen to come with her.

Eric shivered in fear as he thought more about his experiences, last year. He glanced down at the grey sleeves on his arms that were covering his scars from where Elizabeth had experimented on him. They had healed, along with the other injuries that he had, but these were the ones that bothered him the most, since the scars hadn't faded.

"Are you okay, Eric?" Sloan asked, pulling up to the garage.

Eric nodded his head in response as the car pulled to a stop.

"We have talked about this, Eric. Please, use your words."

"I am fine," he lied.

Eric hadn't talked since he was rescued. When he had to talk, he kept it short, even when they were questioning him about his experience with the Shadow Reapers. "Yes." "No." "I don't know." "Sure."

"Thank you. Can you please help me get the groceries out of the trunk?"

They got out of the car and walked to the trunk. Sloan opened it up and grabbed a few bags that were full of groceries. Eric grabbed four bags, two in each hand, and walked across the drive to the side door of the house.

The house very lavish, having six large, white pillars in the front and a large wooden front door that was painted black. Two windows were on either side of the door. It was a house straight out of the history books when they talked about plantations in the South.

The small glass-paneled door on the side of the house that Eric entered led into the enormous kitchen. The walls were a soft yellow, which complimented the white curtains and white granite counters that lined the walls. The white marble floor was still the original floor from when it had been built in the late 1800s.

Eric walked to the island in the middle of the kitchen and sat the bags on it. He made the trip to the car and to the kitchen a few more times before all of the groceries were out of the trunk. A few of the kids that were with them walked in from the living room that was attached and helped put them away.

Eric left them, walking through the large and bright dining room full of students. After entering a small, contemporary-themed library, he picked a book that he'd read a few years ago.

Eric quickly walked back into the dining room and to the glass, French doors that led to the large backyard. As he opened the door, the smell of freshly cut spring grass hit him, making him a bit homesick. The door opened up to an oak deck that stretched from one side of the house to the other side.

The deck was large and open, extending outwards twenty feet from the house. A metal table and chairs were to Eric's right, next to a grill, and a small fireplace that was surrounded by metal folding chairs was to his left as he walked down the stairs to the backyard.

He followed the serpentine dirt and stone path to a little flower garden that was behind the old, red barn on the property that they used for DASR class. The flower garden, which Eric took care of, was enclosed by a white picket fence that was weathering. Glass stepping stones, which Eric made by blasting sand with his firepower, led the way past the sunflowers, daisies, tulips, roses, lavender, and the small herb garden to the large peach tree that had grown.

Eric sat down on the ground, lying against the large tree, put his headphones in his ears, turned up the music to maximum volume, and opened the book. Since they moved into the house a few months ago, Eric found himself in this spot more than any other spot on the land. It was his, he took care of this spot with his hands, and it was the only spot that he could get peace and quiet in the busy house.

Eric was almost halfway through the book when he saw movement through the flowers. The feeling of being alone went from comfortable to scary in an instant. He ripped the headphones out of his ears, quietly laid the book down next to him, and pulled out his wand that Sloan had saved for him after the destruction of Aviance.

He swiftly got up on his feet and moved behind the tree for protection. With his right hand holding his wand, and his left holding a fireball, he seemed like he was ready for a fight, but inside he was freaking out with nervous sweat was forming on his forehead.

"Eric, are you back here? Don't be afraid, I brought food!" Marina said in a calm and quiet voice.

Eric extinguished the fireball, put his wand back in his pocket, and walked around the tree.

"You know to text before you come down here when I'm reading." Eric told her as he walked closer to her.

"I did. Check your phone. Anyways, Sloan told me you haven't eaten today, so I brought you this," she said, holding up a brown paper bag. "It's a turkey and cheese sandwich with some chips."

Eric sat back down, and Marina sat down next to him, placing the bag near him. Instead of reaching for the bag, he reached for his phone. He unlocked it, saw the text he missed from Marina, and turned off his music that was still playing.

"Eric, you have to start eating more. You've barely gained any weight back," Marina begged as she pulled out the sandwich and handed it to Eric.

Eric grabbed it, unwrapped it, and took a small bite out of it.

"Thank you!" Marina said with a smile.

It was true that Eric hadn't gain back much of the weight that he'd lost when he was being tortured. He had lost almost fifty pounds there, leaving him at ninety pounds of just skin and bones. In the last couple of months since he had gotten out of the hospital, he had gained back about fifteen pounds.

"Are you doing any better?" Marina asked curiously.

Eric shook his head and continued to eat his sandwich.

"You can talk to us, Eric. We are here for you," she said, placing her hand gently on Eric's arm.

Eric looked at her hand, which was right over the long scars, and pulled his arm away from her as memories of last year flooded his head.

"I'm sorry. I didn't realize that they still hurt."

"They don't. It's just that the memory is still so raw. I know it doesn't make sense, but yeah."

"I understand, Eric." Marina looked out into the backyard for a while before saying, "Hey, you should watch a movie with us, tonight. Maybe, it would cheer you up a little."

Eric thought about it, but then politely declined. "I'd rather just be alone."

"Okay. If you change your mind, movie starts at seven. I'll be making the popcorn, so you know that it will be good."

Marina got back up and left the garden, leaving Eric in peace for a while. He sat and read in the little flower garden for a few more hours. When his eyes got tired from reading, he lay down under the tree and looked up at the clear blue sky through the branches full of budding flowers.

He stayed like this until he could hear Sloan calling him in for dinner. He picked up his book, wrapped his headphones around his phone, and placed it in his pocket. He opened up the gate and walked back up to the house. In the distant fields of what would become wheat and cotton fields, Eric could hear the sound of the spring birds chirping.

The dining room was full of students and the five teachers that were with them: Mrs. Grey, Mr. Goodman, Mr. Smith, Mr. Baker, and Mrs. Baker. Mr. Baker was taking over Telepathy, while his wife was the new Astral Projection teacher. Five darkly stained wooden tables, which were placed in a 'u' shape, took up the open room. The deep red painted walls were bare, but still, the room felt warm.

Eric walked through the tables of people and went into the kitchen to help serve the food.

When Eric stepped in, Sloan nodded his way and said, "You know, this was so much easier when we had the help of the volunteers," meaning the ghosts.

"Eric, can you grab the mashed potatoes?" she asked.

Eric walked over to the large, silver Dutch oven full of Sloan's fluffy, homemade mashed potatoes that was on the stove. He turned the stove off, picked up a towel to cover the hot handles, and carried it back out into the dining room.

"I haven't seen you all day! Where have you been?" Catlin asked, catching up with Eric while carrying a basket of dinner rolls and a tub of butter.

"Yeah, sorry. I went in town with Sloan, and then, I was in the garden."

"Hey, are we okay?" she asked as she set her basket on one of the tables.

"Yes, we are fine."

Eric smiled at her, sat the mashed potatoes down, and took his seat next to her.

"Do you want to take a walk after dinner? Just around the backyard?"

"Sure."

Chapter 3

It was reaching eight o'clock. Eric was outside, leaning against the fence on the porch deck, looking out over the backyard. The doors opened up behind him, and a few seconds later, Catlin had joined him.

Her long blond hair from last year had been cut to her shoulders and dyed a light brown. Her face had a tiny scar that she got from the battle last year on her forehead, which she hid with her bangs. Her hands, which were near Eric's, were pale and thin.

A few months ago, when they thought that Eric was strong enough to hear it, Sloan, Nick, Marina, and Catlin told him what all had happened. Eric remembered Catlin's death, but that was all.

The Catlin that died saving Eric was an Astral Projection, and when she had died, the original Catlin had felt that. Catlin was with another group helping them find any important information, but when her Astral Projection died, she felt that pain. She started screaming in pain, which called attention to the group. Shadow Reapers came, throwing fireballs and potions. Before Catlin had time to throw her own potion, she was hit by falling glass.

"Do you like my new outfit?" she asked, twirling around. She had on new dark brown khaki shorts and an aqua-blue t-shirt.

Eric nodded and continued to look out into the yard.

"How are you not burning up in that?" she asked, pointing to the grey hoodie he had on.

"It covers up the scars."

Catlin grabbed his arm and pulled him down the stairs into the empty back yard.

"I know I've told you before, but those are battle scars. They make you a hero."

They walked a while toward the fields in silence before Eric

232

said, "I'm no hero. These are scars of failure. That's all I am. I'm the one to blame for all of this," he said, gesturing to the house that was behind them.

Catlin noticed the tears that where beginning to form in his eyes and stopped walking.

"Do you know what I noticed about you the first time I met you?" she asked, looking him square in the eyes.

He shook his head, so she continued, "It wasn't your cute, messy hair, the sad and depressed look you had on, or your cute butt." At that comment, Eric's eyes widened, and he blushed. "It was your deep, green eyes. Those eyes were so full of hope, full of kindness, and full of love. I miss those eyes."

"That was two years ago. A lot has changed in those years," he said, turning away from her.

"Eric, I love you, and I know you love me. So, please let me help you," she said softly.

Catlin grabbed his shoulder softly, wrapped her hands around his neck, and leaned in for a kiss. As soon as Eric understood what she was doing, he pushed her away.

"I don't want to get you hurt."

"But that's what love is. It hurts. Every second without you hurts, and every second with you hurts, but it's a good hurt."

Eric turned around and smiled a little. He walked over to her, looking into her light blue eyes, and kissed her lightly. A few seconds later, they parted and continued to walk, holding hands along the way.

"Are you ready for school to start?" Eric asked, changing the subject.

"Not really, but you'll help me, right?"

"Yeah."

This year, there was no grading system. Everyone was getting taught the same thing at the same level. Sloan said that if students needed extra help, she would offer it, but there was no time for teaching the basics, anymore.

"Have you heard anything from your dad or Jamie, recently?"

She shook her head, saying, "I haven't heard anything since January."

"Don't get discouraged. It could mean that they are being safe, hiding from Elizabeth and the Shadow Reapers."

"Or that they've been killed."

"You can't think that way. You have to be optimistic," he said with a smile.

"Why? You never do," she said, coldly.

"That's different. My whole family is dead. I have no reason for hope."

"But you have Sloan, me, and everyone else in that house. We all care about you. That should give you hope."

"Then why doesn't it you?"

She stopped, leaned against the old wooden fence, and looked up at the stars.

"Right now, I'm alone. I only have you and a few friends. And that scares me. If my dad is dead, who am I going to live with? What's going to happen to me? The future seems dark, and it scares me."

Eric squeezed her hand a little tighter. "I know exactly how you feel."

They walked along the property line in silence for a while until Catlin asked, "How are you? No lies."

"It gets better every day. The depression is what hurts the most, though."

"On a scale from one to ten, ten being the worst pain ever, how is it?"

Eric paused thinking about it, and then said, "About a seven."

"That bad?" she asked, holding his hand tighter.

She leaned in closer to him and lightly kissed Eric on his scarred cheek.

"Now?"

"Six and a half."

"A half?" she asked, confused.

"You did it on my cheek and not the lips." He said, giving her a weak smile.

"Well then," Catlin said, leaning in again to kiss him on his soft lips.

"Now?"

"Five."

"Good."

Eric smiled a half smile, pulling Catlin over to the flower garden, which was now lit by a few solar lights he'd bought from town. They sat next to each other, resting their backs on the tree. Eric was staring up at the little bit of sky he could see through the leaves, but Catlin was staring at him, tenderly.

"We've been dating for how long? Three months?" she asked, softly breaking the silence.

"Is this a trick, because three months sounds right?" Eric asked, now looking at her.

"No. I was just making sure. Time just seems to go so fast."

"Really? To me, time seems to be going slower."

"I'm sorry."

"You apologize too much. It's very annoying."

"So do you!" she said, poking him in his side to make him laugh.

"So, since it's been three months, can you promise me something?" she asked after Eric stopped laughing.

"Within reason, yeah."

"No more lying to each other and no more hiding things from each other. Deal?"

"Deal." He said, sealing it with a kiss, "But what's this all about?"

"Well, the other day, I had a vision ab-"

"About me?" he asked, interrupting her, "When was this? Today? Yesterday? How long have you been hiding this from me?"

"It was a few days ago. I told Sloan right after it happened. I wanted to tell you... trust me, Eric, I did."

At this, Eric tried to protest, but Catlin raised her voice louder and continued to speak.

"Sloan had told me that you weren't ready to hear about my vision. It could hurt you more than you already are."

"Please, tell me," he begged, his voice soft and low.

"I don't want to hurt you."

"If it helps us, then please do it."

The night air was cooling, creating goose bumps on their exposed skin.

"If it hurts you, tell me and I'll stop." Eric nodded. "The vision was of you. You were standing on a type of stage. Sloan didn't know what it was when I described it. You were dressed in all black, but the outfit looked like a military officer uniform. Beside you was Elizabeth. She was in a long black dress and had a black diamond crown on her head. My visions, lately, have only been pictures, and I don't know when this happens. There was also a phrase that I heard. 'Viva la coppia reale.' Which translates into -"

"I know what it translates to. Long live the royal couple. What does this mean? Does it mean that we lose? That Elizabeth gets what she wants?" he exclaimed, his voice now loud and bitter.

"Sloan doesn't think so. Because of the way I described your face. You weren't sad, but it's the face you have on when you are usually up to something. That face you make when you are trying to keep something, like the valentine's gift, from me."

"What did Sloan say about this? Did she have any idea of why I would go over to their side?"

"This is the part that you may not like. Sloan says that the vision I had is a plan that she had been forming for a few months, now. She thinks it would be a good move if we sent in some spies. Not a lot, but a group of five, you being one of them."

"How? It's not like we can just walk in there saying 'Hey we have your powers. Let us into your army.' Elizabeth would know something was up. It would never work."

"Sloan says that you would be the easiest to get in. The others would be more difficult. She was suggesting that we would go looking for trouble to find Shadow Reapers. We would make sure that we weren't outnumbered, but we would trap them and then take their identities. Like how they did to you."

"That would never work. I would never do that," Eric said, getting upset by all the memories from last year flooding his head.

Suddenly, the scars on his arms felt like they were on fire. Sweat started to form on his forehead. Blood started to drip from the corner of his mouth as the feeling of being stabbed hit his stomach. Catlin jumped up in fear and screamed as loud as she could for help.

Chapter 4

"Is everything okay?" Elizabeth asked, kindly. Her face had a concerned look on it.

"Not really," Eric responded in a dark and hushed tone.

"Talk to me... what's wrong?"

"I don't really know. I feel upset. Like my body is in pain."

"Do you need to go to the ER?" she asked, quickly getting up off the floor where she was studying with Eric.

"No... I don't think so... I just need to rest, I think."

"What's going on? Please, let me help," she said, helping Eric lay down on his back.

"It honestly feels like I'm dying, but not. Almost like I'm in limbo, or something. It's confusing."

"That's it. I'm calling 9-1-1."

"No. I'm fine."

"No, you're not!" Elizabeth shouted as she picked up her phone.

"No!" Eric shouted back, seeing her start to dial.

Eric threw his arm in her direction, and a small ball of fire flew from his hand toward the phone. When it hit the phone, it exploded in Elizabeth's hands, not harming her.

"What the hell was that?" Elizabeth shouted in fear, getting as far away from him as possible.

"So, they do work if I'm in a dream."

"What are you talking about, Eric? This isn't a dream; this is real life!"

"It is a dream. I know, because you would never call 9-1-1 on me. You always tried to fix me, instead of letting someone else do it, and in reality, you are dead, and I'm all alone. All alone with no parents, no true home, no future, nothing. All because of you."

"What the hell are you talking about? I'm right here, and your parents are at work! Remember? You're mom is a college *professor, and your dad is a doctor. This is real life, Eric."*

"No, it is not! This is all a lie. I have these dreams all the time, except I'm gaining more control over them."

Eric walked over to Elizabeth, who had her hand on the doorknob. He placed his hands on her shoulder and then asked, "Why do you keep asking to be saved? In every dream I have, it always ends with you asking me to save you. Save you from what?"

He face went emotionless and pale. She stared straight at Eric, but it was as if she was looking through him to what was behind him.

"From me, Eric. You have to save me from myself. I know you don't understand, now, but you will soon enough. Now listen, I need you to do something for me. You are going to be faced with some difficult choices when you wake up. No matter how scared you are, you need to choose to leave."

"Leave what?"

"You will understand. But you have to leave. It will all work out in the long run. Trust me, please."

"I do trust you, but I'm not strong enough for all of this. This is all just happening too quickly," he said, looking defeated.

Elizabeth smiled, took his hands, and said, "It will be fine. You will be fine. I love you."

"I love you, too."

"Now, it's time to wake up. Remember what I have told you."

"I will. I will," he said, his eyes starting to feel heavy.

Chapter 5

"How is he?" asked Catlin.

"He will be fine, but we had to block some memories. They were destroying him from the inside, out," Sloan said in a quiet and worried tone.

"How much did you take away?" asked Nick.

"We did not take away any memories. They are all still there, but we isolated and.... Eric, you are awake?" Sloan asked.

"Kinda. My head hurts, a lot. What happened?"

Eric was lying in his bed, surrounded by Sloan, Catlin and a few others, but his vision was too blurry to see faces. He assumed that they were Marina and Nick, but they could have been teachers.

"We were outside walking, and you were showing off, like usual. You had climbed the tree in your garden and got on a branch that you thought was secure. You went out to the edge of it and fell off and hit your head," Catlin told him, lying.

"Trust me, Eric, it sounds worse that it was. You are fine. You didn't break anything. You just have a concussion. Just rest, drink some water, and you will be fine in time for school," Sloan assured him.

"Is there anything you need? Water? Some food?" Catlin asked, sitting on his bed with him.

"No. I think I'm fine. Thanks, though."

"I'm here if you need me."

"Only until curfew, Miss Chamberlin. Eric may be sick, but you are not staying in the boys' room over night. Nick can take over for you."

Eric couldn't see it, but he imagined that Catlin rolled her eyes at that comment. Sloan walked away, leaving the room.

"You scared us. Don't do it again!" Marina commanded.

"I didn't mean to. Sorry," Eric murmured, dejectedly.

"Hey, it's fine. We are just glad you are okay," Nick said to him as he played a game on his phone.

"What game are you playing, now?" Eric asked, regaining his vision a little.

"It's a new one that just came out. And as soon as it did, the Shadow Reapers took it down, but I got to it before they did. It's a game made by a few of my buddies back home, actually. It's called *Shadow Killers.* You have to stop the darkness from covering your screen, and if it covers it, a bunch of Shadow Reapers show up. Then you have to take this light stick, and cut them in half."

"Which is totally incorrect, but it's a good game," Marina said, sounding a little upset about it.

"But it's so addictive. And it continues to get harder the more you play it. The darkness is hard to fight along the way."

"Isn't it, though?" Eric asked with a depressed tone in his voice.

"You okay?" Catlin asked him, getting scared.

"I don't know. I just feel like, for some reason, I should feel depressed and mad. Which makes no sense, but... yeah."

"You have no reason to be depressed or mad. Everything is okay. We are all okay," Marina assured him.

"I know, but I can't help it. It's like a wave of pain and sadness just hit me and washed away all the happy."

Catlin grabbed Eric's hand, intertwining their fingers, then raised his hand up to her lips and kissed it.

"I'm here for you. I always will be. I know I haven't always been in the past, but I'm here, now. I love you," she told him.

"I know you guys are here for me. But you guys can't really help."

"But we can try. We all love you, Eric. Please, just let us help," Nick said, putting away his phone.

"I don't even know why I feel this way, so I don't know how to fix it."

"Do you want anything? Do you want any Tylenol? Or what about some popcorn?"

"No. Can you just get my headphones from my book bag and the book that's in there? And where's my phone?"

Catlin reached behind her to get his phone off the nightstand, while Marina went through his book bag.

When she handed him the book and his headphones she asked, "Do you want us to leave, or what?"

"I don't care. Stay if you want, but I'll just be reading."

Catlin got comfortable next to him in the tiny twin sized bed. Marina sat on the bed next to his, which was Nick's, and Nick left to get one of his extra handheld game consoles for Marina.

They sat in silence for the most part. Every once in a while, Nick would let out a celebratory yell. Catlin rested her head on Eric's boney shoulder and had fallen asleep. When it was reaching 5:00, Mr. Smith in a new grey suit, came into the room and announced that dinner was ready. Marina woke up Catlin, who then woke up Eric.

"Hey, do you want us to bring you up a plate?" Catlin asked in a soft tone.

Eric pulled his head phones out of his ears and said, "No, I'm not really that hungry."

"Okay. If you change your mind, text one of us. I love you," she said, kissing his forehead.

He nodded and then put his headphone back in and watched as they left the room. He placed the book he was reading in the drawer of his nightstand. Out of nowhere, tears started streaming from his eyes.

"What the fuck is wrong with me!?" he yelled to himself. "Why do I feel like complete shit? This just isn't fair. This pain is just too much."

He turned up the music as loud as it could go, hurting his ears. Wiping the tears off his cheeks, he got up off the bed, grabbing some fresh clothes from the draws that were under his bed. He went into the warm, open bathroom near his bed to take a shower, placing his clothes on the wooden stool that was right outside. Stepping into the shower, he started to cry.

"I can't live like this, anymore. I don't want to live, anymore! I just want to die!" he screamed, frustrated at everything.

By the time Eric got done with his shower, his eyes were all red from crying so hard. He grabbed his clothes and changed inside the stall.

"Are you okay?" asked a little kid who was sitting in the windowsill as Eric came out of the stall.

Eric almost jumped out of his skin. He didn't even notice the kid when he walked in.

After catching his breath from being scared, he said, "I'm fine."

"I may be a kid, but I know that you're not fine."

"Who are you, anyway? Why haven't I seen you, before?" Eric asked as he got closer to the boy.

He was small and very skinny. His pale face was skinny and small. Eric couldn't really see his face that well, because the kid was looking outside. His dark brown hair was unkempt and looked like it covered his eyes.

"I'm Mr. Smith's son, Derrick, and you don't see me because I don't want to be seen. I don't really like people."

"Me either," Eric said as he leaned on the wall next to the kid.

"What's wrong? Why do you want to die?"

"You are too young for me to talk to you about it."

"I am eight. I'm old enough to understand depression," he said, bitterly. He extended his long, boney arm out. In the sunlight, Eric could see the fresh cuts on his wrist.

"I'm sorry."

"Don't be. It won't help. Sorry won't bring my mom back."

Derrick and Eric sat there in silence for a few minutes, and then Derrick said, "You may be fine, but you're not happy."

"Not everyone has to be happy."

"True, but being happy feels good."

"Obviously, you don't feel happy, either."

"I try, but the feeling just- happens."

"Like it's a tidal wave of emotions coming down on you, and you find yourself unable to swim."

"Yeah."

"My friends don't get that. They try to be supportive and try to help me, but they can't. They can't fix me, because I'm too broken," Eric said in a defeated tone.

"And all the king's horses and all the king's men couldn't put him back together, again," Derrick recited in a monotone voice.

"Exactly."

"I get you. I get what you're going through, but sometimes, we can't do it alone. Sometimes, we need people. Whatever you are going through, whatever is making you feel like this, it's not worth taking your own life. I found that out the hard way."

"What do you mean?"

"Let's just say this. I will forever be eight."

Eric, who was just staring into space, turned to look at Derrick, but he was gone. The window had fog and ice forming near the corner.

"Can my life get any more messed up?" Eric shrieked, looking up into oblivion, waiting for anyone to answer.

When no one responded, Eric walked out of the bathroom and back to his bed. He lay on his bed, not even putting the covers over him, and looked one of the windows that were near his bed. He stayed like this for a while, until a large group of guys, including Nick, walked into the room

Nick walked over to Eric's bed and pulled the blankets over him.

"You doing okay?" Nick whispered into his ear.

Eric nodded, so Nick left to get ready for bed. Eric stared out the window into the dark night. It was a really dark night... no stars, and no moon, just pitch black. He stared out the window, until his eyelids got too heavy.

Chapter 6

"Rise and shine!" Nick yelled into Eric's ear.

"I'm up! I just don't want to get out of bed," he said, pulling the covers over his head.

"But it's the first day of school! I thought that was your favorite day of the year!" Nick said, sarcastically.

"Yeah, when school was actually school. Here, we learn how to fight for our lives. It's more like boot camp than school."

Eric pushed the covers off and slowly got up out of bed.

"What time is it?" he asked as he stretched.

"Six thirty."

"Why the hell are we up so damned early?"

"We are going on a run before class starts!" Nick said with too much energy for Eric to stand.

"Why are we running?"

"Because Marina is anxious and needs to run, and we figured it would be good for everyone. Get those chemicals going!"

"How many energy drinks have you had, already?" Eric asked as he gathered his clothes.

"Six? Seven?"

"You are going to make your heart stop with that amount of chemicals and sugar in your system."

"Yeah, yeah. Hasn't affected me yet! Come on already!"

"Let me go put shorts on and take some Tylenol. I have a feeling I'm going to need it."

"You have no clue," Nick said so softly that Eric didn't hear.

Eric grabbed an old pair of basketball shorts and went to the bathroom. He changed, brushed his teeth real quick, and grabbed two Tylenol from the medicine cabinet.

When he walked back into the bedroom, Nick was gone, and everyone else was still asleep. He was tempted to go back to bed, but he had ignored his friends enough, lately.

The three of them were waiting for Eric at the bottom of the stairs, all in loose shorts and tank tops. Eric was still in his long sleeve grey shirt. Marina had her soccer ball under her arm and a water bottle in her hand.

"Are we ready?" Marina asked, about to open the front door.

Eric shrugged, not really caring either way. Catlin fixed her high ponytail, smiled at Eric, and then stepped out the front door. Cold, sharp, spring air hit them as they walked out. The fields that surround the property were foggy, and there was dew covering the grass.

"You know, that headband looks stupid," Eric said, pointing at the bright yellow and green sweatband on Nick's head.

"I like it! It makes me feel like I'm actually athletic."

"When was the last time you have seen a professional athlete wear one of those?"

"True, but I've already made the decision to wear it," he said with a grin.

When Marina stepped off the porch, she started to lightly jog in the direction of the driveway. Nick followed close behind her, while Catlin and Eric slowly walked.

"Come on, slow pokes! Even Nick is running!" Marina yelled at them as she picked up the pace.

"This was *your* idea. I will run when I want to," Eric replied.

When Marina reached the end of the driveway, she picked up the pace and started to run around the property. As the others reached the end of the driveway, they started to run after her, the cold air making their chests hurt.

The scenery looked like a painting from an art museum. There was a small wooded area out in the distance that was blurred from the fog. The farmers who were getting ready to plant seeds were working the fields. There was a small pond on the front edge of the property that had a bit of fog above it.

"How—are—you—doing?" Catlin asked out of breath.

"I'm—doing—fine."

"Eric, I know fine doesn't mean fine with you," she said stopping to take a break and a sip of water. She offered it to Eric, but he shook his head. "What's wrong?"

"Nothing. I'm just tired, and this running is only making it worse."

"Do you want to walk for a while?"

"Hey, losers! Keep up!" Marina taunted from a distance,

245

still running.

Eric went ahead and took a swig from Catlin's water bottle and handed it back to her. He took a deep breath and started running, again. Catlin stayed behind to catch her breath.

Eric was almost caught up with Marina and Nick when he saw something out of the corner of his left eye. It was Derrick, in the same outfit he was in the first time Eric saw him, a red t-shirt and blue jeans.

"What are you doing here?" Eric asked him, slowing down a bit.

"I'm here because you want me here. But the real question is why are *you* here?"

Eric stopped running, and asked, "Wait, why do you think I want you here?"

"It doesn't matter why. What matters now is why you think you should be out here."

"I'm out here for my friends. This was their idea."

"But why are you pleasing them? Why do you care if you make them happy, when it's clear that they don't make you happy."

"They do make me happy."

"Are you just saying that to make me disappear, or do you really believe that? Because I can see through you, Eric," Derrick said, looking straight in Eric's eyes.

"They do their best," Eric replied as he began to walk away.

"In a few weeks, you are going to be asked a question. Say yes to it," Derrick said, changing the subject.

"What if I don't want to?"

"I'm dead. A ghost. I can go to any point in time. My mom's imaginary friend as a kid was me. I don't just see the future; I can *go* to the future. Say yes, and everything bad will end. Faster that you might think."

"For all I know, you are a tumor in my brain. You might not even be real."

"I am real. They call me the Angel of Suicide. I come when people need me, and when they no longer need me, I leave, but that's a story for another time," Derrick said as he walked away into the fog.

Eric started running again, trying to keep his distance between Catlin, who was about twenty yards behind him, and

Marina and Nick, who were about fifty yards in front of him. Eric knew that Catlin could catch up to him if she wanted, but he figured she was giving him space.

They were halfway around the property when Eric started to question what Derrick had said to him.

They are my friends, but I'm not happy. But why am I not happy? he asked himself.

I should be happy. Not screaming for joy happy, but happy enough that I don't have to fake a smile to get up in the morning. What's wrong with me? I should be happy that I still am alive, that I still have people who care about me. But I'm not. I'm miserable be—.

"Hey!" Catlin said, interrupting Eric's thoughts. "Just thought— I would check—on you. Do you need—another sip— of water?" she asked, breathing heavy, handing him her water bottle.

Eric took it, although he didn't really need it. He took a few swigs from the half-empty bottle and handed it back.

"Do you want to—slow down some?"

Eric shook his head and continued running a little faster than he was.

"Okay. Well, I'm going—to slow down for a few. If you— need me, I'll be—right behind you."

"Okay."

At this point, Eric's lungs were killing him. A sharp pain covered his chest, and the cold air wasn't helping, at all. His eyes were watering, and he couldn't feel his legs anymore, but he knew he was still running.

Nick and Marina were already reaching the driveway, and Eric could hear them encourage each other to push each other like they always do. Eric watched as Marina ran onto the driveway, closely followed by Nick. They collapsed on the ground, trying to catch their breath. They smiled and started laughing.

Eric arrived at the driveway a few minutes later, closely followed by Catlin. Eric stopped, put his hands on his knees and his head between his legs. His vision was beginning to fade into black when he fell on the ground, trying to take deep breaths.

"Are you okay?" Marina asked.

"Stop—asking—me–that!" Eric barked at them in between

deep breaths.

"He hasn't done any physical activity like that since he got out of the hospital. He probably pushed himself too much," Nick said, pulling a little blue inhaler out of his pocket.

"I didn't know you were asthmatic," Catlin remarked when she saw it.

"I'm not, entirely. It only acts up when I do too much, like running faster than I should. This is just in case I push myself too hard."

Nick placed the inhaler inside of Eric's mouth, pushed down on the cylinder that held the medicine, and said, "Deep breaths."

When the medicine sprayed in Eric's mouth, he took a deep breath, making his lungs hurt more. Nick pushed down again, releasing more of the medicine. It took a few moments, but Eric's lungs began to feel better, and his chest didn't feel so tight.

Catlin sat behind him and pulled him into a sitting position in her lap.

"Deep breaths," she said, running her hands through his thick, long hair.

"I'm okay," Eric weakly said back, still little out of breath.

Catlin helped Eric off the ground, and they walked back up to the house.

"I just realized we never had SATs, this year," Catlin observed.

"That's because there's no new Freshmen, so there was no need for one," Nick told them.

"This year is going to be different, that's for sure," Marina said, chiming in.

Chapter 7

After taking a shower and getting dressed for school, 7:30 found Eric and Nick walking downstairs to breakfast, carrying their book bags with them. They sat next to Marina and Catlin, who were talking to Mr. Smith at their table. When Eric sat next to Catlin, her hand instantly found his. As she turned to him and smiled, he barely noticed the teacher excusing himself to go sit with other teachers.

"Is that a new one? I like it!" she asked, commenting on Eric's bright orange hoodie.

"Not really. I got it a few months ago."

"Is this the first time you have worn it?"

Eric nodded, suddenly feeling nervous that his scars were showing, so he tugged on the sleeves to make sure they went down past his wrists.

Jake DeLinsky and Rose Amber came in with Sloan, carrying breakfast trays. When everyone was seated and all the food and drinks were on the table, Sloan stood up at the head of the table and gave her morning speech.

"Five... Four... Three... Two... One... Thank you for getting quiet. Before we start with our breakfast, I have a few announcements for you. First off, I would like to say that even though we are in a bad time, we should still try to be happy to be alive.

"Secondly, we will be operating differently than what we have been. Students will be taught at the same grade level. This will save time and save lives. I want to say, if you feel confused about what is being taught, or if you feel you need extra practice, please talk to your teacher. Seniors, this doesn't mean that what you are going to learn this year isn't what you learned last year.

"We will be learning more fighting techniques, as well as more charms and potions that you can use in battle to protect yourself and to attack the Shadow Reapers. We will be teaching some advanced techniques; some that we vowed to never teach, but it needs to be done.

"Lastly, you are only permitted to leave the school under certain conditions. You must have at least one teacher with you, you have to have groups larger than three, and you may only leave from ten in the morning to five in the evening. If you do not follow these rules, you may get caught by a Shadow Reaper, and if I find out about it, you can bet that my punishment will be worse that a Shadow Reaper.

"Now, let us eat and be merry!"

"When do we get our schedules, this year?" Nick asked as he grabbed a plate of food.

Catlin quickly raised her hand to get attention.

"Yes, Miss Chamberlin?" Sloan said as she herself sat down to eat.

"When do we get our schedules, this year, since we don't have the ghosts to hand them out?"

"Oh—I just about forgot about that!" She responded, getting up and walking out of the room.

"It's not really like her to forget about something like that," Nick said with a mouthful of food.

"She has a lot of things on her plate. She's stressing a lot, recently, just because of how much things have changed so drastically," Eric informed them.

"In her defense, the ghosts do usually take care of it. She's probably not used to doing all of this by herself," Marina said, chiming in.

"She needs a reward for all the things she does for us and the whole White Knight community," Catlin stated before finishing off her orange juice.

A few silent minutes later, Sloan came back into the room holding a pile full of papers.

"Please, pass the schedules around your table so that everyone gets their schedule. If anyone needs an extra copy, please see me later," Sloan said, walking around to the tables, handing piles off to one of the students.

When Catlin found her schedule, she handed the papers to Eric. He flipped through the papers to find his and handed the papers off to Nick. While Nick was finding his, Catlin and Eric compared their schedules.

"It's so weird not seeing Astral Projection on my schedule. I'm going miss Mr. Day; he was my favorite teacher," Catlin said, an almost depressed tone in her voice.

"It won't be the same without you, Catlin," Nick said to her.

Eric had one class together with Catlin, two with Marina, and had four classes together with Nick. His Fire Manipulation class was only on weekends with Sloan, after their Driver's Education class. Even though the world was changing, they still had to act like normal teenagers, which meant they had to learn how to drive a car.

At 9:00, Breakfast was over, and clean up was done by the students who had first period free. Eric and Nick left Marina and Catlin and headed to the barn where the Defense Against Shadow Reapers class was being held. Mrs. Brown was already at the barn, opening the door for students.

The barn had been renovated since they moved into the house. Before, it was a normal-looking old, red barn. It had horse stables that lined the walls, a small wooden workbench at the far end, and a ladder in the middle that led to the small attic that was full of hay and straw. Now, the stables, workbench, ladder, and attic had been removed.

The inside walls were covered with cement, the thin glass-paned windows were replaced with thick, bullet proof glass, and industrial lights were installed to brighten up the room. Where the workbench once was, stood two of the SRBs that had been recovered from Aviance. Metal benches were placed near the door, facing a chalkboard that was on the wall.

Eric and Nick took a seat near the middle of the room and waited for the rest of the class to show up. The class was filled, like Sloan said, with kids in all three of the grades.

At ten past nine, Mrs. Brown shut the door. When the door was shut, she locked it using a charm.

"Good morning, class. Before we get started today, I need to take attendance to make sure everyone who is supposed to be here, is here," she said, stepping to the front of the class to her metal desk.

She cleared her throat, fixed her grey blazer, and started to call off names that were on her attendance sheet. When every student's name was called, she started class.

"For today, like usual, we will not be practicing with the

bots. We will go over some of the things that we will be learning, proper procedures to do when practicing with the bots, and so on.

"This year, as Sloan mentioned at breakfast, we will be learning some more advanced techniques to use when in battle. These will range from taking out your opponent with different powers, to how to permanently stun your opponent. My favorite thing we will learn this year, which we will get to in a few weeks, is how to properly confuse your opponent.

"There will be no textbook, this year. However, there still will be reading assignments; not a lot, since this is a hands-on class, but there will be a few. For those, I will copy pages out of a textbook I have and will hand them out to you.

"The bots are the same ones we have had, but I want to make it clear that the bots do not replicate what a Shadow Reaper will do in battle. The real Shadow Reapers are stronger, wiser, and can't be switched off. These bots are training tools, designed to help you be ready for a battle when one comes. However, with that being said, I have made a few readjustments to the bots. Their fire will no longer burn your clothing as fast, and it won't spread. We still need to take precautions when using them, just in case this modification backfires.

"This class can be stressful and terrifying, at times. If you get overwhelmed, please talk to me. There is no need for someone to get hurt in the class. We take precautions, but sometimes, accidents happen. If something happens, you need to come to me immediately, and I will help."

Mrs. Brown talked about a few other items and techniques they would learn over the course of the year. She had finished before time class ended, so she let class out a bit early.

The temperature went up from this morning, and was a nice change from the freezing classroom Eric and Nick were just in. The sky was clear and a perfect shade of blue. There was a light breeze that was a refreshing contrast to the hot, humid air.

"What class do you have, next?" Nick asked, opening the door into the house.

"Metamorphosis. Thank you," Eric responded as he walked in.

"Marina is in your class, then! I have a free period now!"

The Metamorphosis classroom was being taught in the

library, which Mr. Goodman wasn't happy about. Since the moment Eric walked in, he could hear him complain about the small room.

"We need space to practice. I can't function like this! Why did Sloan put me in here, when Mr. Smith gets the larger room for his stupid potions."

Eric saw Marina sitting at a table near the back with a short, skinny, redheaded girl, whom Eric recognized as Jessica. She was a Senior who played soccer with Marina. Eric never had talked to her, but she always seemed nice. It seemed like these days, Eric was always trying to avoid people. Less people to hurt and less people to get hurt by.

Eric sat down, and sure enough, they were talking about soccer and the national soccer league. Mr. Goodman shut the blinds and turned on the bright lights. The walls were painted a bright blue; there were white metal shelves on the walls and several round birch wood tables. The windows that looked out onto the front yard usually had a futon under it but were replaced with a little desk for Mr. Goodman.

As he looked around the room waiting for class to start, Eric realized just how bright the library was, and the florescent light bulbs didn't help. It was almost overwhelmingly bright, almost to the point where it was causing Eric to have a headache. As it reached time for class to start, Mr. Goodman shut the door to the room and sat at his desk.

When his watch said 10:10, he started class. He stood up, and everyone immediately got quiet. Marina quickly pulled her notebook and pen out of her bag and placed it on the table.

"Good morning. Since it is the start of a new school year, I feel like it is my duty to go over guidelines in this class; and since it's a new classroom, we will have some new guidelines.

"First off, since most of the space in this room is taken up by other books and furniture, we will have most of our practice days in the garage. We would go outside, but Sloan thinks doing any kind of magic outside of the building could cause trouble. On days when it is impossible to be in the garage, we will move the furniture and make space in here.

"Secondly, if I see a phone, tablet, computer, or any other electronic device, I will take it from you. You are in this class to learn, not to update your tweets and blogs. Your ePads and uPhones are not going to help you in a fight.

"Lastly, I am supposed to remind you that if you need extra help in the class, I am here for you. We will be learning some Metamorphosis techniques that are advanced but could save your life. If you feel challenged, please get help. It could save your life," Mr. Goodman said in a monotone voice.

By the middle of class, Eric tuned out Mr. Goodman and was absent-mindedly drawing in his notebook. Marina noticed and wrote **R u ok** on his notebook.

Eric looked at her and nodded his head.

U sure, she wrote underneath.

Again, Eric nodded. To be honest, he didn't know. He didn't really feel anything at the moment. He just wished the day would be over with, already. He wanted to skip his next class but figured it would look bad to skip on the first day, although every teacher basically goes over the same set of rules on the first day.

Then again, if he skipped, he would get in trouble with Sloan. Eric thought about using an Astral Projection, but he felt too weak for it to work.

Mr. Goodman was ranting on about the room size, again, and had somehow gotten on the subject of public libraries becoming more of a video rental place than a library.

"Mr. Goodman usually is hard to get off topic," Marina whispered.

"He's probably nervous. We all are," whispered Jessica.

"We have a right to be. We are under red alert, constantly," remarked one of the other boys at the desk. "It's all *his* fault," he whispered, but it was still loud enough that Eric heard.

Eric closed his eyes, bowed his head, and tried to hold back the tears.

"That was uncalled for!" Marina yelled at the kid as she put a comforting hand on Eric's back.

"Miss Martin, is there a problem?" Mr. Goodman asked.

"Yes. Yes there is. I am tired of people *always* blaming Eric for everything that has gone on recently!"

"I can stand up for myself. Stop it, please," Eric said in a hushed tone to her.

"Miss Martin, if you interrupt me again, I will remove you from this class. As Mr. James has stated, he can fight his own battles."

Marina sat back down, crossing her arms, giving the guy a look that Eric knew well. It was the *I'm killing you in my head* look. As much as Eric wanted to be mad at her, he knew that she meant well. Mr. Goodman continued on talking about how they will be learning to transform into small objects to hide better. But Eric could still hear the whispered conversations of people. They all blamed him.

"It *is* my fault," he said under his breath.

Chapter 8

Eric decided to skip dinner and head to the garden. His phone had gone off a few times with texts from Catlin and Marina, but he ignored them. He just sat there leaning against the tree trunk and gazing out into the fields. It felt weird to him to find beauty in all this destruction and hate. The sun was setting on the horizon across from Eric, casting an orange haze around the yard.

Yet, there were families right now being murdered, fighting to stay alive, or being *upgraded*, as Elizabeth put it. Like Eric, no one understood Elizabeth's reasoning behind who got an upgrade and who didn't. Even if you volunteered for an upgrade, you weren't guaranteed one. It seemed almost random, but Eric had been doing research on it for a few days.

Eric had asked Marina, who turned out to be a mastermind with computers, to hack into a website. The website belonged to the hospital the Shadow Reapers were using to give the upgrades. He was looking at the records of those individuals who were upgraded to see if there were any connections between each patient.

As Eric was sitting beneath the tree watching the sun set, he couldn't help but think about some of the records he had come across. Family members were taken away from each other, and some died, while others were upgraded. Those who fought the upgrade were still forced to upgrade. There were a few cases where the upgrade failed, and the patients had to be terminated.

Eric pulled out his laptop from his book bag and opened up some of the patient files. He was looking at two people who were recently upgraded. Jeremy Dowes, a twenty-three year old graduate student from Indiana, and Meredith Wheeler, an eighteen year old high school dropout from California. There was no obvious connection between the two people. Eric was going through their records with a fine comb to see what they had in common. They had different weights, heights, and different medical backgrounds. Jeremy had a clean background, never having a surgery or many doctor visits. Meredith had several visits to the emergency room in the past two years, two surgeries, and hundreds of doctor visits in the past five years.

"Why did these two get an upgrade?" Eric asked himself.

Then, he got to the blood type. They were both type A. Eric pulled up a few more records at random and looked at their blood type. A, A, A, AB, AB, A, and AB. Everyone who was getting an upgrade was AB or A.

"Why this blood type, though? Why not go after the type O people, since there are more of them?" Eric asked, recalling some of the facts about blood from his seventh grade biology class.

Then it hit him. His blood type was A. Therefore, it could only be used on those with blood types of A or AB. Eric saved the files to an USB, just in case Elizabeth found out someone was hacking their files.

"What are you doing?" asked Derrick, hanging from a branch above Eric.

"Jesus H. Christ!" Eric screamed as he jumped.

"Sorry."

"I thought you were a Shadow Reaper. I almost killed you!" Eric yelled at him while he put his laptop back.

"Can't kill the dead," Derrick said with a devilish smile.

"Yeah, that's true, but you could in a way."

Derrick gave him a quizzical look and then said, "Explain."

"If you destroy the object that is keeping you here, then your spirit will either move on or die."

"Where did you find that?"

"A book."

"It's not easy to do. The object has to be destroyed a certain way. That's not the case with me, though."

There was a long pause as Derrick got down and sat next to Eric.

"It's dark."

"What's dark?"

"The afterlife."

"Eric!" Nick yelled from the porch.

When Eric turned back to Derrick to ask him what he meant, he had already disappeared.

257

"Eric! Time for our last class!" Nick yelled, again.

Eric quickly shoved his laptop back into his book bag and headed back to the house. He met Nick on the porch, and they walked to the library for their Molecular Immobilization class with Sloan. When they walked in, Mr. Goodman was arguing with Sloan over classrooms. When it was time for class to begin, Sloan, in a bright yellow blouse and lime green pants, sat down in her chair and told him they would discuss the matter, later.

"Good evening, class," Sloan cheerfully said.

"Good evening, Miss Marlin," the class said in unison.

"Now, you all know me well enough to call me Sloan," she announced with a kind smile.

"Now, as I said at breakfast this morning, things have changed. Things are going to be a lot harder this year, and we are going to have to learn fast. If you make mistakes, it's okay. I haven't seen a mistake that I haven't been able to fix, yet," she said with a sweet smile.

Someone towards the front of the room raised their hand.

"Yes," Sloan said to them.

"What exactly are we going to learn, this year?" asked a girl with a very high, squeaky voice.

"First off, we will begin today with some review for the older students, and the younger students will learn some essentials for what we will be learning later on. My goal by the end of the regular school year is to have you *all* using your powers to freeze large amounts of enemies and to focus your powers onto specific areas of the body to freeze only parts."

The room was silent, no one moved, and no one breathed. It was just all so surreal; the fact that they could be attacked without warning. All the other times, they had large numbers, and they had a warning beforehand. Now, it was just them. No one to give them warnings and no one to give them support during the fight.

Sloan noticed the silence and stood up.

"Yes, things are going to be *a lot* different. Yes, it is scary to think about. Yes, lives have been lost. Yes, you have a right to be frightened out of your wits. However, you are safe here. There is mighty power in small numbers. The reason we are teaching you all at the same level is because it will help us all if anything happens. I am not telling you to not be scared. Being scared keeps you on edge.

"If you want someone to talk to, I, along with the other teachers and students, will be here for you. Fear is not something that should be in this house. Am I clear?"

Everyone nodded their heads and Sloan said, "Good, now let's get started."

The students got out of their seats, moved the tables and chairs as far back as they could, and waited for instructions from Sloan. She moved her desk up to the wall and pulled out a large brown bag from under the desk.

"I want you to break into groups of two or three, and when I come around to you, I want you to take three balls out of the bag."

Nick, Eric and Jake DeLinsky, who decided to join them since everyone else had a partner, grabbed three balls out of the bag. The bag had been magically altered to be bigger on the inside to fit all of the soccer balls.

Each of them grabbed a ball, and Sloan told them, "I want each of you to throw the balls in the air and try to freeze them before they hit the ground. The challenge is to freeze the balls, along with your partner."

This was a little out of Eric's range of abilities, even though Sloan had been trying to get him caught up. He thought that Sloan knew it, because as she walked away, she gave him an encouraging smile.

"Who wants to go first?" Jake asked the group.

"Nose goes!" Nick said, placing his finger on his nose in a blink of an eye.

Eric was the last to put his finger on his nose, so unfortunately, he had to go. Jake and Nick took the balls, threw them up in the air, and Eric reacted without a second thought. As soon as the balls were in the air, Eric closed his eyes, and threw up his hands to freeze them. He was successful in freezing two of the balls, but the third ball fell to the ground, and Nick and Jake were still moving.

"Hey, it's okay. Give it another try," Jake said to him.

Eric unfroze the two balls, and Nick caught them as they fell. They waited for Eric to recollect his thoughts and tried again. They tossed the balls in the air, and he tried again, succeeding in only freezing the balls this time.

"I'm finished," he said, defeated.

"That's okay. You gave it your best. Maybe, you can try again after we get done," Jake said with a kind smile.

Eric took the two soccer balls from Jake. Before Jake said he was ready, Eric asked, "Why are you being so kind to me?"

Jake, shocked by the question, asked, "What do you mean?"

"I'm not stupid. I know what you said to me, last year."

"What I said was directed to the Shadow Reaper who took your identity, not you."

"Bull shit. You had no clue that wasn't me," Eric said, trying to keep his voice down and anger in control.

"Eric, what is wrong with you?" Nick asked, placing a hand on his shoulder.

"I'm tired of all this two-faced shit from everyone!" Eric barked in a hushed tone and then threw the balls in the air.

The three balls froze instantly in the air, along with everyone else in the room, besides Sloan and Eric.

"Eric, what's wrong?" Sloan asked, walking towards him.

Eric crossed his arms and said, "Nothing. It's nothing."

Sloan gave him a questionable look and said, "Don't lie to me, Eric. What is troubling you?"

"I'm tired of being the one everyone talks about. Half the people take pity on me, and the other half hate me because I'm a threat. I just want to be left alone. I want to leave."

There was a long silence in the room. Sloan leaned against a table to think.

"I was going to bring this up later, when you had more experience under your belt, but I think now is a good time. Go up to my office after class and we will talk."

Sloan unfroze the room, and class continued. Jake and Nick left Eric alone as they practiced; only talking to each other. When class was over, Eric packed his stuff and left in a hurry. He heard Nick say something to him, but he didn't look back.

Chapter 9

Eric had beaten Sloan to her office, so he sat outside in the hall on the world's most uncomfortable chair. Sloan had bought the stiff, bright yellow, plastic and metal chair from IKEA, because she had a coupon and thought that it could brighten the house up. Eric told Sloan that she didn't need it, but she refused to listen to him. So it sat outside her bedroom and office door and was an eyesore that didn't match any of the other dull pastel colors in the hall.

"Eric, thank you for talking to me," Sloan said as she walked down the hall with several books and folders in her hands.

Eric gave a sound of acknowledgment, stood up, and adjusted his sleeves to make sure they were still covering his scars. Sloan unlocked the door with her key, stepped inside, sat her books down on a white end table that was to the right of the door as they stepped in, and invited Eric inside. The room looked like Sloan modeled it out of a *Southern Living Magazine.*

There was a neatly made queen sized, four post bed across the room with white sheets, two silver nightstands on either side, a silver dresser with a mirror on the grey-blue wall above it and an antique jewelry box on it, and a door that Eric assumed was the bathroom. The walls were bare, except for a few modern and abstract paintings and a coat rack that had a few expensive-looking necklaces hanging on it.

In the middle of the room was a desk that was painted light baby blue, which matched the cushioned chair that sat behind the desk. Two white plastic chairs that looked like the bright yellow one outside sat in front of the desk. Sloan walked over to the desk, sat down, placed some papers into a box on her desk, and then opened up her laptop.

"Shall we get down to business, Mr. James?"

Eric nodded.

"You will most likely not like what I have to say, but we,

the White Knight community and I, think it could work. That this could be the best way to end this war."

"What... is it?" Eric asked, the fear creeping into his voice.

"A few months ago, we had a student report to me that they had a vision of you—"

"Of me?" Eric interrupted, confused because he didn't remember being told by Catlin.

"Yes, of you and Elizabeth. You two were upon a stage together, dressed in traditional Shadow Reaper gear."

"But why?" Eric asked, his voice shaking

"At first, we had thought that this meant we would lose the battle. Upon farther review by Mrs. Grey and I, we find this to be a good thing."

"How is it a good thing?" Eric barked at her.

"That is the last time you interrupt me before I finish. Now, we figured out it was a good thing when Mrs. Grey and one of her students saw your body language. You had a face that I am familiar with from game night." Sloan chuckled, then continued. "From this information, Mrs. Grey, Mr. Smith, a few others from the community, and myself figured out what this vision meant and what events would lead to it.

"You will give yourself up to the Shadow Reapers—"

"What?" Eric yelled as he stood up.

"Sit down, Eric, and let me explain."

Sloan waited for Eric to calm down and sit before she started, again.

"You will go to the Town Hall, request to speak to the head Shadow Reaper there, and tell him who you are. Of course, they will not believe you at first, but that's when you remove the spell that hides your identity. When they see it is actually you, you need to request to speak with Elizabeth.

"Everything has been planned out in great detail. To ensure your safety, you will be on your own. They would be suspicious if a large group came at once. The same goes for once you are at the head Shadow Reaper building."

"You mean I'll be alone through all of it? How will this even work? What am I supposed to do while I'm in there?"

"Yes, you will be alone. While there, you need to dig up as much information as you can on what they are doing. That way, we can figure out a plan to make it stop. You will report back through your parents and the other Spirit Slaves over there. From there, they will deliver your findings to a few ghosts that stayed behind, even after Aviance was destroyed, and then, the ghosts will come to me. Everything is well thought out and planned.

"Eric, I know you never want to step foot in that place, but it is our only hope."

"When?"

"When, what?" Sloan asked.

"When will we start?"

Sloan had a shocked look on her face, paused for a moment, and then said, "You need a few more weeks of schooling first, but July first is when the Shadow Reapers come to upgrade more people."

"So, I have to be ready by July first?"

"Yes."

"I'll do it."

"Are you sure? If you accept, there's no turning back."

"I understand."

"Okay, then. I will start putting things in motion. Thank you, Eric."

"I'm not doing this for you or the White Knights. I'm doing this to avenge my parents."

"Okay."

Before Sloan could say anything else about the plan and the repercussions if anything went wrong, Eric had gotten up and left the room. He shut the door with a little bit more force than he planned on. Marina, Catlin, and Nick were waiting on him by the stairs, tears in their eyes.

Eric noticed but kept on walking. They wanted to say something to him but didn't really know what to say. His friends knew that whatever they could say or do wasn't going to help Eric. As Eric was heading down the stairs, Catlin went to follow but was held back my Marina.

"If he wants you, he will come to you. Give it time," Marina whispered to her.

"I'm afraid that he won't, though," Catlin responded as Eric reached the bottom of the stairs.

Eric left the house and headed to his garden, using his phone as a flashlight, since the sun had set. As he stepped into the garden, he heard rustling come from behind the tree. Eric put his phone in his pocket and slowly walked toward the tree.

There was a tiny source of light sneaking through the flowers, and Eric could see something move.

"Who's there?" Eric yelled as he held one hand out, ready to throw a fireball.

"How many times do I have to tell you that you can't kill me, stupid?"

"Derrick?"

"Who else would it be?"

Eric slowly, still unsure, walked around the tree. There, sitting next to a small, old kerosene lantern was Derrick.

"Why are you giving me that look?" he asked Eric.

Suddenly, Eric was aware of the confused and angry look on his face.

"I'm just confused. Why are you here? I though you just appeared when I was depressed."

"I appear whenever someone needs me."

Eric sat down next to him and stared absent-mindedly out at the sky.

"Did you accept?" Derrick asked, looking at him with a raised eyebrow.

"Accept what?"

"Sloan's plan."

"Oh... that..."

"Did you?" Derrick asked, sounding excited.

"Why do you care?" Eric murmured, bitterly.

"Because I do. Now, tell me!"

"Yes."

"You actually accepted it?" Derrick asked, sounding a little disappointed.

"Yes. For one, you told me to. That and I need to be somewhere that I'm not going to be looked at like I'm either a threat or like I'm a sad puppy."

Derrick stood up, climbed the tree, and sat above Eric on a limb. He lay back, looking up at the stars, swinging his bare feet.

"That will never change. You can't escape from that."

"How did you get so wise? You're only a kid!"

"I'm eight. Even when I was alive, I was smarter than your

average eight year olds. You do have to realize that even though I'm eight, I've been eight for eight years."

Eric looked up at Derrick with a sad, shocked look on his face, with tears in his eyes, and said, "You're my age?"

"Would have been, yes."

"Wow. I'm sorry. I had no clue."

"It's fine. I've accepted it was a choice, a stupid one, but a choice that I have to deal with. You know... I thought it would have gotten rid of the pain and that I could be with my mom. Instead, the pain is stronger, and I will never see my mom, but I've accepted all this, because now I have a job."

"What job is that?"

"To save people who were in my shoes."

"Sounds impossible," Eric absent-mindedly said.

"Everything is possible," Derrick said with an upbeat tone.

"I used to think the same thing. Not so much, anymore."

"The war?"

"Yeah."

Derrick climbed down from the tree and sat in front of Eric.

"When you said yes to Sloan, that was the first step you had to take to make the impossible become possible. You will see, Eric James, that this will change everything. I promise."

Eric raised an eyebrow at him and asked, "What would have happened if I had said no?"

"Then the impossible would still become possible. Elizabeth, sorry, *Queen* Elizabeth and the Shadow Reapers would have won, and life as we know it would be gone."

Derrick got up and started to walk away. Eric watched as his figure disappeared into the darkness. Tears were starting to form in his eyes. He didn't know why, anymore. Tears just happened, these days.

He stayed there for a few hours. When it was getting late and the moon was above him, he decided to go back to the house. The back door was still unlocked, and as he walked in, Eric could hear the soft sound of the TV on in the living room.

Catlin was curled up on the couch with the yellow blanket Eric had gotten her for her birthday in January. Quietly, Eric walked over to the couch, turned the TV off, sat his book bag down, and lay next to her on the couch.

"Hey, you," she whispered, making more room for him on

the tiny couch.

"I'm sorry, did I wake you?"

"No, you're fine. Are you doing okay?"

"I'm great," he said with a smile.

Catlin softly kissed him, and then fell asleep in his arms.

Chapter 10

"**E**lizabeth, what's wrong?" Eric asked as they swung on the porch swing.

It was mid July; the grass was brown from the lack of rain and summer heat, the flower garden was overgrown because it had been too hot to weed, and the sounds of fireworks filled the humid evening.

Eric and Elizabeth were sitting on Eric's front porch in the wooden swing, watching the storm clouds roll in.

"I don't know."

"Babe, please tell me. I know you know. Don't make me tickle it out of you!" Eric said to her as he started ticking her side.

Elizabeth giggled and squirmed and yelled for him to stop.

"Not until you tell me what's wrong!"

"Dad got a job offering in another town!" She revealed in between laughs.

Eric stopped ticking her and moved away from her on the now still swing.

"What?" he asked, looking confused and hurt.

"He got a job offer in the city, which means we would have to leave Dear Knoll."

"Oh," Eric said, hanging his head low and kicking the bush that was in front of the porch.

"I'm sorry, Eric."

"Yup."

Elizabeth tried to comfort him by placing her hand on his, but he moved it closer to his leg. A tear fell from her tan face onto her peach colored sundress.

"When?" he asked.

"When, what?"

"When do you leave?"

"In a few weeks. The house is already sold."

"When were you going to tell me?" he said, turning to

look at her.

"I wanted as much time with you as I could get, and I wanted that time to be happy. If I had told you sooner, we both would be sad."

The wind had stopped, the fireworks had ceased, and not even the psycho neighbor dog was barking. It was the calm before the storm.

"You need to leave," Eric softly said to her, looking as if he just lost a battle.

"But—"

"Leave!" Eric barked at her as he directed her off the porch with his arm.

Elizabeth looked like she was going to say something but gave up. She got off the swing and tried to give Eric a kiss goodbye, but he stopped her by getting up and walking inside the house. Elizabeth stood there for a few moments and then started to leave.

"Eric, what's wrong? Isn't Elizabeth staying for dinner?" his mom asked from the kitchen.

Eric ignored her and walked up the stairs to his bedroom. He slammed the door, knocking a picture off the wall. He turned on his radio, turned the volume as far up as it would go, and laid face down on his bed.

His phone buzzed in his pocket, but instead of even looking at whom texted him, he threw the phone at the wall. As it fell to the floor, the text message appeared on the front screen.

SAVE ME, ERIC. IF YOU TRULY LOVE ME, THEN SAVE ME.

Thunder cracked, shaking the house, and lightning struck, lighting up Eric's room. In the distance, the local tornado siren went off.

Chapter 11

The following Saturday, Eric had a Driver's Education class at 10:00 with Sloan. It wasn't the first time that he had driven, since his dad would let them drive their car around the block every once in a while at night. So, as Eric got behind the wheel, he felt a little bit more confident than Catlin, Nick, and Marina felt as they began their lesson.

"Okay, today I want you to get on the main road and drive to Republic. From there, I want you to get on the interstate and drive to Springfield. Are you okay with doing that?" Sloan asked, getting into the passenger seat.

"Yes, but isn't the interstate a little risky?" Eric replied, adjusting his seat.

"If you get pulled over, you know what to do. All of you do."

Eric tightly gripped the steering wheel, started the car, adjusted the rearview mirror, and started backing out of the driveway.

Eric put as little pressure as possible on the gas pedal while backing out. When he reached the end of the driveway, he pushed on the brake a little harder than he wanted to, causing everyone in the car to jolt forward in their seats.

"Jesus, Eric!" Nick yelled.

Sloan gave Nick a very stern look for using foul language in front of her.

"Sorry," he said, softly.

Suddenly, all the confidence that was in Eric had gone away, and his hands began to shake as he turned the wheel and backed out onto the road. He made a complete stop, changing from reverse into drive, and slowly accelerated up to five miles under the speed limit.

"Eric, the speed limit is 55. You can go a little bit faster," Sloan informed him, kindly.

Eric nodded his head and sped up a little, but as he did, he

269

got nervous and his hands started to shake even more. By doing so, he was causing the car to swerve on the road.

"Eric, take a deep breath. Everything is going to be fine. Nothing is going to go wrong."

"You don't know that! What if I get pulled over by a Shadow Reaper? What if I get killed, before our plan can take action?" Eric asked with his voice shaking.

"You just need to relax, Eric. I listened to the police scanner before we left, and no one is patrolling the town, today. As for the plan—"

"Can we not talk about the *stupid* plan?" Marina barked.

The car was silent after that, besides Sloan telling Eric where to turn every now and then. When they eventually got into town, Eric's knuckles turned white he was gripping the steering wheel so tight. Sloan had told him to take a right at a light, and as he turned, his wheels scrapped the curve, causing the car to jolt and the wheels to make a terrible noise.

"Sorry," Eric said shyly as he straightened up the car.

It took a few more turns and about ten more minutes before he got to the interstate.

"Now, you'll have to start pushing hard on the gas when you turn right, that way, you can reach interstate speed before you get on it," Sloan informed him.

Eric waited for the light to turn green, and then as soon as he turned onto the on-ramp, he pushed hard on the gas pedal. He watched has the speedometer quickly passed the 40, 50, and 60 marks. The car engine growled as Eric reached the speed limit of 70.

"Okay, this lane will end soon, so you'll need to get over to the lane on your left. Switch on your turn signal and check your blind spot before you pull into that lane," Sloan said to him.

Eric looked carefully behind him before he started to turn the steering wheel to pull over into the lane. As he did, he heard a car honk. He looked up into the rearview mirror and saw a police car right behind him on his tail.

"Fuck," Eric mouthed as the cop turned on its lights and siren.

Eric carefully pulled to the side of the road and stopped the car. He kept both hands on the wheel as the cop came up to the window; by that time, sweat was dripping from his forehead.

The cop tapped on the window, and Eric pushed down on the button to make the window go down.

"Do you know why I pulled you over?" asked Sergeant Banks, according to his badge.

"Because I didn't look carefully enough before I switched lanes?"

"Correct. Now, I need your license and registration."

Eric got his wallet from his back pocket, and Sloan handed the cop the registration from the glove department. Eric took his driving permit out, forgetting that the picture on it was that of Aaron Clay Greene and not his, which made Eric even more nervous.

"Are you his mother?" he asked Sloan.

"No, I am his grandmother and also the owner of the car."

"I need to see your ID as well, ma'am."

Sloan pulled her wallet out of her grey purse. As Sloan handed it to him, Eric saw the name and picture on the ID Eric was beginning to question if this was going to work or fail horribly.

The cop took their information and went back to his car.

"This isn't good. He's going to figure out that they are fake names and IDs, and we are going to die!" Eric said, starting to freak out.

"Eric. Calm down. Everything will be fine. If I suspect that something is wrong, then I have a plan," Sloan said, digging through her purse to find her wand.

"A plan?" Marina asked.

"Darling, I have a plan for everything. There is a reason I am Headmistress," she said with a mischievous smile.

It was the first time Eric had seen Sloan smile like that. It felt strange, because it felt out of character for her, but things were changing, and so were people.

"Everything checks out okay, but I will have to give you a ticket for reckless driving, Aaron, which will go on your record," Sergeant Banks said as he handed Eric his ID and his ticket, and Sloan the registration and her ID.

When the cop walked away, Sloan told Eric to wait a few seconds to get back onto the road, until the cop drove away. It took Eric about thirty minutes to get to Springfield, and when he did, Sloan had him pull over at one of the gas station and convenience stores.

Sloan filled up the car with gas, while everyone else got food.

"Are you not talking to me, anymore?" Eric asked them as they walked in.

Catlin turned around, shocked at the question, walked over to him, and hugged him.

"Eric, of course we are! This whole thing is just tough on us. We get you back and you decide to leave us, again."

Eric broke away from the hug, took a step back, and said, "You say that like I had a choice in the first point. I was deceived, imprisoned, and tortured. I had *no* choice. The *only* reason I am going back is to help end this war that if you haven't noticed lately, isn't going so well for our side. You have no say in this."

"So, your friends and family don't get a say in how you risk your life?" Marina asked with a tear falling from her face.

"It's my life," Eric informed her.

"Yes, and we are a part of it, like it or not. I don't know about Catlin or Nick, but I don't want to watch you throw your life away by doing something stupid, like this. But I don't say anything, because I understand it *is* your decision. I have no say, but I thought you would have at least asked us what we thought before making a decision. Guess I was wrong. Guess I was wrong about how you think about us."

By this time, Marina had tears falling down her face. Nick just stood there awkwardly, saying nothing and avoiding eye contact. Catlin still stood a few feet away from Eric, looking hurt.

"Is this the end, then?" Eric asked them.

"No, don't be so thick!" Marina said.

"We still love you, Eric, and we will support you no matter what! We just wished you would have talked to us, first," Catlin said, taking a step toward Eric.

"You will always be our friend, Eric. I knew that the first day I met you," Nick told him.

"You have been through things that make hell look like heaven. We understand that, but so have we. Sometimes, it feels like you don't care about us and what we are going through. It's not all about you," Marina barked at him.

Eric didn't know what to do or what to say. He just stood there, looking at her like a hurt puppy. Eventually, Sloan came over and asked what was going on. Marina left and headed inside the convenience store. Eric turned around and walked to the car.

"What did I miss?" Sloan asked Catlin and Nick.

"Nothing," Nick said, quickly, before walking inside the restaurant.

Eric stayed in the car while everyone else ate. He understood where Marina was coming from. He understood where they were all coming from, but did that gave her the right to say what she said? As he sat in the backseat of the car, he began to think. He barely knew anything about Marina and Nick. He knew more about Catlin than those two combined, and yet, they knew everything about him. It wasn't fair, but Eric didn't know how to fix it, nor did he have the time.

When they came back, it was Catlin's turn to drive, and Sloan had her drive around the city. Eric, Nick, and Marina sat quietly in the backseat. Eric stayed as close to the door as he could and stared out the window. When he felt his phone vibrate, he took it out of his pocket, and saw he had a text from Sloan.

Is everything okay between you three?

Eric quickly responded, **No.**

:(

Chapter 12

Eric woke up the next morning a little bit earlier than usual, even though he had a free day. It was a quiet Sunday morning; most people were still in bed enjoying the rainy weather, but there were still a few students and teachers up. Sloan was one of the few that were up, which didn't surprise Eric, at all. The thing that surprised him was the fact that she was still in her light blue nightgown, and her usually neat grey hair was messy and uncombed.

"Good morning, Sloan," Eric said cautiously as he grabbed a cup of coffee.

"Kids your age shouldn't drink coffee," she informed him.

Eric ignored her and continued pouring the coffee.

"Is everything okay?" she asked as she leaned against the counter and looked at him.

"No, not really, but I'm planning to fix that, soon."

"If you need my help, you know where to find me, Eric."

"Thanks, Sloan."

Eric put some bread in the toaster and sat on the counter as he waited for it to cook. Eric jumped when the toast popped out. He put some butter and cinnamon on the toast, grabbed his cup of coffee, and headed toward the front porch.

Eric was alone on the porch, sitting in the rocking chair and watching as the rain fell straight down. He found rainy mornings calming; the sound, the feel, and the look. He was a little hot in his blue long-sleeve shirt and his sweat pants, but every once in a while, there was a breeze the covered him in cool air.

As Eric sat there sipping his coffee, he tried to think of a way to fix what was going on between him and his friends before he had to leave, which was in a few weeks. He knew they all had a free day today, so Eric knew today was a good day to do *something* about it.

We need to talk, Eric.

The message from Catlin popped up on Eric's phone. When

Eric saw it, his stomach dropped.

Eric finished off his coffee, got up, and went into the house. There, still in her pink tank top and navy blue basketball shorts that she always wore to bed, was Catlin sitting on the bottom stairs.

"What's up?" Eric asked.

Catlin patted the spot next to her, and Eric sat next to her.

"I don't agree with everything that Marina said, yesterday, but I do agree that your biggest problem is that you are a little too obsessed with *you*."

"Are you saying I'm narcissistic?" Eric asked, confused.

"I don't think so," Catlin said, looking lost. "I'm just saying that you don't ask us many personal questions. We know everything about you, but you hardly know us. That's not what any kind of relationship should be like."

"I understand, and I am really sorry."

Catlin reached over and grabbed Eric's hand, then said, "I know you are, Eric, but being sorry isn't going to fix everything. Nick and Marina are really hurt, and you need to do something to make it up to them. We are your friends, but you act like that doesn't mean anything to you, anymore."

Eric let go of her hand and started to get up to leave.

"Where are you going?" she asked, ready to follow him.

"I hear what you are saying. However, I don't know how to fix this."

"Yes, you do. Just talk to them, Eric. That's all they want.'"

"Tell them to meet me in the garden after breakfast," he said as he headed to the dining room.

"Wait! It's raining outside!"

"Tell them to bring an umbrella!" Eric yelled at her as he closed the back door.

Catlin stood there in the hallway for a few seconds, looking confused as to what he had planned. A few older students came down the stairs with Mr. Smith, talking about a potion that they wanted to learn this year that would shrink people. Catlin got out of their way and headed upstairs.

While Eric was sitting under his tree in the garden, he was thinking of what he was going to say to them.

"Sorry for being a crappy friend. Sorry that I was busy being too depressed to pay attention to you. Sorry that shitty crap has happened to everyone," Eric yelled out in a hushed tone.

He knew that no matter what he said, it still wouldn't be enough to fix everything. He knew that if roles were reversed, he wouldn't forgive them. He didn't want to lose them, but he couldn't help but feel them slipping away, no matter what he had planned.

When Eric heard the porch door open and close, he stood up and waited for them to arrive. Catlin, Nick, and Marina all crouched under a large umbrella and quickly ran to the garden. They met Eric, who was now drenched from the rain, and waited for him to talk.

Eric looked each of them in the eyes, took a deep breath and then said, "Everything you said about me is true. I've been selfish. I hardly know you, yet I call you my friends. It's wrong of me to do, and I understand that no matter how much I apologize, I will never make it up to you.

"I've never had actual friends. Growing up, I only had Elizabeth, and before her, I was always alone. I was always the kid that played, ate, and worked by himself. I don't know how to be a friend. I know that this is a stupid excuse for how I treated you, but it's true.

"As for the decision I made about joining the Shadow Reapers, I have no excuse for how I acted. I know I should have talked to you about it. The only thing I can say about it is that I was upset and angry about how I was being treated here by teachers and other students.

"I wish I could make it up to you. I wish that I could start over. I wish there was this big, giant redo button I could push, but there isn't. I know I have to make it up to you, but I don't know how."

The four of them stayed silent; the only noise was the sound of rain and the old, rusty windmill that was spinning. Eric stood there uncomfortably, waiting for them to talk.

Finally, Marina looked at him and said, "Well, I think we found the one thing that you aren't so smart at. Friendship," she said with a giggle.

"All we are asking for, Eric, is that you think of us every once in a while. You deciding to go over to the Shadow Reapers means that we are going to lose you after we just got you back.

We understand why you are doing it; we just don't want to permanently lose you," Nick said.

"You guys aren't going to lose me. We have everything planned out, perfectly. I will live to give you guys hell, again," Eric reinsured them.

"And you know, maybe you could ask us how we are doing every once in a while, so that we know that you care about us, too," Catlin chimed in.

"I am very sorry, guys. I can't promise that I will do better, just because I hate promises, but I will try to do better."

"That's all we ask," Marina said to him as she gave him a hug.

"Good lord, you are soaking wet!" she yelled as she let go.

"Yeah, I know. I need to go change."

"Change, and then come hang out with us in the library," Nick insisted.

Eric nodded his head, and then joined them under the umbrella. By the time they got to the house, the rain got heavier and thunder roared. Eric quickly changed out of his wet clothes and into clean jeans and a thin, green hoodie.

Catlin, Marina, and Nick had combined two square tables and had taken up all of the space on it. Marina and Catlin where working on what looked like a craft project, and Nick had his laptop out playing *Minecraft* while listening to an alternative radio station, online.

"What are you guys doing?" Eric asked as he sat in between Marina and Nick.

"Catlin is working on a project she saw on Pinterest where you take old shirts and make them into skirts," Marina said, still working on her project.

"The only problem is that I can't sew to save my life," she said before she poked herself with the needle, wagging it at him as a tiny bead of blood formed.

"I'm working on a drawing I started a few months ago but never finished," Marina informed him.

Eric looked over and saw that she was recreating a photo that the three of them took in their Freshman year. They were all outside laying on the grass. Eric remembered that day. They had just gotten done playing soccer, and to Marina's surprise, Eric and Catlin won.

277

"I didn't know you could draw!" Eric confessed to her.

"Not well," she said, dismissing the comment.

"Yes you can! That looks just like the picture. And you said your only talent was playing soccer," Eric said, nudging her in her side.

"Thanks. It was something I did with my dad before my sister died and everything went to shit. This painting is actually going to be a going away present for you, if I finish it on time."

"Yes. Yes. Yes!" Nick cheered, disrupting everyone else in the room.

"What happened? Did a zombie drop another carrot?" Catlin asked, giggling.

"No. My team just won the Mega Walls Team Championship!"

"Congrats?" Eric said, unsure of what he was talking about.

"It's a game that someone came up with on *Minecraft* where you have to defend this thing called a Wither that's in your castle. Each of the four teams has one, and your goal is to kill the other Withers. You have a certain amount of time to collect resources within your area, and when the walls fall, you have fifty minutes to kill the Withers," Nick explained.

"And you were in charge of your team?" Eric asked, looking as if he was up to something.

"Yeah," Nick responded, unsure of what he was up to.

"And how many games did you have to win? How many people were you in charge of?"

"Ten games and fifty people. Why?"

"No reason. I was just thinking of a plan, that's all."

"A plan for what?" Marina asked him.

"Well, since I didn't let you help me decide whether or not I should have accepted Sloan's plan, I thought you could help me come up with how to pull this whole thing off," Eric told them.

"How? I don't mean to be the downer, here, but we are just kids," Catlin told him.

"Exactly! Nick can be in charge of getting me in. You guys can be in charge of helping me, once I'm in."

"Again, we are just kids. How are Marina and I going to get in with you? We can't be in the school. We don't have the power to possess fire, like you."

"Well, that's something that Nick can figure out! That way,

you guys feel like you have a part in the decision. And if you and Marina are inside with me, then you guys don't have to worry," Eric said, writing it all down on a paper.

"No, but I'll be worried about all three of you," Nick informed them, looking sad.

"Please, I need your help," Eric begged them.

"Fine," they said.

"Thank you. Thank you *so* much! I know none of this makes up for how I treated you guys, but please know that I'm trying," he told them, trying to make peace with them.

"We know, Eric, and I'm sorry that I bit your head off. You are an *amazing* friend. We just feel that sometimes that this friendship is one sided," Marina said to him.

"I promise that I will be better."

"Thank you," she said, giving him a hug.

"But right now, I have to go talk to Sloan about our plan!"

Chapter 13

"Y ou know what to do when we arrive at the court house, right?" Sloan asked Eric, Marina, Nick, Catlin, Mr. Smith, and Mrs. Grey.

It was 6:35 on July first. Sloan had removed the charm that changed Eric's identity, so Marina was applying some stage makeup to ensure no one would notice him before their plan was put into action.

"You're really good at this," Eric said as Marina held up a mirror for him.

She affixed a silicone mask that changed his skinny face into the face of an old man. She was applying some makeup to the mask to make it more realistic when she said, "Thanks! I was on my high school's makeup crew for plays and musicals."

"Is everyone else out of the house and in the lookdown room?" Sloan asked Mr. Smith and Mrs. Grey, talking about the secret hidden room in the basement.

"Yes. We have moved all the students and remaining teachers down there. They know what to do if we do not return within a day's time," Mrs. Grey informed Sloan.

"Good. Now, just as a reminder, things could easily get messy. I don't think the Shadow Reapers would cause too much harm to citizens, but they did destroy the entire east coast. This could undoubtedly be the last time we will be together." Sloan pushed the sleeve of her white battle robe up her arm to check the time. "It is time for us to leave."

Everyone put the hoods up on their robes and quickly walked out the front door and into the new black Chevy Traverse. Sloan drove with Mr. Smith in the front seat. Eric sat in between Mrs. Grey and Catlin, while Nick and Marina sat in the seats behind them.

Sloan had already figured that they had appeared on the Shadow Reaper's radar, because Sloan had to reverse the identity spell on Eric, so she drove faster than she would have and stuck to the back roads. The car ride was deadly silent; everyone was too nervous to talk. Marina's legs were restless, Catlin picked at her fingernails, Nick just sat there and stared straight ahead, and Eric just wanted to run the other way.

The night before, the four of them sat in the living room and talked all night, too nervous to sleep.

"What happens if we fail?" Nick asked.

"Then, we lose?" Catlin asked.

Eric hung his head.

"You know, the last thing I lost was my baby sister when I was younger, so I'm not used to losing at things," Nick said.

"Neither am I," Marina said, taking a break from running around the room.

"Would you stop running? You are making my dizzy." Eric asked her.

"You know it's my way of dealing with stress."

"We know it's your fucking way of dealing with stress, but we have serious things to talk about here, so sit your fucking ass down!" Catlin yelled at her.

Eric looked at her, terrified. He had never heard Catlin yell before that night. He squeezed her hand tighter to comfort her, but it didn't work.

"Can we all just take a second to seriously talk about what could happen, tomorrow?" Eric asked as calmly as he could.

Marina sat down on the floor underneath Nick, who was sitting on the couch. When everyone was quiet, Eric asked, "I know we are all scared to die, but what else are we afraid of?"

"That I'm never going to get to see Jamie or my dad, again," Catlin said, tearing up.

"My mom and brothers will die just because the Shadow Reapers want to mess with me," Nick coldly said.

"I'm afraid that even if we survive all this, it *still* will not be enough to end the Shadow Reapers. That all these deaths will be for nothing. I'm afraid that the days of good have left us for good," Marina softly answered, staring at the white carpet.

"I thought you were an optimist?" Eric asked her, trying to lighten the mood.

"I'm just as messed up as you, Eric, but unlike you, I choose to fake a smile, rather than affect my friends and family with my

281

depression and anger."

Eric was shocked by her answer. Never in a million years would he have guessed that she was depressed.

"I'm sorry."

"What about you. What are you afraid of?" she asked him.

"I'm afraid that if I fail, you guys will be killed. I'm afraid that you and Nick are never going to get that happy ending that you guys deserve. I'm afraid that Catlin will die trying to save my sorry ass. I'm afraid of everything, to be honest. I was afraid from the second that I heard screaming come out of my bedroom window, and I never stopped being afraid. But I'm not afraid of dying; I never was. I'm afraid of what my death will lead to. I'm supposed to be this magical hero that ends it all. What happens if I can't? I don't want to sound egoistic, but I don't want to fail. I've caused too many deaths, already.

"This is the reason why I haven't really gotten too close with you guys. I don't want Elizabeth to use you guys to get to me. I don't want to lose you, and I felt like if I emotionally stayed away, then it wouldn't hurt so bad if any one of you died. I don't mean that in a bad way. I mean if you guys died, I wouldn't know how to deal with it. I love you guys so much. You helped me through a lot.

"I know more recently, I have been distant, but that's because I honestly didn't know how to talk to you guys. I didn't want you to know just how messed up I was."

When Eric was done talking, Marina and Nick walked over and sat next to him on the couch.

"We don't care how messed up you are. We are your friends, and we told you that from day one. We will always be here for you," Nick told him.

"Listen, we may not always understand exactly what you are going through, but we are all messed up in our own ways. I mean, Nick puts Ranch Dressing on his eggs!"

"Hey! It's a good combo!" Nick said, disrupting Marina.

"And I'm sure you have seen old photos of Catlin, before I gave her the makeover in sixth grade. As for me, I understand your depression, and it does help to talk."

"I know, but I just didn't know where to start," Eric admitted.

"Sometimes, just asking for help is a very good place to

start."

As Eric went to give Marina a tight hug, he saw Derrick standing in the hall.

"I have to go to the bathroom. I'll be right back," he said to them as he got off the couch.

"You're not planning to make a run for it, are you?" Nick asked.

"No. Because I'm... I'm not scared, anymore," Eric responded with a warming smile.

His hollow face was now full of joy and love; his dull and lifeless eyes had become rich and bright, again. He was crying, but those tears weren't there because of sadness or pain. They were because for the first time in months, he felt happy and truly loved.

Eric walked out of the living room and walked to the bathroom that was in the library. Derrick followed close behind him. As soon as Eric was in the bathroom, he shut and locked the door behind him.

"What's up?" Eric asked him.

"Nothing. I'm just here to say my goodbyes," he said with smile.

"Goodbye?" Eric asked, confused.

"You don't need me anymore, silly. I've done my job. You have made peace with your friends, and you are no longer as depressed as you were."

"But... I... I need you!"

"No, you don't. You have your friends. What I saw back there proves it. You've started to open up to them."

"Yes, but—"

"But nothing. I can't do anything to help you, now. If you do need me again, I will sense it. But until that time, this is goodbye," he said as he hugged Eric.

"Thank you for your help. I just wish I could help you," Eric said.

"You can."

"What can I do?" Eric asked, eagerly.

"If you see my mom, tell her I'm doing fine and that I'll hopefully see her, soon. Her name is Melody Smith," Derrick said, handing Eric a photo he got from his back pocket.

"I will," Eric informed him, looking at the photo.

Derrick and his mom where sitting on a swing, outside. She looked to be in her early thirties. She had light brown hair that flowed to her shoulders. Her face was fair and very pretty. She had a small button nose, thin lips, and her eyes were bright blue.

"Thank you, Eric. It will mean a lot to me," Derrick said to him before fading away.

A tear fell from Eric's left eye as he put the photo in the front pocket of his shorts. He was sad that he lost a friend, but was relieved that he left because his job was finished, because that meant that Eric was getting better. Eric left the bathroom and headed back to the living room to join his friends.

Chapter 14

It was near 7:00 by the time they had reached the courthouse in Republic. One by one, they all got out of the car. Sloan and Mr. Smith stayed out by the main doors, while Mrs. Grey, Eric, Catlin, and Marina walked inside the large stone building.

As soon as they walked in, an older woman who was the receptionist greeted them. There were three floors. First floor had all the court filings and other records. Second floor was the court offices and where most of the cops and judges were. The third floor had been cleared out and was being used as the Shadow Reapers department, where they kept their own kinds of records.

"Hello, we need to see the head Shadow Reaper, here. I believe his name is Brandon Evans," Eric told the receptionist.

"Do you have an appointment?" she said, looking at Eric through her very large and thick-lensed glasses.

"No, but I have information on the location of Eric James."

"Oh… uh… let me just give Mr. Evans a call."

She immediately picked up the phone and started dialing a number. Eric looked around the building, which seemed to be dead. Catlin, Marina, Nick, and Mrs. Grey had already disappeared. Hopefully, they hadn't gotten in trouble, yet. As Eric began to think about them, he started to get nervous again, and sweat was beginning to form on his forehead.

When she hung up the phone, she said, "Go on up to the third floor. They will be waiting on you."

Eric walked behind her desk and over to the elevator on the far wall. He pushed the up button and waited patiently for the elevator to come down. The bell chimed a loud tone, announcing its arrival. The doors slowly opened up, and Eric stepped in. He was relieved to see that Catlin was waiting for him. She had changed from her white robe into something a little more casual. Black t-shirt, black skinny jeans, and black

Converse shoes.

"You changed quickly. Are you sure that's going to protect you as much as your robes?" Eric asked her after the doors had closed and he'd hit the button for the third floor.

"Should be."

"I don't see why you had to change clothes."

"The others are there to protect you. I am here to be undercover, just like you. As soon as you give away your true identity, I am the one that is supposed to take you away," Catlin calmly told him.

The elevator bell chimed, again, and the doors slowly opened to reveal a black bricked lobby that had little decoration. Again, there was a receptionist at a small desk that was exceptionally clean and organized. She was young, black-haired, black-eyed, and pale, wearing a black blazer and a black skirt.

"How can the Shadow Reapers help you?" she asked, coldly.

Eric stepped close to her and announced, "I know where Eric James is."

By this time, Catlin had tried to make herself invisible by standing near some people by the water cooler.

"What did you say?" the receptionist asked, shocked.

"I know the whereabouts of Eric James."

The receptionist swiftly got up from her chair and darted to the large, black stained glass door with the words **Brandon Evans** etched in gold lettering. Within a few seconds, a tall and very broad man came marching out of the office. He was wearing an expensive-looking three-piece black suit that matched his black eyes. His pale skin was marked up with scratches and burn marks.

"How do you know where Eric James is?" he asked in a very threatening, deep voice that almost shook the room.

"Because I am Eric James!" Eric announced.

He removed his robe hood, raised a hand up to his face, and peeled of the mask that Marina had put on him. As soon as Brandon Evans understood what was going on, he reached under the desk. A deafening siren went off in the building; all the doors shut with a forceful slam, followed by a loud locking noise. Eric knew it was going to happen, but it still took him by surprise.

On cue, Catlin rushed over, and placed the special handcuffs that the Shadow Reapers used to neutralize magic. They got the handcuffs by pick pocketing them from one of the Shadow Reaper Officials that patrolled the town. Eric was scared out of his mind, but all he did was stare at the Head Shadow Reaper with a cold and wicked smile.

"Get him out of here. Take him to the executioners," he commanded.

Catlin's black eyes widened in fear, and Eric's pulse went out of control. This was something they had not planned for.

"Wait.... Wait... I don't come as a White Knight!" Eric bellowed as three more Shadow Reapers came towards him.

"Then, why the hell are you here?" he asked.

"I'm here to join the Shadow Reapers, not the fight them. The White Knights are holding me back!"

The Head Shadow Reaper just stood there looking at Eric, not believing a single word he was saying.

"Just let me talk to Elizabeth! Please, I beg you!" Eric pleaded, falling to his knees.

"Someone stand this pathetic creature up."

After Catlin helped him up, he said, "Come."

Catlin pushed him forward, a little bit more roughly than she wanted to, since he almost fell on his face. They followed Brandon Evans inside his bare office that was painted a deep red. There was large, antique, black wood desk, which was very organized and insanely clean. The entire room was spotless and very sanitary, and there was a hint of bleach in the air.

Behind the desk, there was a mirror that covered the back wall. They walked over to it, the head Shadow Reaper walked in front of it, and as he took his right hand from the left side of the mirror to the right, he said, "Patefacio portas umbram."

Black smoke formed in the corners and rapidly crawled to the center. The smoke started to swirl when it met, creating a vortex. When it calmed down after a few seconds, the mirror was covered in a black void. Brandon Evans motioned to Catlin to push him toward the new portal. She did as she was told, and as they stepped into it, it felt like they were on fire.

It only took them a few seconds to get through, and when they passed through the other side, they were in Elizabeth's office that had been renovated from the last time Eric had seen it. The portal came out near the main door that was made from red stained glass. The corners had off-white marble columns built in, and the walls where the same deep red color as Brandon's office.

There were several posters on the walls that promoted the upgrades. All of them had Elizabeth's face on it. There were a few grey filing cabinets around the walls. Toward the back of the room, there was a modern glass and black metal desk cluttered with papers and files. Behind the desk sat Elizabeth.

"Well, well, well. Look who has given himself up," she said in a cold, mocking tone.

She stopped her work and stared at Eric with her cold black eyes. She flipped back her hair that was covering the left side of her face, which revealed a large burn mark. Eric gasped at the sight of it.

"Yes," Elizabeth announced, "a gift from your dead slutty girlfriend that she left when she cast that fireball charm at my face."

"Oh, she's not dead," Eric told her.

"Is that so? Well, then she should know that the rest of her family is."

Catlin took a sharp breath in, trying to hide her emotions. It wasn't good enough, though, because Elizabeth noticed and said, "Thank you for your help in delivering him to me. You are dismissed."

Catlin bowed to her and left through the glass door. As soon as she was out, she went and looked for Eric's parents.

Chapter 15

"Now, the question is... why are you here, Eric James?" Elizabeth asked in a cold tone.

"I know you planned for me to be executed if I was found, *but* I come here as an ally. I want to join the Shadow Reapers."

"Now *why* on Earth would you do that? I thought you had it *all* with the White Knights. You were going to be the one that ended us Shadow Reapers," she said in a sarcastic tone.

"You wouldn't get it."

"Try me," she returned, leaning forward.

"Two reasons. The White Knights treated me more like... like a threat than a savor. Here, I'll be treated like anyone else who is here."

"And the second reason?" she inquired.

"Because you need me. I know that you said that you don't need me, anymore. However, think of how much easier things would be with someone next to you," he said to her in a very businesslike manner.

"Are you saying I need a man next to me to rule the world?"

"No, that's not what I mean, at all. I just think it would make you more likeable if you had someone to campaign with, and I can help take some of the stress off you and help with all the paperwork."

Elizabeth reclined back into her chair and thought about it.

"You did always have a talent for public relations," she said with a laugh.

Eric let out a little laugh, just to make things a little bit less stiff and awkward.

"We'll see about it. I'll have to think about it. However, I do think that we could use you just as much as you could use us. You can learn ten times as much as you could with the White Knights. I also can guarantee that you will *live* ten times as long."

Elizabeth raised a hand and slowly flicked it in Eric's direction. The handcuffs disappeared, relieving the pressure on his wrists.

"I don't see you as a threat, but if you make the slightest mistake, I'll have you taken down faster than you can blink."

Eric nodded.

"Today, I will add you into our system. Our school doesn't officially start until August twentieth; however, right now, there are summer classes."

"Are you the principal, or whatever?"

"No. I am simply the one who runs everything. The one in charge of the school system is Shadow Reaper Shrock. She controls everything to do with the school system and what is taught. I will send her your information, and she will get in contact with you, today, about housing. We have had to do some construction work to make room for the increase in students," she announced with a smile. "She will also have you take a test to see where your abilities are and then determine what classes you need to be in."

"Okay. So where are the dorms?"

"First floor is the dining room and kitchen. Second and third floor has a few classrooms. Fourth through the ninth floor are for student living. Tenth through the thirteenth floors are more classrooms. The fourteenth floor is my floor. This is where I live, study, and rule the world," she said with a smile.

Eric couldn't believe how many floors this building had, but he figured most of it was underground, since there weren't any windows.

"Of course, this is just the main campus. There are several others just like this one all over the world."

"Where are we?"

"Washington. Inside Mount St. Helens in Washington. Volcanoes are full of magma, which is such a powerful weapon to harness. Don't you think?"

"But why would you harness it?" Eric asked her, confused.

"Daddy moved us here a few years back, even before I was brought here. He said it helps our Fire Manipulation Power. I figured we could control it just as we do fire," she told him, giving him an evil smile.

"Daddy, as in Vesta?"

"Who else would I call daddy?"

"I don't know... maybe, the one who raised you all your life?"

"Those liars? No. Besides, I had them killed a few years ago."

Eric suddenly felt uncomfortable being in the same room as Elizabeth. He had no clue of what he had gotten himself into. She had changed too much. Eric was beginning to panic.

"If you wouldn't mind leaving now, I have a lot of paperwork to get through by tonight."

Eric nodded his head, trying to hide the nervous look on his face, and walked out of the room. When he was out of Elizabeth's office, he stepped toward the stairs that was in the middle of the square hallway and fell to his knees. He started to breathe uncontrollably heavily.

"Dude, are you okay?" asked a guy that was walking up the stairs.

He had short, blond-reddish hair that was semi messy and semi neat. His face was skinny and long. Freckles covered his cheeks and nose. The more Eric looked at him, the more he felt like he had seen him, before. He was taller than Eric, probably around six feet, and as skinny as Eric was.

"Yeah, I'm fine," Eric told him, standing back up.

The guy took off his glasses, cleaned them on his blue t-shirt, and asked, "Did you just receive an upgrade?"

"No."

"Then, why do you look like you're freaking out?" he said in a mocking tone.

"Do—you—not—know—who—I—am?" Eric asked between deep breaths.

"Nope. Should I?"

Eric shook his head.

"I'm Jeremy Dowes," he stuck a hand out, "Nice to meet you!"

Eric shook his hand, saying, "Eric James."

It took a few millisecond for Eric's brain to place the name with the medical file that Eric had looked at nearly a month ago. The only difference was his face was paler, and his eyes were pitch black.

"How old are you?" Eric asked him.

"Twenty-three, why?"

"Aren't you a little old to be a Shadow Reaper in training?"

"Nah, there are a few people here that are older than me. Although they do limit the upgrades to people between the ages of eleven to twenty five. Anyone older than that, they just use for testing. Or so I've heard."

"How can you say that like it's something that's normal? They are killing people for the hell of it!"

Jeremy leaned in close to Eric and said, "You learn not to question things around here. If you do, you get taken away."

Eric's eyes lit up in fear. There was no way he was going to get out of here, alive. The more he thought of how messed up this plan was, the more he started to regret the decision. He wanted to talk to his friends but had no clue if they have even made it through okay or not.

"Are you sure you're okay?" Jeremy asked, noticing the frightened look on Eric's face.

"I just need to get some fresh air. This place is making me feel claustrophobic."

"Come on," Jeremy said, grabbing Eric's hand.

He guided Eric down the black marble stairs into a grey painted hallway lined with rooms that had class numbers on the solid metal doors. There was another staircase at the end of the hallway that led to a floor that looked like the same as the previous; only the stairs were on the opposite end of the hall. This pattern continued for two more floors, until they came across a floor that had the bedrooms. The walls were still the same grey color as the other floors.

There were bathrooms to the right of the stairs, and the bedrooms were to the right. Eric could see a room at the end of the hall that sounded and looked like a commons room, since there were people coming in and out and the sound of music and people talking.

When they reached the second floor, a small balcony led to a few more classrooms on the other side. Jeremy, still pulling Eric, walked down one more staircase. This one led to a large room with black marble floor, off-white brick walls, and a large navy blue chandelier was hanging from the bottom of the balcony. There were several more posters with Elizabeth's face on the walls. About twenty round, glass tables were placed around the room.

The wall opposite from the stairs had a serving counter and a doorway that looked like it went into the kitchen. Jeremy headed to the wall to their right, which had a massive metal archway that looked like something from a kid's storybook.

"This is the closest thing we have to the outside," he announced as they entered a vast sun-lit room. There were tall hedge bushes on either side of them, and in the center of the room was a round fountain the size of an Olympic pool. The hedge bush went all the way around the fountain, and there were a few small flower boxes and benches around the area.

"The bushes are a maze," Jeremy informed him, "Look up."

Eric looked up and saw the sky was all around the room. No mountains, no trees, no hills, just the sun and the clear blue sky.

"It's a charm. The room is actually dome shaped, but the walls mirror the sky, outside, and the environment in here mirrors the environment outside. So, if it's windy outside, it's windy in here. If it's storming outside, it's storming in here."

"That's cool!" Eric said in awe.

"It's the only beauty I have found here."

Eric walked over to the Roman-style fountain and sat on the edge of it, enjoying the mist and the soft breeze that was blowing.

"Are you sure you're okay? You still look like you're going to pass out."

"Yeah, I'm fine. I just need to digest everything."

"Okay. I have to go. I was on my way to my check up when I ran into you," he said with a laugh.

He waited for Eric to say something, and when it was clear Eric was done, he left.

Eric realized that he was still wearing the white battle robe. He took it off, along with his book bag that was under it. He took out a disposable phone that he bought and shoved the robe into the book bag.

Butter and eggs? he texted to Catlin's disposable phone.

He sat his phone next to him and waited for it to go off.

Bread and milk! she texted back after a few minutes.

Eric breathed a deep sigh of relief. Catlin, Marina, and Nick, who had sneaked in with the help of Eric's parent's help, had all made it here safely and were with Eric's parents. He still didn't know when he was going to see them next, but they were safe.

"Mr. Eric James?" said a tall, skinny, older woman in a black pinstripe skirt and blazer with a white dress shirt.

Her hair was pulled back into a tight bun. She had sharp cheekbones, a foul look on her face, and she carried a brown paper package and a clipboard with a file attached to it.

"Yes?" Eric answered.

"Come with me," she said before she turned around and walked out of the garden.

Eric put his phone in his shorts pocket, grabbed his book bag, and hurried after the woman.

"My name is Beatrix Shrock, but you will address me as Shadow Reaper Shrock. Here is your room assignment, here is your test date, and here is your uniform. We gathered your measurements from the last time you were here. It is to be worn Monday through Friday from the time you wake until you go to sleep," she said, handing him the papers and package, still walking toward the stairs. "That is all for now. Do not be late for your test; otherwise, you will be punished."

Chapter 16

Eric's bedroom was on the fourth floor, bed 10. As he walked near the boys' bedroom, other students kept giving him strange looks. He kept walking toward the bedroom, trying not to care. He pushed open the metal door that said **Boys' Bedroom #1**.

The room was the same grey color as the other walls but packed with bunk beds. Each bed had a number on it, white sheets, and a dresser with the corresponding number to it. The bedroom had about thirty bunks in it and was very crowded, making Eric even more claustrophobic.

Eric found his bed, which was the top bunk, and put his clothes and the uniforms that were in the package in his dresser. He had nothing else to do, so he climbed up to the second bunk, lay down, and stared up at the white painted ceiling and at the glass balls with fire in them that lit the room; the same glass balls that hung everywhere else.

"Are you ready for this?" Elizabeth asked?

They were getting ready to get in line for the Ring Of Fire, a roller coaster that went upside down in a loop and hung you there. It was the annual summer fair, and Elizabeth was trying to talk Eric into going on the roller coaster.

"You know they put these things up over night, right? That can't be safe!" Eric tried to explain to her.

"Babe, they wouldn't have it if it wasn't safe."

"I don't care. I'll just stay here and hold your purse and phone."

"No. You are getting on this ride with me!" she said, laughing as she pulled him into the line.

As soon as they were in line, several large groups of people walked behind them.

"Now, you can't chicken out!" Elizabeth pointed out.

While they waited in the long line, Eric began to bite at his

*fingernails. When Elizabeth noticed, she grabbed his arm.
"You have nothing to be nervous about. These rides are safe. I
promise!"*

*People behind Eric took notice of his behavior and started
to tease him.*

*"Did you hear about the girl that had her feet cut off
because a screw broke while she was on the ride?" asked
someone with a high and annoying voice.*

*"Yes! The same thing happened to another guy, except it
decapitated him. A screw broke, and a wire snapped," said
someone with a more raspy and lower voice.*

"Elizabeth, I can't go on this ride. I don't want to die!"

"Grow up. It's just a ride."

*Elizabeth glanced back at them and shot them a nasty and
evil look. They shut up, instantly, and took a step back. Eric
saw the look she gave, but what he didn't see was that she
threatened them with a fireball that she had in her hand.*

"Thank you," he said under his breath.

Elizabeth nodded her head and leaned in for a kiss.

*"Are you okay? You're freezing," Eric asked after they
broke apart.*

*"I'm fine. I'm not even cold. Maybe, you're the one that's
sick," she said, laughing.*

*"I mean it! You're freezing!" Eric said, placing his hand
on her pale yellow, short sleeved shirt.*

*"You're exaggerating, Eric. I'm not the least bit cold. You
are just trying to find a way out of getting on the
rollercoaster."*

*Maybe, it was just his head playing tricks on him. Or
maybe, it was the heat of the day getting to him. Either way, it
still felt weird, but he decided to drop the issue and just wait in
line.*

*It was about twenty minutes later before they handed their
tickets to the guy operating the ride, who was extremely tan
and fat, wearing a red polo and tan shorts. Elizabeth led Eric
to the front two seats at the beginning of the rollercoaster. Eric
tried to protest, but Elizabeth wouldn't hear it.*

*They had to wait a few more minutes for everyone to get in
their seats and for the guy to check the safety bars that held
them in. When he was finished, he walked over to his station*

and sat on the sun-bleached, red stool. He pushed one of the buttons on the controller, and the ride started.

Eric closed his eyes, and as the roller coaster teetered forward and backwards to gain speed, Eric reached for Elizabeth's hand. As soon as his hand touched her freezing cold hand, she recoiled, saying, "Only pussies hold hands on a roller coaster."

Just as they were gaining enough speed to go all the way around, there was a loud snap, and the top of the track fell to the ground. Time froze; the roller coaster carts were just hanging in mid air.

"You are running out of time, Eric. I know I have made mistakes and didn't always treat you the best, but you have to save me. Things are going to get harder for you. Things will be revealed to you in the next few months, and there will be deaths. Be strong. I love you. Don't give up."

Time sped back up to normal, and screams of horror filled the air; the carts fell to the ground. The rest of the track collapsed, and a cloud of dust surrounded the area.

Eric jolted up, breathing heavily with sweat dripping off his face. His whole body was in pain. He looked around the room, and everyone was gone. It was 12:46, meaning he had missed lunch. His stomach growled, and he thought of the last time he ate, which was two days ago. He had been too nervous to eat, yesterday and this morning.

He got out of the bed and decided to go on a walk. This place was cold, unwelcoming, and there was something about it that just felt wrong. Then again, everything about the Shadow Reapers felt wrong.

Just as he was thinking about this, he saw a sign on the wall that stated: **Be careful, we are listening to your thoughts.** It sent shivers down his back. He never really thought about his telepathic power, mostly because he never used it, except for in class.

"Eric, why aren't you at lunch?" Elizabeth asked, walking towards him.

"I fell asleep."

"Lunch is mandatory to all students."

"Sorry."

"You don't need to know why," she said to him.

"I—I didn't ask why."

"You read the sign. I know you did."

"Okay, that's creepy. Stop."

"Always complaining."

"Sorry."

Elizabeth ignored him and continued down the hall. She was about to enter one of the bedrooms when she said, "Your friend, Jeremy, didn't pass his test, so he was… taken care of. We only accept the finest here at the Shadow Reaper Academy."

Chapter 17

A t 6:00 on the dot Monday morning, a loud alarm went off. No one bothered to explain to Eric what the alarm was for, but everyone got up and headed to the bathroom.

Stupid new people. When are they going to learn how things are run around here, Eric heard from someone when he used his Telepathy power.

He was a bit rusty with it, so he had to try a few times to key into one person. He did this a few times and got the same result. They didn't care about him or who he was. They saw him as disposable, and one person even said he would be gone in a few days.

He grabbed one of his uniforms, toothbrush and toothpaste, and a comb from his dresser, and followed the other boys to the bathroom across the hall. It was covered in obsidian tile. There were twenty-five shower stalls on the left and right walls that had red towels hanging on the outside of the doors. In the middle of the room, there were sinks lined back to back, with double-sided mirrors hanging from the ceiling along with several more of the glass balls with fire in them.

Eric placed his clothes outside of the stall like everyone else, stepped into one of the shower stalls, and to his surprise, he found a toilet sitting right under the showerhead.

"Don't complain. Just get used to it," said the guy next to him.

Eric quickly showered and changed into his uniform. Black dress pants, black dress shirt, and a black vest. He fixed his hair and tried to make it as neat as he could, without gel. Then, he brushed his teeth.

It's the eyes.

And the skin.

What's up with him?

He still feels other emotions. Why is he still here?

Eric heard them talk about him. Of course, they wouldn't

299

say any of it out loud, because that would be rude, even for a Shadow Reaper. Eric hurried out of there and headed toward the dining room. His test was right after breakfast in room 1006.

The dining room wasn't crowded yet, but it had a few dozen people in it. Eric looked at the kitchen and saw a few Spirit Slaves working. Eric sat down at an empty table close to a back corner and people-watched for a few. It seemed to Eric that everyone generally looked the same. Sure, there were some height and weight differences, but everyone was dressed the same and had the same haircuts.

Guys parted their hair on the side and combed it over. Most of them had their sleeves neatly rolled up past their elbows. Girls seemed to have a choice between a long-sleeve black dress that fell just below the knees or black dress pants and a black long-sleeved blouse. Their hair was shoulder length and either held back by a black headband or pulled onto a ponytail.

As time got closer to 8:00, the room was filling up, and as seats were filling up, people began to sit with Eric.

At 8:00 sharp, another alarm went off, and everyone got up and walked to the counter to get food. He grabbed a white tray and waited to get food, staring down at his tray as he stayed in line.

"Breakfast croissant?" asked a familiar voice.

Eric looked up to see his mom, nodding at her as she handed him a foil-wrapped sandwich. He continued on, grabbed a glass of water, and went back to sit at his seat. He unwrapped his sandwich, and underneath the foil, he found a piece of paper.

Tonight @ 10. Travel quickly and quietly.

He quickly shoved the note in his pants pocket and ate his meal, keeping to himself. When he was done with his sandwich, he placed his tray and cup above a trashcan with a few other dirty utensils. There was still half an hour of breakfast, but Eric left to go to the testing room.

Eric had about ten minutes left by the time he got to room 1006 up on the tenth floor. Knocking on the door, softly, he waited for someone to answer.

"Come in," said the familiar, cold, monotone voice of Shadow Reaper Shrock.

Eric slowly opened the door to the cold, sterile-looking room that was half full of student desks and a bare teacher's desk toward the front of the room. Eric figured that the rest of the area was for practice. There were no decorations, no windows; just a few of the glass balls with fire in them to light the room.

Most of the desks were already full with students, and Shadow Reaper Shrock was sitting at the teacher's desk. Eric walked over to one of the desks that were towards the front of the room. The desk had two pencils and a packet that was faced down on it.

The alarm rang at 9:00, and Shadow Reaper Shrock stood up, fixed her black blazer, and cleared her throat.

"You have fifty minutes to finish the test. The test itself is comprised of three hundred and fifty questions; fifty questions for each subject. The subjects include Fire Manipulation, Dark Magic, Telepathy, Battle Techniques, Metamorphosis, Molecular Immobility, and Potions.

"After you are done, you will turn in your test to me. I will grade it and will find you later today with your results. You will also get an information packet on how to order supplies for class and your login information for the school website. Now, please turn your packets over and begin the test."

Eric turned his test over and began. He thought it was weird that it was testing knowledge of the powers and not actually testing the usage of the powers. Eric figured that most of the people in this room had just received their upgrade, so he didn't understand why they had to take the test. After all, they would have no knowledge of any kinds of magic, until now.

Yet, by the time Eric was about two hundred questions in, most of them had turned in their test. Time was running out, and Eric still had about half the test to get through. Luckily, most of them were multiple-choice questions, so Eric quickly rushed through the rest of the test.

"Ten minutes left."

Eric hurried through the last couple sections of the test and turned in his test before time was up. As he handed in his test, Shadow Reaper Shrock gave him a very displeased look.

He left the classroom and went upstairs to see if Elizabeth was in her office.

"Come on in, Eric," she said as he approached the door.

He opened the door and stepped a few feet into the room.

"Are you busy?" he asked her.

"I'm always busy. What is it that you want?" she asked him, sounding annoyed.

"I don't look like everyone else here."

"There's not much we can do about that. We can't make you paler, and we can't do anything about your eyes. You'll just have to get used to it. If I'm being honest, I would miss your green eyes if we could."

"I think we could use my looks as a publicity move, as well. Not saying that I look like a model or anything, just saying that because I look normal, it could get more people to like us. I was just afraid that people here might not like it."

"If they don't like the way I run things, then they can be terminated. I do, however, think that your idea could work. We've used CGI for my appearance on camera, but you would be good for personal meetings. Come, take a seat."

When Eric sat down in the chair across from her, she said, "I have been planning a world tour to get more people to agree to upgrades."

"That's a good plan, but how are you going to do it?"

"If you don't agree, you are killed."

"That's just going to frighten more people. More people are just going to revolt against you. Why don't we have some meet and greets and some public speeches?"

"What would I say?" she asked, curious.

"Something about what you hope to accomplish at the end. As of right now, it's not clear, at all. Maybe, assure the people that the upgrade is harmless, that it will in fact improve their lives. Say things that will make you seem less hostile and more warm."

"I see. It would help our numbers."

"I could help write the speeches."

"What would you get out of it?"

"Nothing. I just want to do my duty as a Shadow Reaper."

"Maybe, you're not as useless as I had thought."

"Thanks," he said, not sure if that was a complement or an insult. "Now, first things first. What is your goal?"

"To end all wars and create a world where there is nothing but Shadow Reapers."

"Okay. So, we will say your goal is to ensure peace and

equality for all, and bettering lives by offering upgrades to people. Our slogan could be something along the lines of 'Utopia is no longer just a dream!'"

"That sounds cheesy."

"But people fall for cheesy."

"If this fails, it will be on you."

"I understand. So, when is the world tour?"

"It starts in a few weeks on July twenty-fifth and will last a month. The first stop is Seattle. You will be in charge of my speeches for each spot. I will get with those who are in charge of scheduling and get back to you about your ideas. Is that all?"

"One more thing. Did you mean what you said, last year? About our relationship being one big lie."

"It's sad that that even bothers you," she said, mockingly.

"I was in love with you, and I thought you really did love me. You know what it did to me when your parents told me you were kidnapped? It broke me. I didn't eat. I didn't sleep. All I could do was cry."

"Which is what makes you weak. But yes. What I said last year was true. Our relationship was a lie. To be fair, we were only in middle school. You had to realize that nothing would be long-term. When Vesta found out that I knew you and that you were in love with me, it filled him with glee. It made capturing you easier."

"Wow, you really are heartless," Eric said, getting mad.

"I am my father's daughter. It's what makes a Shadow Reaper."

"I've noticed. Everyone here seems to only have one emotion. Hate."

"We made some changes to your blood for the upgrades. Removing all other emotions other than hate was one of them. Anyone who fails in that aspect of the test will be terminated."

"There's just one more thing I don't understand. You. Why didn't you kill me when you had the chance, last year? You had many opportunities. You also had many opportunities to kill the White Knights. Why not just finish everything when you had the chance?"

"Vesta had it all planned. Even down to his death, which is why he didn't put up a fight. He made the White Knights think that they had won by killing him, and then after he was dead, I took control. The plan was never to kill you. You were going to join us one way or another. We didn't kill the White Knights, because they are not a threat. They are weak and small in numbers. Why kill something that is already dying?"

Eric sat there, not knowing what to say or do. None of it was making sense. He was even more confused than ever, so he got up and left the room without saying goodbye to Elizabeth. He didn't know where he was going to go. He had no one to talk to here. He had nowhere that felt safe and comforting to him.

When he got out of Elizabeth's office, he started walking, but as he got further away, he started running. Still had no clue where he was going, but it felt better than doing nothing. A few people yelled at him to stop. Others gave him hateful looks, and Eric just about lost it all.

Chapter 18

Eric ended up just staying in the garden until 8:00, when a couple Shadow Reaper Officials came around to enforce the curfew. Eric walked up to the bedroom on the fourth floor and got into his bed and waited until 9:45. At that time, he grabbed his wand from his dresser and quietly headed out of the room. Eric was shocked that there wasn't anyone patrolling the halls.

He put socks on to make sure that his feet didn't make sounds on the marble floors. Every time he ran into a stairway, he double-checked to make sure no one was coming before he went down. The garden was dark and quiet, besides the sound of rushing water from the fountain.

Eric entered the maze and followed the path back to the very back. There, sitting on a wood bench, was his mom and dad, Catlin, Marina, and Nick. Eric started running toward them to hug them. It was weird to Eric; they were translucent, yet they were solid. Sure, for his friends it was just a charm, but it wasn't for his parents.

"It's complicated," Eric's dad explained. "We are technically dead, but we have a physical presence. We can feel, touch, smell, and age, but we don't breathe or bleed."

"Zombies," Nick informed them.

"Kind of, but we are see-through, and we can't be killed by a shot to the head," his dad responded.

When things calmed down and they stopped hugging, Eric's mom asked, "Do you have any information, yet?"

"Yes. I know what Elizabeth's plan is."

"How?" Nick asked, surprised.

"She told me, because she made me her PR person, and I'm helping with her world tour that she's doing."

Eric explained everything that he and Elizabeth had discussed from the first day, up until the conversation they had today.

"Is she insane?" Catlin exclaimed very loudly.

"Does she realize that it's not going to work?" asked Nick.

"Honestly, it seems like she genuinely is. Every time I'm in the same room, I get these really weird vibes. She kills for the hell of it. Who does that?" Eric asked.

No one answered him. They just sat there. Catlin broke the silence first by saying, "I saw my mom. I nearly gave her a heart attack, if she could get one. I explained everything to her and asked her if she had seen Jamie or dad, but she hasn't."

"That's good news, though! It means that they're still safe," Eric said, comforting her.

"How are you doing?" Marina asked him.

"Okay. I'm just trying to get used to things, here. *Everything* is so much different from Aviance. I was just getting used to things there. I don't know if I'm going to make it through this."

"Do you have your wand, hun?" Eric's mom asked.

He took his wand from his sweatpants pocket and handed it to her.

"What's in it?" she asked.

"Crystal, sage, and lavender."

"The things you put into your wand symbolize what your true characteristics are. They are your favorite things for a reason. If they weren't, then the potion wouldn't have worked. The crystal you used it agate, which stands for strength. The sage stands for wisdom. The lavender stands for devotion. You will make it through this. You all will."

"Why did you hide it from me?" Eric asked his parents.

"What?" his dad asked, confused.

"You guys had magical powers, even though you weren't supposed to. Why did you hide it from me?"

"Your mom and I did have to give up our powers to be with each other. However, we did so temporarily."

"We knew that we would eventually be attacked by one side or another, and that if we had a child, so would it, even if we didn't have powers," his mom informed him.

"We had some help from our families to ensure that we would keep our powers. We didn't know how long it would last or if you would even have powers by the time you were born. Honestly Eric, we had no clue you had powers. You never showed any sign of them. We never told you about our powers to keep you safe," his dad finished, a frown creasing his face.

"We are sorry, Eric. We can only imagine how you feel," his mom softly said, placing a hand on his shoulder.

"It was hard, at first. I was very confused and *very* depressed, but my friends helped me a lot. And one day, I hope I can help them like they helped me," Eric said, looking at them.

"But seriously, how does Elizabeth think this is all going to work, and how is doing all of this by herself? She's only sixteen!" Nick said.

"She's not doing this by herself. As far as I can tell, she's really not head of anything. She delegates everything to other people," Eric informed them.

"Then, who are we after?" asked Marina.

"She is still the queen, so if we take her out, it will be easier to take out the rest. As for if she thinks her plan will work, she seems positive it will. She will do anything to make it work," Eric conceded.

"Please, be careful, Eric," Catlin said to him.

"I will. I am doing my best to make everyone safe. Now, Elizabeth is planning a world tour to get more support for the upgrades. It starts in a few weeks. Nick, I will try to get the details to you as soon as I can. I think that the kickoff party and speech would be a good opportunity to strike back."

"I will need to see blueprints of the venue, assuming that it's not going to be here. I would also like a list of all that's invited. Once I have that, I'll start to make a plan and see if I can get in contact with Sloan. Marina and Catlin have been getting some strange visions about the next few months," Nick informed them.

"There wasn't much in my vision, but I saw a cliff with a figure standing near the edge," Catlin said.

"You're not going to like what I saw. I know Catlin didn't," Marina told him.

"What is it?" Eric asked, scared.

"Well, for one, I saw a lot of red. I couldn't really make anything out, just the color. Secondly, I saw what looked like an announcement for a wedding. The names on it were Eric Arthur James and Elizabeth Mary Williams."

Fear filled Eric's eyes. "No… Why?" he asked.

Marina shrugged her shoulders, looking just as confused as

everyone else. There was a moment of silence, before Eric spoke, again.

"There's one thing I don't understand. Why would you try to get rid of my memories of this place?"

"How do you know about that?" Marina asked, shocked.

"As soon as I stepped into this place, the memories flooded in."

"Eric, Sloan had to. They were destroying you. Something Elizabeth did to you," Nick told him.

"I just don't understand. I know you did it to help me, but what did you think would happen when I came here?"

"We honestly had no clue what would happen. We had plans if anything did happen. We were hoping that the memories wouldn't come back, but we had planned for the worst. The worst being the memories came back and destroyed you. If that had happened, we were basically fucked," Marina said to him.

"Excuse me?" Eric's mom said to her.

"Sorry."

She gave Marina a stern look, and then, turned to Eric and said, "All that matters is that you are okay for now."

"However, Sloan fears that they could still trigger and cause your body to start destroying itself, again. If that happens, we won't be able to save you, again," Catlin confessed.

"Like my mom said, I'm fine for now. I remember how I felt before that attack happened. If it happens, again, I'll come find you. Promise. I'm not mad, at all. I just didn't understand why you guys didn't say anything about it."

"We didn't know if anything had happened until you mentioned it. We assumed that your memories were still blocked. Catlin said you acted okay that day," Nick explained.

"My poker face is a good one. I didn't want to show any emotion that could compromise our situation. But it was scary. All the images and pain," Eric said as tears started to fall.

"Eric," Catlin said as she moved to sit next to him, "we know it's scary for you. We can't even begin to imagine the things you went through. It's going to be hard, but please try to get through this. It will all be over soon, and then, you can try to put this all behind you."

As the time reached midnight, Eric left his parents and friends and headed back to the bedroom. But before he left, he asked his parents if they would do something for him.

"Can you do a favor for a friend of mine?" he asked after his friends had left.

"We will try our best, son," his father said to him.

"Can you tell Melody Smith that her son is doing well and that she shouldn't worry? She is a Spirit Slave, here."

Eric handed the photo that Derrick had given Eric over to his parents. They promised they would try to help, hugged and kissed Eric, and then left. Eric stayed in the maze for a little while longer, looking up at the stars.

He was happy that his questions were finally answered, but he was still confused and a bit worried about the memories of last year. The thing he didn't tell them was that the memories were causing him pain, but he was just trying to ignore them as much as he could and to just bottle up the pain.

After all, they did the right thing by helping him. He just had mixed feelings about the whole thing. He was mad that they risked his life by not knowing what would happen and that they tried to hide memories from him, but he was happy that they were honest with him and didn't continue to lie. The next few weeks were going to be challenging, hard, and scary, but Eric was ready.

Chapter 19

A week later, and the Shadow Reapers were celebrating another victory in a battle against the White Knights. Eric had gotten a message from Sloan through an email address saying that if anything was going to happen, it needed to happen, soon.

Our situation is getting worse. Mrs. Grey hadn't predicted the attack. Our numbers are dwindling quite rapidly, and with it, so are our powers. Nick has informed me of the plan. We are trying to get as many reinforcements as we can, but it doesn't look good.

Marina had set up Eric's computer the next time they met to hack into the Shadow Reaper Official's records and military files. He sent what he could about military standings, statistics, records, and plans to Sloan over email, then Eric had messed with some of the statistics that just came in that were being sent to Elizabeth.

When Elizabeth got a hold of the new reports, she had Eric come up to her office to talk about the tour and what they can do about numbers.

"Support is down, and so are the numbers of upgrades. We need to accelerate our plans. We need an idea that can help us. Are you going to be that person to do it, or are you incompetent?" Elizabeth asked him.

Eric was going to hate himself for suggesting it, but he said, "If you want numbers to increase for support, you could make yourself more likeable if you found a partner."

"A partner?" Elizabeth asked, intrigued.

"The media is always about couples. Who's with who? You know?"

"And you think that it should be with you?"

"Well, I am very likable."

Elizabeth sat back in her chair and thought about it. Before she had the chance to say anything, Eric said, "And the media also loves a wedding. Who's invited? What is the bride wearing? What is the dress going to look like? Where is it going to be? All that stuff. It's good publicity."

"Just to make this clear. You are suggesting that two sixteen year olds get married?"

"You are Queen of everybody of land and everybody of water."

"True, and it would be a scandal. *Everybody* loves a scandal. However, this marriage will not be real. It does *not* mean anything."

"Trust me, I understand. After all, you tortured me for *months*! Have you *seen* the scars that I have? Why would I want it to be real?" he spat, bitterly.

"If anything goes wrong, you know what I'm capable of," she threatened.

"Yes, and I am reminded of that every day."

A cold, creepy smile grew on Elizabeth's face.

"Pain will drive you, Eric. It will be the fuel of your hatred. And that hatred will help you become more like us. Soon, you won't feel anything other than that. Once you're full of nothing but hate, your eyes will turn pitch black like everyone else's. After all, they eyes are the key to a person's soul."

"That would never happen to me," he said, instantly.

"But it's already happening, my dear Eric. Your eyes are darker than they were two years ago."

Fear spread across his body, remembering what Catlin said about his eyes.

"Don't be scared, Eric dear. It's a good change. You were too depressing, anyways. Always have been 'Oh poor me, I'm so misunderstood. I don't know where I belong in life'," she mocked him.

"Shut the *fuck* up."

"There we go. *Feel* that rage! *Fuel* that anger! Soon, you will be like the rest of us. And there's no way of stopping it."

Eric's head started to hurt, and white pain spread across his body. His eyes felt like they were on fire.

"Stop trying to fight it, Eric. If you fight it, then it will kill you. I can tell that someone tried to stop it from spreading, before, but that only made it stronger. Who blocked it? Sloan? Yep, looks like her handiwork."

"Get—out—of—my—head!" Eric shouted at her.

"You are weak. You would be killed, immediately, if you were anybody else."

Eric opened his eyes that still felt like they were on fire, burst out of his chair, leaned over Elizabeth's desk, and reached for her throat. A fire whip extended from his hand, tightly wrapping around Elizabeth's neck. Her neck snapped, she grabbed Eric's arm, and pushed him. Eric flew across the room, hitting his back hard against the wall.

The whip disappeared, and Eric's body was frozen.

"Is this how you treat your soon-to-be bride? Funny... I don't recall you being into whips and chains in the bedroom when we were dating."

"Oh-"

"Go fuck yourself. God, could you get any more predictable," she said as she snapped her neck back into place, "You look like hell, by the way."

"Unfreeze me."

"But you look so good just slumped there."

Eric just stared at her, giving her a menacing look. Finally, after a few minutes, she said with a laugh, "Would you stop glaring at me with those black hole eyes of yours? It's creepy."

"No!" he screamed.

A disturbingly wide smile grew on Elizabeth's face.

"Welcome to the Shadow Reaper Academy, and congratulations on becoming a Shadow Reaper."

Elizabeth unfroze Eric's body, but he still sat there, unmoving.

She grabbed a little compact mirror from a desk drawer, walked over to Eric, handed it to him, and said, "Don't believe me, look for yourself."

Eric took the mirror from her, and sure enough, his eyes had turned pitch black. There was no color in them at all; no white, no green. Just pure blackness.

"Make it go away!" Eric shouted at her.

"Too late. What is done is done. There is no turning back, now."

Eric felt like he was going to cry, but nothing came out, which made him even more angry. He couldn't cry, because he couldn't feel sadness, anymore. When he thought about it, he couldn't feel anything but hate.

"Why did you do this to me?"

"I didn't do anything to you. All of this was inside of you, from your father's side, waiting to be released. You just have been too afraid to let it come out."

"Liar!"

"I may hate you, but I am no liar."

Elizabeth opened up the door to the hallway. "You are dismissed. Come back tomorrow afternoon, and we will discuss more of the tour."

Eric stood up, walked out of her office, and headed to the garden where Catlin and Nick were waiting for him.

"Eric?" Catlin asked as he approached them.

"Yeah, it's me. You don't want to know," he said when he saw them stare at him.

Catlin walked over to him, gently placed a hand on his face, and asked, "What happened? Are you okay?"

Eric placed his hand on hers, and she gasped.

"What's wrong?" Eric asked, stepping back.

"You're ice cold!"

"I'm fine. Honestly. If I wasn't, I would tell you guys."

Nick and Catlin looked at each other as if to say, *Should we believe him?*

"Are there any updates on your side?" Eric asked them.

Nick cleared his throat and said, "There was an attack on one of our larger forces. That's why Marina isn't here. Her mother was one of the lives lost, and her dad was badly injured, but he escaped."

"Any word from your families?" Eric asked them.

Catlin shook her head, and Nick said, "My mother is with family somewhere in Canada with my brothers, but my dad killed himself to save them."

"I'm sorry. I really am. And Catlin, I haven't found anything about your dad or sister in the records. They are completely off the grid, which is good. It means Elizabeth doesn't know about them."

"But she could use me as leverage to get to them."

"No. She doesn't work like that. She would just kill them," he said bluntly. "Anyways, since things are getting worse, what does Sloan think we should do?"

"Well, since our numbers are depleting fast, along with our magic, she suggests that we use forces outside of magic. Which is something that is being debated right now," Nick informed him.

"What kind of outside forces?" Eric asked intrigued.

Catlin sat down on a bench, crossed her arms, and said, "Guns, bombs, and other explosives."

"That's not a bad idea, actually. We wouldn't be expecting it," Eric said.

"*We?* Since when have the Shadow Reapers become a *we* to you?" Nick interrogated him.

"Since I started looking like them. Now, why are they debating this? This is the best idea you guys have had in weeks."

"Well, you know, some people aren't comfortable putting guns in the hands of kids."

"There are two people in life. Those who shoot, and those who get shot," he said, coldly.

"Eric Arthur James! How dare you!" Catlin yelled.

"Tell Sloan that she has my support. I have another meeting with Elizabeth about the tour, tomorrow. I will meet you again, after that," Eric said before he left.

Chapter 20

"**Y**ou don't have much more time, Eric," Elizabeth said as they lay on the grass outside in Eric's backyard, watching the spring clouds roll over the sun.

"What are you talking about?"

"Don't play dumb. I know that you know what I'm talking about."

"I already have your birthday present, and our anniversary isn't for another month. I don't know what you're talking about."

Elizabeth sat up. "Think hard. Think about Catlin, and Nick, and Marina. Think about Sloan. Think about the White Knights and the Shadow Reapers. Think about how much you really hate me."

"What are you talking about?"

"God, you are so dimwitted. I hope that you will remember this when you wake up."

"What are you talking about?"

"Just listen. I'm not really here. I am what is left of Elizabeth's soul. It's complicated, but I'm here to help you. So please, listen to me."

"What are you even talking about?" Eric asked, convinced he had lost his mind.

"You have to stop me; the real me. You have to kill me. I know that's going to be hard for you, but if you kill me, then things are going to be a lot easier for the White Knights. You see, after Vesta was killed, all his powers went to Elizabeth, something that he had control over. Because she has his powers, she is linked to every Shadow Reaper out there, including you.

"If you kill the power source, it will weaken them, significantly, giving you a more significant chance to win this war. When you kill Elizabeth, it will be like turning off the lights in the brains of the Shadow Reapers.

"Elizabeth hasn't set up anyone to be the heir of her powers, so there's no one else to worry about. Without her, the Shadow Reapers won't stand a chance."

"I just don't understand any of this!"

Elizabeth leaned down to kiss him; first on his forehead and then on his lips.

"I know you don't, sweetie, but it will all make sense when you wake up. Now, this will probably be the last time we talk, ever. Because I'm growing too weak to contact you, and if all goes as planned, Elizabeth will be dead, soon. With her death, comes my freedom."

"Freedom?"

"Just because you're a Shadow Reaper and your soul has been removed, doesn't mean it's gone, forever. You can always get it back. It takes a while, and it takes a lot of effort, but it can happen. But until that time, your soul is stuck in a sort of limbo. And if you wait too long, if you don't try hard enough, then it will die.

"When you sleep, your consciousness is easier to get into. That is how I've been communicating with you, but I'm not always guaranteed to be able to fully intervene and communicate with you, and most of the time, like now, you don't understand what I'm talking about."

"Elizabeth, have you gone insane? You aren't making any *sense to me."*

"Save me, Eric. Please. I love you," Elizabeth pled.

The sky turned dark, and the surrounding area turned pitch black. Eric couldn't see anything. He jumped up on his feet and reached out to find Elizabeth, but he couldn't feel anything. The grass beneath his bare feet turned into what felt like smooth concrete. The warm air that had filled the air was still, cold, and smelt stale.

"Elizabeth!" he shouted.

Unexpectedly, when he took another step, the floor was no longer there, and he fell down. Darkness still surrounded him as he fell, and the longer he fell, the more he felt afraid. He had no clue what was up, what was down, and he had no clue what direction he was falling. He could see nothing and feel nothing but the wind that surrounded him.

Eric woke up the next morning at 4:39, gasping for air. He almost fell out of his bed when he jolted up so he could catch his breath. The more he breathed in, the more of the images of his dreamed flooded his head. He grabbed the cell phone he'd been using to text his friends with.

Meet me in garden. Now. He sent them.

Eric quietly got out of bed and headed straight to the garden, not really caring how much noise he made. When he got to the garden, he walked to the spot in the maze where they usually met. He waited for a few moments and checked the phone. There weren't any more text, so he decided to call.

"Come on… Come one… Pick up… Pick up…"

Catlin picked up the phone after a few rings, "What's wrong?" she asked frantically.

"Just meet me in our spot as soon as you can!" he whispered and then hung up.

Eric sat there; looking at the fake stars in the fake sky and waited for them to show up. About ten minutes later, his friends came rushing in. Eric explained to them what had happened in his dream."

"It doesn't make sense!" he said to them.

"But don't you see, it does!" Nick said to him.

"Has everyone gone insane, but me?" Eric almost yelled.

"No! Remember Freshman year when Mrs. Grey told you that the Elizabeth that you knew was dead?"

Eric nodded his head, not really knowing where this is going. "But she was wrong. She is alive."

"But her soul is dying."

"That's why Mrs. Grey couldn't find her, because if someone loses their soul, then it's like they aren't alive," Catlin said to him.

"But that doesn't explain how she got that way, or what's all is going on." Eric said to them.

"Mrs. Grey told us about what happens if we lose our soul, last year. It's not pretty."

"Yeah. It's happened to me!" Eric shouted at her.

She stepped closer to him, placed a hand on his face, and said, "No, it hasn't. Not yet. What you feel is just anger and hate, but I can tell there is still love, happiness, and pain still in you. If you had truly lost your soul, you'd be like everyone else, here.

Emotionless. Just bodies ready to fight in the war.

"When someone loses their soul, they go through several stages. You grow cold, ice cold. So cold your skin turns snow white. Your eyes not only become pitch black, but they also become hollow looking. Have you ever looked directly into Elizabeth's eyes?"

Eric shook his head.

"Next time, you should. But don't look too long. It's like looking into a black hole," she said, continuing, "After their eyes become hollow, they begin to become emotionless. It's like they are walking zombies, except they can talk, learn, and eat. The one thing they lose, though, is the ability to think for themselves, which is probably how Elizabeth is connecting herself to them and why her soul told you it would be easier to kill the rest after she's dead."

"It's like in the first Star Wars movie, when Anakin Skywalker took out the droid control ship," Nick said.

"Geek," Marina mumbled under her breath.

"Once your soul is removed, it slowly starts to die. Some are stronger than others. If it dies, you will be stuck like that, until you die. No one knows what happens to you, after that," Catlin informed Eric.

"But how is her soul contacting me?" Eric asked, confused.

"I thought you were the smart one," Marina teased.

"I'm not smart about all this magic stuff, yet! Remember, I lost a year!"

"Well, she has always contacted you through dreams, because when you are asleep and dreaming, the line between reality and limbo becomes blurred. That's why when you dream, you have dreams about those you have lost, and they feel so real. So, these dreams that you've been having have been Elizabeth's spirit. Not her."

"Does she know this?" Eric asked, scared.

"That's probably how she found you and got you to trust her. She was using that to get into your head, Freshman year," Nick told him.

"Do you think she's *still* aware of it?" Eric asked.

"I don't know. Elizabeth could. After all, her soul is saying that you need to kill her."

"Eric, you know you don't have to do it, alone. We can help

you," Marina said.

"No. I don't want to endanger you anymore than I already have. She would get too suspicious if there was anybody but her and I. When things start heating up, I want you to promise me that you guys will leave. Please," Eric begged them.

"We couldn't abandon you, dude," Nick said.

"You have to."

"Why?" Catlin asked.

"Just promise me," Eric said forcefully.

"Okay," Marina said, looking down.

"Fine," Nick said, sounding defeated.

"No!" Catlin protested.

"Always are the stubborn one, aren't you," Eric said, smiling.

"Yes, I am. And I refuse to leave you. Especially if you plan on doing something so epically stupid."

"I just want to make sure you are safe."

"Trust me. I can take care of myself."

"Noted," he said before he kissed her, making Nick say, "Get a room."

"Promise me you won't get yourself killed," he said after they broke apart.

"Only if you promise they same thing."

"Deal."

They hugged, kissed, and then they left. Eric waited a few minutes before he left, just in case someone was out there watching. He knew he wasn't going to be able to sleep, anymore, so he took his time walking back to his bed. Along the way, he kept thinking of how fast things were moving. Soon, he'd be in battle, alongside his friends once again, and he knew more lives where going to be lost.

He wished he could go back- back to the time when magic didn't exist for him, where he was happy. Sure, he wouldn't have the friends he had now, but he wouldn't have all these scars and lives on him. He wouldn't have to kill the girl he once thought he was in love with.

That thought made him laugh. If only he knew what he knew, now. That their whole relationship was a lie... that she never loved him the way he loved her... that it was all an act. Which didn't really surprise him; after all, they were in middle school.

"Get over it," he said, talking to himself.

When he got back to his bed, he lay on his covers, stared up at the ceiling and thought of what was going to be happening in just a few weeks.

Chapter 21

"So, is everything in place? You have my speeches written?" Elizabeth asked him.

It was a few days later, and Eric had been working non-stop on details for the tour. They were hitting all the major cities in the US and visiting the capitals for all seven continents, from London, Paris, Berlin, Moscow, Winnipeg, Toronto, and so one, staying two days and having two public speeches in each and two public meet-ups.

"Yes. Everything is in order. Everything is planned down to the second. Security is on the highest level. If someone does anything or thinks about doing anything that could be seen as a threat, they will be disposed of. On the spot."

"Excellent, but what about the venues? I want as many bodies there as possible."

"We got the largest in the cities as we could, but I also have it set up that your speeches will be broadcasted on every television and on every radio within the state. That way, everyone will know what you have to say."

"Don't forget what I said, Eric. If anything fails, you will die. But before I kill you, I will make you a witness to your friends' death, since I know that they are alive and well. I *will* find them. And you *will* watch while I slowly burn their bodies to ash."

Eric nodded his head, saying, "Understood."

Elizabeth dismissed him with a wave of her hand. Eric got up and left her office. He had a fitting for a tux with a person who was called Shadow Reaper Greene in room 705. He had been meeting with a lot of different people in the past week, organizing all the speeches, booking the sites where Elizabeth would be giving her speeches and meet-ups, meeting with security forces, and also meeting with a few of the White Knight forces through Astral Projection.

They were almost ready for the battle. Many people within

the White Knight community were not pleased with the plans but agreed to help, anyway. Many of the older White Knights were against having Nick in charge of the mission, since he was still a teenager, but Sloan stood her position by saying that he was one of the brightest students with a talent for strategy.

Nick, Marina, and Catlin had all left with all of the records that Eric could get for them. They didn't go too far away; just to downtown Seattle. There, Sloan, Mr. Smith, Mrs. Grey, Miss Carton, and a few other teachers from different countries had taken refuge in an abandoned warehouse, where they prepared with the many students and Numes that had volunteered.

Within the week, Eric had visited them there a few times.

"Eric, it is *so* good to see you, again," Sloan said, giving him a warm hug.

Her face looked like she hadn't slept in a few weeks. She was wearing the White Knight's white battle robes. Her long, grey hair was pulled back into a French bun, and a tiny silver tiara was on her head. Eric never asked why she wore them; he just assumed it resembled that she was someone in charge. Like a general with his badges.

Even though it was just an Astral Projection, Eric's power had gotten strong enough to feel things and to look more opaque. They were in a small lobby room that was dark. The floor was covered in moss, and weeds had grown through the cracks. The white painted walls were dirty and graffitied, with a main door that had the glass broken in and a weathered wooden board that covered it.

"It's good to see you, too," he said, hugging her tightly.

They stayed like that for a while, before Eric broke away. "So, has Nick caught you up to speed on everything?"

"Yes," Sloan said as she started walking towards a rusty metal door. "Nick has informed all of us. I was just about to update some of the teachers of the foreign countries, who had arrived just before you did."

"How many reinforcements do we have?" Eric asked as they walked down a small metal stairway in a dark hall.

"We already have around three hundred White Knights from around the world and about two hundred Numes."

"You do understand that we will still be incredibly outnumbered. Ten to one."

"I do understand that, Eric, but I do believe that we have the upper hand, here."

"I hope so."

"Eric, you have changed. I'm afraid it has *not* been for the better," she said sadly, stopping at the bottom of the stairs.

"So? I'm still a good fighter," he contended.

Sloan opened another rusty door, revealing a colossal, bright room, saying, "Remember whose side you're on, Eric. Remember all of the lives that have been lost to get to this point."

Eric didn't say anything, after that. Sloan gave him a stern look, and then, walked into the room.

The room was separated into four quadrants by tape on the ground; each housing different groups of people working on various things. Some were working on combat skills with the SRBs, some working on shooting guns, some working on magic techniques, and others were hurdling around a very large oak table.

As they approached the area with the large oak table, Eric noticed that there were several metal doors around the room. Two people in white robes walked out of one of the doors near the table, walking towards Sloan and Eric.

"I am very glad to see you made it here safely," Sloan said to the taller of the two, extending a hand to greet them.

The woman pulled back the hood of her robe, revealing long black hair and a skinny, pale face, before shaking Sloan's hand.

"It was a challenge, but we made it," she replied to Sloan in a heavy German accent.

"Eric, this is Ava Müller. She is the Headmistress of the Berlin division of their White Knight school."

"It's nice to meet you," Eric said kindly, reaching his hand out.

Ava ignored his kind gesture, saying, "So, it is you who is responsible for the many deaths."

"I'm also the one who's trying to end it," he said, raising his voice.

"Frau Müller, we are here to come together peacefully to—"

"We are here to end a young girl's life in order to end the Shadow Reapers," Ava said, interrupting Sloan.

"Wait, hold up," Eric said taking a step back. "Are you

seriously saying that you feel bad for killing the person who is guilty for the millions of deaths?"

"I am saying that the girl is only sixteen. Haven't there been enough deaths?"

"We are trying to end a war. Ending battles will always have its casualties."

"Enough," Sloan interjected, "Right now, we have to make our final plans for the battle."

Sloan guided them to the table. Ava sat down in an empty seat, and Sloan and Eric took their spots next to Nick and Mr. Smith.

"Five... Four... Three... Two... One... Thank you for getting quiet," Sloan said, getting everyone's attention, "We only have a few days left before what could be the last battle. If we win this, it will be the last of the Shadow Reapers. If we lose, it will be the end of the White Knights."

An eerie silence filled the space, and the air became hard to breathe.

"We need everyone to be on the same page. We need everything to run smoothly. We need to win this battle." Sloan waited a few minutes to see if anyone had anything to say before she continued, "Now, Eric is in charge of the event for the Shadow Reapers. He has supplied us with a way in."

"Yes," Eric said, taking over. "Since it's a public event, we are encouraging everyone to come. However, if security sees any known White Knight there, you will be taken out, immediately. As we are speaking, I'm trying to erase names and photos from the database. If it doesn't work, there is a secret service entrance in the basement. It's a little harder to get to from the outside, but security doesn't know about it.

"Once you are inside, you just need to stay quiet and wait for the signal, which will be provided by Nick Walters and his team. Towards the beginning of the event, after Elizabeth gives her welcoming speech, I will interrupt her by asking her to marry me. The ring that I will give to her will have a charm on it. This charm, provided by Mr. Smith and his team, will basically render her powers useless."

"Basically?" a woman with a Russian accent asked, skeptical.

"Yes," Mr. Smith answered her. "The charm will dampen

324

her powers as long as she has the ring on."

"Once she has the ring on," Eric said, "that's when all power to the building will be cut off. During that time, I will get Elizabeth out of the building, and she will be my responsibility, and I will take care of her."

"After they are out of the building," Nick said, now taking over, "it will be up to us. The Shadow Reaper's power will be weaker, since they won't be connected to Elizabeth, so it will be a little bit easier to take them down."

"Wait, why are we listening to these... these *kids*?" said an angry older man.

"These *kids* are the brightest of the bunch. It is because of these kids that we are still alive," Sloan said, defending them.

"It's because of these kids that we are in this spot," yelled Ava.

"Enough, Ava. Yes, these kids are young, but they are no way inexperienced. I trust them with my life," Sloan argued.

"I don't think we should be taking battle orders from teenagers!" yelled someone else.

"Listen!" Sloan yelled. "Eric James, Nick Walters, Marina Martin, and Catlin Chamberlin have all risked their lives for us to get to this point. Without them and their skills, we would not be here.

"Eric is risking his life to get us the information we need to end this war. Nick is using his strategy skills to help us win this battle. Marina is helping us hack into their security and computers, that night. Catlin has had training from her father, who is a Federal Bureau of Investigation agent, and she is helping us with teaching the Nume volunteers how to shoot and handle guns, even though she is against using guns."

"What makes them qualified over anyone else?" shouted someone.

"As I said, before, they have teams. They are not working alone. They each have teams made up of strong, brave, and wise members of our community."

Before anyone could say anything else, Eric said, "Do you know what burning flesh smells like?"

A few of them around the table nodded their heads.

"Okay. Do you know what it's like to know that the smell is coming from your parents, or even yourself?"

Heads were hanging, angry faces replaced with sad ones.

"Do you know what it's like to everyday wake up and realize that the nightmare you had... was real? Do you know how it feels to be cut open and experimented on?"

Eric waited for anyone to say anything.

"No? Well I do, and I have the scars to prove it," he said, pulling up his sleeves.

There were surprised, sharp inhales from around the table.

"Do you know how it feels to be looked at like you are the cause of all of this? To feel the hatred from people when they look at you?

"I'm not the only one that has had damage done to them. Each of you has a story to tell. Loved ones lost and killed. But you have to realize that these *kids* that you are talking about have gone through the same thing.

"Catlin's mom died at the hands of Shadow Reapers, and she doesn't know if her dad or sister is dead, captured, or alive. Shadow Reapers killed Marina's older sister when she herself was only five. After she was killed, her dad committed suicide, knowing that there was no way of getting her back. Shadow Reapers attacked Nick's family, too. They took his one-year-old sister's life and just recently, they took his dad's life after he sacrificed himself to save Nick's mom and brothers.

"Just because we are young, does *not* mean that we have not experienced pain, suffering, and hate."

"So, after you propose and the lights go off, what are the plans," asked Ava.

Chapter 22

"I don't know why you ever wanted to be a teacher," Elizabeth said to Eric as they walked around the colossal theater for tonight's speeches. "You really do have a gift for Public Relations. I mean, *look* at this place!"

The theater lobby had several posters of Elizabeth that promoted the upgrades, saying **Put the 'I' in fight, and get an upgrade!** or **Help us create the Utopia by getting an upgrade!** Eric was showing Elizabeth where her dressing room was and where she would walk on stage.

The dressing rooms were in the back, behind the stage, each complete with a private bathroom, lounge area, a closet, and a large collection of mirrors. There was also a large, green room that had a bar and several couches, chairs, and coffee tables.

A line-up was placed at both stage entrances, dressing rooms, and at the green room. At 7:00 sharp, Elizabeth would give a welcoming speech. At 7:30, Shadow Reaper Andrews would give a speech about joining the forces. At 8:00, Shadow Reaper Jean would give a speech about the classes. At 8:30, Elizabeth would come back out to talk about her plans for the Shadow Reapers. At 9:00, there would be a small Q&A with the audience.

Eric had walked Elizabeth to her dressing room. There, Eric handed her copies of her speeches out of a folder.

"You don't need to memorize this, but I do recommend that you go through it a few times, before tonight," Eric said to her.

"Are we not doing rehearsals in a few hours, anyways?"

"Yes, but the speeches are long. It would be wise if you familiarized yourself with them, before we went live."

"Fine. I'll look at them when I get a chance."

Eric was just about out of the room when Elizabeth added, "Do you have the ring?"

"Like I said, *everything* is in order."

Eric walked out, shut the door, and headed to the basement.

A drunken construction worker had cut off the basement after renovations in the 1950s, so the only way into the basement was the door outside. However, Nick had reviewed the blueprints of the building, both from now and before the renovation, and found a small service door that led to the basement that was covered up with cement bricks in the loading dock.

Eric used the *Vanesco* charm on the bricks to make them go away. The wooden door was rotten and fell off the hinges as soon as Eric pushed on it. The hallway was dark, filled with old cobwebs, and the stairs felt like they would give out at any moment.

"Pila lucis," Eric said, flicking his wand at the ceiling, which created a small but bright ball of light.

"Fortitudo," he said, flicking it at the stairs, so they would hold up a little bit longer.

He headed down the stairs, until he reached another door. He knocked three times, waited a few moments, and then, knocked two more times. He heard some shuffling, and the door slowly opened. A hand quickly reached out, grabbed Eric's wrist, and twisted his arm behind his back. The person jumped on Eric's back, making him fall to the ground. Eric fought back, swinging his foot back and knocking the person off him. He then flipped over, holding the attacker's arms on the ground and sitting on their chest.

Catlin's face lit up when she saw it was Eric.

"Hey there!" she greeted him.

Eric bent down and kissed her.

"What's with the attacking? I thought you said you weren't into all that," he asked, jokingly.

Catlin laughed. "You can't be too sure. I didn't know if it was you, or not."

"How can you still be sure?"

"With this!"

Catlin swiftly kicked Eric off of her, knocking him to a wall. She grabbed a flask out of her back pants pocket and splashed it on him. When nothing happen, she said "You passed the test."

"What was that? It smells awful!"

"A potion to remove any Metamorphoses or shape shifting

charms."

"Smart move," he said, following Catlin into the room.

"We're taking *a lot* of precautions."

The room was dark, but Eric could make out the faces of those in the basement. They were scared, anxious, and some even looked sad. Catlin took Eric to where Sloan was.

"Is everything ready?" she asked Eric.

"Everything is in order. Is everyone ready?"

"Yes, some. Most are frightened and afraid, but they are ready to fight."

"They know what to do and when to do it?"

"Yes. Marina's team is already hacking into the system. Nick and his team are ready to act. Everyone and everything is ready."

Eric nodded his head. Sloan reached out and placed a hand on his shoulder.

"Eric, are you okay?" she asked gently.

Eric paused, deciding whether or not to tell the truth.

"I know what I have to do. I don't like it, but I have to do it."

Sloan gave him a kind and warm smile. She hugged him tight, holding him for a long time.

"You know that you don't have to do this, alone. Although we can't see the outcome is for tonight, I know that you don't have to do it alone," she informed him.

"What do you mean?"

"We have been trying to see the outcome of this war since the beginning. No one has been able to. Wars are too unpredictable to see the consequence."

"So, you have no clue if we will be successful, tonight."

"I do not. However, I have hope that we will. I'm sorry, Eric."

"It will be okay. Things will turn out for the better. Even if the Shadow Reapers win, we will most likely be killed, so we won't have to deal with the aftermath of Elizabeth's plan."

Sloan hugged him one more time, saying, "You've grown up so much since we first met."

"Thank you."

"For what?"

"For always being there, for understanding, for helping me, and for trying your best to protect me."

"I always protect my students."

"I love you."

"I love you too, Eric."

Even though the room was dark, Eric could feel his eyes changing from black to green, again. It was a subtle change; his eyes still looked black, but they had a hint of green in them, now.

"If you change your mind and decide you want help for your part of the plan, let us know," Sloan said.

Eric nodded, again, and hugged her. He feared it would be the last time that he would get to hug her.

"Eric, can we talk?" Catlin asked, tapping on his shoulder.

Eric let go of Sloan, they said their goodbyes, and Catlin grabbed Eric's hand and pulled him towards a part of the room that was empty, besides a few people.

"I think we should say something, before it's too late and we might not get a chance to, later," she said.

"What do you mean?"

"Like our goodbyes."

Eric was shocked. Two people walked closer to them, and as they did, Eric realized they were Nick and Marina.

"This may be the last time that the four of us may be together," Nick said.

"Stop it!"

"We're just being realistic here, Eric. Sure, the plans sound fool-proof, but we never know," Marina said to him.

"I don't like goodbyes!" Eric yelled at them.

"No one does, but it would be nice to say something, just in case something happens," Catlin said.

There was a silence amongst the group.

"I'm sorry," Eric said, looking down.

"All is forgiven," Marina said, hugging him.

"I love you guys, so much. I couldn't have asked for better friends. You guys were there from the start, and I'm sorry that I've treated you like shit," Eric said, starting to cry.

"Hey, no more tears. Like Marina said, all is forgiven," Catlin said.

"You've been an awesome friend too, Eric, believe it or not. You are like a brother to me," Nick said.

"Listen, guys, if things are on our side and we make it

through this, then I *promise* things are going to be different between us. I want to be the friend that you guys deserve."

"You are that, already. I'm sorry that we ever fought in the first place," Marina said, hugging him.

"If things do *not* end on our side, though, I just want you guys to know that I love you. Thank you for being the best friends a girl could have," Marina said, almost breaking down in tears.

"Can we not say goodbye? I don't like that word. It means we'll never see each other, again. I want to stay optimistic here and think that after tonight, we'll still be here," Nick told them.

"I'm just being realistic," Catlin said to him.

This shocked Eric. Catlin and Marina had always been the optimistic ones; always happy, always cheerful, and always trying to ignore the bad vibes, as Catlin once told Eric. But these last few weeks had really changed her. Everyone, really. Eric's stomach felt heavy and upset.

"Can I ask you guys something?" Eric implored.

"Ask away, man," Nick replied.

"It's about tonight."

Chapter 23

"Welcome and thank you *all* for coming!" Elizabeth announced, greeting the thousands in the audience and the thousands more listening over radio and watching on their televisions.

Every seat in the theater was filled, and Eric was standing offstage, watching Elizabeth give her speech. He watched her stand in her black silk gown that was covered in different sized black pearls. Her hair was curled and flowed down her back, and her bangs covered most of the burn marks on her face. A small, but prominent, black diamond tiara was on her head.

Eric noticed that she was no longer the girl that he had met back in middle school. He remembered when she gave her first speech in their Speech Class. Even though she was one of the more popular girls, she was still nervous about getting in front of a crowd and talking. Not anymore, or if she was, she was hiding it well. This Elizabeth spoke with confidence as she looked out into the crowd.

"Tonight, you will hear from several Shadow Reapers about what we plan to achieve within the next few months. You will also learn about the upgrades and what is entailed, what an average day at the Shadow Reaper Academy is like, and we will end with a lovely Q and A with me! At the end of the night, if you still have questions or concerns, you can fill out a form that will be available by requests out in the lobby."

She continued for a little bit longer, saying how glad she was to see everyone there in a very fake tone and how happy it made her feel that people took their time to come listen to what she had to say. She was finishing up thanking everyone for coming out, once again, which was Eric's cue to come out.

Eric, dressed in a black formal military commander uniform with fake medals that had been pinned to the jacket to make Eric look more official and noteworthy, started to walk out on stage.

"Excuse me, Queen Elizabeth Williams of the Shadow

Reapers. I'm sorry to interrupt you, but there is something important that I need to ask you," he said, tapping her on the shoulder.

She turned around to look at him and gasped when he got down on one knee. He pulled out a tiny velvet case from an inside pocket of his uniform jacket and held it out to her.

"Will you do me the honor of being with me for the rest of our lives?"

Elizabeth nodded her head, saying, "Yes! A thousand times, yes!"

Eric opened the box to reveal a black diamond surrounded my black pearls on an onyx band. He took it out and slid in on her finger. He stood back up, hugged her, and then kissed her.

The audience applauded them, standing up to cheer for them, yelling, "Viva la coppia reale." Elizabeth turned back to the audience, holding Eric's hand, saying, "Thank you, all!"

After she said that, there was a thunderous bang that shook the whole theater. The lights that surrounded the stage and the sitting area exploded, sending glass flying everywhere, scratching Eric and Elizabeth's faces and bodies. Screams of cheer quickly turned to screams of terror.

Elizabeth and Eric both reached for their wands, shouting, "Lumen," and sending two large flickering balls of light into the air.

Elizabeth violently gasped when she saw what was now in front of her. Every single member in the audience now had a white robe on.

"This can't be. It's impossible!" Elizabeth murmured.

"Oh yes, Elizabeth. It is possible," said Sloan, whose face appeared on the screen behind them.

"How?" Elizabeth asked, her face looking more terrified than it ever had.

"We were waiting for the perfect moment to surprise you, and this seemed like the perfect time. I am very sorry to interrupt your world tour and engagement ceremony. Now, before you run out and try to send your troops on us, I have a few things to say.

"Since you won't get the opportunity to tell the people of the world what you are planning, I'll do the favor.

"The Queen, here, after she gets enough people to say yes to the upgrades, and the update is successful, plans on killing every human that hasn't had a successful upgrade to create a more peaceful world. A world full of only Shadow Reapers.

"But here is the thing, Miss Williams. Spoiled children do *not* always get what they want. You may have tried as hard as you could, but you failed. You tried to knock us down with every fiber of your being, yet here we are, stronger than ever. You have failed."

As Sloan finished her speech, Shadow Reapers started to come in the room from behind the stage and the other exits. The sounds of guns reloading filled the air. White Knights were ready to attack, some with firearms and others with wands.

"I will give you a chance, Elizabeth. Call off your men and surrender, and no blood will be spilled," Sloan said to her.

"Never! The daughter of Vesta De'Lore will never surrender to the White Knights."

"Don't say we never gave you a chance to save yourself," Sloan said in a calm, yet threatening, voice.

"Elizabeth, I think we should leave, now," Eric whispered to her.

She grabbed his hand, and he guided her off stage. Muffled gunfire and screams started to ring out as soon as they were off stage.

"Did you know about this?" Elizabeth asked him.

Eric ignored her and kept pulling her towards one of the side exits.

"What is going on? I demand to know!"

"Resera!" Eric shouted, swinging his wand at a blue Ford Escape.

A large explosion went off behind them; Eric tried not to think of what was going on in there as Shadow Reapers and White Knights came rushing out of the building after them. He opened the car door and shoved Elizabeth in the car, closing the door on the bottom of her dress.

"Where are you taking me?" she screamed.

"Incendere machinam," he said after getting into the driver's seat.

The car started, blasting them with cold air from the air conditioner. Eric put the car in reverse and pressed hard on the gas, hitting a few of the Shadow Reapers. Elizabeth screamed in terror and confusion. He put the car in drive, and then, pressed hard again on the gas pedal, driving over the sidewalk to get on the road.

He drove down the crowded city streets for about twenty minutes, avoiding as many red lights as he could by using his Molecular Immobilization powers to freeze the cars in his way. He got on the interstate and continued driving for thirty minutes.

"Where the *hell* are you taking me?" Elizabeth asked, flinging her hands as if to cast a charm on him.

"What... What is going on?"

A cruel and evil smile crawled onto Eric's face, and he chuckled as she fought to find out what was going on.

"I should have never doubted you, Eric," she said, utterly terrified.

"Oh, for the love of god, would you just shut the hell up, woman!" Eric yelled at her as he increased his speed.

Eric got off the interstate and headed towards Snoqualmie.

"Why are we here?" Elizabeth asked, fear filling her voice.

"You will find out, soon enough."

Chapter 24

hey arrived at an old Inn near the Snoqualmie Pass Ski Resort. Eric pulled to a stop at a little hiking trail that was on the Inn property.

"I don't like where this is headed, Eric."

He turned to look at her, and coldly said, "Oh... you really shouldn't."

He jumped out of the car, walked around the car, and pulled open the passenger's door.

Elizabeth screamed in pain as Eric jerked her out of the car.

"Morere!" she shouted, pointing her wand at him.

Eric just stood there, laughing at her.

"What did you *do* to me? Why aren't my powers working?"

"It's the ring. It's dampening your powers, rendering you powerless."

Elizabeth relentlessly tried to take off the engagement ring, but it was no use.

"It also binds to your skin. So, good luck trying to get it off."

I have to get out of here. I have to run. I have to. Eric heard her say in her head.

Eric froze her, instantly. He slowly walked over to her, saying, "What happened to the confident and angry Elizabeth that you were just a few hours ago?"

Eric picked her up and tossed her over his shoulder and started walking down the wooded trail. There were a few old and faded signs warning him about the cliff edges, but he ignored them and continued on. When he got to the cliff edge, he sat Elizabeth back down.

He dress was badly torn now, missing half the pearls. Her hair was messy with twigs and leaves in it, and her feet were bare. There were tiny cuts that were bleeding all over her arms and a few on her face.

Eric unfroze her, and as she regained control over her body, she just about fell over the side of the cliff.

"Don't talk. You've talked enough. It's my turn to talk, now," Eric told her as he paced back and forth in front of her.

"Your plan was always destined to fail. You get that, right? You never underestimate the White Knights. You may have killed most of us, but that only made us stronger.

"You know you can't create a peaceful world, right? No matter how equal you make *everyone*, there will always be people to rebel against *something*! No matter how much you try to control them. You especially are always going to fail, because there will *always* be war, hate, crime, and suffering. And you can't end all of that by adding even more of that.

"You want to create a peaceful world by ending it. Do you not see how fucked up that is?" he yelled at her.

A gust of wind rushed by them, making the trees sway.

"And how to you plan to stop me? You don't strike me as a murderer, Eric James."

"Anyone can be a murderer if they're pushed hard enough. And we both know you've killed enough of my friends and family to push me to the limit, but I don't plan on doing it, alone. No, you see, I invited a few friends to help me, because you also pushed them to that limit."

From the bushes behind Eric came Catlin, Marina, and Nick, all pointing their wands at Elizabeth.

"What... are you too weak to do it yourself?" she asked, mockingly.

"True, you have made me feel very weak, very small, and very useless. But there are a few things I've learned through all of this. One, I'm stronger than you ever will be. Two, I'm not as stupid as you made me believe I am. Three, I am loved."

"If you say so, but that still doesn't answer my question."

Nick froze Elizabeth from her neck down.

"You see, you hurt our friend, and if that wasn't enough for us to want to kill you, you also came for our families," Marina said to her.

"Do you know how the Molecular Immobilization power works, Elizabeth? For living and breathing creatures, it freezes the mussels, essentially making you paralyzed. But it doesn't stop your organs from working, and it doesn't stop you from feeling things," Nick informed her.

"So, our plan is to hurt you as much as you hurt us," Catlin said to her.

"One cut at a time," Eric said, coldly.

They each waited for Elizabeth to say something, being fueled by adrenaline, fear, and anger.

Catlin stepped toward Elizabeth, wand still pointed right at her face.

"Catlin. Poor, poor, Catlin. Not the brightest of the bunch. And now that I'm thinking about it, what are you for? What do you do? Are you just the damsel in distress for Eric?"

"Oh, fuck you, bitch!" Catlin yelled.

She raised her wand, and yelled, "Incisus!" as she flipped it in the direction of her face.

A large cut formed from the left side of her head, all the way to her right shoulder. Elizabeth screamed in terror and pain. Another cut ripped across her chest, making blood pour down the front of her dress

"That is for my mom, my dad, and my sister."

Catlin stepped back in line with Nick and Marina, still pointing her wand at Elizabeth's face.

Marina stepped up next.

"What, nothing to say to me?" Marina asked her.

"When you die, ask your father how it felt when the rope snapped his neck," she responded to Marina.

Marina's hand was trembling in anger, and a tear was falling down her face.

She pulled back her wand, using her Metamorphosis to transform it into long, silver broadsword. She grabbed it with both hands, and yelled, "This is for my dad and for my sister!" before plunging it toward Elizabeth's stomach. When Marina pulled out the sword from Elizabeth's stomach, it turned back into her wand

Blood started to drip out of the corner of Elizabeth's mouth, which still held a cruel smile.

Nick didn't even give her time to say anything to him. He swung his wand at her, screaming, "Pulmones pleni luto."

Elizabeth started choking and coughing. Spitting up blood and what looked like chunks of dirt. Her black eyes looked like they were about to pop out of her head.

"That is for my dad and my baby sister, you cold hearted

fucker!"

He looked at Eric and said, "Finish her off."

Eric walked up to her, dropping his wand on the ground, tears filling his eyes.

"Nick, unfreeze her," he told her.

"But—"

"Do it!"

Nick unfroze her, and Elizabeth fell to her knees. One hand on the ground supporting her, and the other around her throat as she struggled to breath.

Eric picked her up to support her, and then hugged her.

"I'm sorry. I'm sorry that it took me so long to save you," he whispered into her ear.

He covered his body in flames, covering her body too. Elizabeth screamed a very high-pitched yell. She tried to fight him, but he held her tight.

"This for my parents," he yelled.

Eric leaned against her, pushing her off the cliff with his burning body still attached. Together, they fell onto the shallow and rocky waters, far below.

Epilogue

About a month later, all remaining Shadow Reaper troops had been depleted. With the success of the final battle, Sloan had announced Elizabeth's death with the help of Eric James, Catlin Chamberlin, Nick Walters, and Marina Martin, as well as the end of the Shadow Reapers and the destruction of their bases and schools all over the world. With the destruction of the bases came the freedom of the Spirit Slaves, who now continued their journey to the afterlife.

Sloan had decided to bring the Fire Manipulation course back to Aviance, to compensate for all of those who had been *upgraded*. There was a debate within the community about what to do with those who were still in the Shadow Reaper Academy and hadn't yet been brainwashed by Elizabeth. Some wanted to have all of them disposed of, since they were considered *scientific experiments* and *unstable*. Others wanted them treated like everyone else, saying they were manipulated and had no choice but to be upgraded.

"Those who have had an upgrade will be given the opportunity to study at Aviance under my supervision. Shall there be an incident with one of these students, then I will decide how to deal with them," Sloan told the White Knight community.

With a fear of another witch-hunt, now that magic was once again exposed, there was a movement to go back underground and hide from the Numes. With that in mind, it was decided that Aviance be rebuilt in a different location, within the mountains of northern Michigan.

As for Eric, Catlin, Nick, and Marina, it was the end; the end of a time of war and a beginning of a time of peace.

After Elizabeth was killed, Eric lost his Astral Projection power, something he was still recovering from. He was no longer having the dreams of Elizabeth anymore, which made him relieved. He was finally getting a good night's rest, and his eyes had returned back to their normal shade of deep green.

He also upheld his promise of being a better friend. He no longer held things in. Their friendship had never been tighter. Things for Eric have become a lot easier, and he was happier. He still missed his mom and dad, but he was happy knowing that they were no longer Spirit Slaves.

Catlin's father and sister made contact with her a few weeks after the battle. They had escaped to a base in Africa, where he had some contacts. He didn't want to endanger Catlin by telling her where they were hiding. She didn't care about the details; she was just happy they were still alive.

With September approaching and regular school approaching, Sloan was in a hurry to move everything from the house in Missouri back to the East Coast, which was still getting repaired.

"You know, part of me doesn't want to leave this house. It is a great house," Sloan said to Eric with a hint of sadness in her voice.

They were leaning against the trunk of her black Avenger, with the rest of their boxes inside, looking at the large plantation-style house.

"I'm going to miss that garden. I did a lot of work in that garden."

"You should help Mr. Smith with the garden he uses for his class. I know he'd appreciate it," she suggested.

Eric's cellphone went off, notifying him of a new text from Catlin.

I miss you! <3

I miss you too, Catlin. <3 We just got the last of our stuff, and we are headed home, soon.

About the Author

Joseph Alan Workinger currently is studying for his Bachelors degree for Professional and Public writing in Indianapolis, Indiana. After he finishes his degree, he plans on starting his career publishing and continuing to write more books.

Joseph grew up in the small town of Greentown, Indiana. There, he went to the local high school and found the inspiration for most of the characters in this book. Other inspirations and help came from his friends, Allison and Amber, and publisher, Selina, whom he would like to thank. Without their help, involvement, and criticism, this wouldn't be possible.

For more information about Joseph, or to contact him, you can follow him on twitter, at: **https://twitter.com/J_A_W16**

Or tumblr, at:

http://writing-my-way-to-new-york.tumblr.com